Middle Night

Middle Night

by
Eleanor K. Gustafson

To Jen —
" You are now
and forever known..."
Ellie Gustafson

Copyright © 2000 by Eleanor K. Gustafson

All rights reserved.
No part of this book may be reproduced, stored in a retrieval system, or transmitted by any means, electronic, mechanical, photocopying, recording, or otherwise, without written permission from the author.

ISBN: 1-58721-742-2

1stBooks – rev. 7/3/00

About the Book

MIDDLE NIGHT
A feast celebrating the high day of the sun; until now, a gentle time for extended families to reflect on the mistakes of the past and hopes for the future . . .

ROSILLUM
A rare mineral noted for its extraordinary effect when tasted. Seductive enough to make one do most anything for the tiniest lick. Driss, a charismatic and determined young man, and his friends scour the land for a contraband cache of rosillum . . .

CHARRI
A disfigured young woman who is searching for something more basic than rosillum—a name, a *real* name.

MIDDLE NIGHT, ROSILLUM, and CHARRI
A catastrophic convergence of good and evil that ultimately presents Driss with a choice: the way of life or the way of death.

This is a book that will both entertain and challenge the reader. The author conveys the excitement of an old-fashioned treasure hunt, as well as the contemplation of truth, without reference to this world. It is a book dark with power and deep with hope—a description of redemption in a new and intriguing context.

—Louise Midwood, B.A. English Literature and Fine Arts History, Master of Theological Studies

*To Debby, whose loving insistence on excellence
breathed flesh onto the dry bones of Arlony.*

**Man cannot
name himself**

**He waits for God
or Satan
to tell him
who he is**

Reprinted from *The Secret Trees,* by Luci Shaw, © 1976. Used by permission of Harold Shaw Publishers, Wheaton, IL 60189

*Whatever exists has already been named,
and what is has been known.*
                                           Ecclesiastes 6:10

PROLOGUE

According to Arlonian legend, an old liggeth prospector, down on his luck, had little but a sore back to show for months of tunneling. The particular vein he'd been chasing seemed more "rose mud," as they called it, than liggeth. He'd seen a pocket or two of the pesky stuff in other mines, but here it all but replaced the prized fuel. Rose mud wasn't really mud, or it might have made decorative bricks for house construction. As the miner scratched his head over how to turn his misbegotten yield into bread, he considered its properties: beautiful color, light weight, soft and malleable like lead. But for sheer usefulness, lead had it all over rose mud.

Beautiful color . . . bracelets, maybe. But even children ridiculed his attempt at jewelry making. He plodded from street to street, belly crying for bread as he listened to the litany of objections to the odd substance: unlike liggeth, it wouldn't burn; it turned to dust if you tried to smelt it; too soft for tools, cooking pots, or anything useful. "Can't eat it nor plow with it," one farmer complained. "No good to me."

"Well, sir," said the miner, "true enough it won't plow, but I can't say for a fact it won't eat, and I'm hungry enough to try." So saying, he fished a small piece from his bucket and ran his tongue across the lustrous surface.

In that instant, rosillum became a precious metal.

Rosillum. Rare and unique enough to scheme and fight and kill for. It spawned more than one war on the continent of North Lailand. Arlony in particular, being rich in liggeth, bore the brunt of a hundred-year conflict called the "Green Wars." Its neighbor Swendia, sniffing the air for extra income, attacked without warning and pushed Arlony's commander-in-chief and his army halfway across the country. The war seesawed for decades, mostly in Arlony but sometimes in Swendia. Only after their last-ditch effort at Harloon Paddock did Arlony win back its original real estate.

In the two centuries following that war, prospectors by the thousand scoured the other three continents, with little success.

Even Great Zelland, rich in gems and other minerals but too fiercely wild to settle, drew adventurers to death or poverty, blinded by the lure of rosillum.

Since the time of the miner's serendipitous discovery, rosillum has fascinated kings and fools, humanitarians and fiends. Its seductive power, though, remains inextricably bound to the essence of evil.

The good folk of Arlony—drovers and farm wives, people close to the land who feed off the beauty of Arlony—these folk know little of rosillum. But they know the evil that surrounds it. Though it appears only as an ill-defined smudge or an earth tremor too deep to feel, they understand that it threatens the very foundation of their land. They speak of this in hushed tones over back fences. And they talk only to each other; who would dare go higher? Even if some bold fellow did gather courage to approach either Claeman on the one hand or Sigurth on the other in Arlony's current civil war; even if this bold fellow could articulate the people's concerns, who could say whether one or both of these topmost apples wouldn't have worms? Enough that the good folk of Arlony recognized the smudge for what it was and did their best to keep "youngers" out of harm's way.

1

The wagon bounced with abandon as the team pounded down the ledgy roadway. Driss glanced over his shoulder with grim satisfaction. Alert trackers studying the ground might have caught his turnoff, but not the riders he'd left in the dust. They were half drunk and nine-tenths witless—the kind that would chase an empty road up the mountain until their nags dropped. If he could keep his own horses on their feet for another quarter-mile, they could rest a bit and head back to rejoin the others.

Moans from under the wagon canopy cut through the clatter. "Comfortable, love?" he shouted toward the triangular opening.

"You're killing me!"

With a puckish grin he slapped the reins one last time. "I could arrange a swap with them, if you'd rather. I get to drive away in one piece—" He jammed himself between seat and floor board against a spine-cracking jolt. "—you get a nice, smooth ride to wherever. They might even pay me something in the bargain."

"Driss, you're a fiend! I hate you!"

He pulled the lathered team to a trot. "Okay, fellas, whoa down. Easy!" Sides heaving, the matched grays tossed flecks of foam and blew nervously.

On the edge of a broad, open shelf broken only by a knoll, they halted in a grove of gnarled, twisted camblors that seemed defiant against any show of spring leaves. Rays of an early sun muscled through tight-stretched clouds like prisoners straining against bars. Driss jumped from the wagon and moved to the horses' heads, stroking their steaming necks. "Easy, Toggen; good girl, Lady. You did well. Cool down, now; cool down."

As he unfastened the traces, a woman's head emerged from the canopy. Her face, though nearly perfect in beauty, reflected the hardness of the road. A frown sat comfortably on it.

"You think more of your damned horses than you do me. Every bone in my body is broken, but do you care?" Her fingers worked through a tumbled mass of black hair.

"Better your bones than theirs!" Driss laughed in her direction. "You're the cushy-comfort lady. Without horses you'd have only blisters to jewel your toes. Of course," he added, "if you're tired of the trip and drunk T'ribboners don't suit your fancy, we could settle you in a nice little croft in the hills, with a farm boy to service you when he's not done in from his work."

"Oh, shut up!"

The man left the trace and reached out a hand. "Come, Rona, climb down, and we'll walk the horses. You know I'm just playing with you." His frank, open face offered affection to soothe Rona's ire. "This is just a glitch. In less than an hour we'll find the others and be on our way to wealth, ease, pleasure—your heart's desire, my love."

"And yours. Don't pretend you're doing this for my sake. I know you too well, Drissan. Once you find the rosillum . . ."

He pulled her down, his gold-flecked eyes feeding on the unblemished whiteness of her skin, the classic symmetry of her features. "Rona, dear, you're far too beautiful for me to throw to mongrels as you fear. More likely, you'll get tired of me. Stick with me, love, and I'll set you up like a queen. You'll stagger under rosillum circlets and arm bands. You'll sleep on rosillum and dream of the moon. And every year on the anniversary of this day, we'll break out a jeweled cask of rosillum just for licking. In seconds we'll be carried past the moon to stars beyond stars."

With the ingenuous grace of a kitten, Rona melted against him, rubbing her face against the satiny fabric of his maroon vest. Her fingers walked up his chin, his cheek, and fastened in his thick, dark curls. Driss closed his eyes, his own hands exploring the sensuous curve of her body. His mouth met hers, and for a moment their bodies drew urgently together.

A cough from one of the horses brought Driss back, and he pulled away reluctantly. "Come, my sweet. The horses mustn't stand, or we'll lose our transportation. See that little hill over there, tight to the mountain? By the time we circle it, they'll be fit to travel. They did well by us; we'll do well by them." He slapped a dappled rump affectionately.

Their escape road, if indeed it was a road, had disappeared on the open shelf. To the left lay a steep drop-off, but the mountain extended a protective wing partway around its rim. The wash of soil from this encircling arm had, over eons beyond measure, created a natural, sloping amphitheater, and an imaginative eye might see in the flat-topped mound Driss had pointed out a platform from which vast crowds could be addressed.

The travelers had their minds on other things, however. They meandered toward the gap between knoll and mountain, Driss leading the horses, and Rona keeping a prudent distance from the lathered beasts.

"Driss, one of the things I like about you—well, maybe two things—"

Driss laughed. "Only two?"

Her mouth twitched provocatively. "Only two at a time. Maybe tonight I'll think of two more."

They topped a greening rise, Driss listening around Lady to Rona's list. Suddenly, one of the horses planted his feet and jerked back with a snort. Driss was caught off balance. "Toggen!" he roared irritably, yanking the rein. "Giddap!" His eye still on the horse, he moved on, stepping over a low, humped rock.

He didn't see it, that long, thick shadow that lay beyond the rock. Within the shadow his foot met only emptiness. His other leg buckled, and the rocky hump knocked the breath out of him.

His body teetered on the edge of the void—half in, half out. He might yet have clawed his way out, had he time to think. Gravity, though, was against him. Gravity—and his maroon vest. The smoothness that pleased Rona glided down the rock face. Inch by inch it fed him to the darkness.

2

The sun struggled up a winding valley. Its reluctant rays, normally ravenous after their night-long fast, had little appetite this morning for bits of fog scattered along the greening hillsides. Clouds mantled the western horizon, obscuring a looming mountain peak.

Two travelers emerged from the wretched crofter's cottage that had sheltered them from the night. The older, a slender woman of twenty-four, clutched a thin brown cloak against the morning chill. With it she shielded the lower part of her face, as well as a bundle held protectively on her left arm.

The younger, a daisy-eyed girl not yet in her teens, strode forth with none of the cautious restraint of her companion. A yellow cape fell about an otherwise indifferent dress, and from the grand way she swung her shoulders, it still prickled with the glory of newness. The necessities of their journey rode in a small cloth pack on her back and a basket over her arm.

On gaining the road, they both glanced at the sky to read the day's prospects.

"Clouds a'ready!" the young girl grumbled. "Most likely it'll come a-drizzle-drazzle before noon!"

"Oh, I don't think so, Roanna. Yes, spring can mean showers. But the clouds are tight to the mountain, and even though the sun is—well, russet, almost, it seems—"

"Oh, Aunt, don't say that word. It's unlucky!" Roanna shivered under some inner cue.

The woman turned away uncomfortably. "Roanna, please. Just Charri. I've asked you not to call me Aunt. I have no nieces, no family, no relatives, no name—" Her voice faltered, and she lifted the fold from her bundle. "No one except my child . . . my precious baby."

Anxiety lined Charri's face as she touched the tiny, pale forehead. "Oh, my little one," she crooned, "my lovely little flower, be strong, be hungry. You sleep so long and eat so little! Couldn't you suckle a few swallows? We'll stop in a bit. You shall cry for both breasts, and your cheeks will take on the pink of bria blossoms." Her fingers stroked the baby's face. "So beautiful, so perfect. Not like your mother... Yet you haven't a name, either, until I find mine. Unless . . . a claimer . . ." She sighed and covered the child once again. This time, though, she did not hide her own face.

Roanna took no notice of the angry scar that reached from Charri's right cheekbone across the corner of her mouth. Instead, she surveyed her prospects for diversion in the miles that lay ahead.

"Aunt, how far to Lorenth? D'you expect there'll be lads there? Shall we see fine ladies in Dunkir carriages? Perhaps even soldiers?"

Charri smiled. "Do you care whether the soldiers are Russetmen or T'ribboners?"

Again Roanna shivered on cue, wrinkling her saucy, upturned nose. "Oh, Aunt, don't be sayin' that! My ma calls 'em 'the dark ones.' She never says that word. Though—" She hesitated. "The dark ones are more han'some than T'ribboners, 'specially those that shave their heads. Don't they look fearsome, Aunt?"

"*Charri*, Roanna," the woman murmured. "Which ones are you talking about? I've never seen Russetmen—excuse me—'dark ones' with shaved heads."

"Oh, no. Only T'ribboners do that. Ma says taking hair off up there makes things down lower grow. She says—"

"Roanna," Charri interrupted firmly, "when we get to Lorenth, you will take the basket and go from shop to shop, but you must buy only what we need. Unless we're careful, our money won't stretch. We have half of Arlony to cross. It's not a huge country, but big enough on foot. We must at least make Chadwich and the tinker's wife—if we find no one before that who knows my name."

Roanna remained quiet—abnormally quiet—for a whole minute. Then she spoke her thoughts. "Aunt, Arlony ain't the same as the world, is it?"

Charri smiled. "Of course not. Arlony is a country. It's one of many on the continent of North Lailand. We left Swendia yesterday. Do you remember the man at the border who asked questions and gave us a paper? Swendia is our country, and it lies east of Arlony." Charri pointed behind them. "Arlony isn't so very different from home. Except for higher mountains." She glanced grimly at the notch that loomed black and leafless above them. "People on foot and the green of spring both climb slowly. And up north— Maybe you know about Ramah to the north where Sigurth lives? You have heard of Sigurth, haven't you? Leader of T'ribboners?"

Roanna nodded knowingly.

"Well, above Ramah there's another countr—"

"But I thought a content was the world, and Arlony was—"

"Con-ti-nent, Roanna. No, the world has four continents divided by great oceans. We live on North Lailand, which has many countries and many people. South Lailand has a lot, too, because it's warm and mostly flat. Did you ever eat greensweet melon, Roanna?"

"Oh, yes! Once we had one on Middle Night. It was so good we got in a fight, and soon it wasn't nuthin' but mush. We cried, all ten of us."

"I should think you would—in shame!" Charri tightened her lips. "Such delectable eating, ruined by greedy children. The melons grow in South Lailand, but they take a long time to ripen, long enough for ships to bring them to this continent for us to enjoy. They cost a lot, though; poor people get only a taste now and again."

Charri shifted the baby to her other arm to ease a sudden pang. *I cried, too, over greensweet melon I couldn't have. . . .* But she lifted her chin resolutely and continued her geography lesson.

"Another continent, Great Zelland, is far, far away but has no settled countries. It's very large, with more volcanoes and earthquakes than we have. It's so far and so dangerous, hardly anyone ever goes there. Some do, I guess, trying to get rich. Plenty of treasure there, though not much rosillum, they say. Most of those who go never make it back. Such a waste!" Charri lapsed into silence, her inner eye scanning the contorted landscape of a continent that could lure strong, able, and otherwise sensible men to certain death. She shook her head sadly. "Kravesta," she went on, "the fourth continent, is a little closer but cold and wild. Hardly anyone wants to live there, either."

"Not even soldiers or fine ladies?" Roanna ground her nose with the heel of her hand. "You said, Aunt, I could buy me somethin' special—a ribbon, maybe. The color of the year. What year is it, Aunt?"

Charri sighed. "This is an orange year, Roanna, the Ninety-First Year of the Earthquake."

"What earthquake? The orange one?"

"Yes—no." Charri blinked her eyes in confusion. "A North Lailand earthquake, Roanna. The earthquake isn't orange, the year—this year is orange. It's the Ninety-First Year of the Earthquake—an orange year. Last year was a blue year. Yes, I did say you could buy something, but I didn't necessarily mean in Lorenth. Somewhere—maybe on our way back—we'll either buy or find a ribbon or something like it, just for you. We won't have enough for food, though, if we spend free in every town."

Again Roanna fell silent, gestating another question. "Aunt, if Sigurth leads T'ribboners, who leads the 'dark ones'?"

"Claeman leads Rus—the 'dark ones.' "

"Does he live at Ramah?"

"No, he lives in the west, high in a mountain fortress. They say there's always been a Claeman there and always a Sigurth in Ramah as far back as anyone can remember."

Roanna looked incredulous. "Even as far back as people near to dying can remember? They'd be very, *very* old!"

Charri smiled and shook her head. "No. If they were father and son and grandson and on down, they could still have the same names and not be—"

"Aunt, look!" Roanna pointed up the road. "Riders a-comin'! Fast! Do y' suppose it's 'dark ones' coming after us?"

Inch by inch, into a black hole. Everything seemed to stop while Driss hung on the edge, his brain racing through alternatives. *The other side . . . too far away, can't even touch it. Hang on, Driss . . . but to what?* When he first fell, one rein caught on a harness hame and ripped from his hand, leaving him with a single rein to hold, if it didn't break—or slip. Sweaty hands, greasy leather, oiled just last week in preparation for the trip. *Inch by inch . . . Let go of the rein and dig in with my fingers?* But into what? Rock? Last year's weeds? *No. Fingers won't do it. Maybe Rona . . . forget it. Damn. Damn the slippery rein.* But it did connect him to two tons of horseflesh—horses that didn't want to fall into a dark shadow.

The shadow tightened its grip. He did, too—convulsively. By now, Lady was rearing and plunging along with Toggen. The uncoordinated action of the terrified animals alternately jerked him upward and dropped him further in.

Rona, shrieking frantically after being knocked down by Lady—prudent distance notwithstanding—scrambled up the knoll on hands and knees.

Driss kicked both legs, trying to gain leverage. He peered over his shoulder into the depth.

What he saw made him kick even more wildly.

"Back!" he bellowed to the horses, a new edge to his voice. "Back!"

His voice signaled even more panic to the animals.

"Rona! *Help me!*"

He slid further—from waist to shoulders, from shoulders to neck. Then—slowly, agonizingly—downward became upward. Either his command to the horses had begun to register in their dim minds, or they instinctively decided on a more orderly retreat. Inch by inch upward on his stomach, each breath a gasping grunt, he willed his screaming muscles to hold as the animals dragged him to solid ground.

The horses halted, wild-eyed, pawing nervously. Driss lay motionless, fingers still frozen to the rein.

Rona stopped shrieking but kept away from the horses. Once she saw Driss breathing and still in one piece, she sat down to assess her own personal damage. "I can't believe this! We're hardly across the border of Arlony, and already we've been chased by a pack of wolfcats and mauled by deranged horses!"

Yes, thought Driss. *Wolfcats. Wolfcats worked me over. Am I even alive? Can't move. Can I think? Name—Drissan. Age?*

Who cares? Year? Ninety-First Year of the Earthquake. Country of origin? Swendia. But she said Arlony. What are you doing in Arlony? Rosillum, but don't tell Claeman. Or anyone else. Ooh—my body . . . every nerve, every muscle. Wolfcats screaming, clawing . . .

"Driss, are you all right? You're not saying anything. I must say I'm surprised. You *pride* yourself in being such a wonderful horseman. Well, I certainly wouldn't call this wonderful. Look at me . . . horse slop all over my arm—my whole side, for that matter. Look what it did to my robe."

Look what's down there, Rona. Look down. Look down. How many down there? A hundred? A thousand? What is this place? For beggar's sake, look at what's in the bottom of that hole!

"And my legs. They were already purple from banging around the wagon. Now they're scratched, my elbow scraped—bleeding, even. Rosillum or no . . . Driss, you seem to be *trying* to get me to walk out on you. Are you all right? I wish you'd talk to me."

Driss turned over, teeth clenched against a groan. "Walk out on me, " he repeated mechanically. His lips, still white, twisted wryly. "Yes, Rona, my beauty—tenderhearted, full of pity, brimming with compassion. You might have had to walk out, at that."

3

The mid-morning arrival of Driss and Rona at the concealed campsite caused an uproar. Rolind on his self-appointed watch spotted them first. With every fold of his belted tunic in precise military order and his iron-stiff mustache twitching under the magnitude of his news, he marched crisply to Jonn, a comfortably homely man dressed in comfortably homely brown. Younger than Rolind by some twenty years, Jonn had been pacing anxiously around the loaded carriage and cook wagon.

"Lieutenant." Rolind saluted. "I believe the general is coming. I sighted the canopy wagon from the lookout, and they appear headed toward our bivouac."

Relief warred with annoyance in the physiognomic disarray that was Jonn's face. "About time. With this late a start, we'll be lucky to get anywhere near Lorenth by nightfall. Thank you, Rolind," he added as the older man continued to stand at attention. "And you needn't call me 'Lieutenant' or Driss 'General'; this isn't an army, you know."

"Yes, sir; very good, sir."

Jonn shook his head and turned to pass the word. "Treese . . . Bren . . . Keltie! They're coming! Rolind just spotted them."

By the time the dappled grays trotted into the wooded campsite, the entire group had gathered in welcome. Two women and six other men stood with Jonn and Rolind. Three children bounced up and down in excitement, while a fourth looked on warily. Dropping stiffly from the wagon, Driss tossed the reins to a lanky, brown-headed lad. "Here you go, Amarl. Unhitch the team and let them loose on some grub after they've cooled. They did a bit of work this morning."

Driss helped Rona down, then turned to the clamoring children. With a roar of mock ferocity, he tossed the youngest over his shoulder—and regretted it immediately. "Benzel, lad, I always knew you'd strip my skin off someday. Now you've done it." He pulled up his shirt to show an enormous bruise and assorted abrasions. The other two children were unimpressed and joined the attack. "Hey!" Driss yelped, staggering under a second climber. "Cut it out! Benzel, call off your sister. Nessa, stop. You're breaking my leg! Mercy, Vilda! Stop! I escape one death, only to . . . hallo! Who's that?" As he tried to detach the trio, he spotted a scrawny, thin-chested boy watching intently from a safe vantagepoint near one of the women.

"This is Steph." The woman stroked the youngster's head. Ragged and wise, the child looked back at her with eyes unfathomable in mirth and kindliness. "He found us. Said he heard one of the mules calling his name."

She hurried on at Driss's look of alarm. "It's all right; nobody's following. We checked everything. Treese and Keltie took the rifles and waited near the road to make sure he wasn't a decoy. He really was alone. He told us he'd been with a couple different families but didn't like them, so he took off on his own."

Driss twirled the leather ties on his scarred vest, weighing the possible threat, then jerked his head up and looked at her narrowly. "What was that about the mules, Celine?"

Celine laughed. "I wondered if you really heard." She turned to the child. "Tell him, Steph. Tell Driss what the mules said and why you came in."

As horsemen emerged from a crease in the mountain, Charri stiffened and pushed Roanna off the road, throwing a fold of her brown cloak over her to help the shrubbery tone down the girl's yellow cape. She tucked her own head into invisibility.

With empty jugs banging behind the saddles, the riders swept toward them in a lather. Just short of the women's hiding place they jerked their wild-eyed mounts to an uneasy standstill. Tattered stubs of blue, purple, and green ribbons on arms and legs identified them as T'ribboner soldiers. Their appearance and mood made Charri wonder if they'd been on the short end of a two-day battle. They milled about, cursing sourly.

"Mus' be here somewheres. They gotta be!"

Charri's heart pounded as she squeezed Roanna, who was squirming in fear. Her infant stirred, as well. *Please, baby;*

please stay asleep, Charri implored silently. *This is not the time for hunger. A few minutes. A few minutes. Stay still now. Hush . . .*

"I tol' you, they went the other way!"

"Sure, they went the other way. We went the other way after them but didn't find them, did we? They circled. Must've. Hot bird in a cage like that don't just go *hoosh!* off in the air. Some damn hot-bird trick. Git goin'!"

The speaker flailed the others with his quirt, and the band clattered down the mountain.

Roanna craned her stubby neck after them. "T'ribboners! Oh, Aunt, do you s'pose one of 'em was Sigurth?" Such a thought apparently vaporized her fear.

Charri smiled shakily. "I doubt it. I'm sure the T'ribboner commander-in-chief would look more respectable than those riders!"

The encounter made the two—especially Charri—more watchful as they inched up the steep, wooded slope that lay between them and the town of Lorenth.

The day wore on, punctuated by frequent stops for rest and refreshment. The mewling of the infant was easily stilled by a mouthful of milk, to the dismay and discomfort of its mother. No amount of coaxing brought relief to the overflowing breasts, and when the heat of the climb forced off the brown cloak, her dress beneath clung tight and dark to the exaggerated contours of her body.

Between responses to Roanna's chatter, Charri drew strands of long, cinnamon hair off her damp neck and let her mind range over the assortment of hopes that had set her on this journey. She knew they were mostly wisps of smoke: the tinker's wife; a remote "cousin," so called; a neighbor who had moved away fifteen years ago. What could these people possibly remember— even if Charri did find them—about an obscure Arlonian woman who died soon after giving birth in Swendia? Would they remember the child's name after all these years? So important, a name; more important, even, than a footmark to an Arlonian. Only those who hadn't a name knew just how important.

An even wispier hope lurked deep within. *Glinneth . . . Glinneth . . .* Nothing more than the name, yet in the face of the friend in Swendia who had spoken it, she had felt—fleetingly—the substance of hope. Who was he, where was he—

"Aunt, we keep on passin' cottages. Shouldn't we be lookin' for a place?" Roanna's humid face held tired hopefulness. "Looks like it'll pour out rain any minute now."

Charri halted, the mist-shrouded mountain still looming implacably over them. The damp air, though cool, added more moisture to her face. A sullen stillness, strange to springtime, exaggerated the pounding in her ears. She sighed, then scanned the leaden sky, gauging the amount of daylight left. Looking down at her dress, she smiled wryly. "If it did rain I doubt I could get much wetter. But you, child . . . yes, we should look soon. We may not find welcome at the first house, and it wouldn't do to be out in the rain all night. You watch now for our house, one with chickens pecking around barrels, and baskets by the door. Even if their roof is weedy, they'll have food to share. And you, my baby," she crooned, turning to the weightless bundle in her arms, "you shall find laughter in the whiskers of a cat or the bleat of a new lamb."

The three crept along the mountain road, the word *Glinneth* casting a tiny gleam over the shadows in Charri's heart.

As evening came on, clouds gathered moisture and gloom to feed on during the night. High on the west side of the mountain the rider of an enormous gray stallion picked his way up a shadowy brook, the horse's hooves, like barrel lids, smacking tiered pools of water. An elaborate whistle from somewhere above brought the stallion's head up with an inquiring nicker. When the rider whistled his response, a figure stepped out from a darkening ledge.

The rider rose on his stirrups. "Ho, Durk! There you are. I've kept you waiting. And in such weather."

A youth, dwarfed by the dappled stallion, grasped the hand extended. "No matter. I was late myself. My mare threw a shoe, so I left her below, rather than risk a cracked hoof." He smoothed the massive neck with awe. The horse nipped his tunic.

"Your manners, Venge!" scolded the rider indulgently. "A fine mount, Durk, but a horse of strength often finds diversion in bad habits. Do you remember the little gelding last week?"

"The one Vlian addressed as 'Your Excellency, Lord Mayor of All Vices'?"

"The very one. A fitting title. Strong and quick. He would curse having to carry the likes of me but could do it well enough. You have news, son?"

"Yes. They seem to have come across at a point some three miles north of the border station. No one actually saw where. And they are sixteen, not fifteen as you heard. They've added a child."

The rider pursed his lips. "Still twelve adults, though."

"Yes." Durk's face took on a quizzical expression. "There is one whose name is *known*." He paused significantly and noted his companion's raised eyebrows.

"How about the others, lad?"

Durk drew a thoughtful breath. "A few may be gold, but most, I'd say, most are empty."

"I see." The man's thick body tilted as the stallion shifted a hind foot. "Any word on the woman with the girl?" He leaned forward, eyes twinkling. "What shall we call her, lad?"

Durk smiled. "I'd call her a bruised bria blossom."

The rider settled back. "Ah! Bruises will heal. Emptiness, though, has no room for health. Too full of itself. The group again—where is it headed?"

"My guess is they'll stay in Lorenth a day or two, maybe longer. But where they're headed . . ." Durk shrugged. "Could be anywhere—south, west, north."

The other man nodded slowly. "*Known*." He spoke the word with feeling. "A person known can first be emptied, then filled with wholeness."

"I thought you'd be interested in that one." Durk smiled. "Does he have a task? Some part to play in the great conflict?"

The rider did not reply right away but lifted his eyes for a moment to the cloud-entangled treetops. "The great conflict goes on, in and around us all. But a task? Perhaps it's a task just to submit to emptying and then to choose wholeness. But I'd sooner guess most of it will have to be done for him. Our task, Durk."

"What about the others?"

The big man cocked his head roguishly. "You yourself said some were gold but most were empty. They'll sort themselves out."

He picked up the reins, his voice rising over the galvanizing horse. "Wholeness. And bria blossoms, eh, Durk?"

Durk laughed and danced sideways to avoid a mangled foot.

"You need a ride down to your mare. What think you, Venge? Can we carry an extra fly?"

Driss and others of the group stared at the new boy, intrigued by Celine's preposterous words concerning talking mules. Encouraged by her hand stroking his shoulder, Steph looked at these strangers who had taken him in. They seemed friendly, and he approved of Driss's warm, laughing horseplay with the other children. The boy took a big breath, eyes round and solemn on this occasion of speech before the powers. "I wanted t' go to Lorenth—see? And the hill jis' kep' goin' up, and then—" He took another large draft. "Then I heard 'em call to me. They said—"

"This is the mules now?" Driss questioned.

"Yeah, the mules. They said, 'Steph, Steph—' I don't know how they knew my name—I never ever met 'em before—but that's what they said. 'Steph, Steph,' they said—'come on in. This place is okay. The people are nice, and you get grain once in a while, 'specially if you work hard.' So I come in and went over to talk more close, and—and Benzel found me and told his ma." He nodded toward Celine. "And she took my clothes off and washed me up and down, and—and that man—" He pointed to the cook. "That man give me a breakfast bigger 'an I ever, ever had!" His eyes sparkled in the telling of food.

Driss rocked back on his heels, tongue pushing his cheek. "We'll need to keep a tight watch over our mules from now on if they're going to blab to passersby like that! Did the horses contribute to this conversation, too?"

"Sir?"

"I'm sorry." Driss squatted before the boy and took his hands. "Did the horses say anything?"

Another big breath. "Well—" He looked around at the animals, saddled and harnessed for departure, as though Driss had presented him with a test. "I didn't meet 'em all. Your horse Strada giggles a lot. She seems nervous. And Beck and Bock don't like it when Lady and Toggen are gone."

The adults looked at each other, at Steph, and again at each other.

Celine spoke softly, "I didn't tell him the horses' names, or that Strada was Driss's horse. Did you, Jonn?"

Her husband shook his head, and when the children, as well, denied telling the boy, he shrugged. "The kids must've tipped him off. There's got to be an explanation. Whatever," Jonn continued, glancing at the sky, "we need to get rolling. We'll likely hit rain before dark, especially higher on the mountain. What happened, Driss? Another fight with Toggen?"

Driss rubbed his side and looked away from Jonn's compelling eyes. "Well—you might say the rash part of me got carried away. Pretty stupid, actually. Rona and I were at that turnoff overlooking the valley, the one we stopped at yesterday. What a view, especially at night!" Driss tipped back and sighed deliciously. "Lake dressed in moonlight, night larks, soft breeze off the mountain—" Eyes frolicking, his voice dropped to a whisper. "And *Rona.*

"Anyway," he went on, "we got up in plenty of time to get back for breakfast. I had the horses harnessed and set to go when a dozen or so hellbenders came around the switchback above us. An all-night bash in the hill, no doubt. If we'd stayed still, they might not have noticed us. I decided to run for it, so we took off uphill—directly at them. Yeah, yeah." He dropped his eyes from the ring of incredulous faces. "I said it was dumb. Plowed right through. Scattered men and horses over half an acre. One of them saw Rona, and the few still mounted gave chase. We were way ahead but could never have outrun them, drunk or no. That's when it came to me I had holes in my head."

Jonn shook his head wonderingly but said nothing.

"Then I remembered an old trace road we passed yesterday. Looked for it, and sure enough. We ducked down, and they went by. But the horses had run uphill, so we unhitched to walk them a bit."

He stopped and chewed his thumb. "I'm . . . still trying to figure out what happened next." He paused again, then went on briskly. "The short version is, I nearly fell into an earthcrack, and Lady and Toggen pulled me out. That's the short of it." He looked at the circle of intense faces. "The long of it . . ." He stopped with a sigh and forced a smile. "Yeah, the long of it. Someday . . . I'll unravel it and have a grand story. But here we are," he finished, brown eyes crackling once again, "alive, more or less whole, and set to travel. What do you say—shall we pack up and go?"

As they scattered to their tasks, one of the men waited for Driss. Tall and lithe with morosely handsome features, Treese had a good mind—better, perhaps, than either Driss or Jonn. Had he utilized his native authority, he might have commanded men and women alike. But he had no desire to lead or help make decisions. Instead, he grumbled.

"You know, Driss, your love life would do an alley cat proud. On top of that, you—*A*—pull a jackass stunt that only pure luck got you out of, and—*B*—nearly kill yourself in a hole. Rona's not all that dazzling that you wouldn't see an earthcrack. Doesn't the rosillum mean anything to you?"

"Oh, isn't she?" Driss laughed and punched the other man's shoulder. He immediately regretted the move, even before his shin suffered the consequence. Once before—before Jonn thought to warn him—he had felt Treese's dislike of being touched by another person, especially a man. Only certain women were exempt. Treese had perfected a maneuver that seemed a clumsy blunder and for which he always apologized. In truth, the well-aimed, well-timed kick kept him insulated from the foolery of a close-knit group.

"Lighten up, Treese. We'll get it, all right. I know it means a lot. I have my dream, and rosillum is the only thing that can make it happen."

"The *money* from rosillum."

"Yes, the money. Lots of it. Enough to fund our dreams—yours and mine. We're a group of dreamers, Treese, and ours is an ideal team. Some have skills, some have money, but we're hitched together by dreams. Big dreams like mine of exploring Great Zelland. Little dreams like Jonn and Celine's of just getting out of the hole they're in and buying a house. We'll get it, Treese. We'll find Uncle's liggeth mine and carry off his stash of rosillum—right from under Claeman's nose. He'll sit surrounded by Russetmen in that hulking fortress not a mile away and never see us. He probably doesn't know the mine or the rosillum is there, for all it's his real estate."

"Humph!" snorted Treese. "Even if he doesn't, you can be sure he'll monitor us all the way—three teams, three pack mules, four saddle horses, twelve adults—if you can call Amarl an adult—and three kids—no, four, counting Jonn and Celine's latest benevolence.

"Speaking of Claeman," Treese went on, changing the subject, "did you see any of his soldiers on the road?"

Driss shook his head. "No, I think the bunch I hit were T'ribboners, Sigurth's men. Thought I saw ribbons stubs, and they didn't have the dark faces of Russetmen. You're right, though: Claeman's boys will notice us, that's sure. And without a travel permit, we want to stay clear of them. Yes, yes," he said, raising a hand against a sudden hardening in Treese's face, "the permit business. Let's not hash that again. It was a group decision. We talked over the pros and cons of taking Amarl if it meant having to sneak into the country—which, you have to admit, wasn't hard to do. They don't guard the border very well. When we talked it over, you were—"

"The only naysayer. Is that a crime?"

"My guess is, you don't want Amarl along because he irks you. Isn't that true?"

Treese's mouth twitched ambiguously, but he said nothing.

"Sure, he's a nuisance sometimes; what teenager isn't? But most of us felt taking him was worth the risk. A 'donkey-jobber' for the chores all of us hate—you especially. This isn't a dangerous country, Treese. Everyone we know who's traveled in Arlony told us Claeman and his Russetmen won't bother if we mind our own affairs, especially with women and kids along. They'll see us, yes, but the military is after troublemakers, and we're not about to make trouble."

"Rosillum thieves aren't troublemakers?"

"Oh, come on! You know what I mean. Anyway, there won't be a problem."

"What about Sigurth's T'ribboners?"

"They do seem to pop up everywhere, but so far they're more joke than threat. And since they're on the short end of the civil war right now, they don't care two figs about travel permits." Driss looked at Treese and laughed. "Two armies to watch out for just makes the trip more challenging!"

"Just what did happen this morning, Driss?"

Driss shook his head slowly and studied the ground. "It's not so much what happened as what it means. Yes, I did fall into the thing. I was between the horses, talking to Rona, and would've walked right in—it was sort of hidden. But the horses shied, so I only stepped in."

"Oh. That's better? Stepping in instead of walking in?"

"Well, yes. I was able to hang onto one of the reins and eventually got pulled out. But it was closer to a sudden end than I care to come."

"So what's the great philosophical dilemma?"

Driss shrugged. "No dilemma. I just don't know what to make of what I saw. Like bones. Down in the crack. A pile of them. When I first looked over my shoulder, my thought was, "Um, let's not add to that pile.' But when I looked again, I got thinking. Nothing unusual about the earthcrack itself. The quake left lots just like it, some bigger, some smaller. But the bones: what kind were they? Sure, you could say a lot of animals might have tumbled in during the ninety-one years post-Earthquake. But presumably most animals are at least as bright as Toggen. And the skulls—round and six, eight inches long—didn't look like any animals I know about. Then my mind steps back and does a little calculating: What does *round, small,* plus *non-animal* add up to? What's the only thing it could be, Treese? *Children.*" He stopped and gnawed his knuckle.

Treese raised an eyebrow but said nothing.

"Then the big sloping arena and funny little hill that might have been put there for a purpose. People have been there, Treese—lots of people. Not recently. Not this year or last, maybe. But they've been there. *People* plus an *amphitheater* plus *small bones*— Yes, Rolind, what is it?" He looked up as the old soldier halted before them.

"The troops are ready, sir, the duffel loaded, your mount waiting."

"Thanks, Rolind. I'll be right there. Did the rifles get stowed?"

"Yes, sir. I saw to the ordnance myself. All weapons are in their proper place."

"Very good."

Rolind saluted and about-faced smartly.

Treese rolled his eyes as he watched Rolind bark orders to the children. "A fruit basket! More excess baggage than Amarl, even."

Driss shrugged. "No baggage with money attached is excess. He doesn't have as much as Garrick, to be sure, but every bit helps. And he's good with the kids. He drills them, they love it."

"Oh, sure—'Staden—hom—hou—hree!' " Treese mimicked Rolind's military exercises. "And have you noticed? Even the war scars on his face stand at attention when he salutes."

"Oh, come on, Treese, it's not raining yet. Climb out of the gloom crack! Hey, Thilrec!" he shouted to the cook as they jogged toward the waiting caravan, "isn't it lunchtime? Rona and I haven't had breakfast yet!"

The four gamboling children caught his eye, and under his breath he muttered, "Just don't give me anything with small bones in it, thank you."

4

Teenagers have an eye for luxury, and Amarl was the quintessential teen. One of the things that enticed him to join the rosillum seekers was Garrick's Dunkir carriage. Amarl knew his chief responsibility lay with the horses and pack mules; he knew that none in the group was lower than he—not even weird old Rolind; he knew he would seldom, if ever, ride in that ultimate of luxuries, that his berth would never rise above the front of the cook wagon. He knew all that—but hoped still.

So it was on this fine, brisk morning after the night of rain, that Amarl knew rapture. True, he had been invited along on this shopping trip purely for his burden-bearing capabilities: he fit into the carriage more easily than would a pack mule. He would be dumped off with baskets to trudge from stall to stall through the marketplace while Thilrec picked through herbs as fussy cooks do. Garrick, meanwhile, would amuse himself by showing off his high-stepping, blooded bays. Still, those few miles going and coming made it all worthwhile.

Garrick himself was a drawback to the outing. The fleshy, smelly proprietor of all this wealth had nothing else to recommend him. Amarl in particular shied away from close contact. "He's wet all over, inside and out. Burbles on both ends, sweats and smells like a goat, sprays scum when he talks!" When Keltie reminded him of this just before the boy climbed into the carriage, Amarl shrugged roguishly. "Hey, a fellow needs a good soak now and then!"

Lorenth had sprung up along one of several streams that flowed off the mountain. A bustling city, it retained more charm than did Chadwich, its counterpart beyond the next line of mountains. Thick-trunked camblors arched gracefully over the approach road, picking up the curve of three ancient stone bridges spanning the river. Not only were these bridges Pre-Earthquake, they dated back four eras to the Green Wars, that century-long conflict between Arlony and neighboring Swendia from which the rosillum seekers had come. The endurance of these bridges under the ravages of time and the cyclical skirmish of opposing armies spoke well of the craftsmanship of some long-forgotten public-works engineer who rested his faith in ultimate peace.

Garrick held the bays to a slow trot through the camblor arch until he reached the crowded approach to a bridge, then put them into a flashy canter. As a matter of course he kept the Dunkir carriage in top condition, polishing the gold trim daily and wiping mud and dust from its shiny black finish. This day his investment paid handsomely in the form of admiring stares.

They came to the marketplace, that boiling mosaic of colorful canvas, patterned displays of produce, and vocal, gesticulating tradesmen. Stalls and carts and blankets offered wares, exotic and humble, to the throng of shoppers converging on the square. A zestful challenge to the eager shopper, a tedious bore to such as Amarl. He winced at Thilrec's instructions to Garrick: "Be back in three hours. That should give us enough time."

Three hours! What that meant in terms of wait and weight gave the boy a certain boldness that under other circumstances he would never have considered.

"Uh, Thilrec, maybe I could just ride around with Garrick until you've had a chance to look things over. Then I'll come back, and we can zip from stall to stall and pick it up all at once. Wouldn't that be okay?"

"Not okay," Thilrec replied firmly. "You expect me to go around the market twice so you can loll in the carriage. Go all the way back for a handful of garlic, forty pods of kuhnel, a few bundles of parsley? Hang the inconvenience: Amarl wants to play! What do you think we feed you for?"

As he continued lining out Amarl's faults, the boy studied a makeshift tent pole nearby. Concentrating on his spine, he straightened, then bent it in varying degrees, trying to align it with the crooked shaft. This mental game served as the prow of a boat, dividing the force of Thilrec's tirade and allowing it to wash ineffectively around him. When Thilrec again directed his attention to Garrick, Amarl rolled his eyes in relief, suddenly awed by his folly and the complications of alienating the cook.

What you thought around Thilrec didn't much matter, but you couldn't be too careful with your words, especially if you were Amarl. Thilrec was an artist with food. Not only could he dish up consistently fine meals, he did it under conditions few chefs would tolerate.

A man quick of word and action, he also had an artist's temperament, as his assigned helpers—Amarl, Jharne's wife Celine, and Bren's wife Griselle—soon discovered. With his own meticulous methods, he gave a sense of never having left the elegant tavern that had known his service for twelve years. The cook wagon was hardly less impressive than Garrick's Dunkir. Every utensil, every ingredient had its well-scrubbed place, and Thilrec ruled his portable kitchen with despotic hand. If you got on his bad side, you paid. Even now, as Amarl contemplated all that went into food preparation, the cost of gourmet was high.

Leaving Amarl to his donkeywork, Garrick drove from the market area to a stately, tree-lined boulevard paralleling the river. He began a well-practiced maneuver, clicking his tongue, muttering to himself and greeting important-looking persons with noisy presumption—all with specific purpose. His flashy carriage seldom failed to gain him a companion—female preferred—to wile away his free time. Without this prop, he would have received only scorn. Money, though, was Garrick's friend.

He had method as well. First he would drive his circuit, looking over possibilities, then zero in on likely prospects. He expected and received many rejections, but a thirty-three-year layer of thick, oily skin served him well.

On this day he had surveyed and bawled greeting to only five candidates when he spotted a woman who looked familiar. Her brown dress and coarse cloak told of hard times, making her accessible to Garrick. But her face and the creative lines of the dress set her off as a woman of experience with men. That part gave him pause.

After a couple of passes that finally caught her attention, he pulled up and jumped down, flicking a coin at a passing urchin to hold the restless bays.

"Oh, my—if it isn't—well, I say, it's been so long since I last saw you that—you know, when I saw you as I was driving by in my Dunkir, I said to myself, 'You know, that looks just like—' and what a surprise it is to meet you again! Would you like to go for a ride in my Dunkir?"

He bobbed up and down and offered a soft, wet hand, a bit shaken by the woman's presence and the effect of her trim, low-cut dress.

Her calculating look took in everything, and she returned a careful smile. "Ah, yes! Garrick, I believe—or is it Garrish? You're Drissan's friend, aren't you?"

"You remember!" He writhed delightedly. "Has it been two years, three, perhaps, since we saw you last?"

"Since he grew tired of me?" she returned wryly. "How is Drissan? Do you see him often?"

"Oh, yas—yas, indeed!" He stomped and clapped as for a performance. "We're traveling together—a group of us—westward."

"Oh, really! Same direction I'm heading. To Cassia. I have a . . . friend who's setting me up in a job there—a business, really, already established." A hard, inscrutable smile played at her mouth. "You should drop by and see me, honey, if you get that far." With professional disregard for Garrick's corona of foul odors, she drew a well-manicured finger around his face.

He wriggled and sweat and pumped his mouth ineffectively. The woman laughed derisively.

"Where is Drissan now?" she inquired. "Is he here with you?"

Garrick shook his head and tried to direct her toward the carriage. "Perhaps we could ride around a bit, and I could tell you about him."

Again the woman calculated carefully, avoiding direct acceptance or refusal. "Are those dark curls as fetching as ever, and his fine clothes?"

Her one-sided smile seemed to mock men in general, but Garrick took no note of anything except his cleverness in engaging her in conversation, with the distinct possibility of moving her a step further. He tried again.

"I have nearly two hours before picking up Amarl and Thilrec, and—"

"Thilrec! You don't mean Thilrec of Klingen's Tavern? *That* Thilrec?"

Ahh! Unexpected leverage. "Yas—ah, um—we bought Thilrec—that is, we bought his services for this trip."

It worked, and for the next hour, the high-stepping bays drew sufficient attention to satisfy both occupants of the Dunkir carriage.

To retain her company, he measured out information about Driss and kept his trump card—a meeting with Thilrec—until all else had failed.

Finally, however, she had shaken hands with the famous man and proffered her faintly scornful thanks to Garrick.

"Tell Drissan," she murmured, dropping her eyes, "that I have a quiet room over the clothier shop, with an outside stairway in the rear. If he'd like to get together for a chat . . ." She turned away suggestively, then leaned close with a wicked smile.

"And Garrish, honey—the name is Clettie."

5

In an alley behind one of Lorenth's many taverns—an alley strewn with broken bottles and crocks, rain-matted rags, the bloated remains of a dead cat, rotting garbage, and shallow, fetid pools that digested insects and rodents alike—here in this dismal alley a small boy sought recreation. He slunk to a patch of sunlight and glanced nervously over his shoulder at the crusted door he had just exited.

He was no less filthy himself, thin hair caked in random spikes, his ragged shirt and too-small trousers a mottled puce. With one hand he dug at a scab on his leg; with the other he troweled yet another layer of nose paste over his grimy face.

With eyes narrow and dull, he checked his recreational opportunities with seeming haste. And for good reason. From inside the tavern came sounds of exasperation. He cringed but persevered in this tiny moment of freedom, looking desperately for something to make it all worthwhile.

His eye fell on the cat corpse. He lunged toward it and clawed through matted fur, seeking some morsel that might pass for food. Only when the stench grew stronger than the pangs of his belly did he hurl it vengefully at a deathbird, recently landed to scavenge on its own.

The boy had little time for disappointment. The door banged open, and an enormous brute of a woman plunged into the alley.

The lad froze, his natural coloration concealing him amid the debris of the alley.

Not for long. The woman's warring eye circled expertly, and with nostrils blazing she heaved her bulk at astonishing speed across the alley to flatten the boy with her meaty arm.

In a well-practiced ritual of cursing and screams, the child's playtime ended. The crusted door slammed, and before the ground had stopped reverberating, the deathbird got on with its banquet of dead cat.

Lorenth did not agree with Roanna, and she became grossly, disgustingly ill. For perhaps half a minute, Charri considered simply walking away. The girl's mother would scarcely care: with ten children, she had been more than happy when Charri had proposed taking Roanna along as a companion-helper. One less body in the crammed cottage. However, the chains that bound Charri to duty would not permit such easy escape.

When Roanna, sent on errands, failed to return by nightfall to their tiny room over the public livery stable, Charri ventured out in search of her. The market stalls had long since emptied, with only wind left to sweep straw and litter. The few passersby hurrying to their suppers could not remember seeing a girl in a yellow cape.

For two hours she walked up and down every street, taking care to avoid both Russetmen and T'ribboners. Ever since she could remember, her several guardians had threatened her with Russetmen if she was naughty. She intuitively avoided T'ribboners, though for different reasons. Not till she was older had she come to realize that both were soldiers of Arlony, not Swendia, though they often spilled over the border, drifting well beyond the town from which she had come.

It was a small cluster of dark-faced Russetmen that indirectly helped her find Roanna. She had headed uphill to get around this particular band, climbing to where she could see the jeweled city sprawled across the river. The soldiers, however, had also turned and seemed, in the shadow of night, to be following her. She was in Arlony now. The early warnings took on substance. Here on the upper reaches of Lorenth, it would not do to be pushed into mountain wilds at night, especially by Russetmen. Thus she fled down a different street toward the center of town.

A tiny lane she hadn't noticed before seemed to offer a measure of safety. This took her past a small tavern that belched drunken laughter and stinking fumes. She would have hurried by, but mother instinct heard one small sound out of the din that brought her up abruptly. She plunged into the dim recess, anger overriding caution.

The place was not large. A shelf along one wall held leaky barrels of ale and unplattered food of suspicious origin. Tipped benches lay scattered across a carpet of fetid sawdust. The establishment's two lamps played darkly across rough-planked walls.

A number of men stood in a circle, cheering and whistling at some unseen bit of entertainment. Hesitating just a moment to get her bearings, Charri shoved between broad shoulders to grasp Roanna, the tipsy center of attention.

Just as she laid hands on her, she became aware of the girl's wretched state and backed off in horror. Roanna had been stuffed with food and drink to the point of volcanic return. What was worse, her clothing, her hair, her shoes were covered with vomit.

Despite her condition, Roanna babbled blissfully. "Oh, Aunt," she cried in the same drunken tone Charri had heard from outside, "you've come to the pardy! You've . . . you've—" She broke off and clutched her middle as a new wave of misery hit. "Oh, Aunt! I be . . . sick!"

Dismayed, Charri watched her retch as the onlookers, well seasoned with T'ribboners, roared in laughter.

That was the moment she considered walking away from Roanna. After all, her own sick baby was quite enough to worry about.

One of the men tipped the child into this new pool of corruption and rolled her about in it. Charri, baby clutched under the shielding cloak, jerked the man by the hair, fury blazing from her eyes. For once heedless of her scar and drawing her slender frame tall, she fastened him with furnace heat—this she-bear, this defending warrior with her back to the city gate, this steel measuring rod against which the rough T'ribboner appeared bent and flaccid. A wave of astonished silence fell over the group. Without a word, Charri drew Roanna up and all but carried her out the door, ignoring the filth ruining her own clothing.

While this was going on, a small figure cut crab-like around the shadowy edge of the room. With head tucked into what little shirt was left him, the boy who earlier had sought recreation in the alley scuttled between benches. He rode the crest of the wave in front of Charri and Roanna, unseen by anyone else. He stayed just far enough ahead to keep from being stepped on, yet close enough to avoid notice, a maneuver that appeared well practiced.

Charri, shaking from anger and the comprehension of her audacity, halted under the street lamp after a few steps of this strange parade.

"Please," she said to the boy, "get out of our way. We must leave here quickly!"

The lad took hold of her skirt and looked at her dumbly, plaintively. His nose still bubbled, and he had the added color of a black eye and a fresh cut on his cheekbone. Around his neck hung a collar of blue, purple, and green, plaited from some soldier's ribbons, the streamers forming a sort of leash.

This strange ribbon collar, though not something Charri had actually seen before, set something astir in her subconscious. Something someone had told her not long ago . . . She shivered and tried to pull away, but the lad placed himself underfoot and would not be dislodged. He continued to tug in wordless pleading.

"I'm sorry," Charri said, "I can't help you. I have nothing to give you. Please. Get out of the way."

Roanna continued to weep loudly, with occasional halts to drain her stomach, not particular about where or on whom.

Charri, after trying vainly to keep her moving, finally stopped in exasperation and pushed the boy firmly from her.

"You must leave us! I can't help you. I have nothing to give! Go away!"

Her efforts to shake him off got unexpected help from three T'ribboners heading for the tavern. With a look of terror on seeing them, the lad turned abruptly and dove toward the nearest darkness.

Not before being spotted by the soldiers. They leapt baying after him, and with uncomfortable relief Charri saw them all disappear into the black void.

With the boy out of the way and her anger cooled by the night air, she had only old, familiar resentments to lay at rest. Disagreeable tasks had ever been her lot, but by gritting her teeth, she always managed to muddle through somehow.

Never mind that water—several buckets of it—would need to be hauled from the nearest public well; never mind that she had no tub for such a quantity of clothes; never mind that

Roanna would be in no condition to watch the baby while she did all this; never mind that the better part of two days would be required for washing and drying.

Life was hard, but she could tie the baby in a sling and get on with it. This had long been her calling, perhaps even her name. One tiny morsel of comfort: whatever her lot, however hard her name, it would never be as distressing as that of the desperate child and his ribbon collar.

6

Early the following morning, Driss made preparations for his assignation with Clettie in Lorenth. He drew Treese aside to strike a bargain, nervous over how it might be received.

To get the precious rosillum, Driss needed Treese and the qualities he offered. Jonn had recommended him, and as Treese's tastes lay well beyond his own resources, he in turn had jumped at Driss's invitation. In addition to his intelligence, Treese was levelheaded, unafraid, an excellent horseman, and—of more immediate benefit—good with women. An impeccable dresser with a cool, almost icy temperament, he had only to ask, and a woman would do anything for one of his rare smiles.

And they were rare. This gloomy tendency was his only flaw. While women fell at his feet, men walked carefully—and learned not to touch him. He sometimes on principle opposed things he favored, and this left Driss with the tricky business of managing a resourceful grouch.

Now Driss faced a test of his personnel management. "Treese, I'll be straight with you. I'm planning to go into town today and tonight with Garrick, Bren, and Keltie. Jonn has agreed to watch over things—keep the troops happy." He smiled nervously. "Anyway, in exchange for your not going with us, I'd like you to take Rona in hand for the day—and night. There's probably a nice place up river."

He watched Treese apprehensively and was not heartened when the latter pasted his tall, slender frame against the red bark of a sarrel tree and gazed dispassionately over the encampment. "She's a man's woman, Treese. A high-strung horse—like Strada. She needs a practiced handler, someone who understands women. Curry her the wrong way, her ears go back. But the right touch—everything a man could want, Treese."

He paused uncomfortably but met only silence. Driss was about to try another tack when Treese turned with a fraction of a smile.

"What would you say if I told you I was a jump ahead of you?"

Now it was Driss's turn to back off and kick dirt. No, he didn't like it at all, but this game had infinite variations. Treese had won an advantage, but play would continue. Besides, the only alternative was to forget Clettie and tend his fences. That would be even harder to swallow.

On their way into town, the four men came upon the smoking remains of a house fire. A chimney towered above the rubble—a stark, self-conscious survivor of the blaze. Washtubs and night-slops pails lay exposed in the wreckage, the private functions of life laid open like torn undergarments for everyone to see. Some women wept, while men kicked the cooler timbers.

Driss, Bren, and Keltie jumped from the carriage and approached a bent, gnarled bystander. "What happened?" Driss asked. "Anybody hurt?"

"Aye." The old man nodded, his rubbery jaw crunching toward a hawk nose. "Threebody. A lad and his sister tried to save the old grandmother. They was all three of 'em killed." He shook his head. "A shame, such a shame! Come right down on 'em, it did. Never had a chance. 'Twas set, too," he went on. "Feller made the mistake of standin' about watchin' the flames. Before he knew what come on 'im, five Russet soldiers grabbed aholt and drug him off, a-fetchin' and a-screamin'. He knowed as well as the rest of us he'd get a good whuppin' for such a deed."

The old man rubbed his whiskers thoughtfully. "Them Russet fellers, they don't put up with no nonsense—not like T'ribbonmen. But I was weepin' glad they got fire-settin' feller. Can't tell: my place'd maybe be next!"

They continued to stare at the ruin in morbid fascination until Garrick broke the spell by backing the team from the lineup of vehicles. "Well." Driss shrugged. "Nothing we can do, I guess. Might's well move along."

After stabling the carriage and bays, they walked toward the town market that seemed vibrantly untouched by the tragedy. Vendors lined the area with crates of chickens, ropes of shallots—the ordinary, the exotic. Children, drunk on market-day freedom, jumped and chased until parental hands shook them sober. The turbulence of the square gathered and transposed ragged strains of dissonance into a bracing, contrapuntal song of commerce. More than children became drunk on its power.

Lorenth was an occupied city and had been for much of its history. Lying near the border of Arlony, the city had endured the seesaw fortunes of the Green Wars, with Swendia and Arlony by turn controlling its stone bridges. When Arlony's civil war erupted a hundred and twenty years later, war-weary Lorenth again sighed and accepted its military lot. Claeman's army was currently in control and kept close watch on all activities, as the old man had hinted.

"But if Claeman and his Russet guys own this place," Bren wondered, his lean-hipped frame dwarfed next to Keltie, "how come T'ribboners hang about? Look over there: the third bunch since we got in town. You wouldn't think to see any here where Russetmen are thicker'n needles on a kung tree."

Garrick cleared his throat. "As I see it," he began pompously, "and since I come to Arlony frequently, I probably understand these things better than you fellows. As I see it—"

"What's this?" Keltie's head snapped up eagerly. "An Arlony expert?"

Driss looked up suspiciously but said nothing. Keltie was as solid and dependable as his bull heft suggested, with a deep cleft that split his chin and a smile like a warm coat on a chilly day. But his dislike for Garrick drove him to tease, weakening the group's fragile respect for their patron.

Garrick rose to Keltie's bait. "Yas. Some of the people I spend hours talking with say Claeman was a fool for not wiping out every last T'ribboner when he had the chance."

"Huh!" grunted Driss. "Maybe he couldn't wipe them out. Anyway, who's to say whether Claeman or Sigurth is better for the country?"

"Yas! Who *can* say?" Garrick crowed. "When Sigurth overran the country after his Middle Night attack, many folks felt they'd been liberated. Claeman was too strict, they said; no fun. Now, some other people I spend hours talking with think Claeman wants to keep Sigurth and T'ribs where he can see 'em."

Keltie's broad-set eyes gleamed blue in a wreath of curly hair. "Okay, you say we got two he-goats here. One—Sigurth—attacks on Middle Night, the biggest holiday of the year; the other—Claeman—beats him off with dark-faced soldiers and laws against havin' fun." He stopped. "Hey! Look there." He pointed to a stubby wagon drawn by three mismatched pairs of tattered donkeys and ponies. A vertical, ladder-like structure in the middle of the wagon held rolls of fabric or carpeting. "Y'don't see rigs like that in Swendia!"

All eyes turned to watch the strange conveyance and its colorful driver. Long of hair, beard, tooth, and eyebrow, he wore a red-striped shirt with matching turban and broad ankle bands.

"Do you suppose he's one of the old Arls?" Driss mused.

"Could be," Bren said. "If they're like Swens, they're *strange*. Talked to one once. Couldn't hardly understand him. He told me some sayings that go back to the Green Wars, maybe earlier. Like to frizzle your hair." Bren thrust his hands in his pockets.

"Well?" said Keltie. "Don't just leave us hangin'. Tell us what he said."

Bren shrugged. "Well . . . like . . . well, he made it rhyme, but I don't remember that part. Somethin' like, 'A blood sign during first-quarter moon means a younger'll get stole and cooked by full.' "

"And eaten?"

"Cut it, Keltie!" said Driss "That's not funny."

"Well, that'd frizzle my hair. What else?" Keltie turned back to Bren.

"Let me think. Somethin' like, 'Strike stone, strike wood, strike bone, drink blood.' " His face twitched. "Makes you glad you're not a Swen."

Garrick shouldered back into the interrupted conversation. "Like I was saying," he said, "early in the civil war—not Green Wars now," he admonished; "the civil war, more recent. Sigurth laid his groundwork. Do y'know how Sigurth laid his groundwork? First, he gave out chickens."

"C'mon, Gare. Chickens?"

"Yas. Chickens, money, wine—all to poor people. Farm help. Anything. Win 'em over; get 'em on his side. A favor here, a favor— Brought good will into Sigurth's corner."

"That how you got your Dunkir?" Keltie winked at Bren.

"No," Garrick sighed, "though considering who I am, I could be of *substantial* . . .

"Then brothels," he went on, "for men with money, y'know? Worked on how repressed they'd been under Claeman. Set houses up all over the . . . Good businessman, Sigurth."

Driss snorted. "Nothing like good, lusty whores for the economy!"

"Whores and liquor. Keep everybody happy—rich and poor. Yas."

He stabbed the air. "The *second* stratagem was his massive attack. *Massive.* On Middle Night. Caught 'em by surprise. Overran the country.

"Yas . . . yas." Garrick gazed off through his whirling mind. "Claeman fought back and finally got the upper hand, but Sigurth keeps scratching away. Claeman says his line and claim go back to the country's founding, and therefore he's the rightful . . . But who can say if that's true—hum?

"And Sigurth," he continued, face gleaming with the moisture of importance, "he says the people are with him. He's more reasonable and open minded, and he should rule. Did y'know," Garrick went on with lightning irrelevance, "that T'ribboners are big on parties?"

Just then a black-winged bee singled out Garrick, drawn to the cloud of tiny flies around his head. Garrick swatted at it and went on, scarcely missing a beat.

"Yas. Partying sets 'em off from Russetmen. They drink and fight around big fires all night. More'n one comes back dead." He clucked.

Keltie whistled.

"But they love kids, I hear," Garrick went on. "Especially lone ones."

The bee circled back, diving enthusiastically into the flies. Garrick, mistaking its intentions, flailed ardently and inadvertently whacked a passing pedestrian. Bee and pedestrian both returned the compliment—with a vengeance.

Keltie and Bren howled with laughter; Driss did not. Between Garrick's bombast and Keltie's ridicule, his head was thumping. So far, Garrick hadn't caught on, but if he did, how much would he tolerate before deciding to invest his capital elsewhere? Garrick was as hungry for money as any of them, but he could be huffy. "You're okay, Garrick," he said, hauling the yowling victim to his feet. "We'll get you dusted off here. Where'd it get you? Ah. One sting; not bad. Tell us more about T'ribboner parties. They love kids, you say?"

"Yas, yas. That's right. Hum. Give 'em good things to eat, fancy neckbands braided out of their tri-colored ribbons. Yas. Just last week I heard—"

"Huh!" Driss interrupted. "Those neckbands you're talking about are called 'collars of doom.' They mark those children for—"

"No!" Garrick scoffed. "That's not . . . My friends say it's a party game. Fun for kids, fun for everybody. Only fuddy-duddies would . . ." He frowned suddenly. "There are strange things, though. Rock scratchings. Runes, that's what they call 'em. These runes scare the britches off locals, but nobody'll talk about 'em. And if I with all my experience don't know . . ." He clattered his throat in a vague sort of way.

Keltie's face stiffened, and while Garrick rattled on, he leaned toward Driss. "Garrick don't know the half of it. His runes somehow tie in with some stuff they call 'zill.' That much I know. But don't ask me what zill is."

"Where'd you hear that?" asked Driss. "From the old Arls?"

Keltie grinned. "Hey, I got people I spend hours talkin' with, too."

He turned back to Garrick. "I'm tellin' you, old lad, you're all over the map here. First it's civil war, then Middle Night and back to chickens and whores, and end up at a party. You been leadin' a squirrel chase, but you never get us back to the beginning. Way back. Like with juice."

"Juice?"

Driss, his mouth open to turn Keltie off once and for all, closed it again.

"Juice. It's what starts wars. Now, I'm the one tellin' you here, so pay attention."

Keltie inflated himself to Garrick proportion. "In the beginning was juice. In men it come out as *spit* if they was just passin' time, or *froth* if they was tearin' each other apart. Mostly they spit, but every few years they'd froth through every pig sty and pickle orchard. Women, now, in them juice leaks out their eyes and maybe some other places. But the point is, y'gotta start at the beginning. Green Wars come before the civil war, and—"

"I said we weren't talking about the Green Wars," Garrick shouted. "I was talking civil war. I said that. You think I don't know—"

"Sure, you know," said Keltie sweetly. "You know everything. You said that, too. But I'm sayin' y'gotta keep things in order. Green Wars first. Over a hundred years first. Then a Peace Era, then a string of Disaster Eras, but don't ask me what kind of disasters. Jonn'd know. He takes a history pill every day. Anyway, endin' with the Earthquake Era. *Then* comes the civil war. Hey, I know these things; I listen to Jonn."

Yes, Keltie, listen to Jonn. Jonn knows more than Garrick, more than Driss, even. You didn't get the juice idea from Jonn, but it's a place to start.

Juice, as in *rain*—a driving, slanting downpour that hides all but the bony outline of a mountain. Mist shrouds bones—the bones of men and women who once lived and loved on that mountain but who are forever lost in the murk.

Juice, as in the *river of time* that layers silt over ancient shards of living, breathing history. Trace the mighty flood back, Keltie, back to tributaries and rivers, to streams and rocky brooklets, back—back to runoffs high on mountain slopes.

Who were these ancestral springs, the scraggy, knurled Arls and Swens who glowered from smoky hovels, painted themselves fierce, and thumped taut wolfcat hides? They ate and fought in ever-widening streams until their strife joined that of the Claemans and Sigurths of those days in a major tributary called the Green Wars. These waters ran crimson at times, sometimes black with treachery, sometimes heroic gold. Here *rain juice*—the personal, everyday events of life—blended with *river juice*—the broad sweep of time—to forever alter history.

Swendia struck the first blow of the Green Wars under cover of Sigurth and Claeman's on-going scrap, then stumbled along for sixty years in this conflict before making any real headway. Finally, they forced the Russet army of Arlony back to Cassia, just miles from Bethzur, Claeman's citadel near the western border, and through a colossal act of treachery, the city fell.

It happened this way.

With the Swendians approaching Cassia, Russet troops mustered a counter-offensive under their most able general. Like other officers of those times, he wore his own special uniform so he'd be easy to see in battle. "Set up a peacock," Garrick brayed, "and even a jackass will follow. It had worked up to then," he went on, "but not this time. Here's the army ready for a surprise counter-attack. The general takes the lead dressed in red with white fur decorations, a horned helmet that half covers— And of course, face grease. That's what makes 'em dark, y'know. Face grease. But this general—known, loved, dressed as usual—turns out he's nothing but a *costume*, an imposter who led the Russetmen into a death trap! How he replaced the real general nobody knows, but through that treachery Arlony lost a third of its army."

He surveyed the effect of his story with satisfaction. "Taught the army a lesson. From that day on, Russet officers never wore face grease or fancy uniforms, and each soldier had to know his officers by sight."

"Is it the Green Wars you're talking about?" A woman full of sadness and deformity sat crumpled on rags, a three-stringed setel across her lap. Long, restless fingers curled the neck of the instrument, skill covering the missing string. Her voice lifted a sample line and held it out to the men. " *'Triona, Triona, my darling, my love—'* You've heard the song about the greatest heroine of the Green Wars, perhaps?" Her soft lips lifted just slightly as she studied the receptivity of each, from Garrick to

Bren to Keltie to Driss, then back to Keltie. *" 'Your heart shines with glory,' "* she sang tentatively, *" 'My heart I lay down.' "* Doe eyes reached for Keltie's heart. He nodded.

She shifted her warped body and began to sing. Her rich, throaty voice spun the tale of a maiden whose Russet lover served Arlony as scout and spy. The maid herself often relayed information to him at their trysting place.

One raw autumn night she bore news of a pending attack by Swendia but found, to her dismay,

The dell was not vacant; a small fire low
Showed a small band of T'ribboners with unrest to sow.

In a lapse of caution, she had already given the signal and received her lover's in return. In moments he would face certain death and perhaps worse. Still unseen, she could've gotten away, leaving her lover to fend for himself. After all, they couldn't torture out of him information he didn't possess.

But an attack by Swendia, totally unanticipated, would devastate the ill-prepared Arlonian forces. Hesitating only seconds, she ran across the tiny clearing to where her lover waited. She threw herself into his arms, whispered the message and then shoved him on his way. The T'ribboners, hard on her heels, stopped, incredulous, as she threw off her robe and ran naked past them, leading a merry chase for at least two precious minutes. Her ruse worked; the T'ribboners forgot the scout and whooped in pursuit until at last, inevitably, they had her.

Her body was found three days later, scarcely recognizable. She had held fast, though, and the Russet army was spared another crushing defeat.

Chords of triumph, fierce and harsh, broke from the setel and shattered alarmingly over the listeners' hearts. Gradually, though, pulling on shifting skeins of light and shadow, the instrument resumed its original haunting pattern as she bound off her well-knit tale.

The battle-scarred mountains wept blood o'er his woe,
His sword measured terror on Arlony's foe.

*In two years two thousand Swendians fell
Ere a wound sent him back to that grave in the dell.
He bowed in his grief till five autumns had slept,
Five layers of leaves stitched his quilt as he wept.
Five years from the day of Triona's great deed,
His eyes closed forever on victory's seed.*

Her head bowed over the final refrain:

*In the dell by the river the birds sing your name;
For here sprang the spark that ignited a flame.
Your scorching defiance forged victory's crown,
Your heart burns with glory—my heart I lay down.*

*Triona, Triona, my darling, my love,
The wind wafts your valor to mountains above.*

The men stood fixed. Finally, Driss drew a breath, motioned to Garrick to give her a coin, then bent with a word of thanks. When he moved away, Garrick pretended not to understand the signal and ambled behind Bren, whistling his own tune. Keltie's jaw stiffened, and he dug for two of his own few coins and eased them into her hand.

He followed the others, thinking hard about juice.

7

"Roanna, you are not going to die. If I thought you were, I wouldn't leave you for a minute. The water trough isn't far; I'll come back as quick as I can."

Wearily, Charri pushed hair from her face with the back of her wrist, then studied her sticky, stinking hands. "I must get water. What's left isn't enough to wash my hands, let alone clothing."

"Ohh, Aunt, my head, my tummy . . . I know I be dyin!"

"Yes." Charri sighed. "I know. Your head aches terribly." *And so does mine,* she didn't add. She leaned to soothe the girl. "Lie as still as you can while I'm gone."

"Please, *please* don't go! Don't leave me!" Roanna began crying and grabbed Charri's hand imploringly. She raised partway off the bed, then fell back, clutching her head and retching yet again.

"You must lie still, Roanna. Moving around only makes it worse."

"But . . . but what if somebody comes in? Somebody might come to hurt me. They might—"

"I'll be gone only a short while. If you're quiet, no one will bother you." Again, she didn't say, *Who would want to?*

"But . . . Aunt—"

"Roanna," Charri said firmly, "I am going for water. I borrowed another pail, and with care, that much water might get our clothing reasonably clean. Not another word. I'll be back soon."

She turned from the blubbering girl, and after tying the sling that held her infant, she picked up the pails, shut the door with understated emphasis, and went down the stairs.

She had not gone far when a feeling of unease came over her. She looked around. Nothing seemed amiss. The livery stable she had just exited, neither the largest nor best in town, tilted into the hill as though clinging desperately to the slope. The lower-level horse clientele were mostly bony and slack lipped, but as

Charri had discovered, seedy hostelries would accommodate slender purses. No, the livery, though far from elegant, was not the source of her unease.

As she wound downhill, even the rough, stony road struck her as unfriendly. Only one point of color relieved the shabbiness: yellow-and-white bonnet flowers boiled down the sides of an old kettle in front of a cookery shop. Charri bent for a golden breath of fragrance. She closed her eyes to savor it, then left it behind and hurried past buildings that leaned toward her as though eavesdropping on her thoughts.

Most of the foot traffic fit the local ambiance, but here and there dark-faced Russetmen climbed or descended. *Or is just one soldier going up and down, watching me?* Charri tightened her grip on the buckets. *Yes, I'm sure of it. That one whose arm looks as though it been broken but hadn't healed right. He just passed me, and now he's coming back. Maybe the others . . .*

She lowered her face and eyes as he passed. When he had gone, she peered about to make sure no other soldiers were in sight, then ducked to the right on a plunging footpath she hoped might cut off the bend in the road. It was steep, but its hazards looked less alarming than reappearing soldiers.

She had not gotten halfway down the shortcut when she heard voices from behind a high, rotting fence. The conversation was low, but the few words she could make out froze her mid-step.

Only for a moment. Eyes wide and frightened, she walked even faster down the rugged slope.

They're talking about us—about Roanna, about me. I know they are.

A tree root caught her hurrying feet. She lurched and clutched her baby convulsively, the clang of her buckets sending her into near panic.

Heart racing, she looked behind her, then bit her lip hard to force calm. *They didn't see me. They're not following. But they're talking about us. They didn't say Roanna's name, just "the girl," but who else could it be? What does it mean?* "Someone might come here to hurt me," Roanna had said when

I left. And I thought, "Who would want to?" But someone does want to. Why do Russetmen want Roanna?

As the path flattened and joined the road, the water trough beside the river came into view. She could see a line of Russet soldiers heading toward it, but these were clearly not the ones who had had their eye on her. With a careful look around, she crossed the last street, still trembling over the hidden speaker's words: *The girl's not with her; just her and the baby goin' for water. She'd be a real prize, that girl, so just make sure you know where she is, that she don't get outta sight.*

Driss, Keltie, Bren, and Garrick walked along the shady bank of the river toward the clothier shop where they were to meet Clettie. As they approached a public latrine, a column of nut-colored Russetmen marched toward them. Driss halted, the implications of stealing rosillum from under Claeman's nose playing along his spine.

"Hmm. I feel a sudden call of nature. You fellows?"

His companions chuckled and followed Driss into the building, but Keltie raised an eyebrow.

"Suppose they're coming here, too. What then?"

Garrick tensed under this specter of bodily harm. "D' you think they might? How would we get away?"

Keltie, his interest in Garrick-baiting revived, pretended alarm. "Dear me! I don't know! If worse comes to worse, I guess we could jump through the toilet holes into the river and—"

"Cut it, Keltie!" Driss cuffed him, patience threadbare and head pounding. The long crackdance Keltie had led Garrick through on the way here didn't seem to have done actual harm, but he was capable of shutting down the better part of their financial backing.

The dark soldiers went on past, but inside, the four found themselves among a group of bantering T'ribboners. Most but not all had shaved their heads and were dressed well but casually in either soldier tunics or belted shirts and short, loose robes, with streamers of blue, purple, and green on arms or thighs. "They match the colors of Sigurth's flag," Garrick had pointed out earlier. "T'ribboners—three, tri-ribbons. Get it?"

The latrine was a stone, semi-enclosed building set low on the north bank of the river. Water flowed through from two sources. The river cleansed the lower level, and an uphill spring filled a circular trough that penetrated an open-gabled wall, providing both outdoor and indoor access to water. Assorted holes and slots ranged along the river side of the facility, and opposite these was a long, wooden bench. On the wall near the water trough, a bit of polished tin served as a mirror.

The men went about their business, keeping cautiously to themselves. As Driss checked himself in the mirror, however, he jumped when a tall T'ribboner clapped him on the back.

Even more startling than the man's jovial approach was his appearance. Driss considered himself more handsome than most, with his dark curls, well-set brown eyes, and good-humored mouth. This man, though, went beyond handsome to a kind of perfection. Every line of his face and body spelled grace and charm. Even his sandy hair and beard seemed exempt from need of comb or scissors. The only discordant note on his face was a set of burning, implacable eyes.

He was clothed more elegantly than the others. "Money?" Bren wondered under his breath. "Rank?" A heavy, square-cowled shirt covered a high-necked undergarment of soft selke leather. Dark trousers and guida boots completed the costume, with the top ends of his ribbons incorporated directly into the fabric covering a well-muscled thigh.

"Getting spruced up for the ladies, eh?" The officer laughed.

Driss grinned weakly in reply.

"Got a good one on the line, do you?"

"Good enough," Driss replied cautiously.

"Is she a beauty?" Laugh lines deepened as he glanced at his companions.

"Of course! What do you take me for?" Driss was wary, not sure where the conversation was going.

The T'ribboners chuckled among themselves, and Garrick began to perspire.

"Come along, now, friend," the fair-haired captain continued. "I'll tell you how we go about women. Sit here on the bench, and we'll tutor you. Not even Glinneth could give more careful instruction." An enigmatic gleam flashed from his eye.

Puzzled, Driss looked at his companions. Glinneth? The man went on.

"A bit of a drink first, hm?" He pulled a jug from a pack, and as it passed down the line, the *glug* of liquid blended with the sound of water being dipped from the outdoor half of the trough.

"Now, then. You walk down the street—one, two, and even three of you. But not four." He passed over Garrick with a mocking twist of his head. "You'll get attention, the kind you want." He sized up their appearance approvingly. "But each beauty you come to, you just . . . walk by." Moving down the bench, he tapped each head with caricatured courtliness, his throaty voice holding the men like a magnet.

"You're looking all the time for . . . just the one. You come to her: fat, scraggled, foul . . . wet."

Ignoring Bren and Keltie's grimaces of disgust, his eyes again played with Garrick. But he backed off gracefully as Driss's face stiffened.

"She is ugly beyond belief, though not old." He turned dramatically. "She is cut off from male . . . companionship and ready—ripe—waiting to be plucked."

Every eye followed as he reached for the imaginary plum. He held it in his hand as he held his audience. "A bottle—maybe two—of the finest wine to start things off. A couple of coin to purchase a bath for her if she needs it." He shot a fleeting glance at Garrick. "You, meanwhile, search out the richest robe you can afford. Now." He straightened with a flourish. "The stage is set. A visit to Klingen's Tavern—though not such fine eating as it used to be—perhaps another bottle, and the night is yours." His voice dropped to an intense whisper. *"Whatever* your heart desires!"

His eyes shot sparks onto tinder. No one moved, each caught in his own prurient inventions.

The soldier straightened slowly so as not to break the spell, then bowed low and ushered his men outside.

On the outdoor half of the circular trough, Charri shuddered again and again as she retied the sling carrying her pale, passive infant. Taking special care in arranging her cloak to conceal the ugly slash across her face, crimson now in anger and fear, she picked up her full buckets and stepped cautiously onto the street.

8

Outside the window of Clettie's small apartment, a spider prepared for guests. The last visitor to come through left a gaping hole in her hospitality, and now the silk-encased remains of her feast swung breeze-blown on the tattered web. She set about making repairs. First the long spokes, then sticky strands tacked in concentric circles to the spokes. When the last filament had been drawn from her spinnerets, she hung motionless on the lacy orb . . . and waited.

Within the house, a soft knock sounded. Clettie, ringed and perfumed, uncoiled from her satiny couch—the most impressive of her few pieces of furniture—and opened the door to see Driss leaning lazily against the jamb. One hand held a bottle, the other a gold medallion on a neck chain.

She stood a moment, her lips tracing the shadow of a smile, and was satisfied to see his eyes widen appreciatively. She had given great care to Driss's color preferences. The green of her long, loose-folded dress was picked up by the suggestion of jade and emerald in her jewelry. She could afford neither but knew how to make do with good effect.

"Hullo, Clettie."

Ah! He hadn't changed. That grin with its characteristic flash of high spirits, the careless verve, the personal magnetism that gave him sovereign command over men and women alike. His alliance with Garrick had not hurt at all. His perfectly muscled form would look good in anything, but as he stood there in a thick-sleeved shirt with its green braid and open neck, she became acutely aware of the need to play her game carefully.

"*Wilcuma*, Drissan. Come in!" She stepped aside, whispers of green drawing him through the door.

Setting his bottle on the petal-and-spice-strewn table, he turned and unhooked the medallion chain. Without a word, he placed it around her neck, then bent to kiss her. She returned his embrace with just the right tentativeness, resisting his pull toward the couch; proper timing was everything.

The gathering night outside began to glitter with its particular black fire, each element orchestrated to tantalize the senses. From across the way came a throaty song of lonely passion, and in seemingly programmed response, a crepuscular insect caromed in blind ecstasy off the web. The spider, however, remained immobile.

Driss sat on the couch. "You got my note and the purse, I see. Your friend met us outside and took charge of the guys. Looked like a ladies' assembly when I came by the room. How many did you come up with? More than one apiece?"

Clettie smiled knowingly. "Enough to 'keep morale high,' as you put it." Even as she spoke, laughter filtered from the adjoining apartment.

Driss's eyes twinkled. "Nothing like good, lusty whores—for the economy, of course!"

"For *your* economy, Driss." Clettie looked at him archly. "You can rest assured that Garrick will consider his money well spent."

As they talked, Clettie laid the aromatic table with an array of food: breads, cheeses, nuts, fruits, and Driss's wine, plus a bottle of her own.

"However did you lure Thilrec away from Klingen?" she asked, settling on the couch beside him.

Driss shrugged. "Money. What else?"

"Garrick's again, I take it."

He nodded absently and broke a round loaf. "Yes . . . but Thilrec's a funny duck. I think he might have come even without Garrick's money. He's a five-tiered tyrant around his wagon; has to have everything just so. But somehow the adventure of it all gets him. Never a word about rain or rough roads or danger. Just the opposite of Amarl, our donkey jobber."

"The boy I saw with Thilrec the other day."

"Yes. We brought him along to help with the animals and food things. You'd think this would be adventure heaven for him. But no—he's lazy, scatterbrained, has fifteen grouches before breakfast— If he lasts another week I'll be surprised."

Clettie raised an eyebrow calculatingly. "He'll last if the rewards make it worth his while . . . like *very* worthwhile."

Driss smiled wryly. "Garrick, I take it, told you some things."

The silvery web outside trembled once again, and the keeper of silk moved quickly to throw a strand. Could she get enough on her prey at the start, she'd have no trouble turning it over and over, encasing it in silken grave cloths. A quick bite would settle it. After flooding it with a strong digestive fluid, she would alternately suck and pump until nothing remained but a dry, mummy-wrapped shell. If she could get that first strand . . .

Clettie reached for a chunk of greensweet melon. "He didn't actually say 'rosillum,' but—"

"But you caught the drift. And you thought it worth your while to let bygones be bygones, is that right?" He kissed her impudently.

As they ate, he told her of his uncle's map and how he'd gotten his support group together.

"Drissan," Clettie asked, pouring another drink and nestling comfortably, "this uncle of yours—what makes you so sure he didn't send you off on a chicken hunt? What if you get there and find somebody else beat you, or that the treasure doesn't even exist? Maybe he just made up a story."

"I'm as sure as anyone can be. 'I guarantee it,' the old man croaked, 'more (wheeze) rosillum (wheeze, wheeze) than ever you can use.' " Driss grinned impishly. "He was dying, you see. I think he meant this to be his crowning joke on cronies who'd been trying for years to worm the secret out of him. He'd never hold the treasure himself, but somehow he felt he'd get it back through me. He laughed so hard at the thought, he started coughing and nearly died on the spot." Driss toyed with a wisp of Clettie's auburn hair.

"Uncle was a strange bird—peculiar . . . if you get what I mean. When I was—oh, maybe twelve, I walked in on him once. He was expecting someone else and met me at the door all dolled up. Talk about mad!" Driss whistled. "I don't think even his wife knew. Anyway, he was so angry he grabbed me and started ripping at my clothes. Took me about ten seconds to size things up and break loose. I left but kept my mouth shut, figuring it was his business, not mine. That was the end of it; he never mentioned it again. Neither did I. He growled a lot, but then, he hated all teenagers, even loveable ones like me." Driss grinned.

Clettie murmured, almost to herself, "Rosillum would oil any man's love life, whatever its shape."

Driss grunted. "All his life he fought, plotted, scrabbled for money. He'd make a little, but it would disappear like water on desert sand. He hated liggeth mining—the dirt, the coughing—but it's all he knew. Then he got lucky. An enormous cache of 'rosegold,' as he called it. Why he couldn't or didn't carry it off with him, I don't know. Maybe he got hurt, or somebody in his party. He never forgot, though. Talked about that rosillum almost every day. For years. But he never could raise the money to go back for it. And of course his lungs were terrible."

Clettie marveled. "Every liggeth man in the world dreams of hitting that mother-lode of rosillum and carrying off his retirement, but I don't know anyone who actually made a strike. That's why I wondered if he had you on a string."

Driss shrugged. "Well, he had the details. The rich, reddish luster you never have to polish. When he found the stuff, first thing he did was lick a piece. He—"

"Really?" Clettie sat up straight. "What happened? I've heard it's potent, but I don't know—"

"Even talking about it made him rhapsodic. 'Climb mountains in seven jumps,' he'd sing, 'a swarm of bees on your tail!' He quit, though, when he saw that spit turns the surface black. He wanted to make a goblet. If you alloy the rosillum, he told me, it'll hold up, but the kick is mostly gone. Crazy stuff. No other metal acts like that."

Clettie rubbed her nose. "They say Glinneth has a rosillum goblet that he uses when—"

"Glinneth? I heard that name just today, but don't know . . . What's so funny?" he asked with some annoyance as Clettie bent to hide her laughter.

"Honey, if you don't know Glinneth, then I'm not the one to tell you about him. He's a bi-i-g man! That's all I'll say."

Her eyes sparked with amusement, but she would only shake her head in response to questions.

"Tell me how you got this . . . this trove hunt going," she said.

"Well, Uncle talked a lot but never would say where or how he came by the rosillum. As I grew, he kept watching me. For a while, like I said, I thought he had it in for me and Jonn, not just because I walked in on him, but because we often pulled crazy stunts. Like the time we stole all the Middle Night food from the larder before anyone was out of bed. He didn't think that was funny. Anyway, I guess when I finally did grow up he saw my love for adventure and knew I had friends who'd back this kind of venture.

"I'll never forget last Feast of Candles," he continued, "on Middle Night. Uncle always had this weird sense of humor. Never appropriate, you know. Either busting out when nothing was funny, or not even smiling while everyone else laughed. Well, that night, his eyes burned. I don't know what was inside his head. I think he knew the end was near and wanted to settle the rosillum business."

Driss cut two slices of cheese and stuffed one in Clettie's mouth. "Feast of Candles being mostly for kids," he said between bites, "it had been years since I'd gone around the family circle. But that Middle Night he called my name and pulled me down to lay hands on my head. 'I claim you!' he quavered. 'You are Drissan, full of zest. Go! Make your claim in my name!'

"Well, everyone kind of snickered, but he was dead serious. He gave me the map, grabbed a candle from the nearest kid, shoved it at me and made me pour wax on his hand. He wasn't happy till I'd clinched the deal by drawing my old mark on the wax. And since he was the oldest person at the gathering, he himself poured water to set the wax. I knew what the ceremony meant, so you'd better believe I was serious, too—more than I'd been in years! But that's when he got laughing and coughing, and I heard afterwards that he literally died laughing—not that night, but a few days later."

Driss leaned over and kissed Clettie repeatedly, his stomach full, his attention beginning to shift. "He died happy, and I'm happy to be on my way."

"On your way . . . to the big time—like me," Clettie purred. "I'm leaving for Cassia tomorrow and will get there days—even weeks—before you. I don't have Thilrec and his fancy needs holding me back." She laughed. "Stop by when you get there. They tell me I'll be in some odd-shaped house— should be easy to find. As though you'd have trouble locating me." She rubbed his chest and played with his chin.

Driss looked at her sharply, his eyes narrowed. Then he laughed and lay back on the satin couch, pulling her with him. "Nice try, sweetheart. Even Garrick doesn't know exactly where we're headed, so he couldn't have told you. I'm not about to, either. You'll find me as hard as granite, as mute as a swan. But you, my lovely gazelle, shall have your share of the rosillum—to lick or wear as you will. But now's it's time for other things."

The insect struggled an instant longer, then broke free, leaving another rift to be repaired.

Night, however, proved a more successful predator as the lights over the clothier shop flickered out. Strand after strand of its soft, sensuous web bound its helpless victims for the digestive process until nothing remained but hollow shells.

9

Rona had had a rather pleasant time with Treese, but she was careful not to communicate that to Driss.

"You lie!" she screeched. "The Dunkir would take wings and fly before it broke down! Garrick's whole life hangs on his precious carriage; he hovers over it every minute. And you try to make me believe that a wheel could fall apart without his noticing the problem coming on? Surely you might have invented a cleverer explanation than that, Driss! You could've had him eating a whole pig and being too sick to move. That's believable. Or Bren might have—"

"Cut it, Rona! Think what you will; we just couldn't make it back, that's all."

"Poor dears. I suppose you slept in the street somewhere, or perhaps the stable boys moved over to give you a bit of hay."

Rona's expertise lay in anger. It went with her raven hair and flawless white skin; her eyes drew fire from it. She knew how to use it to good effect, bludgeoning men into submission, then binding them with manacles of shrewdly dispensed affection.

Her beauty left men in tatters. Tall, with perfect features and a flattering wardrobe, she knew her strength and moved with confidence across the dangerous landscape of their fascination. Years of practice had perfected her strategy, and although Driss was not as firmly in thrall as she might wish, she felt secure enough. Having attached herself to this expedition with its unparalleled opportunities, she couldn't afford to allow its mastermind to stray.

"Was it Clettie? To hear Garrick talk when he got back, he had her sewed up in his own pocket. More likely, she used him to get you. Why didn't you invite her along to share the rosillum? I'm sure if we threw in the old men and boys, we could keep her happily employed. Cheap, odious whore!"

"Rona," Driss began, trying to quiet her wrath with his arms, but she twisted away and scourged him with a cat-o'-nine-tongues.

At the height of the maelstrom, Steph, the newcomer, came near and stood unseen, watching solemnly. After a few minutes, he hopped from the shadows, a mischievous twinkle in his eye, and whispered to Driss, "This is what y'do!"

He turned to Rona, who had stopped talking and was surveying the child with ill-concealed annoyance. From under his cloak he drew out a scraggly, multicolored bouquet and thrust it at her, all the while smiling seraphically.

Driss rocked on his heels, bemused, while Rona writhed. Driss's love for children would tolerate no display of anger toward one of them, but to accept the bouquet was to lose the battle. Finally, after a long, uncomfortable hesitation, she took the flowers stiffly, then stalked off through sun-dappled trees.

Man and boy grinned at each other and whirled in a heady, hilarious dance of victory.

As they walked together back toward camp, Driss reflected. *Maybe the T'ribboner officer was right. A man might get more mileage out of an ugly woman!*

A vehicle did need repair, but not Garrick's Dunkir. Shortly after Rona's blast, Driss, along with Keltie, Bren, and Treese drove the canopy wagon into town, dropping off Amarl to amuse himself while a broken fitting was replaced at the blacksmith shop. *Shop* is perhaps too grand a label. A cave, really—grimy, cluttered, lit only by a slumbering mound of coals that opened its fierce, white-hot eye when breathed on by the forge's great lung. They unhitched the team and left them to doze amid twisted heaps of rusty iron and the sharp clang of metal.

Sooner than expected, Amarl panted uphill, his face wobbling between silly and sheepish. "You won't b'lieve what happened." He hobbled oddly toward the four men waiting by the wagon.

"Not believe what happened?" said Keltie, wrapping an elbow around the boy's neck. "Amarl old lad, nothin' happens to you we couldn't believe. What's the latest?"

Amarl twisted away with his foolish grin. Striking a pose to heighten drama, he balanced on one leg and sketched an elaborate design in the air with his other foot.

"Oh, that's good, Amarl!" said Treese, leaning to inspect the boot. "How'd you manage to tear the sole off, rip the boot halfway around, and do it without mangling your foot?"

Amarl shrugged. "Well, it got caught."

"Got caught." Driss studied the boot. "Could you be more specific?"

The boy shrugged again and wriggled uncomfortably. "Well, I—uh . . ."

Driss sighed, then turned to the men. "Okay, he doesn't want to tell us. Let's figure it out. He went down to the river and was messing along the edge, when he stepped on a wolfcat trap. It scared him and—"

Bren hooted. "Who'd be trappin' wolfcats in Lorenth? And besides, his foot ain't wet nor muddy."

"No," agreed Keltie, "you got it wrong this time, Driss. The river's wrong. Amarl couldn't walk along a river without fallin' in. You know that. Now, this is what I think happened." He rubbed his cleft chin and studied the torn boot. "What happened was . . . I know! There was this girl, see? Amarl was makin' eyes at her, and her old man come along. He had a giant claw wrench in his hand, see? And when he seen Amarl, the girl primpin' and shallyin' around, he roared and lunged and— But Amarl, he got all flustered, that big thing comin' at him, and of course he tripped and fell down, but instead of the wrench grabbin' any bad parts—" Keltie flicked his eyebrows. "It got his foot instead. Well, Amarl's pretty agile, so he kicks and twists and manages to—"

Amarl, who had been busy scooping dirt with his floppy sole and turning red, suddenly spun away and threw himself on the ground, rolling and groaning and laughing.

"Aha!" exclaimed Treese. "Pay dirt! The wench and the wrench."

Amarl shook his head vigorously, but a fatuous grin spoke of truth.

Driss hauled the boy to his feet and dusted him off. "Okay. You don't want to tell us. We get the picture. Whatever happened, your boot's ruined. Did you bring a spare pair?"

Amarl shook his head, tending to a triangle of dust Driss missed.

"Then we'll have to buy a pair. Let's see . . ." He looked toward the cave. "The smith said he wouldn't get to our wagon for half an hour. We got time to hunt up a cobbler. If we're lucky, he may have ready-mades on hand."

Driss stepped into the shadows to gesticulate with the smithy. The five then started down hill, Amarl tripping occasionally over the consequence of his folly.

They crossed the bridge nearest the market area and, after inquiring, turned onto a narrow, winding street. They spotted a sign hung from an oversized boot but halted uncertainly at a distance. A Russetman stood between the cobbler shop and the tavern next door.

"Uh-oh!" said Bren. "Trouble."

Amarl shrugged in assorted patterns and rhythms. "Can't a guy even buy boots in this town?"

Treese grunted. "Not if you're Amarl and have a citizen mark on the bottom of your foot and this soldier happens to be measuring boot customers' patriotism." His voice carried an edge.

Driss pushed them along. "We can't just stare at the guy. He'll start wondering why. Walk on by. We'll look things over and decide what to do."

They ambled nervously past the soldier, a short, slight young fellow whose face grease left large, oval rings around his eyes, either from lack of experience in putting it on or as a joke. His eyes crinkled pleasantly as they passed. Rounding the bend out of view, they halted again. A pushcart of odd scraps rattled toward them, the carter inventing a "hobbler-cobbler" song as he neared the shop.

"Well, what do you think?" asked Bren. "The Russetman seems okay. Small enough—no bigger'n me. Nothin' you guys couldn't handle." He grinned. "Anyways, people was in the shop, and he didn't seem to pay 'em no mind. Just stands there lookin' happy."

Driss chewed his lip, thinking.

"We could just walk up to him," said Treese brightly, "and say, 'Hello there, little man. We'd like you to meet Amarl, a talented young fellow who just chomped his boot to pieces by some means he's too ashamed to admit. We're from Swendia, but he's our token Arlonian, a splendid representative of your coun—"

"Cut it, Treese. You're not helping."

"How about another cobbler?" asked Keltie. "Or do all of 'em have Russetmen standin' by?"

"The man I asked said he knew only two cobblers; the other was on the west side of town, a good three miles."

"There's got to be more'n two cobblers in a town this size. Dozens, likely."

Treese's mouth twitched. "Let's ask Russet Owl."

Keltie hooted. "Russet Owl! That's good!"

"Oh, sure!" said Bren. "With a cobbler shop at his elbow. That's good!"

Driss looked at Bren in disgust. "Don't you know when you're being had? Now, look. The guy isn't bothering people going in and out; we can see that. We could wander in, check for ready-made boots, and if there aren't any, maybe he could make a pair by tomorrow."

Amarl scratched his head and ran the length of his arm under his nose. "All because of a dumb ol' tattoo on the bottom of my foot."

Treese's eyes narrowed and his jaw bulged rhythmically, but Driss stepped in quickly. "That tattoo, Amarl: you may not like it right now, but it's worth plenty to you. It says you're a citizen here in Arlony, and despite what Treese says, that's not a bad thing. These Russetmen we're trying to avoid, and maybe T'ribboners, too—I don't know—they'd protect you and grant you the rights and privileges belonging to a citizen."

"Then why . . . ?"

"It's just that the rest of us aren't citizens, and having you along opens us to all kinds of awkward questions. But being a citizen of Arlony isn't bad in itself."

They moved cautiously around the curve, hoping the Russetman might have moved on, but now he stood inside the broad opening, giving friendly attention to the shoe trade.

Again, heads clustered for consultation.

Treese stood aloof. Then with only a glance at the Russetman, he stuck his hands in his pockets and ambled toward the shop that exhaled leather, oil, polish, and garlic. Nodding to the cobbler, he said, "Got any made-up boots that would fit this— Where'd he go? Come in here, Amarl."

The cobbler, crooked in nose and back and oddly sheathed in scraps that might have come from the pushcart, bobbed his head in response and displayed a toothy smile. Spikes of orange hair poked through holes in a purple cap, and a pair of green eyes gleamed incongruently from a jumbled face. His tongue hit the floor running. "Boots, guidas, shoes, brogues, clogs, weatherns—we have 'em, we have 'em; lots more besides 'em. Them we don't have, we make 'em. Ev'ry day we make 'em what you need. Ev'ry day. Fleegan, first-tier cobbler, that's me." He paused momentarily to fold a piece of leather around a customer's foot, cocking his head to calculate the fit. "This man here, he come ev'ry day, he like my work." He stopped again to scrutinize Amarl. "This the lad here needs boots? This the lad?" The cobbler looked him up and down as though accustomed to measuring feet by body size. He paused, looking oddly at Amarl, then flicked a glance toward the Russetman. "See over there," he said to Treese, flapping an impassioned finger at a pair of boots displayed prominently on a broken crate. "In the middle, in the middle. That boot there—that one, that one. Yes, yes."

"I see, I see," Treese muttered under his breath. "Shut up, shut up!" He turned to Amarl. "Yes, these might do. Stick your foot up here. See if it's close."

Driss and Keltie rolled eyes at each other, then wandered into the shop, trying to appear casual. They weren't heartened by a mysterious exchange of winks between "Russet Owl" and the cobbler, followed by an almost imperceptible nod from the latter, but Treese and Amarl were already measuring boot to boot.

Driss exchanged his own look with Keltie, weighing alternatives. Something was up; he could feel it. The cobbler had stopped chattering and seemed to be paying more attention to the boot inspection than to the fitting operation at his bench. Should they just grab Treese and Amarl and haul them out?

Meanwhile, the Russetman, irrepressible humor on his comical face, stuck his hands in his pockets, began whistling, and meandered past the shop and out of sight.

The men stared after him, not quite trusting the relief they felt.

Just then, a number of T'ribboners, full of spirits, barged from the tavern next door, making everyone jump.

"Will you look at that!" Keltie chuckled. "They probably been waitin' who knows how long for that Russetman to move off. Maybe since—"

Amarl gave a startled yowl. The men turned to see him floating slowly toward the ceiling.

"Amarl!" Driss hollered in alarm. "What are you doing? Cut that out!"

Keltie and Bren tried to grab what they could of the screeching, flailing boy, but his foot caught Bren on the chin and knocked him to the ground. The other men could do little but dance away and shout back.

Treese sized up the situation, then laughed. "Well, well, Amarl. First the wench, then the wrench, and now, if I'm not mistaken, it's the winch."

Even as he spoke, Amarl began to descend, and the others could see a rope playing along the ceiling from high above the jumbled crush of shoemaking material at the rear of the shop.

"Aha, my dears! My apologies, dear sirs!" The cobbler, who had watched this display with hang-jaw interest, dragged his twisted body toward them, neither perturbed nor contrite, but beaming broadly. He received Amarl warmly as the boy's feet touched ground, patting him reassuringly and trying to work loose a sticky, many-barbed gang hook from the back of his broad collar. "It worked this time, Lorssan! It worked!" he shouted at the back wall of the shop, which thumped in response. "It worked! We are happy! Happy!" His teeth lined up like multiple seals on a parchment of excellence.

The little Russetman returned, owl eyes merry over the success of Amarl's flight. He shook pleased hands with the cobbler, then with each of the men in turn. "Fleegan here," he said, pounding the cobbler's humped shoulder with his russet hand, " has been troubled by night thieves. You can see—" He gestured around the shop. "No room here for a proper blind, and by the time he hears the noise from his room, whoosh, they're gone." He smiled modestly. "This little idea of mine, just needed to test it. You boys didn't seem like you'd mind a little joke. At least," he added anxiously, trying to interpret the glazed look on their faces, "we hope you didn't mind."

Bren rubbed his jaw.

"No, no," Driss put in hurriedly with a forced laugh. "Glad to help." He stared hard at the pendulating gang-hook.

"And you, my friend," the cobbler said to Amarl. "You lookin' for boots. You looked at these boots here, these boots that was bait, right here in the middle." He hunched his hump and chuckled delightedly. "They fit you? You tried 'em?"

Amarl shook his head. "They—uh—we measured—" He cleared his throat uncertainly and looked pleadingly at Driss.

"Here. Take your boots off," said the cobbler, "and— Great sun above! No need tellin' us you need a new pair! Here, boy, try 'em on. Try 'em. They look to fit good."

Amarl again appealed anxiously to Driss, who looked hardly less uneasy. Treese moved in, shoving Amarl to the rough stool near the cobbler's bench, and helped him haul off his boots. To Driss's increasing alarm, Treese made no attempt to hide Amarl's foot mark and indeed took perverse satisfaction in holding his ankle so all could see.

"Ah!" exclaimed the cobbler after the boots went on. "Like I say, a perfect fit, yes?"

Amarl walked around gingerly, then strode up and down with growing satisfaction.

"How much are they?" asked Driss, his voice unsteady.

"A fine boot, careful made. See the stitching over top, across the heel? Double stitching here. And this gusset. No cheap boot got this!" He traced a proud finger around the boot. "Excellent boot—excellent. But—" He paused for effect, stretching his deformity proudly. "I give them to you. I give them because you not get mad." His teeth stood forth in bright array. "They fit on the boy perfect. You take 'em. Take 'em. A gift from Fleegan."

Driss, set to bargain, was thrown off balance. Once again, Treese stepped in, nodding diplomatically while trying to keep his face straight. "Quite right, Fleegan—an excellent boot. Where could you find a pair more carefully stitched? And that gusset." He shook his head in dramatic awe. "Your generosity pleases us, sir. Well worth the unusual—uh—flight of fancy. We'll tell everyone we see about Fleegan's excellent shop."

"But not warning thieves what might happen, eh?" He jabbed Treese in the chest, and the men held their corporate breath, expecting the usual shinlash. Treese, however, simply raised an eyebrow and twisted his mouth in faint scorn and continued bowing agreeably.

It was well past noon by the time they could exit gracefully. "I'm starving," Amarl announced at the end of the lane.

"Huh. I should think you would be," said Bren. "Had quite a morning. Is that rain?" He lifted his face.

" 'A *winch* and a *wench* and a giant-clawed *wrench*.' " Treese punched up his catchy rhyme.

"A few drops. Nothing serious. What do you say we pick up a meat roll, then head for the wagon?" Driss said. "Should be done by now."

"Sounds good!" whooped Amarl. "I know just the place! Saw it earlier. And besides," he muttered, the glazed look of happiness returning, "it wasn't a wrench."

The congested bridge did not lend itself to eating. "How come so many people all of a sudden?" said Amarl, irritated over any delay in filling his stomach.

"Middle of the day," replied Driss. "Other people get hungry, too."

At the foot of the blacksmith's hill they passed a knot of milling, shouting T'ribboners. As Treese popped his last bite, the noise crescendoed to near-brawl level. He stopped to look. The others walked on, but their attention was suddenly energized by three soldiers riding directly at them. They scrambled out of the way.

Treese, though, didn't notice until the horses were just yards away. He turned, but surprise immobilized him. The Russetmen tried to avoid him, but an overloaded dray on one side and a woman with three children on the other left him the accident of choice.

10

Four squealing children chased around the cook wagon. From the day he first came, Steph had proven a commendable playmate, introducing new games and adventures into the creative pool. The parents had watched carefully to make sure the boy wasn't overly inventive, but he seemed happy just being with other children.

While the youngsters stalked each other, Garrick growled over the smoldering stubs of the morning fire. Celine and Griselle ignored him and headed for the stream embankment with a basket of dirty laundry.

Jonn, sitting against a tree, lifted his face to the sun's tentative smile, but when it retreated behind a cloud, he returned to the map on his lap. He and Driss had plotted the most direct route across Arlony, but they both agreed that most direct was not always the fastest. They would fine-tune their plan according to local road conditions and intelligence from other travelers. So far their judgment had been good, but the better part of Arlony still lay before them.

The next several days' route was clear enough, but a fork beyond the village of Forsythe presented a choice. They could follow a small river road—winding, with possible washouts—or take a chance on rougher, hillier terrain.

"Hey, there!" Garrick bawled in his direction. "Where's Thilrec gone?"

As Garrick approached, Jonn folded the map and placed it in its waterproof pouch.

"He and Rolind went hunting. Mostly for greens, but they took a gun in case a grouse or something turned up."

"Did both of 'em have to go?"

Jonn laughed. "Well, Rolind can't tell an edible green from skunkweed, and Thilrec can't hit a mountain with a gun. Put them together, though, and you get a good supper. What is it you want, Garrick? Something I can do for you?" Jonn's forcible eyes sought Garrick's, but Garrick ducked behind a tirade.

"Thilrec let the fire go out. He knew how cold it is this morning. You'd think he'd know enough to keep it going. You'd think he'd know I'd be needing it, but no, he just let it go out. And Amarl sneaked off with— You'd *hope* he'd have sense enough to *at least* build a fire before he went."

Jonn sighed with restraint and uncurled himself from the base of the tree. "Okay, Garrick, old lad, let's start you a fire. There's dry wood under that tent cloth over there; Thilrec thought it might shower last night. Tell you what: I'll get the fire going, you can tend it. Fair enough?"

Ten minutes later Jonn sought a more distant tree. He closed his eyes a moment, listening to watery sounds from the brook, happy sounds from the children, and warm sounds from Garrick's fire. *I probably should tell him not to use all the wood,* he thought but instead unfolded his map.

Twenty minutes later, terrified shrieks from the children yanked him to his feet. As he ran from the grove, he saw the entire woodpile on fire, and this in turn threatened the cook wagon.

Garrick was jumping and shouting incoherently, the children were screaming. Only Steph had presence of mind to head for the water bucket on the wagon tailgate. Jonn grabbed the child and shoved him away, then bent his head against the heat and snatched the full pail, plus two empties. He threw the empties toward the children with instructions to get more, then dumped the water on the wagon.

"Garrick!" he shouted. "Help me move the wagon away."

Garrick, however, continued flailing and shouting.

"Damn him!" Jonn snarled at the wagon tongue as he tried ineffectively to pull it. Dropping the tongue, he hauled Garrick over and positioned the latter's hands on the side of the wagon. "Now, push while I pull!" he commanded. Slowly, the wagon moved away from the flames.

His daughter, however, stood rooted and screaming.

"Nessa! Move back! I want to put the wagon there."

By this time Celine and Griselle had clambered up the bank with the other children, all of them crying. Celine almost threw her filled buckets to Jonn and flew to Nessa.

Jonn, chest heaving and sweat running down his face, set the buckets aside and held the children. "It's okay now. We won't waste the water. It'll burn out. It's okay, it's okay."

Later, when things had settled down, Celine stood by her husband, forehead on her palms, eyes closed. Finally she looked at him. "You remember Nessa's nightmare last night?"

Jonn shook his head. "I remember her waking up terrified."

Celine looked at the remaining coals writhing across a bed of ash. "It was a fire, and somebody was trying to push her in."

At the foot of the blacksmith's hill, two of the three Russet horsemen squeezed safely through the narrow gap between pedestrians and the parked wagon, but the third was left with no maneuvering room. Treese, being squarely in the way, bounced off the galloping horse. After lying a moment to get his breath, he scrambled to his feet, sputtering obscenities in the face of three wailing children wrapped in the folds of their mother's skirt.

Not for long. The soldier who had toppled him stopped and turned, and Treese, faced with possible repercussions from obstructing justice, pulled himself together and wiped his face smooth. The Russetman, his horse fighting to rejoin its comrades, simply hollered, "You okay?" At Treese's wave and attempt at a smile, he nodded and swung back to the action at hand.

"Whoosh!" said Bren. "You sure you're okay, Treese?"

Treese didn't answer. Rubbing his shoulder, he stared darkly at the milling scene behind them.

"How come you didn't get out of the way?"

A gun barked from the trouble spot. All five strained to see what was happening.

"I saw something and stopped to look," said Treese. "Some T'ribboners had a kid—or somebody small—who was struggling to get away. They held him tight, laughing, like they were just fooling around, but it wasn't fun for him, that was clear. They seemed to be pawing at his face, but I couldn't really tell."

"Well, there's two guys on the ground," said Keltie, ducking and weaving to peer through the gathering crowd. "One's a T'ribboner and somebody else. Couple Russetmen kneeling by the other one—yeah, could be a kid. Huh!"

"I can't see nothin'," Amarl grumbled.

"Me, neither," said Bren. "Move closer; let's see what's goin' on. Plenty folks there. We wouldn't stick out none."

Driss gazed pensively at the tableau, then stiffened and turned. "The Russetmen are bringing the boy this way," he said tersely. "Let's get out of here. We been noticed enough for one day."

They began the climb to the blacksmith shop. Amarl sighed as he trudged after the men. "She was pretty, all right, but she never stopped to ask *me* if *I* was okay."

11

"Driss, whatcha gonna give me on Middle Night?" Nessa's trauma from the morning's fire seemed to have fallen before more compelling concerns.

Driss pretended to choke on his food. "Middle Night! That's weeks away, and already you're counting presents."

"Huh!" retorted Celine, brushing a fly from her daughter's plate. "You think it's weeks. Look at the sky. Here we are, eating supper in broad daylight. High day of the sun will be on us before you know it, and Feast of Candles."

Steph stopped shoveling food into his mouth and looked up with interest.

Benzel rocked sideways, banging his plate. "Firs' Night, Middle Night, Las' Night; Firs' Night, Middle Night, Las'—"

Jonn reached over Nessa and grabbed the boy's shoulder. "Stop, son. Just eat."

Nessa swayed, too, but sang more discreetly:

Seal my heart in love,
Seal my love in—uh . . .
Seal my love—

"What is it, Mommy?"

" '*In flame,*' " Celine replied after a slight hesitation.

"*. . . in flame,*
Mark my love,
Set my love,
Not—not—

"What is it again, Mommy?"

" '*Nor death can mar its claim.*' We need to practice before Middle Night, don't we?" Celine glanced at Jonn, relieved that the reference to flame hadn't re-ignited their daughter's nightmare.

"Do I still get presents," asked Amarl, "or do I have to give 'em this year?"

Treese snorted. "You mean you hustled presents from your folks for . . . how old are you—fifteen?—three extra years?"

Amarl grinned and hunched a shoulder.

"Come to think of it," Treese growled, gloom lines defining his good looks, "what's to show you ever grew up?"

"Hey," Amarl retorted, "if I'm still a kid, then how about a present?"

Celine, running a practiced eye over the children in the supper circle, stopped at one.

"What's the matter, Steph? Why aren't you eating? You're usually done first."

Steph took another bite to help him formulate words. "Feast of Candles, right? It's only for fam'lies, right?"

"Yeah, Steph, for families." Keltie stroked the thin neck and shoulders with his big hand. "It's families and candles, pitchers of water and huge feasts. Ha! With Thilrec, will we ever feast this year! It's singing and dancing. I got my toule flute and bells all—"

"Wait, Keltie," Driss interrupted. "Hold on. He's saying something else. Steph, when was the last time . . . well, put it this way: were you ever in on a Feast of Candles celebration?"

The boy shifted uneasily. "Naw. I watched a bit of Middle Night through a window once. They was havin' fun. But . . . but only for fam'lies."

A jumble of reassurance rose from the circle. Then Keltie took over, wrapping an arm tight around the lad's head. "Hey, man, this year you're family! You're one of us. You get gifts right along with Nessa and Benzel and Vilda. No more lookin' through windows. And eats! You better practice up, or you'll never plow through the mountain Thilrec'll heap on your plate." Keltie loaded the boy's spoon and crammed it in his mouth.

Steph laughed around the food, spraying it on Benzel.

"Presents for everybody this year!" Keltie shouted.

Keltie finished his meal and was first to leave the circle. After relieving himself of a long, rumbling belch, he took his plate to the cook wagon and swished it through the bucket of dishwater with only token attention to cleanliness. Then he turned with a stomp and began a rhythmic march around the campfire and remaining eaters. "DAH-duh-duh-duh, DAH-duh-duh-duh," thrusting alternate arms and shoulders forward with the beat. Steph gobbled the rest of his food and was quick to take up Keltie's winked invitation. Vilda followed. Nessa and Benzel tried the same maneuver, but Celine pulled them back. "Finish eating first." Keltie turned off Benzel's howl with a crazy face each time he passed the boy.

He changed the marching chant to his standard yodel, "Oh, tel-lee-ti-o-ti-o!" which then picked up standard variations: "Oh, Vil-dee-ti-o-ti-o!" and "Steph-ee-ti-o-ti-o!"

After washing his plate—more thoroughly than had Keltie—Driss joined the parade and plucked up Nessa, stuffing last bits of food into her mouth. Benzel cried again over the pile still on his plate, and on the next pass Driss ate part of it. On the third round he snatched the boy himself. Celine glowered at them but philosophically ate the remaining food to "Ben-zee-ti-o-ti-o" and Driss's extravagant countermelody.

When the game wound down, the children ran off for a last few minutes of play before bedtime. Keltie flopped beside Bren on a mossy slope overhung with bria bushes. Their faces writhed in a sudden spasm of light as Thilrec dumped a plateful of greasy scraps on the fire. Keltie hollered to Bren's wife, who was standing near the cook wagon. "Hey, sweetie, any coffee left?"

Griselle lifted the lid of the heavy, sooted pot and peered in. "Some, but it's pretty dark."

"Well, dump in a little hot water and bring me a cup, how about it?

"Wasn't that somethin' about Steph?" Keltie went on, turning to Bren.

"Yeah," Bren replied, shaking his head. "We don't know much about that kid, do we? He's a strange one. Y'know, I swear he really can talk to horses. He figures things out about 'em before I do, sometimes. Like the other day he said Bock told him he had a sore foot. He wasn't limpin' or nothin', but Steph kep' at me, so I looked. Sure enough, there was a small stone caught in the frog. Nothin' serious, but makes you wonder, don't it?"

The two leaned on their elbows, eyes following the children silhouetted against the campfire.

"So we head out tomorrow, eh?" Keltie asked.

"Yeah . . . maybe. If night don't get us first."

"How come? Thanks, Griselle. Come sit down."

"Well," Bren went on as they made room between them, "Rona's still in a tizzy, for one thing, and it could take—"

"Rona's always in a tizzy," Keltie growled.

"Why's she in a tizzy?" asked Griselle. "*She* had *Treese* all to herself last night. She stinks."

"Speakin' of Treese," Keltie said, looking across Griselle to Bren, "what'd you think—"

Griselle yanked at Bren's sleeve. "Yah. Speakin' of Treese, you did go cheatin' last night. Celine said—"

"Oh, get off my neck," Bren snarled. "You been yawpin' all day. First one, then another said. Pretty soon it'll be Vilda said. Who tells me when you do your cheatin'—hm?"

"Keltie cheats." She turned an accusing look.

Keltie reared back in a pretense of shock. "Me? Cheat? What you talkin' about? I ain't married."

"You cheat on Celine."

"She's Jonn's wife, not mine! You can't—"

"She likes you."

"So? I stay on good terms with all the ladies. Never know when I might need it, sugar." He squeezed her thin shoulders.

"But Jonn's ugly. No wonder Celine cheats. He looks like that dumb statue head we saw last week that somebody started but didn't finish. Jonn looks just like that. Not finished. And he wears ugly clothes. All brown."

"So?" said Bren. "Celine wears brown, too. They don't got money to throw around on clothes, but does that make her ugly? And who—besides you—says she cheats? Far's I can see, she and Jonn are thick."

Griselle looked toward Celine, who was playing a clapping game with the children. "Yeah, she wears brown a lot. Maybe he makes her wear it because he wants her ugly like him."

"My dear wife," Bren said sarcastically, "Celine's not ugly; anyone can see that. And Jonn's not ugly, either. He's smart, a good organizer. Makes things work in the group. He—"

"Invisible, that's what he is," said Griselle. "He's invisible. You take a group of people—any old group—and Jonn plain disappears. Nobody sees him. Except for his eyes. His eyes grab you, make you look at him. Almost like rape. Eye rape."

"Oh, stop!" said Bren. "That's why everybody likes Jonn. He pays attention when you talk. His eyes don't go runnin' off while he listens."

"It's her hair makes her stand out. Her face isn't pretty like mine, just her hair."

"Who you tryin' to kid? Celine's prettier all round and a lot more woman. Jonn's lucky, but then, she got a good husband, too."

"So I'm not pretty! You think—"

"Oh, shut up!"

"Two brown birds," Keltie sang, *"comin' through the green. Two brown birds couldn't be seen. Two brown birds tied in brown together. Two brown birds all of a feath—"*

"Knock it off," said Bren, tossing a clump of moss at him. "You're as bad as her. Change the subject. Get back to the business in town this afternoon. What'd you think of that?"

"Huh," Bren replied. "Treese was lucky is what I think."

Griselle sat up, small even beside her small husband. "What business? What happened on the edge of town?"

"Nuthin' all that much," Bren replied. "We're walkin' along, mindin' our business, when these Russetmen come gallopin' down the street. Straight at us they come. Driss, I thought he was gonna heart die right then, happened so fast. Treese, he's lookin' the other direction at somethin' back of us. Anyway, he turns around and is right in the way. One of the horses knocks him down. Didn't get hurt or nothin', just surprised."

"Surprised, hah!" Keltie broke in. "He was rippin'—*Bhlaff!*" He reared back, sputtering and slapping at a moth that had blundered into his mouth. "Git outta here!" He pawed his face and spit several times.

Bren laughed. "Moths go for the biggest mouth, they say. Yeah, Treese was mad, all right, but not long. That ol' Russetman seen what he done and whipped his horse around. Didn't stop long or even come close. Just near enough to ask if Treese was okay. Close enough, though, for Driss to have another heart spell and for Treese to get over his mad—quick."

"Well, I think it was pretty nice he came back," Griselle said. "Why should Treese get mad?"

The two looked at her but didn't answer.

After a moment Griselle tried another question. "What were they after, if they didn't want Treese?"

"Well, that's the funny thing," Keltie replied. Treese said some T'ribboners was wrestlin' somebody. Achh! Where's my cup? Moth don't taste good." After a swallow of coffee, he spit again and rubbed his mouth hard on his sleeve.

He looked at Bren. "Did you hear Treese tellin' us—no, you and Amarl was up front drivin'. Me and Driss and Treese was in back. Anyway, Treese said he thought maybe they was spekkin' the kid. Looked to him like they was holdin' his nose so they could get his tongue."

"Blechh! Achh!" Griselle doubled over in a sudden paroxysm.

"O-ho!" Bren laughed. "You get spekkered some time or other? Tell us!" He elbowed her playfully.

Griselle rolled her head against her knees and made retching noises.

"Nasty stuff! said Keltie grimly. "I was always big enough so nobody tried it on me. But once I just barely touched my tongue to a cut spekker bulb on a dare, and that was plenty. I didn't yank at my tongue or lick dirt or nothin', but I seen all that happen often enough—worse, even. One kid almost died. His tongue swelled so bad he couldn't breathe. Near scared the skin off the boys that done it."

"That's what get's 'em." Bren clucked. "Chokin' on their tongue. Back where I come from, you get caught spekkin' someone, it's good for a whuppin', at least. And if they do die . . ." He shook his head.

Griselle sat up, shuddering. "Soldiers spekking. Soldiers knocking people over. I don't like 'em. They stink. Back home in Swendia, you hardly see any soldiers, let alone two kinds. Why don't they all go away?"

"Yeah, said Keltie, "first thing y'know, they'll be hornin' in on Feast of Candles, like Garrick said Sigurth did back—" He stopped abruptly and looked at Bren, a sudden change of weather on his face. "Y'know, I just thought somethin'. Somethin' not good."

"Yeah?" said Bren.

"Remember Garrick tellin' us about Sigurth's surprise attack on Middle Night?"

"When he gave away whores and chickens?" Bren laughed.

Keltie wasn't smiling. "Y'know, we got Middle Night comin' up, hardly a month away. What's to say he won't try again? Or maybe somethin' like it? We'll be right in the middle of Arlony about then, the middle of a country that's hosting a civil war—"

"But they're not fightin' now," said Bren. "What makes you think they'll be fightin' then?"

Keltie snorted. "Much they're not fightin'! How do you think Treese got knocked down? He was caught between 'em, and somebody got shot. All those Russetmen in charge should make you feel safer, but—" He shrugged, then lay back, hands linked under his head. "They're the ones that run over a guy!"

"Well, don't get Treese goin' on that!" Bren said. "Or on politics in general, for that matter."

Bren reached for Keltie's cup. He swallowed a mouthful and made a face. "How can you drink that?"

"Beats moth feathers! What's with Treese and politics?"

Bren handed the mug back. "His daddy was a mayor, you know. He grew up in politics and had it up to here. Bribe and be bribed. Deaf to anybody who don't have money, blind to crooked deals. Early on he thought he might take over after his daddy and maybe turn things around, but now he's—"

"You havin' a hot flash? Treese isn't blind," Griselle said. "Or deaf."

Bren looked at her. "What are you talkin' about?"

"You said Treese was blind and deaf."

"I did not. I said . . . no, no, no; now, wait a minute."

"Tweet! Tweet! Tweet!" Keltie traced a circle around his ear.

When the conversation broke up, Griselle noted that Celine was washing and night dressing Vilda along with her own two, a chore that often fell to Celine by default. With a glance toward Bren and Jonn who were going over travel plans, Griselle sauntered from the firelight to where Treese stood head down, leaning on a rock. She slipped beside him, safe from the stinging kick on the shins a man would have received for any show of concern.

"You feelin' bad, honey?" she asked. "How about your eyes? Where do you hurt?"

Treese straightened with a wince, rubbing his arm and shoulder. "I'm okay; just sore."

"Here. Let me rub it for you. Your neck and maybe shoulders? How about your ears? Any moth feathers botherin' you?"

The two melted into the darkened woods.

12

The troop got underway next morning earlier than Bren had predicted. Instead of continuing due west, however, they went north into Lorenth to appease Rona. She loved to shop, and although Driss told her the wagons could not hold a single extra garment, she knew she had the advantage and was determined to use it.

Rather than take the entire entourage into town, they drove to a sunny meadow from which they could walk, leaving Amarl to oversee the animals and equipment. His objection to this arrangement was remarkably foreshortened when Jonn unlocked the gun case and placed one of the weapons in his hands—a charge made even weightier with the accompanying list of instructions and cautions.

The rest of the group set off toward town, the three youngest riding shoulders and Steph dancing beside Driss. Celine and Griselle looked forward to the shopping expedition as much as Rona, but they would visit less exotic markets.

Lorenth seemed unusually full of people this bright spring day, at least south of the river. The air laughed and snapped, giving energy to an ever-widening stream of horsemen and pedestrians. Driss and his companions caught the festive spirit. Griselle, though, grew anxious. "Do you suppose there's a flood?" she wondered, pulling nervously at the cord on her bodice. "Or a fire like the other day?"

"Oh, *really*, Griselle!" Rona snapped.

"Do folks look afraid, my sweet?" Bren said caustically to his wife. "Everybody's happy. Just movin' along."

"Well, maybe they all want sashes and bracelets, and there won't be any left by the time we get to market."

"It's probably some Arlonian holiday we don't know about," said Driss. And if this crowd—mostly men, seems like—want sashes and bracelets, I think we're in the wrong place."

Rolind worried, too, for different reasons. Any mode of relaxation made him wary of unseen danger. He walked apart from the rest, gray eyes darting. The children—a major concern—appeared safe for now. Jonn carried his son Benzel, with Nessa on Keltie. Bren and Griselle's daughter, high on Treese's shoulders, had the best view of all. Vilda—so like her mother. Fair head empty of intelligence, but her fragile charm and innocence made her *vulnerable*; Rolind knew that. Steph, though, was different. Required special attention. Yes, he was hardy, streetwise. But who of the group knew him well enough to be sure of what he might do?

The traffic seemed to be concentrating south of the river away from the center of town, so the women, after asking when to return, cut across the bridge toward the market area.

The men peered ahead to determine the crowd's objective. "Must be downstream on the floodplain," Keltie noted, watching the convergence. "A race, maybe, or fair. Something big."

"Men and kids, mostly," Treese observed. "More likely a race. Or a caucus of T'ribboners. Look at them all!"

While they speculated, Nessa and Vilda became engaged in an exchange with a giant, thick-trunked man who had drawn alongside. He smiled, his crinkled eyes softening the graying fierceness of his bushy beard and eyebrows.

Though dressed in the standard tunic of a soldier, the man wore nothing to identify him with either Sigurth or Claeman. A number of scars on his face and hands, as well as an air of disciplined self-assurance, marked him as a veteran of battles, one who had faced down his own fear and walked away a free man.

The girls returned his smile and added a shy wave. He waved back and contributed a pantomime of a rider on a horse.

This sent the children giggling into their hands, after which they exaggerated their riding motions, pretending to beat their "horses."

By this time Benzel had also caught up the play, and the antics of the "horsemen" began to stir the attention of their mounts. First Treese, then Keltie and Jonn frowned up at the children. Their eyes were drawn thence to the friendly stranger matching them stride for stride.

The face-wrinkling smile captured the men as it had the children.

"*Hweo*, brothers. Glinneth's the name." The soldier stuck out a huge hand to shake all around. "A good band of crico lovers, I see. Which team will you be cheering?"

Driss felt an inner leap. Glinneth, the "Big Man," here in their company?

The interest of the others followed a different track. "Crico?" Keltie asked. "That what's goin' on?"

"Ay, lad!" Glinneth's laughter matched his merry eye. "An important match today. Three of the finest teams in the entire valley. They've played in sundry combinations against each other, but this is the first time all three have met on the field. Some say it'll set new records."

Steph tugged at Driss's arm. "What's crico?"

"Hah! A boy who doesn't know crico! Can it be?" Glinneth reached over and tousled the child's hair. "We'll tell you straightway, little one. Perhaps you know a crico ring—a broken circle of fine wood, the ends rounded and offset?" His hands traced the figure. "Have you seen such, lad?"

Steph nodded enthusiastically. "I found one once, and I saw some being throwed and—and stuff."

"Right. That's just what they do. In the playing arena they roll the ring to their partner, back and forth, trying to get close enough to their goal to hang or throw it onto the crosspiece." He patterned the movements with animated gestures. "Takes great skill to throw it, but one point in five must be made that way or you lose all previous points."

"Has to be rolled, too," Jonn put in. "Can't toss or run with it. At least you're not supposed to." He smiled. "We sometimes did when we were kids."

"Ay, that's right. Crico Major—what we'll have today—isn't like the sandbank game you and I grew up on, lads." Glinneth's great arms took in the older generation. "So much rougher, that kind. At least it was in my day." He laughed ruefully. "They don't allow body-checking in these major games. It's all how you maneuver around your opponents."

"You played serious crico?" Treese showed unusual interest in the conversation, along with surprise that such bulk—albeit lean—could be agile enough for the game.

"Ay, as a young man I had considerable skill in the 'lunge and scour.' " He demonstrated the move. "I could score with it more often than not. Those were the days of the great heroes." His eyes took on a far-off look. "Men like the 'Hingem and Hangem' brothers, as they were called, and the famed Orgon—d'you remember him, lads? He won the longest-known match single-handedly after his partner collapsed. Seventeen hours from start to finish—with time-outs, of course."

Treese snorted. "Seventeen hours! Last man alive wins, never mind the score!"

"Ay, fine players in those years . . ." Again that mellow distance. "But today," he said, shaking his head sorrowfully, "all show, all money. Take care, lads—" He looked at Driss with particular concern as they passed the first of countless betting circles, shallow depressions modeling a crico pit. "Take care you don't fall before those who have a skill greater than crico!"

Driss watched Glinneth closely, feeling strangely drawn to this big man. He could not say why, for they had exchanged only pleasantries. He felt sure Glinneth was interested in him, as well. Maybe he was just uncommonly warm and outgoing—rare in a seasoned soldier, at least the ones Driss had observed. That wasn't the whole of it, though; more than crico was being communicated here. He could sense it.

He could better say what Glinneth's cordiality was not: not shallow, not designed to impress or gain approval. Neither was it weak. No, this man had authority and extraordinary strength; clearly, he could kill. His very size conjured up tales from the time of the Green Wars, of Croaker Thorge and his exploits, apocryphal though they might be.

But what *was* going on here? In less than ten minutes' time, Glinneth had stirred something nameless and deep within Driss, looping an invisible thread around his heart. He could feel it. A silent but perceptible tugging gave the illusion of conversation—not about crico, but about life, this brilliant spring day, the children, love and sex . . . Where are you going, Driss? What are you doing? Is it really worth it all?

Driss shivered and scratched a shoulder to cover his unease.

It must be the scars. This man—this Glinneth—had been through war. But instead of hardening him, it had somehow made him unusually sensitive to people. Yes, that was it—the scars. Those, plus his size and strength. You pay attention to a man that big; you second-guess what he's thinking. At the very least, such a man might be useful in time of trouble. A big friend was an asset. You return his offer of friendship but stick to safe things like spring and children. Don't even think rosillum in his presence, especially about stealing it from Claeman . . . or was that already too late?

They were close enough now to see banks of flags marking the steep-pitched spectator slope of the game pit. At the bottom of this broad cone lay the playing field itself: a seventy-foot circle with three high, horizontal rods facing each other in a great triangle. The uprights holding the rods were decorated with team colors and bits of miscellany—old crico rings that had won championships, a favorite belt or headband, even a bleached animal skull. The bowl-shaped playing circle, slightly concave inside the three goals, had a high, sharply lipped rim to help keep the ring in bounds.

Nessa, Vilda, and Benzel could hardly sit still on their shoulder perches. A sea of people, caught up in the carnival atmosphere, flowed past food booths, hawkers of junk, tumblers and jugglers, and the ubiquitous betting circles manned by T'ribboners. Color everywhere; motion everywhere; and above all, talk of crico everywhere. The Camblors were the favored team, trailed by the Liggeth Miners and Tinkers, in that order.

"Come on in, ladies and gents, git yer chips while they last. Make it big on the Tinkers; make it sure on the Camblors; make it on the Liggeth boys if you're stuck in the middle. C'mon, c'mon, c'mon—pick up a chip here—c'mon, c'mon— Camblors lead the pack—will they win big today? Even bigger money if they wrap it up under two hours. Hey there, gents. How 'bout a chip for the little ones, one for the old man?" The gravel-throated hawker nodded at Rolind.

Glinneth, though, raised his hands and shook his head. But Treese studied the odds hungrily, and Garrick's hands twitched.

Though they bypassed that betmaster, the men began listening to talk around them: scoring patterns, win charts, injuries suffered. Driss watched indulgently, comfortable in his own sense of priority. Gradually, though, he grew uneasy.

By the time they reached the spectator slope, the crowd had packed itself into the lower level, with patchy spaces higher up. Jonn, Keltie, and Treese unloaded the little ones and discussed where to sit. The children tugged hard for lower seats, but some of the men argued for the top to get in and out more easily, their eyes on the betting circles.

"Okay," Driss said finally, "we need to talk about this. You guys want to bet. It's all right by me. Just don't go overboard. We can always use extra cash, but there's too much at stake—" He stopped, suddenly mindful of the stranger in their midst. "We don't want to blow food money on crico, do we?" He looked pointedly at Garrick.

"We got till fourth point to put money down," Keltie reminded them. "By that time, we should have a pretty good picture of how it's gonna go."

"What fun is that?" Treese retorted. "You can't call it gambling if you wait that long."

"No, but it could be money in your pocket. What more do you want?"

"All a matter of principle," Treese returned with a wry grin. "See you around." He ambled off, hands in pockets.

Garrick jiggled up and down, sweat pouring from unshaven jowls.

Driss tried to instill some patience in him. "Wait a while, Garrick, till we see what these fellows look like today. Records aren't everything, you know."

Glinneth nodded. "Ay. Not anything, really. There's much in these games we don't know about. Best not to bet one coin more than you're willing to cast into an earthcrack."

A sudden roar from the crowd shifted their attention to the circle below. One by one, the pairs came onto the playing field and jogged around the perimeter, posturing with victory signals, their loose, multi-paneled robes swirling like giant flowers.

"You'd think they'd break their necks with all that cloth around their ankles," Bren murmured.

"Hah!" exclaimed Glinneth. "I've seen 'em break the other guy's neck. The uniform itself is a weapon. A guy'll get the ring underneath so the others can't tell which way he'll spin it off. No body-blocking allowed, but a well-placed panel of cloth can do considerable damage."

Play got under way in the traditional manner, the six players standing in an outward-facing circle with arms outstretched and wrists clasped tightly. Behind them the carved wood ring lay buried under three inches of sand. The crowd hushed, then exploded as the referee gave his signal and the players dove for possession of the ring.

The children couldn't keep up with the fast-paced action. The players whipped the ring backward and forward, and their feint-and-whirl maneuvers became a blur of motion. The men watched tensely, awed by skillful play that approached an art form.

The highly touted Camblors, or at least their number-one man, appeared to be having an off day. Number two worked hard, but his partner couldn't keep off the ground. The crowd voiced its opinion, especially those whose money rode the team's reputation.

The Tinkers scored first, a magnificent lunge and scour that brought Glinneth to his feet cheering.

"Hah! Did you see that, lads? Almost like he was flying! Good show, good show!"

"What did they do?" cried Steph. "I couldn't see. Did they win?"

"Not yet, son—not yet. Laddie, we need to get closer so you can follow what's going on." Glinneth turned to Driss. "Suppose I take the young ones as far forward as I can. There seems to be some shifting about, now that first blood's been drawn."

Driss agreed readily.

Rolind objected instantly. "Sir—" he began, iron-gray eyebrows forming an unbroken line of concern.

Driss clapped him on the shoulder, wondering at his own lapse in trusting even a kindly stranger. "You go with them, Rolind. Help keep Benzel in line." He flipped the squealing boy upside down.

Glinneth and the two boys cut a wide swath through the mob, leaving an ample wake for Rolind to follow with the girls. Driss watched them settle in a spot just vacated, amused by the tableau of a giant kneeling before Nessa, replacing her shoe.

Bren and Thilrec soon lost interest in the game and wandered off to look at horses. Garrick was interested but couldn't stand still. He stomped and muttered and clapped and gurgled, effectively keeping himself free from the press of the crowd.

Keltie and Jonn, no less than Garrick, were itching to place bets, but with the uneven performance of the favorites, they waited.

The Tinkers scored again and three minutes later made their dazzling throw point that left both Camblors sprawled in the sand.

This rapid development sent the crowd streaming to the betting circles. With only one point before betting closed, an urgency that was almost panic drove the herd up the slope.

Driss tried to calm his men. "Don't sweat it; we're in good shape. We waited long enough to see who was hot, and now we know. The Miners aren't bad, though. Chances are they'll make the next point, and you'll have all kinds of time. Head for a far circle; the lines out there may be shorter. I'll wait here so we don't lose the kids. Keep an eye out for Treese," he called after them.

Driss, waiting alone, began to perspire. Two things worried him: would they get there in time? And would they have sense? He'd forgotten to set a limit, and Garrick was not noted for discretion. Jonn would keep the lid on . . . he hoped. Maybe if they didn't make it at all . . .

Nothing much happened on the field during that long wait, almost as though real play stepped back for a business break. Then, in a move that took everyone's breath away, the Tinkers hung up their fourth point. The crowd close at hand responded wildly, but as an antiphonal echo to the fourth-point gong came the groan of those left standing in line.

Driss paced nervously. It suddenly became very important that the bets had been placed. But why didn't the men come back?

Jonn showed up first, wrinkling his many-angled nose and pulled empty hands from his brown pockets. "The circles were packed—intersecting each other, even. We moved out like you said and split up to triple our coverage, but when fourth point cut off the betting, I couldn't find the other two. There were at least two dozen in front of me. Never had a ghost of a chance."

"Well," Driss sighed, "maybe they had better luck. Maybe—"

A new roar from the crowd drew their attention back to the field. The Camblors had scored much to everyone's surprise. By this time, both of them looked like refugees from a war zone—faces scraped and bloodied, skirt panels tattered. But no longer were they bumbling clowns, getting in each other's way. The spectators rose to their feet as the two took control. Play after astonishing play left everyone gasping, and two more points followed in quick succession.

Garrick and Keltie returned in the ensuing roar, faces lit and pockets rattling with handfuls of chips. "Is that it? Did they win?"

Driss stared at them in pained stupefaction. "Win!" He laughed harshly. "This isn't a game at all. A play, that's what it is, a rotten burlesque! The only winners are the guys who took your money!"

13

"Oh, what a glorious, glorious day!" Celine, clothed in brown and sunshine, lifted her arms as far as her carrying baskets would allow. Tilting her honeyed head first up, then down, she danced a tight circle, swinging exuberant hips.

To Griselle's embarrassment. "You havin' a hot spell? Maybe you want everyone to look at you."

"I don't care who looks. We're in Arlony, in Lorenth with its wonderful markets, and it's spring! We're by ourselves, no children to watch, nothing—"

"You forget Rona. She's here somewhere." Griselle peered around the market square, narrow-set eyes pointing up her small frame. "What would she say?"

"Oh, forget Rona. She doesn't want to be with us, and I don't care what she says." Celine shuffled a few more dance steps, trying on a little tune.

Arlony in springtime, bind flowers to my heart;
Arlony in singtime, grow music in my heart.

She hummed another experimental line, ignoring Griselle's deepening frown.

"You should be singin' about Swendia, not Arlony," Griselle advised, mouth forming a prim triangle. She redid a comb, pulling her hair severely from her thin face into a mane of pale, frowzy curls. "Arlony's not our home. You should sing about where we're citizens . . . well, except for Amarl—"

"I'm not singing about citizens; I'm singing about spring. And besides, Arlony is beautiful. Look at that bank of flowers over there and tree leaves just coming out. Look behind us at the hills we came over, how blue they are. We don't have mountains like that in Swendia."

"It's raining up there; that's why they're blue," sniffed Griselle.

Celine changed the subject. "I'm surprised how few people are shopping. Whatever's happening on the other side of the river gives us plenty of room here." She surveyed the square. "Maybe you don't realize how famous this market is, Griselle. My aunt comes all the way from Coldmeade in Swendia at least once a year. Now, that says something about these shops here!"

"Maybe Coldmeade doesn't have a market. Maybe—"

"No, no. Lorenth has a *better* market. There are things here you can't find anywhere else."

"If you can't find 'em, you don't need 'em."

Celine drew breath to respond but thought better of it. She turned instead to the nearest shopping stall.

Here she found a tidy arrangement of cooking tools, backed by racks of fresh-baked breads, puddings, and crusty supper pies. A knot of round-faced, round-bellied farmwomen nodded colorful scarves and laughed in the warm sun, their chatter as welcoming as the aromas they had carried to market.

"I'm hungry!" cried Griselle, breathing in the essence of grain and sun and butter and spices. "Let's buy a kuhnel bun—one for each."

"Thilrec makes those all the time. Why don't we get something different, something we don't have so often?"

"It couldn't be good if we don't have it often. If it was good—"

"Oh, have a kuhnel bun, then. I think I'll buy a bread roll-up."

"But you like kuhnel buns! You saying these aren't as good as Thilrec's?"

The farmwomen's laughter died under this question of their baking skill.

Celine smiled disarmingly. "Everything looks delicious. Too bad there aren't more people in town to enjoy your goodies."

"Oh, they'll be here, mum, after the game," a dark-haired woman answered. "They'll clean us out quicker 'n pigs in slops."

"Game?" Griselle and Celine looked at each other.

"Crico, mum. Big match today."

"So that's what it was!" Celine laughed. "I'm glad—"

"But Bren said it was a holiday or a flood," Griselle broke in.

"No, he didn't," Celine countered. "You were the one—"

"Hardly a flood, mum." A redheaded, green-scarved woman entered the conversation with a laugh. "And t'ain't a holiday. No holiday till Feast of Candles next moon."

"You're forgettin' Roister Day," said her dark-haired companion.

"So I am. But that one don't hold a candle to Feast of Candles." She chuckled over her pun. "Oh, me," she sighed, "seems just a wee bit ago we had Fast Feast."

Again the two shoppers frowned at each other. "We don't have Fast Feast in Swendia," said Celine.

The redheaded proprietress blew out her cheeks. "Winter Fast Feast? Imagine not knowin' Feast of Candles or Fast Feast!"

"Oh, we have Feast of Candles. And winter Dark Day. Is that what you're talking about?"

The ruby-faced woman nodded vigorously. "Yes, yes. You fast the short day and feast the next when the sun turns?"

"Something like that. Mostly we sing quiet songs one day and jubilant ones the next. And such a feast! Bigger, even, than Middle Night."

The dark-haired woman pursed her lips and squinted darkly as three T'ribboners walked past. She dropped her voice. "Well, we know who fasts and who feasts around here." Her head nodded and shook with heavy import.

The other woman leaned forward. "Claeman's Russeters, they start off the fastin'," she whispered conspiratorially, "and Sigurth's T'ribboners lead the feastin'!"

A third round woman pushed in. "Now, it ain't so simple as all that. It's not just like that. Russetmen—"

"Oh, I know," replied the red one, "Russetmen, they eat the house down too, but on rightful days. Not like the others. The others, they have their affairs off in the hills, and it ain't no fastin' they do." She nodded and bobbed even more than her dark neighbor.

"What do you mean?" asked Celine, her curiosity spiked by these mysterious communications.

The three farmwomen looked at each other significantly. The redhead bent her bulk close to her audience.

"Wheest! There's things goes on in dark places, on high hills, in wild dingles, in earthcracks—one earthcrack in perticaler, other side of the mountain. The Green Wars, they ain't over, not in some ways. They say ribbons didn't fight the Green Wars, but they's things worse 'n fightin'. They made up their own ways, the ways of hurt and harm, of givin' over to fire—"

"And ash children," put in another.

"Ay, ash children, yes. Ashes that make zill. These ways go far back. And today—yes, today they still has ribbons onto 'em." Her mouth drew a hard, straight line.

Redhead nodded vigorously and pursed her lips. "There. Wheest, now. We told you. Keep yer youngers close, keep out of hills and dingles, and watch for ribbons where they don't belong."

After buying their bread, Celine and Griselle wandered in the luxury of time through shop and stall. They discussed the farmwomen.

"I think they're mostly superstitious," Celine said. 'I doubt they can read or write, so what else to do but stand around and scare each other?"

"What's zill?"

Celine shrugged. "I have no idea. I think she was talking about something that went on in the Green Wars."

"Well, I don't remember the Green Wars. Do you?"

"Of course not. That was long before the Great Earthquake."

"Well, how do the women know about them, then?"

Celine didn't answer. Her attention was drawn to a shop with an astonishing variety of baskets. Celine knew baskets. She had come from a basket-making family and had made many of the packing panniers and arm baskets for the trip. She knew weaving excellence, and she saw it right there before her.

She saw herself, too, as a child, sitting cross-legged at the rear of the shop, struggling to make the strands come together in utility and beauty. But on closer look, the child in this shop had none of the brightness, the verve of the young Celine. Long, straggled hair covered her face as she bent over her work. Dressed in a nondescript sack, she seemed a crow's nest among the handsome baskets. Her fingers tugged awkwardly at the strands of a shoulder pannier, dogged persistence her only talent.

Celine could see no one else in the shop. Perhaps the owner, expecting a poor business day, had gone off to the crico game. Whatever, it appeared that sales and production would be down today.

Celine had just drawn breath to ask about prices when she saw the small, thin shoulders bend even lower and begin to shake. The strands had become hopelessly snarled, and the girl gave way under this final frustration. Celine stepped forward. "Oh, my dear!" she clucked sympathetically. "It has gotten away from you, hasn't it? Here. Let's see if I can put it right and get you going again."

She undid the worst of the bungled work, putting the loose strands back into the soaking tub. Then, humming a little song to fuel her nimble fingers, she chose two new strands, shook off excess water, and began the pattern once again, altering it to suit the child's capability.

"Watch the order of colors. I'll go slow so you can follow. See? Now, you do it, and I'll help.

The child, smearing her eyes and sniffling doubtfully, picked up the work without a word and began again.

Griselle pulled nervously at her dress and made short forays away from the basket shop. "I see a scarf and ribbon shop. Let's go."

Enticement failing, she tried intimidation. "Celine, a soldier's watching us! Across the way. See?"

"It's their business to watch the marketplace. We're doing nothing wrong."

"But a Russetman. You can't sit in somebody's shop like you owned it."

But Celine would not be dislodged. The child had begun to catch the basket pattern, her streaked face working up a shy smile. But as the basket took form, a shapeless man of enormous lips and bald head thumped across the square. He saw Celine with the baskets and began howling accusations in assorted languages. "Thief! *Plaguen!* Troubler!" Celine scrambled to her feet, shoving the child protectively behind her.

"Sir, you must be the owner of this—"

The man's roaring marshaled the attention of curious passersby. When Griselle saw two Russetmen, as well, hurrying toward them, she yanked the dress cord across her shallow bosom. "Hurry! They're almost here!" She pulled ineffectively at Celine's arm. Then, with hands to her head, she tried to break through the crowd, only to be stopped by the soldiers. "Celine! Help me!"

But Celine stood tall, the child tight behind her, and stared defiantly at her accuser. "Pig!" she spat out. "What do you mean, setting this poor girl to a task way beyond her, then leaving her to struggle alone?"

"Missacrotte! Vexotte!" he hurled back, his torrid body radiating a thick rancidity.

The dark-faced soldiers pushed through the growing throng, dragging Griselle, who was screaming and fighting.

"Griselle, stop that!" Celine commanded. "We have only to tell them the truth."

"Yes," said one of the soldiers firmly, "the truth. Suppose we start with you." He turned to Griselle and released his hold as though fearful of breaking a bone.

For a moment it seemed she might try again to escape, but she rubbed her arm, redid her comb, and drew a shaky breath.

"Well," she began, "we were afraid of the flood, and we came in here because it looked dry, and—"

Celine closed her eyes in despair. *"Griselle!* The truth!"

"That is the truth! Don't you remember, we talked about a flood, and everybody was runnin' away, and—"

Celine shook her head in disbelief. "Sir," she said to the closer Russetman, "don't listen to her; she doesn't know what she's talking about. Please let me explain."

Mistrust set the soldier's face. "Ma'am, first let me tell you what this looks like to me, and others is sayin' the same thing. After I lines it out, we'll see how floods fits the story. This is how it looks. You two ladies is walkin' up and down the market.

You sees this shop with nobody here but a kid. An easy mark, you thinks. One of you cozies up to the kid while the other walks around to find the best baskets. But before she can make her pick and ease out the shop while the kid is bein' kept busy, the owner sees from across the market and comes over. Now. How does that fit your flood?"

Celine's jaw tightened. "Sir," she said, "I want you to look at this child." She pulled the girl—reluctant, afraid—from behind her skirt, keeping an arm close around her. "Look at her. See the condition she's in—dirty, frightened. These sores on her arms and legs. Look at them! If she's this man's daughter, he should be jailed. If she just works for him—well, shouldn't he be punished just the same? Sir, if there's any justice, I beg you to see to this child, and never mind what that man says."

The Russetman looked the girl over but turned back to Celine. "What you say may be true enough, but that don't mean you wasn't tryin' to take advantage and filch baskets."

"I was trying to help her. I know basket making. She's just a beginner. But he set her at a shoulder pannier—you probably wouldn't know how hard that is to make—with a design that would scramble an experienced basketer. That's just mean!"

"She lies!" the shop owner fumed, spraying saliva in an indiscriminate circle. "I take de bes' care of leetle Rivca here. She been seek. Dat why she look so. De lady lies!"

"She's not lying!" Griselle shouted. "She's—"

Celine turned on her. "Griselle, you've said enough. Keep still!"

The Russetman raised his eyebrows. "Maybe we should hear what your friend has to say."

Celine sighed. "If you want to hear about a flood that doesn't exist, go right ahead; if you want to find out what happened, ignore her."

Griselle sniffed in protest, and the soldier, suppressing a smile, nodded for Celine to continue.

"The girl was in tears when I came along, so I sat down and undid the snarl. Then I altered the design to something she could handle. Look at it now." Celine reached back for the workpiece and held it proudly for the soldiers to inspect. "I just got her started, and she did this much by herself. Isn't it good work?"

"Hah!" exclaimed the owner. "Dese women thieves. Da girl, she change de basket. She wreck it! Lazy *ingrato!*"

The Russetmen looked at each other uncertainly. Then one of them squatted down to face the child. The girl shrank back from the dark face into the brown folds of Celine's skirt.

"Don't be fearful, lass. I won't hurt you. I just want you to tell me what this lady done when she come in your shop."

Celine held her breath. The child had not said a single word the whole time they'd been with her. Would she say anything now? What if she couldn't talk?

After a long, uncertain silence, the child looked up at Celine with pleading eyes and whispered, "She helped me."

Celine closed her eyes and squeezed the child.

The second Russetman leaned to the first and whispered in his ear. The soldier nodded and stood, addressing Celine. "Ma'am, if you have skill in basketing like you say, maybe you wouldn't mind showin' us how you do it."

Celine almost hugged him in relief and delight. Her oval face dimpling, she sank cross-legged to the floor. A shaft of sun haloed the thick coils of her honey-colored hair as she took up humming with the unfinished basket, fingers poking and pulling damp reed weavers around stiff spokes, dexterously introducing new colors. Clearly she was a master.

She had not long to work before everyone but the fat-lipped shop owner began nodding and smiling.

"Right you are, ma'am," said one of the soldiers; "a right fine basketer. Sorry to have inconvenienced you. You and your friend can go. Just keep out of the way of them floods," he admonished with a wink toward his companion.

He began clearing the way for Celine and Griselle to leave the shop, but Celine stood firm, her arm holding the child tight to her side. "I will not leave unless the child comes with me," she said. "She's not safe here. This isn't a proper place for her to grow and learn. I have a daughter, and I would want someone to do for Nessa . . ." She stopped and bit her lip.

The shop owner threw up his hands. "No, no, no, no! *Loguando, no!* She mine! She my business! Look," he went on, noting the creeping hardness of the soldiers' faces, "I have daughter, too. You think I not care? The leetle one, she bembo to me!"

Celine's face stiffened, also. "He admits she isn't his daughter! I will not leave her here." She turned her plea to the crowd. "You know this man; you know how he treats the child. Would you leave your daughter in his hands? Would you?"

Griselle began to fidget again, but Celine, tense and shaking, ignored her.

The soldiers conferred briefly, then turned to Celine. "We have daughters, too, and we wouldn't want 'em here, neither." His face grease seemed to darken a shade, and he added gruffly, "We know what happens to children in these . . . and other places."

Celine eyes widened, the farmwomen's "hills and dingles" and "keepin' youngers close" rising before her.

The soldier straightened and squinted at Celine as though seeing her for the first time. "You say you want to take the child. You have a husband? A home?"

Celine kept her face in order, but her mind began racing. Much more was at stake here than just the child's welfare. When she had taken in Steph, there had been no one to make unsettling inquiries. Here, though, just doing their duty, these Russetmen could bring down the whole enterprise. She fought to appear unperturbed.

"You're right. The child needs a settled home, with love and care and good food." With iron control she looked the soldiers straight in their eyes. "She needs sunshine, a chance to run and play—things many women here would love to give her." Again she faced the crowd and waved her hand confidently . . . hoping.

As if on cue, a young, sad-faced woman moved forward and reached out a timid hand. "Please, sir, I'll take the child. My daughter . . . died three months ago, and I have emptiness in my heart. Please . . . ?"

The soldiers looked automatically to Celine and read relief as approval. They turned back to the woman. "Yes. We'll talk more of it. Perhaps in your home. You have a husband? What does he do? You have enough food—a cow, maybe, for milk?"

The child wept at being separated from Celine, but the hearthunger of the foster mother enveloped her, and the transfer was made.

"And you, sir," the Russetman said to the shopkeeper, "you'll come with us. For a talk."

Griselle turned mean as the two continued their tour of the marketplace. "Wait'll Driss hears what you almost did," she said, redoing her bodice cord. "And that woman. You're a pushover for tears. She'll take the kid and work her worse'n old Fat Lips."

"I'm just glad that woman was there!" Celine said fervently. "I wanted the child, I really did, but I suddenly realized—"

"Oh, sure. You wanted her. Where would we 've put her? Maybe you'd drop Steph off and take her on. It's a good thing you did realize, all right!"

Celine began humming again, this time a biting tune.

Griselle rummaged in her basket. "Now maybe I can finish this." She unwrapped her half-eaten kuhnel bun and bit into it, animal satisfaction softening the hard lines of her face. "Mmm!"

They came to a war memorial, the kind found in almost any sizeable town. An ugly, graceless pile of stone, it bore an ornate, flowery tribute encompassing warriors throughout the whole of Arlony's history. At its base sat a large receptacle for gifts, money, or pictures to honor the dead.

A blind man sat cross-legged nearby, an old Russetman, face still proudly darkened. Head tipped up and back straight, he held a grimy, shredded basket. With the patience of long infirmity, he rocked sideways—gently, rhythmically, smiling on an empty world.

The women gazed at the sheer bulk of the memorial. Several people came as they watched. One placed flowers, another a piece of paper—perhaps a letter—which she read one last time before laying it reverently in the receptacle. From somewhere beyond them, a child's voice lined out a sad, beautiful tune that evoked for Celine a sobbing sorrow for women and children everywhere whose lives are unbearably tragic.

"A big show," Griselle muttered as the mourners moved away. "They want people to feel sorry for them. That's what they want."

"Suppose Bren had been killed in a war. Would you feel that way then?" Celine asked tartly.

"He's a teamster, not a soldier, so how could he be killed?" Griselle retorted. "Besides, if the Green Wars were all that long ago, there'd be nobody left to feel bad."

Celine sighed, her eyes following the sweep of a broom. When the man drew close, she spoke to him. "You keep this place beautifully! Did you fight in any of the wars listed here?" She pointed at the inscription on the monument.

"Ay, ma'am, I did at that." He straightened proudly. "The Civil War and long before it."

Gray of head and watery of eye, he wore what looked like a soldier's tunic, clean but heavily patched. *An old, old uniform,* thought Celine. *Poverty . . . or just loyalty?*

"Folks think soldiers don't do a lot in peacetime," he continued in his thin, hollow tone, "but let me tell you, we never rested much, even before the Civil War, no ma'am!"

Celine's eyes sparked. Whatever came out of this primed pump had to be more conversationally promising than the best of Griselle.

"Now, take T'ribboners. Always troublesome, even in the Green Wars." He shook his head.

Griselle leaped to the fray. "What're you sayin'? T'ribs never fought in the Green Wars. They stayed out. My grandfather—"

The old soldier hooted. "On the bottom of my boot they stayed out! Oh, they bowed to Claeman straight off but then melted into wood and mountain where nobody could get 'em easy. There in the dark, they went to work. Caused more trouble than if they'd fought outright. Terrorized the whole country, they did."

"Well," huffed Griselle, her shoulders swinging indignantly, "my grandfather was a T'ribboner, but he moved to Swendia, and he said—"

"Swendia, too. T'ribs weren't just in this country. Stirred trouble all over. Did you know foot markings started because of the mischief going on between countries? Arlony needed some way to know just who was who."

Celine's face had grown solemn as she listened. "Some shop women just told us something like what you're saying. They also talked about . . . things," she added lamely, "that maybe happen today."

"What kind of things?"

"Well . . . they mentioned earthcracks and fires and ash children . . ."

The old man nodded vigorously. "Ay, they happen. Not a lot, mind you. Not everywhere; not here especially. But it does happen. Just enough to let you know they still do their nasty work." He spit figuratively. "And it's all rooted in the Green Wars. Green Wars and rosillum. Where rosillum's thickest, that's where you find trouble's thickest. Now, I can't say there's never been trouble here in Lorenth. No. I can't say that. But I can say for a fact no T'ribboner comes close to *this* place." Again he straightened proudly in salute of four glorious eras of military tradition. "We see to that!"

As the keeper of the monument resumed his sweeping and Celine turned to go, Griselle stood a moment longer, wadding her bun wrapper spitefully. Then she stepped toward the monument and tossed the wrapper on top of the flowers and letters. She turned away, then hesitated. Retrieving the paper from the receptacle, she flipped it instead into the blind man's basket.

14

That the Camblors' sudden recovery was no minor fluke became obvious, and the crowd, now heavily invested in the Tinkers, fell silent. Every impact, every raspy breath of the tired crico players carried to the topmost spectators. Point four for the Camblors came on another lunge and scour, even more spectacular than the Tinkers' first score. Driss looked down toward the children and saw Glinneth leap up, a solitary gleam in a darkling sea.

They still had not made their throw point, however, and the Tinkers had. Spirits picked up after several failed attempts, and then the Liggeth Miners made their first score.

Keltie kicked the ground, tension deepening the cleft of his chin. "Is this some kind of dance: 'First I take four steps; now it's your turn'?"

The end came mercifully. The Camblors' number one man made a backward flip to the Miner nearest the Camblor goal, seemingly by mistake, then took advantage of the latter's surprise and tiredness and got possession in superb scoring position, with no one guarding. The ring arched up and grabbed, and the game was over.

The Camblors leaped and hugged each other, cheered by the few who had either not bothered to switch their chips or had been caught in line by fourth point.

Driss took a big breath. "Okay. How much did we lose?"

Garrick hunched uncomfortably, but Jonn cut in. "Treese isn't back yet. He was going to bet on the Camblors—as a matter of principle. Ha! If he did—"

"If he did," Keltie growled, "we've lost only half our bankroll, instead of three-quarters." He pulled out a handful of purple chips and let them dribble to the ground.

They watched Glinneth and Rolind climb toward them with the children. Heaviness dragged at Driss's shoulders, and he steeled himself against the inevitable "I told you so." For the sake of the kids, however, he managed a weak smile.

Glinneth looked from face to face, taking in the situation, but said nothing. After a moment he put an arm around Driss's shoulders and drew him aside.

"I'm sorry, laddie. I really am. I wish the game had turned out better for you. I have a little money with me." He pulled a small pouch from his pocket. "But it wouldn't go far amongst so many. If you're in a serious way, I could take you to friends who'd put you up and provide work—at good pay—to make up your losses in short order. Wouldn't be charity," he added quickly in response to the stiffening in Driss's face, "and no one need know who's behind it or where this came from." He fingered the pouch. "Just between you and me; an unexpected change of plans. What d'you say, lad?"

The thread tugged once again at Driss's heart. Like a spider's prey he was being bound, one loop at a time, only Glinneth's web was more fragile than a spider's, a web Driss could destroy with a mere frown.

The silent conversation accompanying the tugs, though, frightened him into a wild inclination to cut and run. As hungry as Driss was for it, Glinneth's friendship with its hidden probing questions—especially ones concerning goals and motives—could in the long run cost him the rosillum.

Reluctantly, he cut the invisible thread. "Thank you, Glinneth; you're kind, very kind. But we're probably not as bad off as we think. Jonn still has his money, and Treese left before the game to bet on the Camblors. He may have made up what we lost." He affected another sickly smile.

Glinneth looked into Driss's eyes and saw. With a small sigh he retired the pouch.

Nessa squatted to examine an object on the ground. "Look what I found!" she crowed, holding up a cheap souvenir crico ring. The other children crowded close.

"Hah!" roared Glinneth, taking it in his hands. "A splendid ring, almost as fine as the great Orgon's. Come, lads." He motioned to them all. "Let's redeem the day with a bit of fun." Grabbing a child under each arm, he strode down the slope toward the playing field.

The men stared glumly after him, mired in despondency, but as Benzel pulled at them and Steph skipped behind Glinneth's yard-wide back, a spark of interest began to grow. Within minutes they were caught up in a wild, rule-free version of crico where by creative scoring methods, all came out winners.

When it came time to part, Glinneth lifted the children one by one, covering each with kisses.

When he came to Vilda, she put her hands on either side of his bushy head and looked closely at his forehead.

"Why . . . why is that line?" she asked, running her forefinger along one of Glinneth's many scars.

"Hah! That line—that one right there," he exclaimed, rubbing the spot, "is a special mark of love, little one. Like at Middle Night, the mark you and the others put on wax. D'you remember doing that last year? It's almost time again, isn't it?"

Vilda nodded gravely but continued examining the scar. "Does it hurt?"

Glinneth shook his head with a smile. "Once it did. My enemy drew it in hatred, but I bear it in love." He stroked the child's hair. "I bear it for you, for Benzel, for Nessa and Steph. I'm a soldier, you see. A good soldier tries to protect little children. Sometimes he can't, but this mark reminds me to do my best for them."

As Vilda wrapped her arms around the great neck, Glinneth hugged her in return and rumbled a familiar baby song.

> *Gizzy cry, Gizzy moan,*
> *Roll on the floor;*
> *Your knee is all bloodied,*
> *Your elbow is sore.*
>
> *Gizzy wink, Gizzy smile,*
> *Laugh, little one;*
> *We'll wash it and bind it*
> *And rock in the sun.*

With a final kiss he disengaged Vilda's arms and set her down, then went from man to man with a warm handshake and a straight look in the eye.

Last of all, he laid his enormous hand on Driss's shoulder. "Drissan, my son—" He stopped suddenly, his heart on his face, then turned quickly and jogged down the road.

Driss watched after him, annoyed by an uncharacteristic lump in his throat. Like an earthquake, Glinneth—the "Big Man"—had upheaved Driss's emotions into a new watershed. He felt as though his life now flowed in two distinct directions.

Even a mother's stubbornness could not forestall death's inexorable approach. The infant, pale and clammy, lay limp in Charri's arms, tiny breaths coming with heart-stopping irregularity.

"My child, my baby! Please be better! Please keep breathing!" Charri bent over her bundle, anxiety tight in her voice.

"Oh, Roanna, I can't tell if she's breathing!" She stopped and laid the tiny form on the ground, heedless of marketplace traffic, and tore at the wrapping. Shoulders shaking with silent sobs, she rubbed the little chest and limbs, trying to stir the spark of life.

Celine and Griselle, baskets heavy with parcels, halted at the sight.

"Changing wetcloth in the middle of the street?" Griselle murmured incredulously.

Celine frowned. "No . . . something's wrong. The woman's crying. Here. Hold this." She dumped her basket in Griselle's arms and crossed the cobbled square.

"Wait!" Griselle cried in annoyance. "You can't do that! Why are you . . . ?"

Celine pushed aside the blubbering Roanna and bent over mother and child.

"Is the little one ill?"

Charri looked up in surprise, her body trembling. "Death is here," she faltered, "and I can't stop it! She seemed better this morning, so we started out at high sun, hoping to travel a few miles before night. But now . . ." She broke into sobs.

Celine put an arm around her and looked closely at the infant. "Poor thing! So tiny. How old is she?"

"Nearly . . . four weeks."

"Where is it you're going?"

Charri drew a shaky breath. "I'm . . . trying to find friends, trying . . . I'm sorry." She blew her nose. "You see, the child has no name because . . . I have no name. I must find . . . before she dies, someone . . . who knew my mother, or . . ." She broke down. "Oh, I don't know what to do! Please, little one." She turned back to rub the tiny chest. *"Please . . ."*

Griselle had come over—reluctantly—and the two women looked at each other. "Must be a healer somewhere in town," Griselle suggested hopefully, then muttered to Celine, "so we can get outta here."

"No!"

Charri's vehemence startled them.

"I'll have no part with healers." Her hand traveled to the scar on her face. "They'd only make her suffer. I'd rather she die than that . . . except for her name . . ."

Again the women exchanged looks. Griselle rolled her eyes and sighed noisily. Without a word Celine rewrapped the infant and gathered it up. "Come. I am claiming her, and I will name her. You must stay with us, at least for today."

Silently, she hoped Driss would cooperate. He should be grateful she wasn't bringing yet another child.

On reaching the wagons, they found things a bit touchy. On top of the losses incurred by Garrick and Keltie, Treese had changed his mind as well as his principles and was tree-thumping furious. Rona too had much to say. She had brought back fewer parcels than she would have liked, but with the new financial crisis in mind, Driss assailed her. "Here we are with less than half the money we need to get where we're going, and you blow a good part of it on clothes!"

"Oh. The men lose their bets, and I'm to blame. Is that it? I'm supposed to see what's going on two miles away and adjust my spending accordingly. I'm supposed to make up for a bunch of snail-brained high-rollers." She arched her brows in a way she knew Driss hated. "Just how are we to get on, anyway? What happened to Rolind's money? Did he gamble, too? Maybe I'll have to put myself out for hire. There's an idea, hm?"

Driss clamped his jaw, words barely escaping his set teeth. "You know full well we've been traveling on Rolind's money, and there's not much left. Garrick still has a little, but not enough—that's the point."

"That's the point!" Rona huffed, turning toward the wagon. "The point is that you're all a bunch of niggardly turnips, and you can have your rotten old clothes!" She hurled them, one by one, at Driss.

After a prudent interval, Celine drew Driss aside to explain Charri's situation and won disgruntled consent. Satisfied with that, she settled the newcomers on a blanket in the warm afternoon sun and gratefully accepted Thilrec's offer of a late lunch.

At first, Charri would not eat. Celine set the bowl aside and took the woman's hands. "Charri, look at me," she commanded.

The other responded reluctantly.

"Your little one is going to die. We know that. She's too far gone to save. We can only love her through death and be strong for her sake. I promise you, she will not die without a name. Now, please. Eat a little soup. You'll feel better."

The woman gave way to tears, and Celine drew her close.

Not for long. Charri straightened and forced a smile. "Thank you," she murmured, then picked up the bowl and ate.

Celine took the naming seriously. She had claimed the baby, a transaction far more weighty than simply helping someone in need. She would extend to that child the essence of who and what Celine herself was. Naming gave identity, but claiming forged a fundamental link between claimer and claimed. What the claimer was, the one claimed would become. Celine, therefore, had to search her own heart for an appropriate symbol of her claim. She asked questions of Charri and consulted Jonn and even Driss, who by this time had shown some sympathetic interest in the strangers' plight. He had already decided to delay departure at least till morning.

Something else settled over Celine, something just beyond vision, just out of reach. Was it simply the vicarious horror of a mother having to bear death in her arms? She had, of course, tested death's weight in her mind many times. What mother hadn't? No, something else, a black fog seeping into her heart, the unspeakable side of this present horror: What if circumstances *prevented* a mother from holding her child in the hour of its death? What then?

She shuddered violently and twisted away from her thoughts and into Driss with such force that he had to grab her to keep them both from falling. "Are you all right, Celine?" He looked at her closely. "You're white as ash. What's the matter?"

Celine took deep breaths and leaned her head against Driss, fighting for control. She attempted a smile. "I'm sorry. I don't know what came over me. Are we nearly ready?"

The naming was a solemn affair. In accord with ancient custom, the group gathered near Thilrec's cooking fire, with Celine, Roanna, and Charri kneeling around the infant. Gently, Celine pulled back the wrap and uncovered the tiny chest. Rolind, as the oldest, handed her a thin stick, still smoking from the fire. Celine first touched it to her own arm, then to the child's chest. She began to chant. "Little one, you are Amara—immortal. You are now and forever known, the outworking of what has been from the beginning. This seal on my arm and on your heart binds us in love."

She bent and kissed the baby, then covered her carefully and placed her in Charri's arms.

No one moved. Charri rocked back and forth, her face glowing. "Oh, my baby, my Amara—conceived in wickedness, brought forth in want. Now you are loved, you are named. Sleep, my child, my beloved. . . . Such beauty, such wisdom in sleep . . . my little one . . . Amara . . . Amara."

Just minutes later the tiny spark went out, but no one wept—not then. Without a word, Celine took the little bundle and helped Charri to her feet. Slowly, slowly, they walked to the canopy wagon to prepare for burial.

Griselle brought water, Steph and Nessa an arm load of sweet fern, and Jonn a piece of tent cloth. The sewing basket yielded needle and thread.

As Celine finished the last loving stitch, Rolind returned, warm from shoveling, and nodded to Driss. Driss then, with solemn compassion, walked to Charri and stood silent as she held her swaddled child one last time, rocking tenderly.

"May I?" he asked gently, holding out his arms.

Charri nodded dumbly and with supreme effort gave it over.

Rolind went first, ramrod straight with shovel in hand like a weapon, followed by Driss and the body, then Celine and Charri. The others, carrying such flowers and greens as they had located, fell in behind. The distant lament of a woe bird appropriately countered the cheerful chorus overhead as the group processed slowly through the woods to a tiny knoll carpeted with cradle cap.

Rolind called a halt and with cool, military detachment gave orders for the placement of the body and the solemn filing by with flowers.

When all had passed by, Celine broke under the weight of the day's emotion. But it was Charri, not Griselle directly alongside, who reached through her own grief—almost, it seemed, from long practice—to bear her through black fog back to camp.

Rolind stood stiffly at attention until the last mourner had blended into the trees, then he too watered each shovelful that filled the tiny grave.

15

Charri had too much milk, and Amarl knew just what to do about it. "My sister had the same problem," he whispered solemnly, "and she had to find someone to drink just a little every day. There's this rule, y'see: if your own baby can't do it, it's got to be an opposite sex person. That's just the way it is," he finished authoritatively as Charri's eyes widened. "It sort of balances off the counterparts. Now, you and I could go back in the woods a ways while they finish breakfast. Won't take long. I'll have to finish loadin' the mules and help hitch, but I'd be glad to give you a hand while I got a few minutes. If you stay wet like that all day, you'll catch cold."

Charri looked away uncomfortably, weighing his air of earnest solicitude against seeming nonsense. Above all, she did not want to offend her benefactors. "Thank you—Amarl, is it?—but I don't know . . ."

Driss, heading across the meadow to saddle Strada, took note of the tête-à-tête. Always suspicious of Amarl's intentions, he sized up the situation and sent the youth scuttling to his chores.

"Are you all right?" he inquired of Charri, shifting the saddle to his shoulder. "Amarl bothering you?"

Charri blushed, attempting to hide both her face and wet clothing. "No. Not really. He was trying to be helpful . . . I think."

Driss raised his eyebrows. "Hmph! I bet. Why don't you talk to Celine. She, at least, won't give you flim-flam."

They got under way in less than an hour after the sun came up, Jonn leading the procession on his bay mare Lina, his most valuable possession. He and Driss had grown up together in Swendia. Though smaller than Driss in more than just size, his good sense made him an excellent choice as Driss's chief advisor. His rough-hewn face would never be called handsome, but a straightforward, look-you-in-the-eye virility drew attention and respect, if not the awe Treese inspired. And whereas Treese announced himself with geometric designs and banded sleeves, Jonn blended with the landscape in his brown cowl shirt over a tight undergarment. Griselle's description of him as *invisible* was kinder than her *shabby* or *brown-cheap* designations, but he did in fact dress according to his means. No one ever remarked about his appearance, but everyone valued his presence.

As they valued Celine. She dressed "brown-cheap," as well, but embellished her family's clothing with love and cheer and imagination.

Today, Driss positioned Strada behind Jonn, but he seldom stayed in line, preferring to range up and down, overseeing the entire entourage. Keltie followed on Jangles, and the heavy equipment came next: Thilrec driving the cook wagon with its matched blacks, Beck and Bock; the three pack mules on a rope attached to the wagon; Bren on the canopy wagon behind the mules; Garrick's Dunkir and white-footed bays. Treese rode rear guard on Floxie, a portly, intelligent sorrel.

Of all the horses, Driss's Strada was most striking. A deep liver chestnut with luxuriant mane and tail, she pranced coquettishly, nostrils flaring and tail arched, the early sun glinting off her burnished coat. After the long holiday, she snorted against restraint in a graceful, in-place canter.

Driss felt completed on his splendid mare. She symbolized everything he believed in and bore in her rippling muscles the sufficient means of carrying him, body and soul, through to his goal. She was his glory—despite performance flaws. Unpredictable, flighty, prone to stumble, Driss could never fully relax on her. But then, he seldom wanted to. Beauty—in both horses and women—had its price; Driss was willing to pay.

Jangles, Keltie's brown-and-white gelding, plodded along at the other end of equine elegance. An old, wise horse, he had little to recommend him in the way of looks, but spirit and steadiness made him one of the more valuable of the saddle horses. The children especially loved Jangles, and Keltie often had one or another on the saddle in front of him.

Griselle and Celine rode the canopy wagon, using travel time to sew and repair equipment. The addition of Charri and Roanna squeezed them a bit, but Charri's skill with a needle made her welcome, even if Roanna was a "yip-yappin' nuisance," according to Griselle.

Rona was the exception among the women. Early in the trip—at night and in bed—she had requisitioned special accommodations. "Oh, Driss," she moaned as he explored her forehead, her chin, her neck, "Such a headache tonight from that awful wagon. It jounces horribly. And Vilda crabbed all day. I felt like a broom packed in with bins and baskets—a charwoman. And sewing—can you imagine a needle in my fingers?"

Driss halted his exploratory kissing only momentarily. "What's the alternative? The cook wagon's no better, and you can't stand Garrick. Want to ride Strada, and I'll put up with Garrick?"

"Driss, you're silly!" she said, cheek dimpling. "Garrick *might* be tolerated—" Her finger played across his lips.

"Packaged in a Dunkir. Is that it? There are the kids, too; they take turns with Garrick." He kissed her nose.

"Well, at least they'd insulate me from Garrick. I wouldn't have to talk to him as much. Please, Driss, could we try it?" She captured his head before it disappeared beneath the blanket and drew his mouth to hers, at the same time stuffing the well-worn headache under her pillow for future use.

Charri had profited from a good night's sleep. The baby had been named and buried in far grander company than she could have dreamed. Relief energized her, making her talkative and less self-conscious.

She was curious about Glinneth, having heard the men discuss him while breaking camp. She asked questions as they traveled, but the women had only hearsay to pass along.

"Ask Driss," Celine suggested. "He seems to know the most about him."

Charri dropped her head. *I'd sooner face a wolfcat than ask anything of Driss,* she thought. *Are there wolfcats in Arlony? So different here ... Driss ... Driss. Even his name. It sounds kind. He's been kind—very kind. Not like ... But no—we'll ask no questions. We came at an awkward time, and we're a bother.*

The head of the caravan shouldn't be bothered with silly questions.

Over the rattle of the wagon and clatter of horses, she told the others of her past, of her longing for information about her parents. She had been brought up by a wretched series of surrogates, the first of which was responsible for her scar.

"Old Father came home drunk one night," she said, trying to keep her voice even. "I began crying. He pulled a stick from the fire and hit me so I'd stop. It wasn't so terrible a burn, but Old Mother—she fancied herself a healer—swore by fox manure for burns . . . and this is what came of it."

She looked down with sudden concentration on the shirt in her lap.

"How awful!" clucked Griselle. "How old were you? Do you remember it?"

"Oh, yes! The stick burned my mind as well as my face. I was just under three and right then became old. I also became *Charri* because I'd been charred. I don't remember what they called me before that—*goose-girl* or maybe *girl.*

"I didn't stay there. They gave me away to another couple in the same town, but that home wasn't much better. They put me on the streets as a vendor—'women's trade,' they called it. I sold everything from flowers and seedcakes to . . . to—well, other things. At the time I didn't know . . . People felt sorry for me; I was good for business."

Celine shook her head sympathetically. "Wasn't anyone kind to you? You wouldn't be so sweet if somebody hadn't helped you now and again."

"There were some, yes," she responded quickly, a small smile nibbling at the hurt in her eyes. "In every place, an aunt or neighbor, a dear friend . . ." She paused in sweet-sad reflection. "As though they'd been put there just for me. They gave comfort and strength, taught me to read and write. My one great happiness." This awareness of good fortune softened her face. "They helped me see that I didn't have to become like the people around me, that I could walk above the bad." She sewed rapidly for a moment.

"In the next move I got away from the street, but they kept me in the kitchen so I wouldn't be seen. They were cruel, too, but in different ways."

"So you ran away and had a baby," suggested Griselle, spinning the story in her mind.

Charri shook her head grimly. "No. Men . . . look away, at least most of them . . ." Again she dropped her eyes. "An uncle—what else can I call him?—well . . . I guess you . . . can guess . . ."

"He got you pregnant?" Celine prompted.

She nodded. "I didn't know . . . I thought he was just being kind. Men didn't usually—"

"Well," Celine said tartly, "I hope you marked him—with a good one!"

"Marked him?" Charri's voice wavered uncertainly. "I don't know what you mean."

Celine looked up sharply, incredulous. "You don't know . . . ? Child, child, how can you be such an innocent after all you've been through? I'm sorry," she added quickly, reaching for Charri's arm. "I don't mean to scold. I'm just surprised, that's all."

For a moment Celine watched the bobbing heads of Garrick's bays directly behind them, then removed the shirt from Charri's hands. "This isn't pleasant conversation, Charri, but you need to know some things. And it won't hurt Roanna to listen, either."

Roanna wriggled forward. "Oh, I know about markin', I do! My ma says when a man comes on and you don't want him to, and his pizzle's big and—"

"Roanna! Charri shook the child. "You must not talk so!"

"But Aunt—"

Griselle tittered, and Celine tried not to laugh. "Roanna's right, Charri," she said. "Her mother did well by her. A woman has the right to mark a raping man anywhere she can, with her fingernails or whatever, deep enough to make a scar. That way she has a claim over him if she can say where and with what she marked him. It's a dangerous game; you can get killed. And it doesn't always work, especially if the scar disappears. But at least you have a chance if there's a baby. If you'd known, maybe you could have made him take care of you and Amara."

Charri bent her head. "Would I have wanted someone like that?"

"Well, that's the question." Celine paused.

"Of course," she added, "any woman who'd mark a man after they agreed to get together—well, she'd be pretty low. That man could never trust her out of his sight."

"Humph!" Griselle muttered into her lap. "Sex is nothin' but a bag of bubble seeds, anyway!"

A hint of mockery played across Celine's face. "Since when? You were leading Treese a merry chase the other night. He get away from you?"

Griselle pressed her lips tight and sewed rapidly.

Driss moved behind the wagon, Strada tossing her head impatiently. "How's everything? You all okay? Charri? Roanna?"

Roanna simpered and fluttered her eyelids, but Charri looked up gratefully. "Thank you, yes."

"Not working you too hard, are they?"

"No, I like to sew. Thank you."

Satisfied, he swung back to talk with Rona for a while.

Driss remained detached at first, acknowledging the newcomers' presence but taking only paternalistic interest in them. This changed, though, the day he hurt his arm.

They had decided to camp by a river. Thilrec gave the children fishing poles and a quota, and Driss helped Jonn unload the wagon. Jonn slid the heavy food box down the tailgate just as Driss saw Rona casting her own lures in Treese's direction. The box plowed an angry furrow the length of his arm. The abrasion was more painful than serious, but he ate little supper, pacing in misery and muttering about the forgotten kung balm. "Who was in charge of curatives, anyway? You'd think that'd be first to go in the box."

Charri watched from a distance, then spoke to Celine. "You can make kung balm, you know, or something like it. Not like what you buy, but it works. It's a job, though."

Celine's mouth tightened. "If he'd been paying attention, he wouldn't have gotten hurt. 'It's Jonn's fault. It's Treese's fault. It's Rona's fault.' He argued for twenty minutes about whose fault it was!" She shook her head. "He'll never admit anything's his fault. Oh, well, if he can stick it out till tomorrow, one of the fellows can pop into a town. Driss'll be all right; he just wants attention. I'll talk to him."

Driss sat hunched against a tree. Celine knelt to inspect the bandage and said, "Tomorrow we'll send Keltie or Treese for some balm. Can you hang on till then? Charri says she knows how to make it, but it's pretty late for that sort of project."

"So what's time?" he snapped. "It's not your arm that's screaming."

"Come on, Driss. Be a *little* stoical." But he waved her off.

When Celine returned to the wagon, Charri had already gone.

"She borrowed a knife," Thilrec reported, "and took her travel basket. Wanted me to leave a pot out and some fire."

Celine tightened the line of her mouth and shot a baleful glance at Driss. "Men are such babies!"

Charri walked briskly through the damp woods bordering the river. The day had been long and trying, even apart from Driss's accident. A rainy chill had gnawed their tempers, making Vilda and Benzel so obnoxious that Driss decreed they walk until the caravan stopped for lunch. Charri had taken it on herself to chaperone the forced march, as no one else relished slopping through mud. The two slept well after that, but Nessa and Steph—too old for naps—had kept her busy thinking up games and songs. She would dream little this night—if the night lasted long enough to sleep at all.

Kung trees were relatively common, especially near water, and yielded more than just balm. Bark from the roots, dried and ground, became part of the special coffee blend that brewed over each morning's campfire. And in small, watered doses, kung balm served as a calming agent for convulsions.

Charri's task was to find a kung tree with the right sort of bark. Without an axe she could not cut into a large one, and soft, young bark would not do. Finally, she found a furrowed tree with bark sufficiently loose.

Rather than haul the entire load to camp, she decided to scrape the inner bark there in the woods, even though it meant an extra hour of sitting on wet ground. Her fingers ached and bled when she finished, but she had enough of the creamy pulp to make a small batch of salve.

She needed a further ingredient: one good-sized collar root or two smaller ones. She'd seen a plant on the way in but couldn't locate it again in the failing light. As she crawled wearily on hands and knees, her hand fell on the prize. She dug carefully with her knife, hoping Thilrec would forgive a little dullness. With glad heart she pulled out the large, curled root.

When she returned, only Celine, Rolind, Keltie, and of course Driss, were still up. Rolind and Keltie showed initial interest in Charri's brew, but they soon turned yawning away to drape tent cloth over a wagon tongue, not trusting the weather enough to sleep in the open.

"Don't wait up, Celine. It's just a matter of stirring and testing. Please go on to bed."

With only half-hearted objections, the older woman gave Charri an encouraging pat and crawled between Jonn and Benzel in the sleep wagon.

Driss wandered aimlessly, coming by the fire occasionally but saying nothing. Charri continued stirring and fighting sleep as the mixture concentrated. When it reached a certain thickness, she pounded herself into alertness. The entire night's work could be lost by a moment's inattention. Every few minutes she swirled a driblet in a bowl of water, watching in the dim light for the bits to thread together. When at last they did, she pulled the pot from the fire and began beating the contents with a spoon. When the mix was smooth enough, she leaned back, rubbing her face.

Now she wished Celine were still up. Should she waken her? Perhaps she should just hand it to Driss. He wasn't helpless.

But he was. First she would have to undo the bandage. Did it look all right? It certainly felt terrible. He was no good with his left hand, so would she please . . . ?

Charri, her face throbbing under cover of dark, smoothed the cream down the abrasion, trying to avoid touching his arm any more than necessary. Driss grimaced throughout the operation but began to relax as the ointment took effect.

Charri watched with satisfaction, then bent to rewind the bandage, replacing the bloodied inner part with a clean piece of cloth.

Driss lay with eyes closed, body and arm limp in relief. Charri again faced the perplexity of touching him.

"Please—can you hold your arm up?"

He rolled his head negatively.

She waited, face thumping again, but he lay still.

"Sir, if you will just—"

"I'm not 'sir,' " he murmured. "Driss. We don't need another Rolind, thank you."

"Please—I just want to finish bandaging your arm—"

"Then do it. Just don't expect help."

Charri chewed her lip, all too conscious of his body—the splatters of mud on his legs and guida boots, the size of his arms, the man smell. She sighed uncomfortably, then gingerly raised his arm and juggled it through to completion.

He continued unmoving. Charri sat back, uncertain over the next proprieties.

"Perhaps if you went to bed now, you'd be able to sleep," she offered.

"I'll sleep here. Just put another stick on the fire."

"You'll be cold; the fire'll go out."

He opened his eyes at the possibilities in that statement.

Charri went into a panic. She rose quickly, pulled a blanket from the canopy wagon and held it out. "This isn't yours, but it'll do for now."

His eyelids only flickered this time, and he made no response.

Annoyance edged Charri's voice. "I'll lay it over, but you should have part of it under you, too." She turned with a brisk good night, not even bothering to replenish the fire.

"Charri."

His voice stopped her, and she looked back reluctantly.

"Thank you."

The blanket she had given him was her own, and she huddled under her cloak between the children, shivering out the remainder of the night.

16

An idea came to Driss that night that took care of his pain more effectively than kung balm. *Look for an ugly woman,* the T'ribboner had said; *she'll be lonely, ripe, waiting to be plucked. A little kindness, and the night is yours—whatever your heart desires!*

The fruit had fallen into his lap.

The plan took shape overnight, and action came with the dawn. Charri must tend his arm; she must feed him breakfast, he all the while feigning weakness and distress. The plan was thwarted temporarily when the prospect of a whole day among a wagonload of women justified his rising from the dead to mount Strada.

That opened Charri's eyes and made her back off as his personal nursemaid.

This unexpected resistance made him rethink the plan and take Rona into consideration, as well. She'd been intoxicating of late, but still, he must tread carefully. He began to watch for opportunities.

The first came early one morning, just as light began separating shape from shadow. Driss crawled from his blanket, thinking himself the first one up. But on his return from the men's "watering place," he saw Charri on a little knoll, gazing over the misty meadow with its grazing animals. She didn't hear his approach, and he stopped to study her. Her left side was toward him, effectively hiding her scar. She had only hand-smoothed her cinnamon hair, and the soft morning breeze gathered stray strands, experimenting with different arrangements around her face. Driss approved them all. Hers was a soft, rounded beauty. Not like Rona. Not an explosion of color and motion, a bracing sharpness that took your breath away, a leaping, whirling kitten with claws. That was Rona, but not Charri. Charri had more the qualities of an excellent horse, like Keltie's Jangles. Sound. Gentle. Patient. Willing to work. That was Charri. Like Jangles, she wasn't much to look at . . . or was she?

In that instant he apprehended a fatal flaw in the plan. She was not ugly: she only thought herself so. Her scar tarnished her beauty, but it was there. Nevertheless, as a person thinks, so she is; it still might work.

He cleared his throat.

"Oh!" She jumped even so. "I didn't think anyone was up." Her hand automatically went to her face.

Driss drew in great drafts of morning dampness. "Beautiful, isn't it?" he murmured, laying a safe, comfortable track for her to talk on.

"Oh, yes!" Her eyes sparkled, and her hand fell away. "My favorite time of year. Everything comes alive: birds and flowers, plants pushing out of death, great leaves from tiny buds. Smell the breeze!" She took a big breath, and Driss was not unaware of the rise and fall of her chest. "New leaves . . . fair green! I would like a dress that color someday. Thin as mist, layer upon layer of filmy, fair green . . ."

She stopped, suddenly aware of the company her thoughts were keeping.

Driss eased her along skillfully. "See how trees slice the mist where the sun shines through them?" He pointed. "Dark and light streaks—one sets off the other."

"Yes . . . yes." Her voice again became dreamy. "Spring . . . so beautiful, so fair. Yet . . . darkness, too. Mosquitoes and scorpion flies—the dark side of the season."

Driss chuckled agreeably. "Beauty has its price, its flaw." He looked directly at her. "But maybe the flaw sets it off and shows it for what it is."

He moved quickly to safer ground before she had a chance to react, and as they strolled back to the wakening camp, Driss felt he had made a good beginning.

That same day, in the evening, several of the group sat late around the campfire, deep in a discussion of names and what they meant. Some argued that the meaning given at Naming shapes the person's life and outlook. Others said the person makes the name.

"Look at my name," said Driss. "It's got two meanings: *zest* and *known.* Now, which is me? Rather obvious, isn't it? What's *known* mean?"

"Yes," Keltie shot back, "but the ones who named you—parents or whoever—maybe they was zesty and figured you'd be, too. Anybody with half a brain could come up with a name that'd fit in the long run."

"My name means *gray-eyed one,*" Griselle put in. "If babies are born with blue eyes, how'd they know mine were gonna be gray?"

"Maybe you were a wondrous anomaly, the exception that proves the rule," said Treese. He put his arm around her slender shoulders with a teasing glance at Bren, who eyed them suspiciously. "Or else," he added, going nose to nose with her, "they peeled back the blue and saw nothing underneath but dull, empty gray!"

Treese's thinly veiled contempt was plain to all but Griselle.

The discussion fell apart when Garrick took the floor and held forth on his potential as *fighter king.* Keltie drifted away and pulled out his toule flute, and beyond the rim of firelight, his tune enticed others to a circle of song.

Charri had remained silent through this discussion, but two days later she pursued it with Driss. The conversation came after Thilrec recruited a number of hands—mostly women and children—to forage for fresh greens and edible roots. As they set out with gathering sacks, Driss felt a sudden compulsion to lend moral support to his flock. Within five minutes he had effectively herded one ewe away from the rest and had Charri all to himself.

After a few desultory exchanges over the lively bird chorus overhead, Charri fell silent. Driss watched carefully out of the corner of his eye, giving plenty of room.

"May I ask a question?" she finally ventured.

"Of course."

"The other night, when you were speaking of Name—" She hesitated.

"Yes?"

"Well, I've often thought . . . I think on it a lot because I don't have one, and I don't believe I ever heard anyone talk about it like that." Words were coming in a rush now. "It's been on my mind ever since, and I wondered if sometime we could..."

"Let's talk now. You should've jumped in. Here's someone whose peace of mind hangs on naming, and we didn't ask your opinion. I'm sorry."

She bent to examine a plant, cinnamon hair hiding a pleased smile.

"What do you think is tied up in a name?" he asked.

She drew a big breath. "Well, Name to me is the—the rock base of a person, almost the seat of power. Without a name—or I should say, without Name, you don't—"

"Why do you say *Name* and *a* name? I never heard anyone do that."

"Really? Most people I know—well . . . at least close friends—have always said that. I thought everyone did."

"Then you have talked about it with others."

"Well—yes and no. It's just sort of background, if you know what I mean. Babies being named. Parents handing down Name to their children, or a claimer does if something happens to the parents. *Name* is what gives you . . . well, it tells who you are, identifies you. *A* name simply sets you apart from other people."

Driss looked at her with new interest. Clearly, this woman had something other than sex and shopping in her head. "But you're looking for something to set you apart. Doesn't *Charri* do that? If I didn't know what it meant to you, it'd be pretty."

She shook her head. "That's not it. *Charri* is just a label. Name goes deeper. Like your name. You seemed to say the other night that *zest* describes you better than *known*. Certainly you're *zest;* anyone can see that. You're like that wonderful, mysterious spice Thilrec puts in stew." She lifted a root from the dank soil, shaking leaf mold over an embarrassed smile. "But maybe *known* will come out later, a . . . a fuller picture of who you are." She trembled so from nervous excitement that her hands could scarcely hold the knife.

Driss looked across the meadow, weighing her words, then turned suddenly. "Do you see yourself as a person or not a person? Now, I don't—"

She laughed. "I know what you mean, and I don't even have to think before answering. No, until I can find Name, I'm not a person. That much I'm sure of." Her chin lifted slightly.

"How can that be? You're intelligent, you're pretty, and you have all the people-things everyone else does. Why do you think you're not a person?"

Charri shook her head and stooped to another plant. When she straightened, hurt had pooled in her eyes.

"After the death of my parents—whoever they were—I had no claimer and therefore no name. Each year when Middle Night came, I felt left out: the only unnamed child and no one who cared." She paused.

"Once . . . an orphan girl came, three years old, much prettier than I. On Middle Night, they had a big fight over who would claim her and give her a name. I tried to pretend it didn't matter, but inside . . . I was screaming and beating on everyone in the circle. But even if I'd done it out loud, it wouldn't have made any difference; they hardly knew I existed, for all the work I did for them."

She took a big breath and, pulling herself tall, went on briskly. "Yes . . . without a name—without Name—I have no power, no roots, no . . . no source. In the old days they gave names to wells and springs, even to pillars that held up great buildings. *Established* or *Strength*—names like that. They understood how important such things were—symbols, like life itself. Name interprets who a person is, what's really inside."

Driss watched her with growing admiration. This woman—packaged in "brown-cheap," as Griselle would call it, stamped as cheap goods by an act of cruelty, worked by greedy guardians as cheap labor, effaced to near-invisibility by cheap self-esteem; yet in her Driss saw more substance, more reality than in any other woman he had known. Her face flickered habitually through a standard sequence of fear, worry, grit, tenacity, and sensitivity. The wrench and wring of her life had dulled whatever might attract a man like himself, accustomed as he was to beauty brought into focus by soaps and oils and colors and perfumes. Yet as he watched her now, he could see beneath her latent good looks a different category of beauty, one made visible only under the black light of adversity.

He made a quiet, almost imperceptible shift.

"Even without a name—or Name, if you will—you still have plenty inside. You're still you; lack of Name can't change that. You put yourself down, Charri. Name is important, but just because you happened to be born in rotten circumstances doesn't mean you aren't worth anything. You're a remarkable woman, you know. Heading out with a sick baby, set on somehow getting her named."

Again she busied herself with a root she might otherwise have rejected.

"Charri." He pulled her up after making sure they were alone. "Whoever your mother was, she was beautiful." He spoke gently. "I know you don't believe it, but a scar is only part of who and what you are."

He was no longer feigning interest. In this brief half-hour, Charri had become desirable in her own right. The plan's fatal flaw had expanded from veiled beauty to a kind of nobility, and Driss had never before considered such an alternative to the Ronas of his life. The challenge now was to figure a way to keep both of them compliant and happy. This one, at least—unlike Rona—would be grateful for small things.

Melting music overhead; the smell of cool, damp earth . . . newly dug roots . . . sun on exposed flesh—a woman's flesh. Redolence rose over Driss in a tidal wave of desire. He slid the gathering sack from her shoulder and set it on the ground, aware of the tremor of her body, the inclination in her face. Her eyes, wide and frightened, reached desperately toward him. He put his hands around her head and watched, fascinated, as the blood drained from her face. The T'ribboner captain was absolutely right. Not only was it easy, it aroused his own emotions along a whole new track.

As he drew her face to his, however, she stiffened and twisted away, chest heaving and body trembling.

He moved quickly to her side, surprised at his own voice grown unsteady. "Charri—"

"No!" She ran a few more feet. "Please don't come near me!"

"Charri—please . . . I'm sorry. I didn't mean to upset you. I'm not playing with you, you know. Everything I said is true, and I love and want you. I—"

"Stop!" She whirled around to face him, fiercely stiff. "You belong to Rona. I won't—I will not become a thorn between you. I've had sorrow enough for a lifetime. Please, *please* do not heap more on me!"

Driss backed away, shaken by a double jolt. This rare, different order of beauty he'd happened on had an equally rare but exasperating ability to surrender her own obvious passion to some perceived higher good. He hadn't the least idea how to get around her. "All right," he said finally. "Again, I'm sorry. I promise I won't do or say anything to make you uncomfortable. Please, though—say you forgive me?"

They walked back in a silence that was heavy with regret on both sides. Even the birds, their attention turned to eating, had little to say.

17

Although Amarl never passed up a chance for diversion, he lacked Keltie's breadth of imagination. A thing that Amarl might note with only tepid interest, Keltie would snatch at, possibilities rising fully dressed to his mind.

The mouse was a case in point.

Mice were common intruders. Whenever the band set up camp, these small rodents took advantage of new foraging opportunities, generating spasms in the women, delight in the children, wrath in Thilrec the cook, and annoyance in everyone else.

Although the rodents normally waited till the group had bedded down, at dusk on this particular evening, ten days beyond Lorenth, a sturdy, gray-backed, white-bellied fellow practiced mounting the cook wagon. It may have been young—an adolescent like Amarl—or genetically harebrained. There, plain to see in the glow of the campfire, it worked its way up an outside corner, a perfect target for Amarl, who saw it only as an object lower than himself and batted it to the ground.

A few minutes later: same persevering mouse, different audience. Keltie's eyes widened, his brain churned. With a sly grin, he plucked the furry animal from its runway, and after examining it with keen interest, keeping fingers clear of sharp incisors, he tucked it carefully in his pocket.

The following morning a problem arose.

"Okay," asked Jonn, "do we stay here at Camberill and get still further behind, or do we risk being conspicuous by traveling on a national holiday?"

"What holiday?" Keltie demanded.

"Roister Day. A day we'd as soon forget."

"Oh, yeah," Keltie said, "the day Swendians got whupped in the Green Wars. Who cares? Let's just go."

Rolind straightened. The old soldier was clearly set to launch a protest. "A day of armistice, even for the vanquished, is to be revered; no ordinary day at all. The Green Wars gave both sides many heroes, many stirring battles to remember. I, sir, recommend we devote this day to solemn reflection."

Bren was anxious to move. "What difference will it make? Families will be on outings all over the place. Why would we stand out?"

Treese snorted. "Family outings don't usually require this many wagons and pack mules. You seem to forget we're not registered to travel in Arlony. Plus, there's always Mr. Citizen, the glowing carbuncle in our midst."

Amarl, sensing the sudden shift of attention to his direction, grabbed the last of his breakfast and wandered over. Under pressure of six stares with no explanation, he jammed hands into pockets and hunched his shoulders. "Whud I do now?" he asked sullenly.

In answer, Driss put an affectionate arm lock around Amarl's neck and knuckled his head. "Well, now," he said to the group, releasing the boy, "we could probably use the day to good advantage—along with solemn reflection, of course," he added in Rolind's direction. "Thilrec has been wanting to rearrange the cook wagon, Bren has harness repair, and the kids could use a good romp. So," he finished with a jab to Amarl's shoulder, "we'll lay by today and head out at daybreak while Camberill and the rest of the country sleep off the holiday."

Amarl was Keltie's first victim, a deliberate choice, not so much for his predictable reaction, but for practice and to enlist him in the cause. After feeding and watering his furry catch, Keltie dropped it into a cloth lunch bag. Then, after engaging Amarl in a spurious ground-dog hunt to draw him away from other potential victims, he slipped his active bundle into the pocket of Amarl's cloak and stood back to watch.

At first, nothing happened. Amarl went on jabbering, happy for this sort of attention from an adult and for a break from chores. Then, although words continued to flow, his facial expression began to change. The result was all Keltie could have hoped for.

"What the—?" Amarl looked at his pocket, patted it inquiringly, then thrust his hand in. At which point he ripped off the cloak and threw it several yards away.

Keltie pretended alarm. "What's the matter?"

"There's somethin' in my pocket!"

Keltie frowned. "What d'you mean?" He peered into his own. "I got stuff in my pocket, too."

"Somethin' alive?"

"Alive! What are you talkin' about?"

"It moves. Feels like cloth, but it moves!"

"Let's have a look. Cloth don't move."

They knelt beside the cloak pocket, which pulsated oddly. Keltie pretended helpfulness. "Here. I'll hold it while you pull out whatever or whoever's in there."

"Nuthin' doin'!" Amarl grabbed the cloak and shook it till the cloth packet bounced out and bobbled on the ground.

"A lunch bag!" Keltie crowed. "Thilrec packed you a fresh lunch—*real* fresh! The guy's a genius. Whoever'd think of—"

"That's no lunch, and you know it!"

"Well, if it's not lunch, what is it?"

At this point Keltie became somewhat proprietary for fear that Amarl would inadvertently injure or allow his entertainment to escape. He hovered anxiously, making sure the bag remained upright as Amarl worked it open.

"A mouse! A little ol' mouse!" Amarl whooped.

"Well, lookee there! Who'd believe it? Thilrec serves up weird stuff sometimes, but this tops 'em all! Any bread to go with it?" He peered hopefully into the bag. "Well, that's an oversight. You'd think he'd at least throw in a piece of fruit or some leftover fool beans. Hm. I see fool beans, all right, but they're tiny. And black."

Amarl sat back on his heels, silent, suspicious. "Keltie, you did this, didn't you?"

"Me? Would I give you mouse for lunch?" But laughter got the best of him, and Amarl launched himself in revenge.

They rolled only a few seconds before Keltie leaped to secure the mouse. It had exited its cloth prison and sat transfixed in the sudden glare of freedom.

"Get on the other side so he can't get away!" Keltie yelped.

The creature twisted and squirmed valiantly, but the schemers won in the end and popped it back into the bag.

After a lengthy discussion, Keltie left Amarl and the mouse and approached Celine. "Do you have some thread I could borrow?"

"Thread? Need something sewed? Give it to me. Or to Charri. She was looking for something—"

"No, this isn't for sewing. It's for—well, you see, I'd like to make a kind of harness. Tiny, you know; somethin' for the kids." He winked roguishly.

Obligingly, Celine swung up into the sleep wagon and rummaged through the sewing basket. "How's this?" She held up a stick of brown thread. "Do you care about the color?"

"Gray'd be good if you got it, but that'll do."

"I think there's—yes." She emerged with gray in hand. "How much? You wouldn't need the whole thing . . . or do you?"

Keltie shook his head. "A few yards oughta do. Maybe fifty."

"Fifty! This is going to be some harness!"

"Well, reins and all . . . you just never know." He smiled ingratiatingly. "What's left over I'll give back."

"Oh, so that's the 'borrow' part, hm?" Celine eye's twinkled. "Well, you borrow for a kiss." She leaned impudently out of the wagon, lips puckered.

"Oh, well." Keltie grinned. "You want it, you pay the price." He looked around carefully, then pulled Celine's head down and gave her a loud, playful smack, followed by a soft, more kindly kiss.

With a smile, Celine put the gray stick into his hand.

Keltie sauntered away, mentally exempting Celine from his "experiments."

By mid-morning Keltie and Amarl had contrived a comfortable and secure but nearly invisible thread harness and leash for the mouse.

They sallied forth on practice runs, allowing the animal its own choice of food instead of pilfered fare from the cook wagon.

When they had satisfied themselves on the rig's effectiveness, they began prioritizing victims.

"Rona's first," Amarl declared emphatically. "She's got to be first."

"Yeah, she's a good one, but Garrick'd be almost as good."

"Or ol' Shin-cracker. Might crack his face, for once."

"Treese?" Keltie laughed. "He got you *again?* How many times is that?

"Never mind. Forget Treese—unless you like your nose flat. Garrick, now. He'd sing and dance just fine!"

Keltie studied the matter. "Griselle's a screecher, but she wouldn't do near as good as Rona. How about the kids? Steph'd love it, and maybe Benzel. But if we scare the girls, Driss'll have our necks!"

They "did" Garrick first, simply because he had removed himself from the throng and made an easy target. They rigged a double container of kava nuts, a small number in the top layer, with the mouse—munching happily—in the bottom.

Garrick had found a patch of sun where he sat blanket-wrapped in his special chair, reading. In careful choreography, Keltie approached, walking and eating all but a few nuts from the top layer. He extended the container to Garrick, casually tucking thread under a fold of Garrick's blanket.

"Thought you might like some kavas, Garrick, old lad. Thilrec broke out a couple a boxes. We had quite a few, so I can leave these with you, if you like." He glanced at Amarl, positioned at the end of the leash in some suitably distant undergrowth.

Garrick lit up pleasurably at sight of the nuts. "Why, yas, I do believe I— My, they look fine! Kavas. Yas. My favorites."

Keltie turned quickly, wanting to be far away when the explosion came.

"Thanks, Kelt, thanks!" Garrick bawled after the broad back. "I'll remember this!"

You will, indeed, Gare; you will, indeed! Keltie replied silently.

Rona was next. She set herself up perfectly by announcing she wanted to bathe in the sleep wagon and needed water. Amarl hastened to her bidding, dawdling just enough for Keltie to arrange her boudoir. When the water arrived, Keltie left and Rona retired.

"Now," he whispered to Amarl, "we could get a show here if the critter holds off till she undresses!"

It did. They got their show. After a minute of shrieking that brought Driss on a dead run, Rona leaped from the wagon and fell quivering in his arms.

"Something's in there!" she sobbed, her white skin now three shades whiter. "It's got clothes on—a hat! I saw the hat, Driss; I'm not making it up. Please! Get me away from here! It moved . . . with clothes—and a hat!"

Driss struggled out of his cloak while trying to hold and comfort Rona, then wrapped and carried her to a patch of grass.

Keltie turned quickly gallant and entered the wagon in one jump to assure himself that Amarl had already reeled in the high-fashion mouse.

It couldn't last, of course. The children proved to be their downfall, Steph divining right off that Keltie was behind the prank. So before the wrath of the entire camp fell on their heads, they decided to become a traveling mouse and pony show. With a quick word to Thilrec, the most disinterested party, that they were going to check out the holiday's progress in Camberill, they threw a bridle on Jangles and beat a hasty, bareback retreat.

"Okay," Amarl said when they reached the outskirts of the small city, "my turn to be front man. You do the leash; I'll set it up this time."

Keltie nodded agreeably, but the "holiday" in town gave them something other than the mouse to ponder. Far from a solemn, commemorative affair, it appeared more a drinking shindy.

"Huh! So much for sentiment over the Green Wars," Keltie observed. "Better not tell Rolind. He'll leave the country on the spot, takin' what's left of his bundle with him. We shoulda brought Griselle along to tell these boozy T'ribboners they wasn't in the wars and have no right to celebrate."

They rode up and down the streets, sometimes behind, sometimes ahead of a dance line led by street musicians. They stopped to watch a cockfight but gave wide berth to a knife-throwing contest. Then as they drew opposite the public latrine, Amarl slid off the horse and nodded toward it.

"Good idea," grunted Keltie. "I'll wait'll you come back; I don't trust the good citizens here with Jangles."

When they had remounted, Amarl said, "Did you notice that guy in there with the V on his back?"

"No. What about him?"

"That marks him as a you-know-what."

"What's a 'you-know-what'?"

"Oh, you know!"

"No, I don't. You think I'm a mind reader? What you talkin' about?"

"A big V, down low on his back. You know."

Keltie shrugged, shaking his head, but their attention was drawn by a sudden deployment of Russetmen around the town.

"There you have it." Keltie grinned. "Just like Garrick says: Claeman don't like anyone havin' fun!"

Suddenly Amarl jabbed Keltie. "Stop and let me off. I got a trillious idea. Take the thread stick and run it behind that shack over there. Keep it low so nobody trips."

Keltie did as instructed, then waited while Amarl made his plant, doubts growing within him about the boy's "idea." He could hear the dance-line, but the only people in sight were three dark-faced soldiers that had dropped off the larger detachment. He began to perspire, though the afternoon was cool.

Finally, Amarl came running and slithered in next to Keltie.

"What are you doing?" rasped Keltie. "Those are Russetmen, dingo!"

"Man! What a boom! Yeah, I know. C'mon, reel 'er in before one of 'em grabs it."

They pulled, this time less concerned over the creature's comfort than for their own safety. As the soldiers' whooping laughter followed hard on the mouse, the two haulers almost abandoned the project to take flight on Jangles. Fortunately, a scream from the direction of the knife throwers drew the soldiers' attention.

As Keltie gathered in the hapless mouse, he turned on Amarl. "You outta your mind with a stunt like that? If they'd caught you, what then?"

Amarl grinned foolishly. "Well, they didn't, did they?"

"Listen to me. The bunch of us are illegal here in Arlony—all but you. You're a citizen with a properly marked foot, but in this case that's not good. Think what it means." Keltie blew himself up in mime of a Russet officer. "'What's a strong lad like you doin', if not in the army? Which side are you on, m' boy—Claeman's or Sigurth's?' Yeah—" Keltie leaned close and glared at Amarl. "Which side *are* you on, anyway? Tell me!"

Amarl shrugged. "How should I know?" he mumbled.

"Well, you better think about it. Say the wrong thing, and you could wind up either in Claeman's army or his dungeon.

"Just because you haven't lived here since you was born," Keltie went on, "don't mean they couldn't find out. 'Take off your shoes, boy.' That's all it would take; get close enough for 'em to check your foot. Now, Driss said if you got yourself in a mess he'd leave you behind, but that don't mean he actually would. You know he's not like that. Didn't he argue with Treese about the group comin' in without a permit? And if he did stick by you, we'd all be in trouble—big trouble!"

Amarl scrutinized every hair on the mouse, but Keltie continued relentlessly.

"Sure, it's fun to trick soldiers, but you gotta use your head, man! What you just did could of lost us the rosillum."

They sat in silence a moment, staring in unison at the dejected little creature. Then Keltie softened and patted Amarl's shoulder. "C'mon, let's go home."

Amarl's head shot up, prepared for this small crack. "No. Just one more, huh? We passed a couple a T'ribboners, guzzlin' in front of a fire. They'd be too drunk to move. Let's do them. Please, huh?"

Keltie shrugged and sighed. "Okay. But one hint of trouble and we're outta here. The mouse can fend for hisself."

They rigged the mouse for its finest hour—hat, cloak, and beribboned legs and tail. Taking no chances, they decided to use two leashes so they wouldn't have to get close to the soldiers for the plant.

"You wait here till I get on the other side," Amarl ordered. "I'll jerk the thread three times; then let 'im go. Okay?"

"Okay, but *be careful!*"

On cue, Keltie released the mouse and fed out the remaining thread, gauging the length that would place the act center stage. After a moment, he heard a satisfying "Whuff! Wha's that?" His view of the two soldiers unobstructed, he settled back to watch, pushing and pulling in rhythm with Amarl.

"Whuff!" he heard again. "A dam' mouse!"

"Naww," drawled the other. "Ain' a mouse. Ain' a mouse. Naww!"

Then, too suddenly to anticipate or do anything about, one of the soldiers lunged full length and grabbed the unfortunate animal. Keltie and Amarl both jerked reflexively, snapping the thread. Holding the limp lines foolishly, they watched in rigid horror.

The T'ribboners held their catch, apparently unimpressed with its trappings. One of them, bony and hook-nosed, pulled out a knife and methodically flicked off the decorations. He held the squirming rodent high before the fire, then with eyes redder than coals, he threaded the point of his blade through layers of loose skin, again holding his victim aloft in a perverted salute.

"To th' Green Warssh!" he bellowed. "To th' Green Warssh!" the other echoed. Without a tremor the knife descended slowly, slowly into the fire, until the quivering animal was still at last.

Keltie and Amarl rode back to camp in silence. Before dismounting in the gathering gloom, Keltie spoke. "Even if Driss isn't mad about Rona, even if he asks about how we did it and all, we won't say much. And we won't say anything about Russetmen.

He didn't have to add, "—or T'ribboners."

18

Garrick's bed fell from a pack mule and no one noticed until mid-morning. Under protest, Keltie rode back to search for it, knowing full well that such a fine item would have been scooped up on the bounce.

When he returned empty-handed, Garrick stomped and cursed Amarl.

"Not my fault!" Amarl yelped. "I don't have nothin' to do with your dumb ol' bed!"

"You do the pack animals; you should've seen it wasn't on right."

"Looked okay to me. You rolled and tied it on. Why you blamin' me?" The pain of injustice took on dramatic overtones in Amarl's voice.

"Look," Jonn said, "the bed's gone; finding whose fault it is won't bring it back. We have extra blankets—"

"Extra blanket," Celine corrected her husband; "only one."

"Well, one's enough; it's all any of us has. I know, I know," Jonn went on, overriding Garrick's litany of deprivation, "a blanket's not a feather bed, but what can we do? A replacement would cost more than we have to spare."

"We'll get you another, Garrick, old lad," Driss reassured him. "You'll have top priority just as soon as we turn rosillum into goods."

As if losing the bed wasn't enough, the axle of the cook wagon shattered the next day when a dead branch fell across the road and sent Beck and Bock onto a rock outcrop. The wagon did not tip over—by the sheerest margin—but equipment and food tumbled into a disheartening mess.

This time the heat turned on Garrick when Bren exploded. "I wanted to bring extra axles and wheels, but no—Garrick had to have a three-layer bed, a chair to help him relax on off days, special soap, his own—"

"Cut it, Bren," Driss ordered. "Like Jonn said, jawing won't change things. Sure, it's clear now what we should've done, but we figured there'd be towns along the way to get parts if we needed them. So let's quit blaming and decide what to do."

The map gave little encouragement. Greentree, the nearest city, lay four days away. Eight days' extra travel, they decided, was too high a price for the cook wagon. "Each day lost now means hotter temperatures in the desert beyond Chadwich," Jonn said. "The east slope of the mountain will be bad enough, but beyond the range it's a furnace and can only get worse."

"All right, we need to be creative," Driss replied. "Could we make do with only the canopy wagon? We'd have to leave a few things."

"Like?" demanded Garrick.

"Well, I don't know exactly." Driss picked through his thoughts for a tactful way to nominate Garrick's chair as the first item to scrap. "We'd work it out, maybe shift a few things to the carriage, the canopy wagon taking the rest of what we can't do without. I think we could keep most of the bins and pots, though," he added with a weather eye to the cook.

Actually, Thilrec seemed most philosophic of them all. He shrugged and set about salvaging his goods, ready to make do with shared space.

Garrick, though, saw the shape of things and fussed interminably.

Rona had choice words, too. "It's her fault!" she declared vindictively, pointing across the road at Charri kneeling at her basket. "Everything was fine till she came along. She brought bad luck."

Driss ground his teeth at her strident tone and looked nervously toward Charri. After their disastrous talk he had given her space, as well as carefully packaged signals of friendship. He was pleased to see her settle down after a few tense days, but now . . . Had she heard Rona's blast? Her eyes dropped, but that wasn't unusual.

Charri had heard. She didn't make her move, though, until they reached Greentree four days later. She and Roanna had taken to walking with Steph and Nessa much of the time to alleviate crowding. On the last day, after the children had tired and returned to the carriage, she took advantage of diversionary sights on the outskirts of the city to lag behind and ease Roanna down a bypass. When Driss discovered their absence, he headed—just as she hoped—into town, combing the streets until evening forced him back.

Rona felt it prudent to keep her distance that night—from Celine, as well as from Driss.

Although he hadn't found Charri, Driss did locate a horse dealer. The following morning he took Beck and Bock to see what they might fetch. Much to Amarl's disgust. He had had four glorious days to charge up and down the road on one or the other, bareback, with a makeshift rope bridle. Driss had tried to put Charri and Roanna on the horses, but Charri said she preferred walking. In truth, she wouldn't have minded if she were not certain she'd be under Driss and Strada's proprietary care.

Bren went with Driss, riding Floxie and leading Bock. Bren looked awkward on horseback, a clothes peg in the saddle. He knew horses from the ground up, though, and as an expert teamster, he would see to a fair price.

Driss, grasping after every possible advantage, dressed carefully in his high-necked shirt and maroon weskit that still bore scars from his slide into the earthcrack. Although Strada would have set him off well, she would make the two-mile trip more exciting than he cared to face just then. For prudence' sake, he borrowed Keltie's Jangles.

Both he and Bren regretted having to sell the team. The big blacks had served them well for nearly two hundred miles, and now after four days of pulling nothing heavier than Amarl, they pranced along, blowing softly with each step, heads high and alert, white-ankled legs folding smartly.

The men could smell the sales lot before they saw it. Unlike well-kept stables with their pleasant savor of horseflesh, hay, grain, and leather, this place had such a raised band of rancid, urine-soaked dung that the horses there, tied as they were to a rope fence, tilted downhill. An assortment of rack-hipped, limp-necked nags dozed in this unsavory feculence, ignoring a stallion trumpeting hopefully from a distant post.

The sales lot had attracted a number of buyers, but Driss and Bren's hearts sank at the mean-looking lot. "I wouldn't sell my runt pig to that one," Bren whispered, pointing to a whip-wielding T'ribboner.

Driss nodded. "And there isn't a one of 'em that looks to have money in his pocket."

The blacks stood apart from the other horses, head to tail in the warm sunlight, swishing flies, scratching each other's necks. A number of prospective purchasers looked them over but offered ridiculous prices. The two men shook their heads adamantly. "I'd as soon keep them to switch off with the grays as to throw them away on these louts!" Driss said.

Just before noon they leaned in discouragement against the warm fragrance of the torpid horses, snatches of conversation drifting their way. To their left two young dolts hunched lovingly over a jug. Their long, ropy hair and clothing, all of which were seasoned with stable debris, marked them as sales lot menials. They seemed to be talking about the recent Roister Day celebration and its connection with Harloon Paddock, site of the battle that had decided the Green Wars.

"There's a new one!" Driss said to Bren. "Did you know it was really Swendia—not Arlony—that won the battle that day? Swendia won fair and square, so these guys say, but Arlony poisoned wells, and Swendians died by the—"

"Vlian, lad," a new voice boomed from behind the team, "I've a mind to stand those louts on their heads and plant 'em in dung since their brains seem stuck in their feet. We'd be doing 'em a favor, don't y'think?"

Dress and Bren saw the two "historians" freeze at the appearance of somebody they themselves had not yet seen. Something in the voice, though, brought Driss's head up, and he stepped out to have a look.

His heart leaped. "Glinneth!" he cried. "Is that really you?"

"Drissan, lad, *hweo*! And Bren, isn't it? I can hardly believe it!" He clapped the men heartily. Then he turned and strode toward the unwashed pair. Although they tried to scrabble away, he snatched both and dragged them to the team. "Come, louts," he ordered. "Come hear the true tale of Harloon Paddock. Lads," he said to Driss and Bren, "you'll not mind my using your horses for an instruction bench, will you?"

With a hand for each, he perched the ashen scholars on the broad black backs—backwards. "Just so they won't ride away on us, eh?" Glinneth's eyes crinkled.

"Now then," said Glinneth. "Learn of Arlony's finest hour. Harloon Paddock, a tiny patch of ground enclosed by stone and brush, a turnout for two, maybe three horses. It had served its humble purpose for several Harloon generations and was unfortunate enough to fall in the path of two warring armies. Here, though, the sheer will of a single man turned the tide of the entire hundred-year conflict."

Glinneth, hands behind his back, strode up and down. "After a string of defeats, Arlony was again being pushed across the country—for the third time. Even faithful Russet lads were losing heart, sick from watching their fathers and their sons die those many years. The general over that section of the army—Lorin was his name—he was tired, too. He'd had a career full of bad luck, but he made bad judgments, as well. Hadn't distinguished himself. But that day in Harloon Paddock, something snapped in him. He'd had his fill of defeat, and he'd take no more. He drew his line in that horse pen. With flame in his eye and fire in his belly, he turned stone and brush into bedrock and would not be moved. 'Lose Harloon Paddock,' he thundered, 'and Arlony is lost. But *we will not lose Harloon Paddock*. From this day on, *Arlony lives!*' And that was the rallying cry. 'Arlony lives!' Let's hear it, lads, 'Arlony lives!' " Glinneth prodded the two into a weak chorus that had to be pumped to satisfactory volume. Driss, Bren, and Vlian clapped approvingly.

"Six blood-drenched days they fought with swords and hewers. The line of battle moved forward and back several times but never fell behind the paddock. General Lorin was everywhere, carrying coals of valor, stoking fiery passion. Three horses were cut from under him, and he himself lost a fair bit of blood, but he kept at it, and the flames spread, touching off countless acts of courage and heroism. At one point, ranks had thinned to critical point. Reinforcements were on the way, but could the warriors hold till they got there?"

Glinneth shook his head slowly, thinking, perhaps, of times he himself had been in such a situation. He thumped the leg of the near "rider," which made the fellow jerk convulsively. "When y'run out of firewood, lad, sometimes y'have to start burning the house. And that's just what that general did. He ignited the spirit of nine of his best warriors, two swords and a hewer in each of three groups, instructed them to sneak into the middle of three Swendia divisions and start fighting. Somehow they did and fought so wildly the Swendians thought three separate armies had come on 'em, and confusion made the plan all the more effective. Only two of the nine warriors survived, but with incoming troops to bolster the flames, that little paddock blazed in a fury that scorched the entire Swendian force. The cry rang from every hill that day. What did they cry, lads?" Glinneth looked up expectantly and was rewarded with the forced enthusiasm of "Arlony lives!"

Glinneth nodded approvingly, then hauled the two off the horses. "Now then, louts." He looked them over with only pretend sternness, brushing a shirt and dusting hair. "Run along, and let's hear no more tales of Arlony poisoning wells!"

The two turned and bolted, the rope fence seizing their haste and flipping them into the muck.

Driss shook his head. "What a pair! And what a story! I never heard—" He stopped, hauling himself back from a reference to his own Swendian understanding of the battle, and made a rapid adjustment. "I never heard all those details." He glanced nervously at Bren, but the latter prudently kept his mouth shut and nodded enthusiastically.

"Ay, lad, the turning point of a long war."

"Did he die—that general?" asked Vlian.

"Ay, he did. He lived till the end, but once he heard that great victory shout, he lay down at last to sleep and never woke up. He'd finished his job."

Driss shivered. "Gives me skin bumps. I guess he finally distinguished himself!"

"Ay. General Lorin. A name forever branded on the hearts of faithful Arlonians." He gazed across one hundred and seventy-odd years of history. "But you, lads. What brings you to the sale lot? This fine team is yours?"

"Yes. We lost a wagon a few days back. Had no choice but to sell the horses. You looking to buy?"

"Ay, lad—Vlian and I." He put an arm around his companion's shoulder. "We need a couple of sturdy animals and had almost decided to hold funeral over the poor beasts here when we spotted these. What are you asking?"

Driss and Bren looked at each other, the prospect of selling to Glinneth making Driss uncomfortable.

"Come, lads." The big man laughed. "These are valuable animals. You must have a sum in mind. What is it—five hundred, six hundred coin?"

Bren's eyes bulged. They hadn't expected to get half that.

Driss shook his head. "I couldn't take that kind of money from you. I'd gladly skin those ghouls over there," he added sourly, nodding toward the knot around the salemaster, "if I could bring myself to sell to them at all."

"Ay, lad," Glinneth agreed, "they're hard on creatures, to be sure. But all of us use them, and sometimes they suffer even at our hands. This is a fine pair, eh, Vlian?" He ran his hand along the broad back and down a leg to lift a bucket-sized foot. He straightened and thumped the dark rump approvingly and watched as his young friend trotted the horses up and down, their necks arched and nostrils flared.

"What think you, Vlian? Are they worth six hundred coin?"

"Every bit, sir. A bargain, even. They've had good care and are none the worse for the work they've done. Prime condition." He smoothed Beck's neck and patted the broad chest.

"All right, done!" And Glinneth measured out the price into grateful and almost disbelieving hands.

After a brief chat and a solemn farewell to the team, Driss and Bren parted from Glinneth and his friend and headed into town to shop.

Silence hung between them as they packed the saddlebags and remounted. On regaining the highway, they stopped uncertainly over a sudden concentration of Russetmen. They decided to try a back road, hardly more than a trail, that seemed headed in the right direction. About a mile out of town, they pulled up again, their way blocked by a detachment of Russetmen. A column of foot soldiers moved across the road like a passing shadow.

"What's goin' on?" Bren muttered. "They're all over the place!"

"They haven't seen us," Driss said. "Let's duck uphill till they clear out."

They glided through the shielding forest and came on a bluff overlooking a hidden valley with no visible roads. The valley was full of Russetmen, with more entering on every side. They seemed to be gathering, but it became apparent that the entire body was heading north.

"Toward Twin Mountain, looks to me," Bren murmured and pointed. "See the line of dust out on the plain? This is some operation!"

"Ha! Maybe they're headed for Harloon Paddock. That's up north somewhere, near Ramah. They're not marching on Greentree, anyway, and it's safe to say they're not looking for us—not with that size army!" His horse, stretching for stray leaves, jerked Driss forward, but his eyes stayed on the pageant below. "Why are they going that way? That's tough wilderness, Bren. Thorny scrub and bog. I know from the map." He shook his head. "Why would they choose a route like that unless they don't want anyone to know?" He turned with a twisted smile. "Has it occurred to you, Bren, we may be the only ones who know about this? Now, that's irony!" he said, chuckling. "Watch out, Sigurth. It's Harloon Paddock for coffee, Ramah for supper!"

Bren sat silent and small on Floxie's wide back, so different from long-legged Treese. His somber eyes followed the parade of foot soldiers, horsemen, and wagons, an occasional neigh the only sound from below. "That many men and so quiet! Hard to watch, though. Every last team looks like Beck and Bock. See the white-footed blacks in that column over there?"

Driss looked at him. "They're in good hands, Bren; I'm sure of that."

When they finally got back, they found camp in a dither. Garrick had packed up everything belonging to him—including most of the remaining money—and had driven off.

19

As much as Rona despised Garrick, she wished him back. Up till now, the group had drawn on Rolind's money to fund the trip, so even though Garrick had lost a modest fortune on the crico game, he still had enough to keep things comfortable for a woman accustomed to such. Without him the picture looked bleak.

She even agreed to ride with Driss into town—on a horse—hardly her favorite mode of transportation. Strada and Lina were both beyond her capability and Jangles far too plebeian, so he settled her on round, sleek Floxie, with Treese growling in the background.

"I know I can talk him back to us," Rona asserted as they approached town, "if we can find him."

"You didn't have much luck talking him out of leaving."

"I was asleep. Nobody woke me till he actually drove off."

Driss sighed with tired annoyance. The sun was already setting under a yellow dome with its dirty tentacles of circling showers. Night would be on shortly. The prospect of searching the entire city of Greentree at this hour, most likely in rain, made him wish they'd waited till morning. Every passing minute, though, lessened their chance of finding Garrick.

Of course, he hoped to flush two birds at once. Charri was quite likely in town. She'd be harder to find, though—no carriage, no horse, nothing but a maid and a basket.

They checked livery stables first, then hostelries and eating establishments, with no success.

"Okay," Driss pronounced wearily, preparing to remount in the lamp-lit courtyard of the last inn, "that's the easy part. Now the real work begins. Are you still game, or shall we come back in the morning?"

Before Rona could answer, a voice spoke out of the gloom.

"Ah, Drissan. And your lovely lady!"

Driss took his foot from the stirrup and turned to look.

A tall, well-clad T'ribboner moved lazily toward him. "You have eaten and are just leaving?"

Driss's face hardened as he recognized the mesmeric picture-painter of the public latrine in Lorenth. Charri had cut and run, and this man was to blame. Not only had his ugly-woman theory backfired, it had set Driss up for hurt and shame, both foreign to him, at least regarding women.

"You know my name."

"Ah, yes. I know everything that's worth the trouble. Your journey has been watched—attentively—by more than one rabbit hunter, you know."

A tingle went up Driss's neck. *A rabbit hunt. Driss the rabbit.* But what of this hunter? The man's face, his clothing, the way he carried himself, maybe even his smile . . . *Am I jealous of him?* His eyes, though. And voice. In anyone else, you'd think it softly cordial, magnetic. But in him . . . *Maybe it's his eyes. If he kept them shut, you'd see just this attractive, fair-haired guy who makes things happen, somebody you'd take along in a minute, if he'd come.* But his eyes weren't shut, and in the dim light of the courtyard they seemed to Driss like windows on a furnace.

Even his well-ordered teeth glinted in the darkness. "I have your interests at heart, Drissan, and am prepared to help as I can. You have eaten, my lady?" The man held out a hand to Rona.

She shook her head with an ingratiating smile. "No. We're looking for a friend. His name is Garrick, and he drives a Dunkir with a fine team of bays. Have you seen him, by chance?"

The man's eyebrows raised, taking in far more than Driss wanted to give.

"Ah!"

Just that, nothing more, yet Driss felt their whole plan lay suddenly exposed to this man.

"Garrick, yes. An important man. Without him . . ." He shook his head sympathetically.

He turned to Driss, smoothing Strada's chiseled face. "Perhaps, though, you and I could be of mutual assistance. I could use someone like you, traveling cross-country, to report on the movements of, say . . . Russetmen. Neither of us have much love for them, I dare say." He chucked Driss's arm. "And it would be worth a coin or two to have this information coming in. Then you could forget Garrick. Which would break neither of your hearts," he added, flashing his white smile at Rona. "Am I right?"

Driss drew a breath, the silent Russet army parading through his mind. He had information, all right—information that Power and Influence here was willing to pay cash for.

What were the implications of such a deal, though? If this man—could it possibly be Sigurth himself? Again his scalp tingled. If this person of authority had been watching them, would not Claeman be even more attentive? The T'ribboner had hinted as much. A freebooter with a side interest in spying could get himself into a haystack of trouble.

Still, their chances of finding Garrick seemed slim, with the most promising places to look already exhausted.

He shifted uncertainly. "Let me chew on this. Garrick must be somewhere. Not being one to endure hardship," he added wryly, "he wouldn't go far on an empty stomach. We'll look a bit further, then maybe we could talk."

As Driss swung up on Strada, the T'ribboner took Floxie's bridle and stroked the sorrel neck, a hint of mockery in his eyes. "Perhaps your lady would like to dine while you search. That would give you more flexibility and her more comfort. What say you, Rona, my dear?"

Rona slid down at once at the pull of his voice and smile.

Driss ground his teeth and clapped Strada into a surprised canter, leaving the two to dispose of Floxie as they could.

He returned two hours later, anger tempered by sober reflection on their financial picture. Here it was only the end of May and Rolind's money nearly gone. The princely sum Glinneth paid them for Beck and Bock seemed to wither and shrink against their remaining trip needs. They had come halfway already, but desert lay beyond the next range of mountains, and expenses would rise. They'd no longer be able to scavenge greens and roots; forage for the animals would become scarce.

They needed money. This man—whoever he was—had it to give.

But everything within him balked at such a deal. Even leaving eyes, voice, and his misfortune with Charri out of the picture, T'ribboners in general seemed a nasty lot, more abhorrent than Russetmen. And this particular T'ribboner grated on him. A general at least, if not Commander-in-Chief. But unlike Glinneth—or even Rolind—this man had no scars, nothing to tie him to the harsh business of war. Driss had never seen Claeman to test his theory, but it could well be that ultimate power dwelt far from the line of battle and rested safe and comfortable in mansions of ease—at least when not out hunting rabbits for amusement.

Driss had been used once by this man; he didn't want it to happen again. But money was money, and he needed it now. And if his information about the Russet army kept Claeman busy and off his own back for a while, so much the better.

He turned reluctantly, angrily, into the cobbled stable yard. As the first drops of rain spattered the dust, he gave orders for Floxie to be readied while he fetched Rona.

The transaction took only a quarter of an hour. Driss gave as little as would satisfy—the number of men and wagons, what weapons were visible, the direction of travel—hating himself the while. However, the pouch he received would, with a little prudence, carry them to their destination—barring further breakdowns or defections. All the way back to camp, though, he fought an impulse to scatter the contents along the dark, wet roadway.

On their return, he barked Amarl out of a sound sleep to care for the horses and tossed the bag to Jonn without a word of explanation. Not until he had heated water and scrubbed his hands and face did he fall into bed.

Rona slipped into her blanket, treasuring a small, secret smile.

Rolind had listened closely to Driss and Bren's account of the Russet army. His military responsibility weighed heavily, especially against the recent setbacks—loss of money, equipment, and people—that were making everyone short. This peevishness worried him.

"The enemy uses such circumstances," he warned. "They take advantage of any breach in the ranks. We must be watchful; we must prepare. They may post intelligence along our route, perhaps even set an ambush."

The lines on Driss's face deepened. *Intelligence! You don't know the half of it, old man! Sigurth—or whoever that guy is—knows us right down to the color of our nose cloths!* But he forced a smile. "You're right, Rolind. We are vulnerable, and we depend on you to report anything unusual as we go along. By the way, you're doing a fine job with the children. Do you think they could take some extra drill on the road as we travel?" He was thinking of tight accommodations, particularly for Rona's sake.

Rolind snapped at the idea. He lined the youngsters according to age—Steph first, then Nessa, Vilda, and Benzel—and had them marching several times a day. They loved it and paraded proudly under his barked orders.

"Command—attenHUN! Hrope—HARH! Hrope—HRING! Staden—hom—hou—hree; staden—hom—hou—hree . . ." The motley band trooped behind their general, carrying whatever weapons of warfare—assorted sticks or clubs, or in Vilda's case, her tattered rag doll. Rolind fussed at this. Such unmilitary behavior drove him to every disciplinary trick up his well-ordered sleeve, to no avail: strength of will is no proof against a child's tears.

Steph likewise tested the old soldier by breaking loose now and then with a crico move that Glinneth had taught him. Exasperated, Rolind would confiscate the old battered ring and hold it until the children had performed to his satisfaction.

As they traveled, they came across unsettling things. Nothing unusual in itself—a burned-over patch of woods, a peculiar symbol scratched in the dirt—but the repetition and cumulation began to gnaw at them.

"You don't think much about one fire," Celine said darkly as they sat eating lunch at the edge of a charred field, "but *six* in two days?"

"Huh!" replied Griselle. "Maybe they store fire crazies here. One county of the whole nation set aside for fire bugs, where they can set all the fires they want, then sit and watch 'em." An impulsive breeze sent a blackened tumble flower cartwheeling across her lap. Griselle slapped its sooty footprints from her dress as though they were fire ants. "The whole business stinks, if you ask me."

"Yes, Griselle." Celine laughed. "Where's your flood when we need it?" But her smile faded. "It's those piles of ashes in the shape of children I don't like. Why would anyone do that? The farm women at Lorenth talked about them. 'Ash children,' they said." She tipped Benzel's face to wipe away crumbs, then stopped. "Ash children—and zill. Jonn—" She turned toward her husband. "Jonn, what's zill?"

"Zill?" He rubbed his eyes in weary concentration. "Never heard of it. Why do you ask?"

Bren swallowed the last of his kuhnel bun, balding forehead knotted. "Some guy yesterday mentioned zill. Said all this business was Feast of Candles comin' up. But that don't make sense, neither. Everybody I know goes soft on Feast days. Not this kind of stuff."

"Well, zill has something to do with ash children and maybe with Feast of Candles. It's—I don't think I really want to know what it is, but somehow . . . somehow I think we should."

A full stomach did not relieve Jonn's unease. When the cortège started moving again, he pulled even with Strada. "I don't like it, Driss. There's something in the . . . well, I was going to say 'air,' but it's more like the ground. Like riding over it might start another fire, trees flaming up behind us." The angle of his forehead steepened under the press of anxiety.

"Cut it, Jonn," Driss snapped. "That kind of talk just sets the women off. They're touchy enough already."

"Huh!" Jonn flared back. "You sense it, too; don't deny it. Yesterday you said you felt the same as when you looked into that earthcrack. But now you want to close your eyes and hope it goes away. Well, it's not going. I couldn't swear to it, but I think we're being followed."

"Oh, great! We're being followed. Why don't you ride up and down the line and shout the good news? Even if we were—which I doubt—what can we do about it?"

"Come on, Driss! There's plenty we can do. We have guns. But they won't do any good in the bottom of the wagon."

Driss ran a hand over his haggard face. "All right, maybe we should get them out. But as soon as we do, everyone'll tense up even more." He also agreed to a night watch, divided among the six men.

Jonn's presentiment took substance in the form of a small band of horsemen that stayed with them day after day, keeping well behind—a disturbing presence.

Finally they struck, in the middle of the night.

The alertness of Rolind, the only one with conviction enough to keep him awake through an entire shift, saved them from losing all the horses, instead of just one. His warning cry as he fired his weapon brought the rest out of their blankets in time to see shadowy figures gallop away.

A quick check revealed that several of the horses had been cut loose, but Strada was the only one missing. Driss raged and stormed and was all for leaping bareback on Lina to go after them, but Jonn wouldn't give over his mare without others as backup. By the time they had met his provisos and found bridles in the dark, it hardly seemed worth it. They did their best, though, Bren and Amarl pressing even the indignant grays into service.

By daybreak, Driss had decided what to do. The town of Peerce lay just ahead. He dug into the clothing box and pulled out his midnight-blue Wooten cloak, laying it—sadly, reluctantly—in Amarl's hands.

"Take this into town and get me a horse with it. I can't spare anyone else. We need every man for defense."

Amarl's eyes bulged.

"The cloak is worth a hundred coin at least, but you may have to look for someone who'll give you that in trade. Now, remember." He straightened the lad and looked at him squarely. "I don't much care what the horse looks like, but it has to be sound and dependable. You got that? If nothing happens here, we'll move out and meet you along the road to Peerce."

Amarl, solemn with this unexpected trust, did not even object to having to walk the seven miles to town. Despite the promise of a warm day, he settled the thick, luxurious cloak on his shoulders and swaggered cavalierly toward the road, the new-risen sun glinting off the silver plaiting.

"Keep your wits about you," Jonn admonished. "If you spot trouble, get off the road and out of sight. *We need that horse!*"

The others settled down to an uneasy breakfast, weighing their options. They hadn't long to ponder. As Bren harnessed the team, a bullet ricocheted off a tree.

"Get down!" Driss shouted, the bile of fear riding a surge of excitement as he seized the gun propped nearby.

Bren grabbed the grays and pulled them from the line of fire, Treese covering their removal. Keltie sprinted toward the women and children, but Rolind, gun in hand, had preceded him and was herding them with measured calmness to a safer place. "Hrope—HARH! Staden—hom—hou—hree . . ." Vilda's doll, left behind, caused the only hitch. At her outcry, Keltie snatched it from the wagon and tossed it to Rolind.

Camped as they were by a stream, with a wooded hill behind and a rise across the brook from where the shot had come, their situation did not lend itself to good defense. A tangle of brush and fallen trees at the base of the hill provided only flimsy cover for the women and children.

They had just three guns. It had seemed enough at the start, but the men left unarmed felt helpless and vulnerable. Keltie kept the marksmen supplied with ammunition, while Jonn, Bren, and Thilrec pulled the horses downstream to a rocky, protected glen—safer, at least for the moment.

The shooting was sporadic, neither side having a clear view of the other. Suddenly, however, the battle erupted on all sides, a hiss of fire coming from the hill behind, as well as from across the brook.

"Damn!" Driss groaned. "They circled around!"

He glanced toward the brush pile and wagon. "They'll want the horses first," he shouted to Treese, "then the wagon. There's plenty in it, even without Garrick's stuff. Try to cover Jonn and Bren. Rolind's across the brook; I'll cover the front here."

They fired at anything that shivered in the breeze, trying to pinpoint the location of their adversaries, but nothing much happened to show either gain or loss. Sweat poured down Driss's face as the minutes ticked by.

Then, out of the corner of his eye, he saw Treese ambling toward him, hands in his pockets, gun slung on his arm.

"You fool!" he hissed. "Get down! What are you trying to do?"

Treese shrugged with a half grin. "Check it yourself. The bullets are twenty feet over our heads. There hasn't one been aimed at us since that first attack."

Driss drew up cautiously to his knees and looked around. "Huh. You're right! What's going on?"

"I dunno. Somebody's fighting, but no one seems interested in us."

Even as they talked, it became clear the battle had moved upstream, the combatants beyond range of doing damage to Driss.

"I'll be damned. Rolind!" he shouted. "Hold your fire. It's over!"

The old soldier rose cautiously but would not allow the women and children to emerge from the tangle until he had convinced himself that the enemy had indeed retreated.

"Congratulations, sir!" He strode over and saluted warmly. "A superb victory. Not a single casualty, not a horse lost nor any of the dunnage. Splendid job!"

As they got underway, however, Driss felt a bit silly and insignificant. A war had swirled around his head, he had risen to the fight, but his own little popguns had hardly been noticed.

20

June 7

Dear Driss,

By the time you read this, I'll be far away, so don't even try to follow.

Not that you'd want to. I mean about as much to you as a clean shirt. You'll pick up some stray puppy in the next town to keep you warm at night, someone who doesn't mind being stuffed into ONE wagon crammed with people and junk. You may find it harder to attract a companion who'll put up with being shoved in a rabbit warren and shot over. It'll be MONTHS before my nerves heal. I was never so frightened in my life, and that bat-faced moron Griselle kept trying to hide under me. If I'd only known that the attack was part of the PLAN, I wouldn't have minded so much.

I'm not talking about your precious plan, Driss. SOMEONE ELSE'S PLAN was more creative and far reaching. You didn't think your little war meant anything. Well, it might have meant a lot. Things were supposed to turn around for the better. Somebody Special was supposed to step in.

The PLAN would've worked for everybody's good—including yours. Even you, Driss, bent on YOUR way of getting the rosillum, would've seen the benefits of partnership with the highest and best in the land. We'd ride the new wave of progress, not the stifling ways of the old. And if the PLAN had worked, it would've meant only a TINY change in your travel agenda.

But of course it didn't work. Your "guardians"—whoever they were—sneaked up behind us and RUINED the whole thing. Attacked my friends and drove them upstream. I was lucky to find them again.

Someday you may realize how much your pig-headedness cost. For instance, with one stroke, the problem of having to hide from every last soldier along the way would've been cut straight in half. Plus you'd have had money to throw under the horses' hooves, if you wanted. Well, too bad; it's shattered glass now.

Things might've been different, you know, if you'd been the TINIEST bit sympathetic to my needs. I would've skipped my "appointment" and stayed with you. But no—you were too busy counting bullets after the fight. I gave you a chance; when we did talk my tears were real. You didn't care, though. 'It's over now; you're all right,' you said, patting my head. Patting ME—Rona—on the head! Condescending tomcat! I'm well rid of you.

You can blame yourself for the missing gun. Both Rolind and Treese put theirs away carefully, but yours stood right there against the wagon in anybody's reach. The way I look at it, the gun is better off in other, less careless hands (my final contribution to childcare and housekeeping).

Consider my leaving as one more loss, like Strada, the cook wagon, the Dunkir, and the FINAL STRAW—your glorious Wooten, so thick and silken. REALLY, Drissan, you have to admit—there's not much worth staying around for these days.

Maybe we'll meet again, maybe not. If you ever get the rosillum, you might look me up, just for old times' sake.

<u>Formerly</u> yours,
Rona

With a great show of disgust, Driss slapped the team into a lumbering trot, not much caring whether the eyesore tied far behind the pack animals followed along or not.

Earlier, when they met Amarl returning with the fruit of his bartering skill in hand, Driss had delivered his mind.

"You traded my Wooten cloak—worth at *least* a hundred coin—you traded it for that runty, sow-eared, sway-bellied sack of shin splints?"

Amarl grinned foolishly under the sting of Driss's tongue but stoutly defended his purchase. "You said you didn't care what it looked like. The guy admitted straight out it was the ugliest horse you'd ever lay eyes on, but he'd do the most for you, once you got used to him."

"Get *used* to him! We'll be lucky to *live* through him! Just on principle, he eats anyone who happens within five yards of him!"

"Well, the guy said you kinda had to watch out . . ."

Furious, Driss launched himself at Amarl, who yelped in fright and ran behind the wagon. Jonn and Treese, much amused, pulled Driss off and with a prudent eye to their own mounts set about persuading him to accept the fortunes of horse trading.

"Look at it this way," Jonn said, laughing. "He'll be an easy keeper. And if another horse gets stolen, it most likely won't be yours!"

"Yes," put in Treese, "we can use a horse that's handy with his fists. A couple of weeks ago," he said, winking at Thilrec, "we were wishing for some glue to fix the cook wagon. With this critter along, we've got the basic ingredients—self-contained, self-transporting!"

Thus the new horse became known as Glue.

Driss was not amused. He refused to ride this wretched replacement for his beautiful mare. And when threats and bribes failed to gain a swap from Jonn, Treese, or Keltie, he chose to take Bren's place driving the wagon, towing the little gelding on a long rope.

This arrangement chafed on all sides, crowding the wagon passengers and tying Driss to the sedate pace of the team and pack animals. These latter creatures suffered much from the newcomer's ill-disposed mouth, and after two hours of squealing, kicking, and tangling, Driss gave up.

"All right, you randy-camped mongoose!" He pulled up the team and jumped down stiffly. "Where's my saddle? Even a bad horse is better than sitting on a wagon all day."

The decision to ride Glue, however, was not quite the same as actually doing it. First came the matter of untangling him from among the unhappy mules. That left him at the end of a long rope in excellent range for charging all comers. Stiff legged, head snaked down, teeth at the ready, he looked every bit like a stallion herding mares.

Bren laughed. "He may be a gelding, but he don't know it. Looks like they got his number a bit late in life. We'll see who mounts who!"

"Pig-eyed rooster!" Driss fumed. "Keltie, fetch another rope. I'll get on him if I have to nail his mouth shut and tie his hind legs to a tree!"

It didn't come to that, though. Once he was snubbed close, they saddled and bridled him with only token retaliation. With Keltie and Bren at his head, Driss mounted gingerly, half expecting a bucking spree to top off all other vices. But the little horse became all business, ready for action, ears moving alertly. He responded quickly to rein and heel, and with grudging admiration, Driss put him through his paces.

"Watch this!" he crowed, reining the loping horse from side to side. "I hardly touch his neck and he turns on a leaf!"

As they pushed on, each new revelation of the horse's merits helped repair Amarl's spirits.

"A quick walk," Driss purred, "a fast trot. Canters like a rocking chair. But why does he have to look like such a ghoul, with a pitched roof for a rump and the neck of a camel? What would Rona say if she saw me on this?"

Backing away from any discussion of Rona, Amarl turned to Griselle. "I knew it all along!" he confided happily. "I knew he'd be a good horse. The guy who sold it to me—I just knew he'd do right by us. Huge guy, big muscles. And his eyes . . . well, I just knew we couldn't go wrong!"

The terrain altered dramatically. Trees and green fields gave way to near-desert conditions on the lee side of the mountain. Their way became tiresome over the long, parched, uphill climb. Few towns and villages lay beyond Peerce, and the group was forced to rely on their own diminishing food supply. At water holes, they fought to hold the animals back until Thilrec and Amarl had filled the jugs. The late spring sun beat mercilessly, and though they would gladly have traveled at night, the lack of cover gave no place to rest during the heat of day.

The women and children suffered most, stuck under the hot, dusty canopy. Vilda grew flushed and dizzy. Griselle was too taken up with her own complaints to tend her daughter, so Celine kept damp cloths on the child's head. With water scarce, they hoped for relief over the approaching pass.

Near the top, the air became cooler and trees more plentiful, but still they found no water. Glue became restless, tossing his head and prancing sideways. Driss finally shrugged. "I guess we'll ride ahead and reconnoiter."

Bren watched the horse with interest. "Go with it, Driss. He may know more than we do."

The horse pulled hard against the bit, head high, ears forward. When they reached the top, he ducked suddenly to the left, away from the road.

"Hey! What are you doing?"

He fought for control, unnerved at the horse's unexpected fury. Animal instinct proved correct, though, and by a short but precipitous route they entered a lush green valley nestled beneath a shoulder of the mountain. Glue galloped straight for the stream and plunged in, sucking up great drafts and pawing liquid onto his hot belly.

Driss flung himself from the horse into the water, laughing and drinking and splashing, then remounted and set out to find a less alarming entrance for the others.

An hour later, Driss and Jonn leaned against the wagon, sipping coffee and gazing up the sloping valley. The children's happy squeals floated across the idyllic scene. "Good pasture, plenty of water," Driss noted. "And if we're lucky, Thilrec will come up with greens, maybe even tubers or dawnweed buds. It's uncanny how he locates wild food!"

"Um," Jonn grunted, his face softened under the soothing hand of relief. "Sounds good to me, especially if you throw in a few squirrels and maybe some milden mushrooms. What couldn't he do with those!"

"Jonn, you don't know how glad I am to be here, just to rest and let the kids play. It's been a long two weeks since Garrick took off. This is ideal—high on the wet side of the mountain, tucked away where no one'll bother us. It's only June—what—fourteenth? We can afford to stay here a few days. The animals need a good—Steph!" He broke off. "Get away from that horse!

He's not one you should talk to. Go see Jangles. Amarl, chase Glue away from where the kids are playing."

Steph ran toward the wagon. "Oh, please, Driss. Please let me talk to Glue? He says so many funny things. He don't like that name, y'know. He'd rather be called 'Your Excellency'."

"Oh, is that so? Well, His Excellency is not safe for you to be around."

"No, it's *'Your* Excellency'."

"Humph! Who'd believe that? He'll just have to put up with 'Glue'."

"Oh, he don't really mind." The lad shrugged. "He's bery smart, you know. He told me he was ready to buck you off if you hadn't gave in on the best way to this place. And he says there's people all around us—soldiers, he thinks—but he don't know what they're doin'."

The two men looked up sharply at the surrounding hills, then back at each other foolishly. Jonn rubbed the boy's head. "Steph, go play now, and just leave the horses alone. They worked hard today and need to eat."

The group pitched camp at the edge of a hardwood grove halfway up the valley. The stream ran close, and Rolind spotted a deer trail he thought might yield fresh meat.

After dinner, Thilrec had his fire roaring in celebration of plentiful firewood. A pot of coffee hung to the side. The children were playing in the brook, and the mothers scolded them for getting wet just before bedtime. Keltie, high up among the trees, sat playing his toule flute, while Bren leaned against a rock outcrop, his sun-peeled face lined with weariness. Driss wandered aimlessly downstream, chipping stones in the laughing waters.

Suddenly, a shout brought his head up. "Driss! Look!"

His eyes followed Treese's arm, pointing to the shoulder high above. A dozen soldiers lined the ridge. He whirled around, searching the barren hill opposite, the one they had just come over. At least ten more stood forth—silent, unmoving, shining orange in the setting sun.

21

Charri and Roanna crossed the same line of mountains by a less direct route to the north. A pleasant, broad-faced miller and his wife had offered a ride, their course following the Cangley River that bisected the range. Not only did the woman and girl benefit from cooler, easier passage, the kindly tradesfolk thought they might be able to arrange another ride that would get them at least partway to Chadwich. Yes, the miller's wife had once met a tinker's wife from Chadwich—at a fair, she thought—but the acquaintance being only casual, she could give no other information.

On the day they departed the miller's dusty establishment, a most astonishing chain of events took place. The miller had instructed them to walk through town and wait near the farrier's shop. The miller's brother would meet them there and carry them to an iron smelter not far from Chadwich.

After receiving Charri's thanks for their kindness, the good folk drew her into a floury embrace with no regard to her deformity. Charri and Roanna waved until out of sight, then made their way across town.

The neigh of a horse and the sharp song of metal on metal led them to the farrier. They had just settled under a tree when a youth, clad in coarse shirt and trousers of rusty brown, drove toward them with a cart and pair of donkeys.

Charri and Roanna looked at each other. "This can't be the one," whispered Charri. "A *donkey* cart? He looks more like the miller's son than his brother!"

"It don't look like the right one," Roanna replied, "yet he's a-lookin' and a-smilin' as though it was. Right han'some, ain't he?" The girl pulled a strand of hair over her shoulder, curling it coyly.

"You must be Charri." The lad smiled as he drew abreast with his little team. "And your companion is . . . ?"

"This is Roanna."

"How do you both do? My name is Durk, and I am to take you south as close to Chadwich as I dare venture, these being troubled times." His grin looked anything but troubled. "I scarce think anyone will bother, though. Slow, humble things are mostly overlooked."

Roanna's eyes widened at the mention of trouble, but Durk snatched up their baskets and had them settled in the wicker cart before either had time for further questions.

The lad—younger than Charri and dressed even more poorly—had a lean, tight body, wide-set eyes, and scraggly brown hair that would have disgraced a less handsome face. Roanna was smitten.

The team matched their driver. The animals were sturdy enough, but their harness had been patched and spliced and seemed more rope than leather. Having neither bridles nor reins, they were steered by taps from Durk's long stick. The cart itself, a woven basket with two benches and an opening for the step-up, had seen hard use.

As they jogged past scattered cottages on the edge of town, following the south fork of the Cangley River, Durk guided the conversation away from the immediate and obvious—where they were going, how he happened to be carrying them, and was he indeed the miller's brother? Instead, he launched into inventive commentary on people and places they passed and soon had leftover questions swept from their minds.

His eyes were seldom still, especially after they left the west-flowing river and headed south. He scanned everything, scrutinized each passing vehicle—and provided miles of preposterous entertainment.

"That ground dog over there—" Durk kicked Roanna's foot and pointed. "You think that's a wild animal, but it's really just escaped from the Lady Malygoo's carriage, that one we just passed, the one you looked at so close." He winked at Charri. "A fine lady, spread across three seats, with a forlorn little pup squished in somehow.

"Now, the Lady Malygoo has a sore complaint. 'Oh, Grainger, dear,' she mewls. That's what she calls the pup—Grainger. 'Oh, Grainger, I have the air on my 'foot'." Durk pronounced it like *boot*. "You must take it away.' And Grainger dear is molded around the offended 'foot.' After a moment or two of that, the arm grows weary, and 'Grainger dear' converts to a cushion. Now, a cushion to the Lady Malygoo," he went on, green eyes dancing, "is not to be borne. That's why you saw Grainger hustling in the opposite direction, so accustomed was he to change that taking on the shape of a ground dog was nothing to him, nothing at all."

Initially, Roanna sat in awe of Durk, but this quickly evaporated. First she switched to his side of the basket because of the sun in her eyes. Then she wriggled against him to wave flies from his face, or drew patterns with her finger on his back—to Charri's chagrin. But the lad's high-spirited rejoinders scuttled her designs without the least hurt to her feelings. Charri's regard for the boy rose steadily, and she hardly bothered to pinch Roanna or frown.

The air sang around them. Sunshine and clouds rolled across the hills and ripening fields with the regularity of waves against the shore. City girl that she was, Charri drank in the intense beauty of this farming district. *How different from Swendia! Back home farms are flat, and not many trees. Mountains make such a difference. The colors . . . deep green to fair green to blue to purple and then the sky.*

"Roanna, do you see that little girl over there with sheep?"

"Yeah. What's she doin'?"

"She must be taking care of them. She has a stick in her hand."

"Does she whup 'em?"

"I think she's taking them down the lane to pasture. And the man—her father, do you think? Maybe he's off to market with those cows. He has a stick, too, and a dog." *Poor Roanna. She knows less than I do about farm life and what it means. When you live in a city, you just don't realize . . .*

Charri leaned back against the wicker, her eye taking in not just hills and farms and cottages and cattle drovers, but the magnitude, the supreme importance of farm life. Here, beyond the picturesque, the stereotype, lay rhythm, focus, pain. These agricultural centers knit into the fabric of society—her society—

were both dependent and depended upon. They represented the basics of life: earth, work, weather, eating, drinking, the making and utilization of manure. The very health of Arlony or of Swendia—her own health, in fact—lay in the tilth of the land.

It lay also in the integrity of its emotional landscape. Behind each river and sunset and song lay some secret, hidden prompting that could unlock the puzzle of life, if only a person had leisure enough to trace it to its source. Charri tipped her head back and closed her eyes, thinking about Driss, searching out her own emotions, feeling the sun, listening to the happy chatter of Durk and Roanna.

When she opened them again, the laughter had faded from Durk's face. Concentrating on a disturbance ahead, he halted the donkeys. After a moment of study, he winked conspiratorially and tapped them off the road and behind a low hill. "A little detour won't hurt them or us." Moving easily through the trackless rough, they soon regained the road some distance beyond whatever he had sought to avoid.

In mid-afternoon they stopped and pulled well away from the road to rest and to allow the donkeys to graze. Durk had only coarse bread with him, so Charri offered some of the miller's bounty.

As they ate, Durk made small talk. When he mentioned the name "Glinneth," however, Charri jumped almost perceptibly. She looked up and was surprised to see him watching her intently.

"Oh, do you know Glinneth?" she asked eagerly.

"Yes . . . a good friend," he responded carefully. "When did you see him last?"

"I never did, actually. I heard a little of him while I was still at home, and just recently some . . . friends told me how wonderfully kind he is."

Despite heroic effort, her face would turn red.

Durk looked off toward the road, chewing his bread abstractedly. "He's a soldier, you know, and soldiers cannot always be kind." Again his eyes fastened on her.

"Yes, I suppose that's true." Charri frowned. What was he after? Why would he say that? "These friends saw him only a couple of times. I suppose he was off duty or something."

Durk snorted. "Glinneth is never off duty. It just looks that way." He stared at the scrubby hillside, then began gathering the baskets. "If you do see him, keep in mind—especially you with your big brown eyes—" He poked Roanna playfully. "Keep in mind that he *is* a soldier."

Though directed at Roanna, Charri knew the advice was intended for her. The words troubled her.

Back on the road, the people they passed looked grim. Horsemen went by without the customary wave or greeting. Carters often gave warnings or mysterious gesticulations. Durk became increasingly watchful, making more and more detours. His humor held but became forced, distracted.

Approaching the road to Chadwich, they turned cautiously. Now, instead of pointing out things of interest, Durk began a silly discussion of boys. Charri looked at him in surprise, but as her eyes were not as easily diverted as Roanna's, she grasped his design to draw their attention inward.

Something had happened here, something dreadful, as though an army had churned through. Pastoral beauty was shattered; violence had raped the rustic integrity. While Roanna responded to Durk's prattle, Charri studied the flotsam along the road—and found reason to shudder.

It was not the torn roadway, nor even the shredded brush and trees that alarmed her, although the roadway resembled a battlefield. Amid the general mayhem, she saw discarded items she herself had once sold as an innocent child. She saw strange marks on boulders and tree trunks, and in one place ragged, red letters spelling "ZILL." The word startled her, frightened her, but she didn't quite know why. Something long ago . . . "zill" . . . "rozil" . . . She shook her head. It wouldn't come, but she did understand the lesser symbols all too well. The people she lived with years ago had thought them hilarious, but who ever explained such jokes to a child?

Now her eyes were opened, and she marveled that she had survived the hazards of ignorance. Children did not fare well at the hands of bad men. She knew that from experience; now it stood out fully dimensioned.

When "ash children" began showing up, old-wives tales suddenly came alive. Singly, in pairs, or in groups, these crude, wood-ash effigies lined the edge of the road. Some were decorated with a child's cloak or tiny shoe. Many had ribbon collars at the neck.

Of all this cumulated horror, it was these tattered circlets of ribbon at the necks of ash children that moved upon Charri almost like a subliminal earthquake, hardly noticed at the time, yet the tremors grew and grew, threatening to bury her under an avalanche of shame. Mercifully, the specific shape of this shame did not visit her until later. Enough for now that some nameless evil—an evil quite possibly spelled z-i-l-l—lay hidden in the ashes.

Durk returned her distraught, questioning look with the barest shake of his head and went on exposing the emptiness of Roanna's head.

Just before sundown in the midst of what seemed yet another detour, Durk halted the donkeys alongside a thicket and began unloading baskets. "This, I'm sad to say, is as far as I can go. Before night falls, I must be clear of this place. You'll be safe, though. Good water, comfortable place to bed down," he said, testing the springy ground, "and good cover. No wolfcats here or other wild animals—" He paused significantly. "Provided you stay well hid till daybreak. You're not afraid?" He looked closely at Charri.

She understood. *This place is thick with danger. But if I let him know I'm afraid, he'll feel he has to stay. And maybe it's more dangerous here for him than for us.* "No," she lied with a smile. "Roanna and I have slept out many nights. This is a good spot. Thank you."

He checked around once more, then gave careful instructions for getting to Chadwich.

Still he lingered. "You may hear things tonight, most likely from afar. Don't fear for yourselves. Shut out the noises, and don't leave the thicket, especially Roanna." He said this with unsettling emphasis. "Though she's saucy enough to pass as a grownup." He chucked the simpering girl's chin.

"One other thing," he went on more seriously, "Chadwich—well, you could say most of the towns west of here are not good places to wander in. You do have a person to go to, a place to stay? Whatever you do, don't stay outdoors overnight in any of those towns. I think you know what I mean."

Charri nodded, eyes comprehending and confused. The perplexity that had only nibbled on her nerves at the beginning of this strange day began to feast at its close. Nothing had gone as she thought it would.

Just before leaving, Durk sent Roanna to draw a drink for him. As the girl went off, he slipped a paper to Charri. "I was commissioned to give you this. Read it quickly, memorize it, then destroy it completely—not one letter left on another. Above all, do not tell Roanna of it. Do you understand?" Again that look.

Charri trembled under the intensity of his whisper, then nodded. With a smile that did not quite instill the confidence he intended, Durk clasped her two hands between his, then leaped into the donkey cart and swatted the sturdy little team. "Remember," he called back softly, "he's a soldier!"

Roanna returned with the water, her jaw hanging as she watched the disappearing cart. "He wanted water and didn't even wait!"

Charri smiled. "I think he forgot in his rush to get home in time for supper. I'll have a sip, though. Is it as tasty as it looks?"

Charri lay rigid in the dark, eyes tight against the fiery glow from every hilltop. All the old tales about children and Middle Night took over her mind like strangler vine in mid-summer. That it was only First Night—June 20—did not ease her fears.

In an attempt to shut out the sounds knifing her heart, she mentally reexamined the note, already destroyed, its words scrawled in haste.

"You have a name; that much I know, but I cannot tell it . . ."

Does it mean he doesn't know it, or that he knows but can't tell me? And how will I recognize the right kung grove where I'm to meet him? Are there no other such groves where two roads intersect?

22

Except for Amarl and the children, hardly anyone slept that first night in the lush valley. The second night the men alternated watches. The third night Keltie volunteered to stay up but fell asleep shortly after midnight.

Each evening, though—trees etched black against a glass-clear band of purple, yellow, and green; soft breezes heavy with the subtle odors and longings of old memories—here against this gift of twilight, the orange soldiers lined the ridges to watch the little band, then melted silently away.

Rolind pushed hard for sending up a detachment to chase them off, but Driss pointed out that two guns and a short supply of bullets wasn't much of a show of arms.

Discounting this rather major concern, the valley was a paradise, a welcome respite after their dry, harried approach from the east. The men rested, the children played, the women washed or aired everything made of cloth. Amarl leaped bareback on whatever horse—except Glue—however many times he thought he could get away with, and tore around the meadow in sheer exuberance. Celine said over and over, "Wouldn't Charri love this place?" Celine had all but danced when Rona left, but she sorely missed her gentle and gracious sewing companion.

Early one evening, before the sunset pageantry on the cliffs above, Keltie hustled the children down the slope from the supper circle and engaged them in mysterious whispers and snickerings. A short while later they lined up behind Keltie's "DAH-duh-duh-duh" and beat a noisy, circuitous way back to the group still lounging around the campfire.

"All right, pupils, sit!" Keltie ordered.

The children settled in a row, giggling and wiggling under some unbearable delight.

"Now." He addressed the adults. "It's my opinion that these youngsters here haven't been gettin' enough teachin'. They don't hardly know nothin' about—"

"*You* fancy yourself a teacher?" Treese asked incredulously.

Keltie turned a withering look on him but otherwise ignored the interruption. "They hardly know nothin' about this country we're in, when it was founded, who rules it—stuff like that. Now, we fellows had Garrick, but these poor tads was in blissful ignorance—isn't that right, kids?"

The children nodded with a new wave of jostling.

"So. Tonight we're gonna show you what they've learned so far. Now, you gotta keep still till the lesson's done, or we'll have to start all over." He turned to the children. "Ready, guys? Okay, first question: Benzel, who lives in Bethzur, a big orange fortress to the west?"

The boy twisted self-consciously with a mighty grin. "Sigurth!"

"Good, good." Ignoring frowns from his adult audience, Keltie turned to the next child in line. "Vilda, who is Sigurth's little brother?"

"Claeman!" she piped. "An'—an' he wears blue, purple and green ribbons in his hair!"

"Excellent!" responded Keltie. "All right, Nessa, here's a hard one. What—"

"Now, wait a minute!" Driss broke in. "What are you teaching these kids? *Sigurth* in Claeman's fortress, *Claeman* wearing T'ribboner ribbons. You'll get them—"

Keltie turned on him sharply. "Didn't I tell you to keep still? You're destroyin' my discipline. Nessa, what color was the Green Wars?"

Steph jumped up, aggrieved. "That was mine! You said I—"

"Whoops. Okay, Steph, you can all answer it. What color?"

The four youngsters bounced up and down, shouting, "Brown! Brown! Brown!"

The trick unmasked, Driss came at them with a fierce growl, and the children fled screaming down the grassy slope. Driss caught first one, then another. Over and over they rolled, shouting in pure happiness.

Spring had just come to full maturity here in the highlands, wrapping the valley in tender green. Each day Driss climbed the stream to where he could see the long distance westward, beyond blue and purple to where reddish lumps intruded on the hazy plain. Here, high above camp, beneath a bria bush weighted with pink blossoms, the brook crept from a rocky hollow through a series of shallow, mossy pools. Lofty camblors arched overhead, a cascade of melody pouring from their tops. The spring sun, mother warm, mother gentle, drew intoxicating vapors from the earth.

Here in this lonely, lovely overlook, Charri came upon Driss. He felt her gentle touch when a bria bloom settled on the arm she had tended. In the rippling grass he saw the green dress she so wanted. He glimpsed her graceful form in the swaying branches. *She was drawn to me. I know it; I saw it in her face. If she were here, she'd be won so easily. She couldn't help herself.*

He groaned. The exquisite beauty of this fountainhead beat on his heart and filled him with intense desire, yet at the same time it washed peace through his soul. Thunder and lightning of physical pain broke over him as the two fronts of desire and tranquility collided.

"Treese, I've got to have a woman! Rona's been gone—how long now? I'm desperate!"

The two walked along the stream under glittering starlight, while the others sang and clapped around a roaring campfire.

"You and Amarl," Treese grunted, "burdened as he is with the full measure of progeny between his legs. Practicing to be a woman killer, he says. This morning while you were doing whatever you do upstream, he tore around the valley bellowing, 'He knows every move, he rides like a deer, he speaks a secret language.' "

Driss looked at Treese plaintively. "Celine, or even Griselle..."

"There you go. Griselle would do well by you." His bitter tone scratched the darkness between them. "You're talking to the wrong gander, old pal! I'm not your agent. Go see Jonn or Bren."

"But you have—"

"So I have, and I managed it by myself. You want a woman—go bag one on your own."

He didn't, though. Jonn was a friend from way back. He couldn't even drop hints in that direction, though he would have jumped at an opportunity. In their younger days, he and Jonn had both gone "bargain hunting." Not now, though; especially not this trip. Driss suspected that Keltie might have slipped through, but in this sex wasteland no bargains were available—to anyone. Griselle was a write-off in every man's book, and Bren, suddenly possessive, had become a testy stallion guarding his mare. Maybe Uncle had taken to "dress-up sex" for want of available women. Well, that sort of thing wasn't for Driss, no matter how starved he was.

But some woman, any woman. *Charri* . . . Her heart was iron, though. Even if she were here, it would take more than spring's madness to get to her.

Why was she so put off? She'd done it before—willingly, it seems. Sure, the guy took advantage of her, but it was still sex.

He wished he could forget her. What good was she? The exact opposite of Rona and Clettie—unsophisticated, vulnerable, ugly. No . . . not ugly. Block out the scar and there was still her forehead and chin, her arms, the luster of her eyes . . . *But looks and availability are only part. Any woman worth her keep in robes and jewelry could give a man body and bed. Charri would be more, much more.* <u>Patient and gentle</u>: *What did that kung balm cost her in patience alone? Her fingers on my arm . . . She didn't want to touch me.* He smiled, recalling her dilemma. *Watching her squirm did more for me than the kung balm. If I were really sick, though—the runs or throwing up—she'd be there with me. The only one, most likely. What's a little puke to all she's put up with? She'd be a tough lady to shock—that way, anyway. As long as it's not sex.* <u>Makes do with very little</u>: *Can you picture Rona setting out on foot over two countries with a sick infant and only what she and a scatterbrained helper could carry?* <u>Loyal to principle</u>: *Damn her principles!* But maybe principle gives love a leg up. He knew that underneath her principles her love for him was there: he'd seen it in her face that day of his great blunder. New love, fresh as spring, unjaded. He closed his eyes and writhed under the driving fecundity of that fair green valley. Whatever love it was, he needed it—now. *Charri, oh, Charri! Where are you?*

He thought back to the start of the trip. Ten horses, three conveyances, three pack animals, plus all the accouterments. Losing Garrick's money had hurt them badly, though no one missed Garrick himself. They lost a bundle on the crico game, too. If he'd foreseen Garrick desertion, he probably would have accepted at least Glinneth's money, if not his offer of work.

Rona was gone, and his mare. If he could keep one, which would he choose? For that matter, given a choice, would it be Rona or Charri?

Rona . . . Strada: aristocrats, unpredictable. Charri . . . Glue: you couldn't compare them except in looks; by nature they were opposites . . . perhaps. Glue, it seemed, held endless surprises. *Your Excellency,* indeed! *Oh, Steph, you're our greatest gain through all this!*

He lay back, studying the canopy overhead. Tall camblors, dark against a rose-tinted sky, performed a courtly dance in the gentle wind, their lacy crowns touching hands decorously with first one partner, then another. As he gazed, it seemed that he was in those graceful tree tops, along with Charri. He watched in wonder as she glided through the branches, one arm stretched toward him in mute yearning, the other shielding her scar in an elegant, stylized pose. In and out she went, face and body both offering and entreating love. He could see himself reach out to take her, but she slipped past, first bending low, then raising head and arms in slow, fluid movements. Grace, always grace.

She turned away, looking over her shoulder as though inviting him to join her dance. He wanted to. He desperately wanted to but didn't know this slow-motion dance. Awkward, clumsy, hasty, he could catch neither the rhythm nor the steps. He pounded his fists on his ineffective legs. Why couldn't he get it—he, Driss, dancemaster at every festival and wedding? Of all of his friends, only Keltie was better. But here, with Charri's steps rising and falling in slow, seductive motion, he felt more like Garrick—a fool, a sweat-soaked bumbler. Always she inclined toward him, encouraging, willing him to keep trying. But when finally he did get close enough to touch her arm, it shattered in tiny pieces and drifted in a cloud through the branches. Her flowing movement never faltered, never lost its intensity of love. He kept on in desperation, but his attempts soon reduced her to curves swaying against the sky. Soon even those were gone. He was gone. Driss lay devastated. Could rosillum ever compensate for such loss?

The breeze died, and the holes in the lace became rosegold scattered across a velvety blanket of Wooten. He reached up to grasp a handful, then closed his eyes. *So near, yet out of reach. Can anything so far away be worth all this? Maybe . . . just maybe.* He sighed, but his eyes found a focus beyond the treetops. *Yes. It will be worth it. And when we get the rosegold, just watch the changes. We'll see how fast Rona comes trundling back to two or three Dunkirs and Wootens by the dozen! I'll do away with the court jester's nag and buy the classiest mare I can find—from Claeman himself, if I have to! Even Charri will think twice about running out on me.*

He rolled over on the pungent moss and peered into one of the pools. Blossoms floating on the surface competed with his reflection, and he felt vaguely annoyed. He looked all right—hair and features, what he could see of them—but the current twisted and shrank his image. Two more bria blooms hit the water, and when they floated away, the gentle swirl left deep, black sockets where his eyeballs should have been. He drew back with a shudder and covered his face.

23

"All right, we're ready." Driss tightened his saddle cinch, keeping predatory teeth at bay by means of a short off rein. "Jonn and I will check the draw that leads out of the valley to see if it's passable. It'll save a couple of hours if we don't have to go back to the pass to get on the road. If you don't hear from us, follow in an hour. We'll wait for you."

Bren nodded, an eye on Amarl's sluggish efforts to load the mules.

"If we get separated," Driss went on, "we'll meet tonight at the foot of the mountain, this side of the river."

Both horses pawed nervously, tossing their heads. Jonn swung onto his big mare and settled into the comfortable creak of leather. "Watch out, Nessa, Vilda," he warned. "Keep back."

"Daddy, you and Driss will come in time for tonight?" Nessa implored as Celine pulled at her.

"We'll see you long before then, I hope."

"No." Nessa shook her hands for emphasis. "I mean *tonight.*"

"Tonight?" Jonn looked blankly at his wife. "What's tonight?"

Celine returned a baleful glance. "How could you forget? With all the making and collecting—"

"Feast of Candles!" Jonn knocked his head with the heel of his hand. "June 20—First Night. I'm sorry. I wasn't thinking."

"Don't they do Feast of Candles in Arlony, Daddy?"

"Sure they do, honey, just like at home." He stroked his restless mare's neck. "Even if we did get held up, we'd still have two more days to celebrate. We'll be together tomorrow, for sure, the big night!" Jonn smiled reassuringly.

Driss grinned at the young ones. "Do you have a present for me?"

The little eyes danced. "Yes! But we won't tell!"

"Ha! I won't like it. I want only snake hair or a squirrel's egg."

The girls exchanged puzzled looks until Steph hooted. "Snake hair! Squirrel's eggs!" The children squealed deliciously.

With a relieved smile, Jonn leaned to kiss Celine, and the two men swung around to canter down the grassy slope.

The valley gave way to a green-carpeted wood dotted with pink, yellow, and white flowers. Jonn on his tall, rangy bay towered over Driss, to the latter's chagrin.

"Hot water back there, Jonn," Driss remarked. "Nearly got scalded."

"Feast of Candles, you mean? Did you remember it was tonight?"

"We-ell . . ." Driss smiled uncomfortably. "It wasn't on top of my mind. It's your fault, you know," he added with a grin.

"My fault what?"

"Back when we were little, when Feast of Candles was everything, rocks would sprout wings before we'd let anyone forget!"

"Why is that my fault? I remember Aunt Een getting after you for trying to find the presents."

Driss laughed. "Aunt Een. No sense of humor. I can still hear her warble First Night Song—

> *"Soft light, old light,*
> *Keeper of the year,*
> *Speak our fame or sorry shame*
> *Ere summer height draws near.*

"She kept track of our 'sorry shame,' all right. Not my favorite part."

He jabbed a finger at Jonn. "Your fault was making fun of Aunt Een and the ritual. I caught on real quick. Feast of Candles is for kids and Old Ones, I learned, but the time comes to smarten up and make jokes."

"Not my fault," said Jonn firmly. "You were always the lead guy in mischief, not me. And I liked it that way. You got us into trouble; I had someone to blame."

"Oh, that's how it worked!" Driss laughed. "But you always were smarter—way smarter."

"Nah. In numbers, maybe, but—"

"And became a numbers instructor. And like Keltie says, you take a history pill every day. But what am I? I can't sell cloth all my life. I have places to go, things to do."

"What ever happened to the Great Zelland plan? You were going to explore the continent, establish a colony, raise Wooten sheep—"

Driss looked at him. "That's why I'm after the rosillum. I thought you realized that. Great Zelland's a tough place to colonize. Housing is difficult in that wind and low temperatures, and fuel's a problem with wood, coal and liggeth being so scarce. Then food. How much can you grow in such a short summer? Sure, Swendia offers subsidies to prospective settlers—they want a piece of the pie, obviously—but it's a pittance. Of course, they'd distinguish anyone who settles in Swendia's name. What d'you say, Jonn?" He grinned. "You and me: chief and vice-chief of—what'll we call our province?"

Jonn laughed. "I'll have to think about that!"

"But even with the problems," Driss went on, "there's still a fortune to be made in mining and trading. And Wooten. I know Wooten would take off there. The harsher the climate, the finer the wool. With rosillum to fund ships and supplies, our investment would double—maybe triple—in no time.

"But first," he said, "first, the rosillum. When Uncle dangled his lure, I studied the map—every river, valley, hill, and desert the whole breadth of Arlony. And with the best men I could find to help me—"

"Except having to drag their families along."

"Yes, but families seem almost a boon here. People wave. Even Russetmen seem to look on us kindly. Did Celine need much coaxing to come along?"

"Not as much as you'd think. She knew how badly I wanted to go, how badly we need—" He stopped abruptly.

Driss looked up sympathetically. "Yeah, numbers instructors don't get rich, do they?"

Jonn shrugged. "Well, this was a good chance in many ways. We like new places, and Celine looked forward to the market in Lorenth. Arlony's a beautiful country with its mountains and rivers, and the kids would learn a lot. It just seemed good to her, too."

"You got a woman there, Jonn!"

"Yeah, she's a spunky lady." He tried to contain his pride, but it leaked into every line of his face.

They rode along, conversation falling before the musical joust in the treetops as spring birds vied for territory. "It's hard to leave this place," Driss reflected wistfully. "If it weren't for Claeman's monkeys gawking over our shoulders every night, I could be happy in a place like this," he said, grinning, "if we'd brought a few extra women."

Jonn grunted. "I thought for a while you wouldn't make it, that we'd have to bury you under a marker. 'He died of lust.' But you managed to keep out of my feed trough."

Driss smiled uncomfortably.

After several minutes of silence, Driss spoke. "You know, they believed it, every word."

"Who?"

"The Old Ones. A bunch of killjoys, I thought then. Now I see what it meant to them. It was more than ritual. They'd call it a holy, happy solemnity."

Jonn laughed. "My! You have mellowed!"

Driss fell silent, Charri's belief in Name and her desire to be claimed suddenly fleshing out the ancient rite. He sighed. "We need to make it a good celebration this year, Jonn—for the kids."

Jonn looked down at him. "Yes—for the kids."

The two rode down the mountain, weighing the disadvantages of the shortcut. It had once seen use as a road, and by clearing the largest debris, the wagon could make it through, albeit slowly. They weren't far from the other road, but would the long, smoother way get them there any faster?

Driss scratched his head. "I don't know. It almost seems—"

Suddenly Jonn pulled up sharply. "We got trouble!"

Coming uphill on horseback were about a dozen laughing, bantering soldiers—Claeman's, from their tawny uniforms.

"They haven't seen us yet," Jonn whispered. "You go that way, I'll go this. They'll see our tracks, but maybe they'll follow only one of us."

"Right. We can at least draw them away from the wagon. Whoever gets out first, circle back for the group and head down—the smooth way!"

Jonn moved to the right toward the road. Driss, though, went ahead several more yards, then set Glue into a noisy gallop off to the left. Just as he hoped, the contingent stopped at the sound, then turned in pursuit.

Now, old bag of bones, let's see what kind of match you are for Claeman's finest!

Horse and rider were rested and ready to lead a merry chase down the steep slope, Glue jumping downed trees and scrambling nimbly over rocky outcrops. Before long, all but two of Claeman's men had fallen back, but these stuck close, not giving quarter.

Driss, though, asked for none. He took Glue over a broad, fallen kung tree, then looked back to see one of the riders tangled ignominiously in its branches.

The other cleared it, though, and with some fifty yards separating them, they came out along the rim of a steep, almost sheer shale slide. As the two horsemen raced parallel to this drop-off, Driss considered his chances. This was turning into a flat-out horse race, and the gap was narrowing. Only one path led directly out of harm's way, but could he pull it off?

He reined abruptly, heart pounding, then turned Glue to the cliff. Would the horse plant his feet and go no further . . . or break both their necks?

The little gelding put his head down almost to the ground, ears working attentively, then took a halting step forward. Stiff legged and virtually sitting on his rump, he hopped and slid down the gravelly cliff, giving a snorting little buck at the bottom before galloping off.

Driss looked back, but his pursuer just sat on top, arm out in salute. Exhilarated, Driss returned the salute and pulled his weary mount to a trot.

By late afternoon, hunger drove Driss from the sheltered meadow where he had stopped to rest. Glue had fed well, but human fodder was limited to a couple of overgrown fiddleheads and a half-dozen sweetberries. Jonn had food in his saddlebag, but they had not thought to divide it.

Driss saddled the gelding, who was more waspish than usual at being recalled to duty. "You've got more in your belly than I do, old man," Driss told him petulantly. "Besides, after this morning, don't you think we could be more kindly disposed toward each other?"

Driss had made his precipitous descent on the southwest slope of the mountain, but in attempting to work back toward the road, he found the way blocked by a ridge jutting into the river plain. Fewer trees were on this side, and long, grassy meadows wrapped around the scrubby tumble of boulders spilling off the shoulder. Too tired for rock climbing, he worked parallel to the ridge, hoping for a trail or an easier grade.

Suddenly, something exploded out of the brush directly in front of him. Glue leaped sideways, with Driss scrambling to stay seated. A small, wild cow and her calf turned from flight to stare and stomp their indignation.

"Whoosh!" exclaimed Driss, stroking his nervous, snorting horse. "Next time, at least moo to warn us!"

He started on but then turned back in a stroke of hungry creativity.

"Glue, now that formal introductions are out of the way, do you suppose we might persuade her to give us some milk? She's probably a pretty good kicker, but we know all about that, don't we?"

They worked the cow back to a ledge, cutting her escape routes in half. Even so, what seemed a good idea began to appear doubtful. Driss dismounted and tried to loop a rope over the animal's neck, but her horns gave him pause. This was no time for a goring.

Next he tried running Glue alongside and bulldogging her to the ground, but he missed altogether and landed on his face, spitting dirt.

As he remounted, anger begat determination. He had a rope: what was the matter that he couldn't get it around her silly neck?

They stood in a face-off: Driss on his horse, the cow panting, her calf bawling in terror. The cow moved first, and before Driss realized what was happening, Glue was after her. Back and forth he went, head down, legs splayed, keeping her locked in the small area close to the ledge. After Driss recovered from his astonishment and adjusted to the horse's sudden turns and stops, he uncoiled his rope once again. Success came within three tries, and he quickly snubbed the cow to a scrubby tree.

Driss stood back, enormously satisfied, and felt moved to congratulate his mount. By this time, however, Glue had lost interest in all but grazing. Knowing how the horse felt about social frippery, Driss simply bowed in only semi-mock homage to "His Excellency" and lay down until the cow had settled.

Milking went relatively smoothly. After trying to keep the frightened youngster off its mother, Driss finally tied it to the same tree with the other end of the rope. He found a tin cup in his bag, not a very satisfactory receptacle, but with good aim and surprising cooperation from the cow, he filled it several times and drank deeply.

He considered dragging his food supply with him but abandoned the idea after weighing the terrain and distance still to go. Regretfully, he turned the pair loose and watched as they loped into the brush, this time not making the mistake of turning to stare.

Driss bedded early. He couldn't possibly make it to the appointed meeting place, and by morning the band would push on, hoping he would catch up during the day. He wasn't sure just where they'd go, but if he found no trace, he'd return to the foot of the mountain and look for a message.

Sadness sifted over him as the setting sun turned clouds to rosegold. First Night of Feast of Candles, and he was alone. Keltie would be playing a lively tune on his flute, embellished with bells below his knee. The others would sing and dance in a circle until they dropped exhausted and hungry. Thilrec would produce some delectable preparation metamorphosed from plain, common stuff. Tomorrow night's meal would be even finer.

The thought of food fed self-pity. The cow had done well by him, but even a belly full of milk could not stave off savage nips of hunger.

His mind crept unbidden to the lighting of candles, driving him even deeper into gloom. On First Night the three eldest of the group would each light a candle saved from last year and sing their special song.

> *Soft light, old light,*
> *Keeper of the year,*
> *Speak our fame or sorry shame*
> *Ere summer height draws near.*

As the candles burned, they would discuss the year past—the "fame or sorry shame" that Driss so hated as a child—until the tapers burned out.

Tomorrow, though—Middle Night, June 21—was the big one, the high day of the sun. Traditionally, the children would light six candles and carry them solemnly in a circle around the group, singing in quiet joy.

> *Seal my heart in love,*
> *Seal my love in flame,*
> *Mark my love,*
> *Set my love,*
> *Nor death can mar its claim.*

Then they would drip hot wax into the hand of each adult and make a mark significant to that child, if only a thumbprint, to bind the family in love. The oldest able person—Aunt Een had been the fixture for years, and Driss's uncle after her—this old person would come behind with a pitcher of water to pour over the marked wax, symbolizing love's endurance even through the heat of flame. The evening would end with a bottle of the finest wine.

Occasionally, someone would be claimed, either through an unusual circumstance, as in the case of his uncle, or more commonly after the death of a husband or wife. Like the ceremony of naming, this ancient custom gave substance and security to life. The very words, "I claim you," struck a responsive chord in nearly every heart. *Belonging* meant everything; a person cut adrift suffered far more than just personal rupture.

The meadow grew pale as the moon, rising behind the mountain, drew to itself the stored heat of the sun. In the chill of aloneness, Driss thought of Charri and her isolation. For her, Feast of Candles meant harsh memories. Not as bad, perhaps, as the horror stories he and Jonn and assorted cousins told to scare each other when they were kids. Children who had warts, or children with green eyes (the categories changed with the teller) carried off to be cooked over a thousand candles—that sort of thing. He smiled at the delicious, long-forgotten terrors of childhood.

While Middle Night candles burned, gifts would be exchanged—small, token things, centering on the children. Adults seldom gave to each other.

Driss had his gifts for the children in mind, though not all were in hand. Sometime tomorrow he'd find a butterfly for Nessa. Benzel would get a pale green stone he'd picked up some weeks ago, and for Vilda he had strung together a necklace of last year's hollow bubble seeds. She'd probably pop them within five minutes, but that much sheer delight was treasure enough. For Steph he had braided a belt from a blend of horsehair (not Glue's) and tough fibers from the inner bark of a dead camblor.

Rolind, hardened soldier that he was, had labored for weeks on a magnificent doll for the girls and a hand-carved crico ring for the boys. Driss would have expected guns or swords, at least for the boys, but on this occasion Rolind had exposed a tiny crack in his martial bearing.

Oh, the kids! They didn't know, they didn't see what it meant. For them, as it had been for him, gifts were the whole thing. Did it take twenty-eight years to grow into Feast of Candles? He suddenly wished he could kiss Aunt Een.

Last Night would be much like the first, only the candles would be blown out quickly and tucked away to finish their course on next year's First Night. On this final night of the feast they would talk of hopes and dreams for the months to come.

The pale night took on incandescence, the sky's rim aglow with the candles of First Night. Driss sighed and shifted uncomfortably on the lonely ground. Rosillum lay before them, though. Next year's grand celebration would more than make up for tonight's minor deprivation.

> *Soft light, old light,*
> *Keeper of the year . . .*

The mist over the grassy swale had begun to evaporate by the time Driss roused from sleep. He pushed off his raincloak-cum-blanket and crawled to the thin stream nearby to splash life into his dull head. Breakfast wasn't a problem: none was to be had, except for a few scavenged greens grown bitter in the advancing season.

Glue hindered his departure. Something had chewed through the tether rope close to the stake, carrying off the pin fastener that anchored rope to stake. Although the horse had stayed close, he managed to keep just out of reach. By the time Driss cornered him and got a rope on him, he had experienced the effects of tooth, heel, and swampy muck.

He was not in the best of humors, then, as he selected the direction he hoped would intercept the others. Almost immediately, he found the way blocked by a jumble of boulders. To avoid a long detour he swung uphill toward a narrow slot between the rocks and the slope above. While threading this corridor, Glue shied at a shrubby hollow. Driss put a hand on the horse's neck and halted, his eyes following the line of Glue's nervous attention.

"Aha!" he crowed. "So you're the culprit!"

A ground dog writhed under the consequences of its crime. The missing pin fastener was impaled in the roof of its mouth, and the animal's efforts to get rid of it only made matters worse.

In its desperate flailing the creature took little notice of horse and rider.

Driss sat back and watched, deriving grim recompense for his several bruises. Despite their appealing appearance, ground dogs were not his favorite animals. Being rodents, their appetite was unpredictable: the pin fastener attested to that. Then, too, they had a way of leaping high in fright at the approach of a galloping horse. The horse's sudden change of direction often held catastrophic consequences for the rider.

Unless Driss intervened, this particular ground dog had eaten its last meal. He could have caught it easily enough. Stupid creatures, readily cornered, they were the staple of wolfcats and other large beasts. Their only defense lay in an extraordinary aptitude for breeding. It would have cost Driss only a few nips and scratches, and almost he dismounted, almost he followed his instincts. His own bruises weighed in, however, and with grim satisfaction he turned away and pressed Glue into a canter.

Near the bottom of the mountain, he came upon a road that headed west. With a stern word to his growling stomach, he set a comfortable pace that ate miles and what remained of the morning.

Brooks that had run freely on the mountain now dove under cover in the treeless plain. In early afternoon Driss followed the rank growth of such a hidden stream into a small kung grove, looking for water to drink. Sure enough, within the green darkness of the grove he found two small pools.

Driss dismounted and tied Glue away from the water until he himself had taken his drink. It was good water, cold water, that gave mountain freshness to his face and neck.

While Glue drank and pawed coolness onto his belly, Driss lay on a carpet of kung needles, hungry, tired, headachy, but grateful for this small, scrubby oasis. He got up, unfastening his trousers as he headed for the bushes, then jumped at the sound of a woman's voice.

"Driss, oh, Driss! It *is* you!"

Charri! With fingers suddenly gone clumsy he pulled his clothing back together and turned, heart loping.

"What are you doing here?" he asked. "I didn't see you. Were you—"

"I was hiding. I didn't know it was you until you . . . oh, I'm sorry, Driss; I should have waited . . ."

They both laughed, and Driss reached for her hands. He would have drawn her into his arms, but the warning flag was up. "Where are you going? Where's Roanna?"

"Roanna has gone to the village yonder to buy food while I wait for . . . and, uh, she'll meet me back here before evening." Her face colored, and she studied the ground in momentary confusion.

Driss noted this but said nothing.

Charri regained composure and went on hurriedly. "There's new information, maybe, and I'll be trying to find the tinker's wife in Chadwich. She's connected somehow with one of my families.

"But Driss—" Her voice took a new turn. "I met your people early this morning. I came along the north road, and when I got—"

"You saw them?" He gripped her arm with new hope.

"They were worried. Jonn said you'd gotten separated and didn't meet them last night. Are you all right?"

"Did he say where they were headed?"

"Yes. He showed me a map in case I happened to see you. He—"

Driss's eyebrows went up. "Jonn showed you the map? You earned *his* trust!"

Charri wasn't sure whether to be grateful for the compliment or anxious over a new responsibility. She hadn't asked to see the map, after all, and once shown, she couldn't very well erase it from her mind.

Shrugging ambiguously, she stooped and drew on the ground. "You cross the river here, go maybe ten more miles to a flat-topped hill. Just beyond or maybe beside it, Jonn said, is a smaller hill, and they'd set up along the brook between. He was hoping for forage there, and protection."

Driss nodded. "I know where you mean. I'll make it before sundown—if I don't starve first. You don't happen to have food, do you?"

"Yes, I do." She dug through her basket. "Not much, but there's bread and cheese and I think some—"

"Are you sure Roanna will get more? I won't eat this if it's going to put you in want."

She nodded reassuringly. "I've eaten. Besides, I want you to have this. I wish it were more, but—"

"You lend me a great gift. Thank you." He looked at her gratefully, then fell on the bread.

As he ate, Charri's voice took on urgency. "Driss, you must hurry! I've seen things these past two days. An army or something is traveling the same direction as you. You've got to get everyone out of there, especially the children!" Her eyes were wide with horrors just beginning to come into focus.

Driss looked at her closely. "What is it, Charri? What have you seen?"

She covered her face a moment. "Pictures, or signs—I don't know what to call them—some drawn, some made of pebbles in the dirt. "

"Runes, maybe?" Garrick's lecture visited his mind like an unwelcome relative.

"Yes, perhaps. But pictures can't hurt a person," she added, looking beyond him in grim resolve. "I learned long ago how to walk over such things. You keep your eyes up; you look away from their power. But . . . other things, like zill—" Her voice faltered to a distressed whisper. "And ash children. Especially ones with ribbon collars. There's some connection . . ."

Driss frowned. "Zill? Ash children? You mean piles of ashes made to look sort of like—"

"You've seen them, too. They mean something. Ribbon collars . . ."

"I wouldn't take it seriously. Mostly superstitious nonsense."

She shuddered violently. "No, it's not nonsense. And zill, rozil . . . something . . . I don't know . . . But whatever it is, zill is behind it all. And as bad as day is, it's worse at night: fires on every high hill, terrible sounds . . ." She began to cry. "Oh, Driss, you *must* get the children away!"

"You're not making sense. Tell me about zill. What is it? Keltie mentioned it once, but he didn't make sense, either. What do you know about it?"

Her eyes implored him wretchedly. "I can't remember. I only know it's awful! And because of it, children . . ."

He tried once again to hold and comfort her, but she eluded him, stuffing a remaining crust in his pocket.

"Go quickly, Driss!" She fairly shoved him onto Glue. "And be careful!"

He cantered off and turned to wave, but she was no longer looking toward him. Instead, she started around the grove, shielding her eyes against the sun as though watching for someone. Roanna, perhaps? She wasn't due back till sundown.

Uneasy, he pulled up at the top of the rise and swung around just in time to see a man approach on foot from a different direction than the one he had come. Charri ran toward him and reached for his outstretched hands. Every curve of her body inclined toward the stranger as though pulling against ropes of shyness.

Anger pounded through Driss. *An approaching army, eh? Zill. A cheap trick to get me out of the way. She's been waiting, all right—for someone else.*

As he watched, they gesticulated briefly, then turned toward the rise where Driss sat. Charri pointed and the man waved. Then after a quick embrace that melted her reserve, he jogged along the track toward Driss, Charri taking anxious steps in his wake.

Grinding his teeth, Driss swung around haughtily and galloped off.

Below, Charri watched the runner disappear over the rise, then turned slowly into the cool grove, excitement enlivening her face. "He called me his sister. . . . Oh, if only he had stayed a minute longer! He said to go to his home. 'I will find you there,' he said. But *where?* . . . Why didn't Driss wait? Perhaps he didn't see us wave . . . perhaps he'll stop over the hill. Oh, please, both of you—get to the children in time!"

24

The sun had nearly set when Driss, pale and shaken, drew rein at camp. Jonn, relief smoothing his features, reached for the bridle, then ducked as Glue came at him, mouth open and ears laid back.

Driss swatted the horse's head in annoyance and dismounted. Giving the reins to Amarl with instructions to walk but not unsaddle the animal, he turned back to Jonn. "We're in trouble, my friend."

Jonn's head seemed to withdraw into his cowl shirt as they listened to a growing hubbub atop the hill across the brook. "They're on top of us, the whole T'ribboner force. And it's more than muscle flexing. Nobody bothered us on the way here, but you couldn't help knowing something was up. Celine's been jumpy, and Rolind—you can guess the state he's in!" He chewed his lip and frowned. "Where's Claeman and his 'peacekeepers' when we need them?"

"Humph!" Driss retorted bitterly. "Probably still up north, or maybe he's at his damned castle celebrating Middle Night. Besides," he added, "why should Claeman care what T'ribboners do to us?"

"Any chance they'll leave us alone? Just because they're all around doesn't mean they're after us specifically. Remember the other skirmish? We weren't the main target after all."

Driss shook his head wearily. "I think they'll take anyone who happens to be handy. I got through, but I don't know how or why. Maybe they let me pass just so they'd have us all. You may not think they noticed you, but Sigurth has ways of keeping track."

Steph sidled up and looked at Driss accusingly. "Glue says you rode him hard today, and you wouldn't let him have any water."

"Well, Glue lies. We rode hard, all right, but he had as much water as I did and got wetter. Go tell Thilrec I could use a drink right now, and something to eat."

The boy ran off but nearly bumped into Celine carrying a plate of food. "It's cold," she apologized. "The men didn't think we should light a fire."

"Thank you. It's fine." Dropping on a fallen log, Driss rubbed the back of his neck. "Almost too tired to eat," he mumbled, but the food disappeared.

Others gathered around, their questions thick with fear. Driss cut them off. "Let me think a minute!" he snapped, massaging his forehead against the growing noise. "Griselle, take the kids somewhere, will you? Not to bed, though. Not yet, anyway."

Worry etching his face, he watched the four youngsters move away, anxiously bearing their own piece of the uneasy atmosphere.

Driss turned to the rest, weighing his words carefully. "I don't know what chance any of us has, but somehow we've got to get the children to a safer place, even if it's just putting them somewhere away from us."

Eight pairs of eyes widened in stunned silence.

Driss went on. "We can't hide the bunch of us plus horses and equipment, but we could stick the kids somewhere with food. Then if one or more of us gets away, we'll come back and get them."

Celine began to cry. Driss sighed in exasperation. "I know, I know. It's a lousy idea, but right now I can't think of a better one. Can you?"

She shook her head and continued to weep.

The others remained motionless, trying to swallow this new lump of fear. Treese spoke first, his voice controlled, matter-of-fact. "I know a place. Steph found a cave way up the hill. Not much room, but enough for the four of them. Best part, the entrance is practically invisible. Can't see it even when you're right next to it. We could leave food and water, and Steph would keep the others in line."

Celine looked doubtful, but the rest nodded eagerly at this ray of hope.

"I have trained them well," Rolind said proudly. "They are courageous soldiers and will obey their commanding officer."

"Good," returned Driss. "Sounds good. Go whip them into shape and get them on parade as soon as possible. Meanwhile, Keltie, you and Amarl see to the animals. Hide them as best you can. Treese, you and Bren cover the equipment. Celine, tell Thilrec what food to pack for the kids, and you and Griselle gather whatever clothes you think they'll need. Hurry, though; not much daylight left. I'll look to defenses."

When they were alone, Jonn planted himself in front of Driss. "What's with the kids, Driss? What do you know that you're not saying?"

Driss's eyes fell under the force of Jonn's apprehension. "I met Charri today. She—"

"You did!" Jonn lit up. "We saw her, too. Celine tried to get her to stay, but she said she had to meet someone. It wasn't you . . . ? No, I guess not," he hurried on, noting the sudden set of Driss's jaw. "Anyway, she must've told you where to meet us. Once we got here, we realized we couldn't have picked a worse place. What's the matter? Weren't you glad to see her?"

"Yes, of course." Something else held his mind. "We talked. I thought she was stretching things, especially about the children's safety, but after leaving her, I came across the things she'd seen. The bonfires, Jonn—" He looked at his friend. "They're not for warming or cooking or singing around."

"Come on, Driss!" Jonn stiffened in disbelief. "You're talking like an old Arl! That kind of stuff doesn't happen any more, if it ever did. You don't believe those Green War horror stories any more than I do! And this is Feast of Candles, man! Who in their right mind . . . Sure, T'ribboners fool around with runes, probably to scare yokels, but even soldiers keep Middle Night!"

Driss just looked at him. "You don't want to believe it, Jonn. I don't either, but I know what I know. This night especially, whatever's going on over there, the kids are in terrible danger, and zill is behind it. Whatever the stuff is, I get the idea it's tied to rosillum. It has power over man and . . . other things. Some places I rode through were so thick with a sort of . . . stench, I guess you'd call it, that—"

He stopped and rubbed his head.

"That what?"

"Jonn, maybe I was just tired, but at the top of one of those fire hills, I felt almost . . . trapped. Nothing, no one there, but . . . something . . . I sat on Glue, just looking around. He felt it, too; it wasn't just me. Nailed his ears flat and kept tossing his head. I sat there trying to figure it out and saw something move out the corner of my eye. I swung around, but there was only scorched sand and rocks. I rode all over the top of that hill and found nothing alive, but every time I turned away, this thing moved again. I kept circling and looking. Then I discovered what it was."

He paused uncomfortably and swallowed. When he went on, his voice cracked. "It was a rock."

Jonn's face underwent a series of startling alterations.

"I know you think I'm crazy," Driss said more steadily, "and maybe I am, but I'm telling you . . . You could see the hole where the rock had sat and the trench it dug as it moved. It had traveled, I'd say, about seven or eight feet from the hole, and you could tell where it had rested—a little hollow—each time I looked at it."

"Driss—"

"I know. I don't believe it, either. I was probably just tired and seeing things and the rock had been moved earlier. But I saw *something* move on that hill, and the only possibilities were rocks and ashes and burnt sand."

The conviction in his voice made Jonn shudder, but Driss gathered himself. "Enough of that. Enough that we know the kids are in danger. How much ammunition do we have? What good it can possibly do us with only two guns, I don't know. Except, maybe, to cut their ranks by a few before they kill us. We can't assume the battle will pass us by this time."

At half-light, Rolind assembled the children before Driss, who drew them close to make himself heard against the din of the T'ribboners on the hill across the valley.

"Now, as Rolind told you, you're spending the night in your cave. You must stay quiet, no matter what you hear outside. There may be a battle with shooting and shouting, just like at Peerce, but you must not leave the cave unless one of us tells you to. Do you understand?" He went from one to the other, holding their heads between his hands and looking into their eyes.

They nodded solemnly.

"We're asking a lot of you, but you are brave and obedient. Steph is your captain; he's in charge. You're to do as he says. Now, come kiss us all, then fall in behind Rolind."

Driss had already emphasized, to the women especially, the virtue of emotional control, but it was sorely tested as the children filed past with their hugs and kisses. First came Nessa and Benzel, then Vilda. Steph brought up the rear, his eyes sparking with excitement as he stood before Driss. Driss gritted his teeth against his own emotion and pushed back the boy's hair. "Be strong, son. Whatever happens, be strong." He held the lad tight and long.

"Atten—HUN!" barked Rolind. "Staden—hom—hou—hree, staden—hom—hou—hree . . ." They marched off into the gathering gloom.

Celine called after them, her voice tight with anxiety. "Be sure to put on more clothes when you get chilly!"

The fading light gave way to the glow of an enormous bonfire atop the hill opposite. The sound of chanting and dancing grew with the flames, and soon the surrounding countryside echoed with unbridled debauch. Even if the hill had not been uncomfortably close—less than a thousand yards—the noise would still have been overwhelming.

The small band lay close in their appointed place, listening, waiting. "The children are so far away!" Celine whispered, clinging to her husband's hand. *"Why* did we come on this dreadful trip?"

"Only five minutes away," Jonn replied grimly, ignoring the unanswerable; "would they were five hours off. What a way to celebrate Middle Night!"

Thilrec crawled to the women with an object in his hand. "Look what got left behind. I checked earlier to see how many cakes of dried fruit we have left, and it was in the bag, probably for 'munch,' as she calls it. I stuck it in my pocket, meaning to give it to her, then forgot."

Griselle began to cry. "Vilda's doll!"

Driss hissed at Thilrec. "A great time to pull it out! Why didn't you just keep still? Where's your sense, man?"

Rolind removed the floppy doll from Griselle's hands. "I'll take charge and see it's returned at the conclusion of the skirmish."

Driss eyed him gratefully. *Rolind, old man, you're a bit odd, but when the chips are down, you come through.* Aloud he whispered only, "Thanks, old boy!"

The doll was forgotten when a sudden stillness fell across the valley. A voice hailed them—a familiar voice: the voice in the latrine, the voice in the cobbled courtyard where information became money. "Drissan! Halloo! Sigurth here. We're having a little party over this way. Would you and the children care to join us?" Every word rang clear as the night.

Driss put up his hand to signal silence—quite unnecessarily, with everyone lying rigid under the tension.

"Come, now. We'll have a splendid time together: fine food and drink, even some zill, if you stick around long enough.

"That word again!" Griselle squeaked.

"Quiet!"

"We have the zill tower in place, some rosillum tempering. All we need is . . . raw material."

The voice remained silent for several minutes, then began again, still jocular. "Drissan! A bargain for you: if you won't come to our party, send the children. Children love parties! Tell you what: send over the children, and we'll let the rest of you go. How's that for terms—ten for four. Freedom, Drissan. You know you can't get away unless I give leave, like I gave entrance this afternoon. What do you say? Do we have a deal?" Hoots from the crowd punctuated the proposal.

The women turned frightened faces toward Driss. He shook his head and motioned for silence.

Sigurth continued propositioning, but when no reply came, he gave an ultimatum. "One minute more, Drissan. After that we'll help ourselves."

Jonn looked sideways at Driss, but the latter gestured helplessly. "We've done everything we can. The kids are as safe as we could make them. The rest of us don't stand a chance, but

Steph is resourceful. He might just make it out. Treese and Rolind are our best marksmen; they're ready with the guns. They'll take at least five apiece before Sigurth gets to us. All we can do is sit tight and wait—and keep the women quiet."

They waited, one minute . . . five . . . fifteen . . . but nothing happened. Sigurth remained silent, but a chant around the bonfire made them all blanch: "Through the fire—*zill!* Through the fire—*zill!* Through the fire—*zill!*" It pounded relentlessly, building intensity, abrading every nerve.

Suddenly, above the noise, came another sound. Some distance up the hill behind them, a voice spoke commandingly: "Atten-HUN! Staden—hom—hou—hree, staden—hom—hou—hree . . ."

"Where's Rolind?" barked Driss and Jonn simultaneously.

Less than three yards away, Rolind leaped to his feet. "Treachery, sir! Sedition!"

"Stop! Don't come out!" Celine screamed toward the children, but it was too late. Little voices had already joined the counterfeit Rolind. Within seconds, their eager marching chant became screams, and the sound moved rapidly across the valley toward the hill opposite.

"After them!" cried Driss. "We'll get to them or die trying!"

"Wait!" A new voice thundered behind them. "Don't be fools! You can't save them now, and you'll all suffer the same fate!"

"Dammit, dammit, we've *got* to save them!" yelled Driss, stumbling wildly toward the brook.

He got only a few yards, however, before being brought to the ground. The stranger bellowed in his ear over the shrieks of the women, "Think of the others, man! They need you now more than ever!"

At that moment a sudden hush descended across the way, followed by a ghastly wail that sent Keltie reeling against a tree where he dropped to his knees and emptied his stomach.

Driss cursed and clawed at the ground, trying to wrench free, but his captor held tight.

"You cannot help them, laddie. It's all over. They are beyond suffering now. Get a hold of yourself. You've a job to do."

Driss stopped struggling and stared. It was Glinneth.

25

Moonlight fell softly around the lone figure trudging up a hill. At the top, she stopped and looked anxiously toward a glow in the southwest. *Is that where Driss was headed? I saw the map, and it seems . . .* She bit her lip and shuddered. Durk's warning concerning night travel brought her cloak tighter. She would bypass that particular glow by several miles, but would there be others?

For the eleventh time, she reviewed the events of the day in an effort to cap an emotional volcano threatening to bury her.

She had expected Glinneth but not Drissan. Each had acted on her in different ways. When Durk gave her Glinneth's note about meeting at the grove, she'd been nervous and excited. But when Driss appeared at the grove first, her heart had leaped with a dangerous gladness. *Poor man. I embarrassed him!* She smiled whimsically.

But whimsy could not divert the relentless flow of lava lapping at her heels. Her mind was kneading the tavern child into a phantom figure that followed close, grasping, dragging at her, cutting her with his reproachful gaze. No voice, just a silent imploring against the drum of her own heartless words: *I can't help you . . .*

She shuddered. *This will not do; you can't dwell on that child, as wretched as he was, the ribbons at his neck that have something to do with zill. No. Think of the men, think of Glinneth.* Yes, Glinneth . . . warm, full of safe love. Strangers— yet before they parted he had drawn her into his arms. He had hugged her, held her without even glancing at her scar! *Sister, he called me. Driss would not call me that . . . well, he might to get his way. Glinneth, though, wouldn't lie. Only two minutes at most, yet I know him. I can trust him. His eyes . . . Eyes say so much about a person. Driss's eyes, Jonn's eyes . . . Glinneth's are crinkley and warm; not harsh, not sharp. They looked past the scar to me. No words, no signs, yet I knew . . . he knew.*

Why should he go to such trouble, coming to me on foot, even? A man of weighty matters, yet for those few moments he focused all his concern on me.

The note said I have a name. He didn't tell me what it is, but almost . . . almost I can believe I really am a person, like Driss said. A small smile eased her face but quickly faded. *Why didn't I want to tell Driss Glinneth was coming? Driss is not safe. Seeing him, hearing his laughter, standing there with him . . . If I hadn't just finished my flow, I would've thought . . . Such wonderful, beautiful feelings!* She sighed, then gathered herself abruptly. *But wrong for you, Charri; wrong, shameful. Haven't you learned that much? When Uncle . . . I didn't know at the time . . . Old Litta kept telling me, "Charri, don't let men use you. They'll try, so sure I am of it." She told me, but still I didn't know . . . I didn't know that's what she meant. So lovely at first, so lovely, until . . . Oh, my sweet, lovely Amara, you came from the lovely feelings, not from Uncle.*

A wisp of smoke slid along the fitful breeze. Charri lifted her head to the scent and again felt the tug of the child specter. She shuddered at the blackness behind her and willed her mind back onto cold, hard ground.

Now I know about men. But would Driss be like Uncle? He's kind. Gentle. He didn't force me. He could have; no one was near. But he didn't. "I'm sorry," he said. "Please forgive me." Uncle just laughed. But Driss knows I'm nobody. Even if he did love me he'd never marry me. He'd use me, like Litta said. But . . . would that be so bad?

Even as the words formed, her face held the answer. *What am I thinking? Yes, Glinneth is safe, but not Driss. Driss will only break my heart. He makes me deceitful, unsure of myself. But . . . never before was there even one man. Now, two in one day . . . two so different.*

She topped another hill. The glow again, the reminder. A stray jag of lightning angled toward it from a starless patch of sky, though the moon still lit the path where she walked. Except for this one rumble of thunder, no other sound reached her from the glow. Not tonight. Still, she put hands over her ears to block out a horror no distance could erase from her mind.

What had become of Roanna? Durk had worried about the child, and he knew more than his words let on. The little village, so close to the peace of the kung grove, had seemed safe enough for her to shop in. But was it foolish to send her alone, just to get her away before . . . ? No, surely she was all right, just caught by a handsome face.

Oh, Roanna! What shall I do with you? Are you in another tavern? Or will I have to drag you out of the arms of some farm lad this time? Such a trial you are! A child still, a larva, but already thinking like a butterfly. I need you, but I don't need your nonsense. You know how low the food bag is.

Food . . . Driss was hungry, and I was able to give him bread and cheese. If Roanna did buy food, it should get us to Chadwich. And to the tinker's wife, maybe . . . maybe. Will I find the tinker's wife? Will she know or remember anything of my parents? My last hope . . .

My last hope except for Glinneth. Have I forgotten so soon? "Go to my home," he told me. "I will find you. Go . . ."

One last rise, Charri, and beyond lies the village. The glow on the horizon has faded now, its obscene appetite sated. Keep to the moonlight, Charri, through this village . . . and the next . . . and the next . . . Don't think of zill. Don't think of ash children with their collars of doom. Pay no attention to the battered tavern urchin clutching at your garments. Try not to notice that the once-bright ribbons ringing his neck are now tattered, bloodied, scorched. Don't look into his eyes: they are full of death.

Driss strode along the brook, hammering trees with fists running blood. "Why didn't you come sooner?" he cried hoarsely. "With you here, we might have saved them! You told us—told Vilda—a soldier's job was to protect children!"

Glinneth rubbed his burled head, firelight from the adjacent hilltop turning the haggard lines of his face into canyons. "Ay, laddie, I might've come sooner, but my enemy hedged me about after some information was sold him. And today I missed a ride by less than two minutes."

Driss stopped pacing and stared. *Information . . . Sigurth . . .* His stomach knotted.

"But no time for that," Glinneth went on. "You're in great danger. But if you move quickly, you can achieve a good distance before Sigurth turns on you."

"That was you with Charri this afternoon!"

"Ay, lad, but we'll not talk of it. You must—"

"Is she safe?"

"Ay, for now. But you're not. Gather your people. They're shattered. You must give direction, work. For their safety and yours, *you must not lose a moment!*"

Driss sighed dully and turned away. "There's no place to go. We're trapped."

"You'll be safe on the road, at least for a while. Collect what you can, leave the rest, but above all, hurry!"

Driss continued to stare numbly.

Glinneth grabbed his shoulders and shook him gently. "Drissan, lad, d'you trust me? I would not lie or mislead. You'll be safe if you act now. I stake my life on it!" He shuddered under these words, eyes fixed on the fire above them. "My *life*, lad!

"Come, now." Glinneth swung around to the others. "Bren, Treese, Keltie," he roared, "gather the equipment, the horses. You, son—Amarl? Ready the pack animals. Rolind, collect the arms. They won't be needed tonight."

Treese was first to move. With an inarticulate roar he strode toward Jonn and Celine, who stood as stone. Separating them roughly, he half dragged, half carried Jonn toward the horses' hiding place. The others followed his cue—slowly, woodenly at first, then catching Glinneth's urgency as he pleaded and cajoled.

Driss, though, continued to stare at Glinneth, a new horror flaying his heart. *My life, lad; my life!* This man . . . this stranger who had unaccountably invaded Driss's inner stronghold . . . This loving ambush had sneaked up on him, the way Steph . . .

He ground his teeth against a spasm, his eyes bent on fathoming Glinneth. The big warrior was everywhere—hauling the wagon from hiding and heaving heavy sacks on board, hitching the horses, grabbing a surprised Glue before the horse had opportunity to mount a defense.

"Here you are, laddie. Mount up and circle around to get things moving. The women are in the wagon. All else is nearly—"

Driss, though, seized the soldier, his voice thick. "Glinneth, what are you going to do? You said you wouldn't lie—*what are you going to do?*"

Glinneth stopped, face glistening in the moonlight, eyes burning with anguish. "Laddie, if you bear any love for me in your heart, don't ask that question. There are lives to be saved, a battle to fight. Stand with me, Drissan; do your part. Leave questions behind and go from this fearful place. Travel all night. Shout and sing. Close your ears to all sound save that of pursuit. If anyone comes, scatter and hide the best you can. By morning you should be safe, at least more so than here."

After a moment of silent, shared torment, Glinneth enveloped Driss in a crushing embrace, then literally threw him on Glue and slapped the gelding's rump—ignoring a poorly aimed kick.

With a wild, strangled cry, Driss tore around the group, beating them toward the road. Before long, they all joined his shout, "In Name of Steph and Vilda, of Nessa and Benzel! Press on! Press on!"

Driss took one last look behind for sight of Glinneth, but the clearing stood empty and still. *Glinneth . . . friend. What have I done? I sold you into trouble, I turned my back . . . Will the children's lives cost yours as well?*

When the group reached the road and met no interference, just as Glinneth had predicted, they pushed along as instructed, venting helpless rage. Only Driss took note of a roar rising from the fire-lit hill behind them; only he knew what it meant. Tears ran down his face. But when a flash of lightning turned the ravaged band into a tortured tableau, he shouted louder: "In Name of Glinneth! Press on!"

The appearance of Glinneth as he pushed to the inner circle of firelight brought a sudden hush to the frenzy. Even Sigurth stared, momentarily dumbfounded. Then a full-throated howl ascended the great pillar of fire.

"You have come!" whispered Sigurth, the perpetual smile returning. "For Drissan."

"Ay, for Drissan. I have claimed him."

Gloating slid across Sigurth's face. "And I claim you!"

Glinneth shook his head. "No. You have power over me, but no claim. Your power is contained; it is named. You cannot bind me to the evil you are unless I give over to you. You will do what you will, but even killing me gives you no claim."

"You claim him for the rosillum."

"Hah! What does rosillum weigh against love? But you know nothing of that; you have no thirst for love."

Sigurth's eyes glittered. "I thirst for zill. But what do you know of zill, bound as you are to repression and gloom?" He motioned toward a two-tiered structure close by and smiled. "Not quite ready, though laid and poured. Come." He beckoned to Glinneth. "A lesson. First, a bin full of ash from young bone. Must be young, you know, as in four youngsters you may have known." He chuckled unaffectedly. "Needn't fear for your bones, old man—though we'd see them whitened for other reasons." He paused at the explosive chatter of kung branches being thrown on the fire, then resumed. "On top of bone ash goes a sprinkle of rosillum, smelted and ground to a fine powder. And finally, hot liquor over all, leaching out that most superb of all wines—zill. One sip of zill is as superior to licking rosillum as whiskey is to mouse milk." He closed his eyes in ecstasy.

"But you, O foe of pleasure," he went on, "would fight its manufacture. You cannot win, though. Common sense tells us the world is changing. Men want to be free of old shackles, old ways. They want leaders of reason."

Glinneth grunted derisively.

Sigurth looked at him, shrugged as though remotely dissatisfied, and turned back to the business at hand. With the ease of orienting a group of curious visitors, he walked around the tower and pointed out the vat beneath that received the reddish liquid. "What you see there is not zill. Several inches of semi-molten wax floats on top to hold impurities. Must be kept at just the right consistency. And underneath is that wondrous, crystal-red fire of *zill.*" His eyes shot sparks toward the still-sputtering kung needles.

"Pour out a pitcher full, then," roared Glinneth. "We shall both drink: you to your own destruction, I in triumph over it."

Glinneth stared at the conflagration, at the tower, at a smoking kettle of Middle Night candles that fed the vat. Hot wax evidently performed other duties, as well. His eyes took in a miserable huddle of naked, ribbon-necked victims, their bones presumably not needed for this particular batch of zill. Blood running down their legs, they clung together in shock from the double assault of hot wax and the thrusts of men aroused by their screams.

The implications of what he saw pierced him like a red-hot stiletto.

Middle Night. Candles. Dripped wax. A mark. Fine wine.

A terrible grimace sent his head skyward, then curled his torso down. His heart twisted against the iron determination of his will.

Only for a moment. Face pale but fixed, he straightened and strode forward, again leaving Sigurth off-balance, scrambling in his wake. He pulled off his shirt and cast it toward the fire. His massive chest turned pink in the intense heat.

"I open my heart to you, Sigurth," he bellowed. "Pull forth your brand. Pour on your wax. Inscribe what you will. This is Middle Night; neither fire nor flood can quench love!"

He stood with head thrown back and arms raised, a giant dwarfed against this towering blaze that fed on blood lust and children's bones.

The ring of T'ribboners fell strangely quiet. Their celebration had been interrupted, challenged by a new, different weapon. Guns they knew, torture, sacrifice. But this . . . Something was wrong, something they couldn't grasp. Somehow, this man was outmaneuvering them—and Sigurth, as well. Their unease became a pervasive, sickening must that rose over the foulness of a thousand drunken bodies.

Overhead, the moon fell dark. Clouds gathered apace with the contest below, seeking to relieve a mounting static charge. As the ground gathered purple electricity, T'ribboners and rocks alike skittered helplessly, drops of water on a hot griddle. Those who worked at melting candles attributed the crawl of hair on arms and neck to rising excitement. Their teeth chattered in salacious anticipation.

Four burly T'ribboners moved in cautiously to secure their prey. Glinneth shook them off impatiently. "I stand unfettered. If you try to bind me, I shall bind you as well. We shall all feel the mark of hate. Take care!"

The soldiers stepped back, looking anxiously at their leader.

Sigurth waved them off. "Stand alone he shall—if he can!" His laughter rang loud. "Wax!"

By this time the keepers of the kettle could scarcely function. Their ladles shook. Wax slopped under orgasmic frenzy. With an oath, Sigurth knocked them away and took over the task himself.

Glinneth writhed unresisting under the flow of wax upon head and shoulders. Sigurth dipped and poured, dipped and poured, but his exultation began to crumble. "Howl, fiend!" he roared in frustration. "Howl and curse! Turn on me. You know my power. I will have you if I have to kill you!"

Glinneth's mouth stretched in a soundless scream, then clamped shut as he turned fiery eyes on Sigurth. "Power . . . but no . . . claim. I give . . . no handle . . . for claiming. I . . . am . . . *secure!*"

Like an angry, bellowing bull, Sigurth lunged toward the fire for a brand to ignite the wax.

His fury, though, gathered the electricity that had been playing over rocks and T'ribboners and thrust it skyward, triggering the nascent bolt of lightning. A blinding flash ripped the clouds and vaporized the tower. Within seconds a downpour brought the great blaze to a whining flicker.

Love's mark was sealed.

In the ensuing confusion, Glinneth dissolved into the darkness. Sigurth roared after him. "Fire will spring up in every town, every hamlet. *I will prevail!*"

The rain ended as quickly as it had started. T'ribboners milled drunkenly around the aborted zill, licking wax and ash, anything that might hold a bit of fire. Sigurth beat among them with the ladle, trying to whip together a band sober enough to pursue Driss and his company. With the quenching of the fire, his thirst had only intensified. What—against zill—were a handful of miserable gutter pigeons, four children, and only half of Glinneth? He thrust clenched fists at the perfidious sky . . . and howled.

26

The anticipated attack did not come until an hour before dawn, when least expected. The group plodded in numb silence through dry and diminishing foothills, each curled inward with grief. The moon hung low in the west, partly obscured by haze over the distant plain.

Suddenly, Treese galloped from his rear-guard position. "Riders approaching—hard! Maybe ten, but not many more. We got a minute or so to hide."

Driss roused from his reverie. "Keltie, ride ahead and tell Jonn, and the two of you hide to the left. Bren, take the team left, too. There's cover in there. Unhitch and move the horses further back. Thilrec, you and Rolind take the women away from the horses. Amarl, to the right with the mules. Treese, scratch out tracks and help Bren with the wagon. I'll try to draw the riders down the road and then get back somehow. Stay quiet as you can!"

The party melted into the gloom. Driss watched anxiously from the road and gauged the approaching horsemen. At the right instant, he clapped heels to Glue and took off, whistling and shouting behind an imaginary band. He smiled with grim satisfaction on hearing noisy drunkards follow his lead.

A couple of miles down the road, dawn gaining apace, Driss spotted a little-used track down a brushy draw. With a glance behind, he swung onto it, ducking to avoid branches. It turned out to be a foot trail and slow going. Glue, however, was in his element, wriggling through tight places, jogging adroitly over rocky ground.

As day came on, Driss grew nervous. These pursuers, unlike the earlier ones, had caught the turn. Even worse, he found himself in a cut that rose steeply on both sides. There was no veering from the stony runoff down the middle; the only way lay straight ahead. He slithered through undergrowth, face tight to his horse's neck, finally emerging on a dry riverbed that lay deep within a narrow gulch.

Here unease transmogrified into raw fear. A footbridge supported by rough stone pillars had once spanned the gulch. The near section of this had rotted away and had been replaced by a single thick plank, fifteen feet long but only a foot wide. For Driss it might as well have been a tightrope.

His legs trembled like sarrel leaves in a storm. The bank was sheer, the drop stomach wrenching, and he—who had scorned such in Garrick—discovered himself a dry-mouthed coward.

And what of Glue? Even if he could bring himself to walk across, he couldn't manage an obstinate beast, too. He'd hate to lose the horse, and despite his predicament he almost laughed. For all his churlishness, Glue had proved a bargain, even at the price of a Wooten cloak.

Time, though, was running out. Though slower than Driss in getting through, the approaching band left him only minutes to act. He placed a tentative foot on the plank but drew back immediately, knees jelly.

I can't do it! I'll fight Sigurth's men with bare hands if I have to, but I can't go across this plank!

But the horrors of the previous night flashed before him. His flesh quailed at the crashing close behind. *I've got to cross, if it's on hands and knees!*

With a final, regretful pat to Glue—repaid by flattened ears—he closed his eyes and drew a breath, trying to rein in his racing heart. He willed himself onto the plank.

At that instant, high on the scrubby hill to his left, a shepherd's pipe began a haunting melody strung with poignant, twisting intervals. The music had an immediate, curious effect. No longer did Driss see the yawning abyss. Afterward, he could not have said whether the music simply fixed his mind, blotting out everything else, or if it created an illusion of water-scoured rocks rising level with the plank, the way an unfocused stare imposes a raised dimension on a flat pattern. Whatever it was, he walked across easily, despite the plank's sway and hollow clatter. The main part of the bridge, though wider, had no rail; it too swung and rattled. Driss pressed on to the far side, heart in mouth, then tumbled gasping to the ground.

A soft nudge made him yelp in panic. Glue stood over him, ears flicking with curiosity.

Driss laughed hysterically and threw his arms around the horse's neck. "You were the clatter! Am I the only coward?"

He saw movement across the gulch, but the band had not quite broken through the underbrush. "Even across is not safe," he decided grimly. "If that piper will only keep up, I just might do it!"

Looping the reins over a boulder to prevent the horse from following, and pragmatically setting aside questions of musical delusion, he retraced his steps to wrestle with the heavy plank. The piper played, the mirage held, and the board tumbled just as the lead rider reached the bank.

Bullets whistled as Driss negotiated the return trip, but he leaped on Glue, staying low in the saddle.

Across the gulch, the plaintive tune melted into the sun-drenched hillside.

"Oh, one thing more." Treese straightened wearily as he wound up his report.

Driss sat on a rock, head on hands and staring at the ground.

"I think Rolind's going ditsy."

Driss grunted without looking up. "What makes you think he's any worse than the rest of us?"

"Well, the toys, for one thing. He carries them—everywhere. Won't go ten feet from them."

"So? He made them. Not too irregular, under the circumstances."

"It's the old doll and crico ring, not the new. He burned the ones he made. He's also taken to seeing things. Talks to people who aren't there."

"Humph! Steph talks to—" Driss stopped abruptly, his fingers tightening convulsively on his head.

After an uncomfortable silence, Treese sighed and put his hand on Driss's shoulder. "Get some sleep, Driss. The rest of us have dozed, enough to keep going. We need to push on toward Chadwich to get food and something for the animals. There's not enough forage for the work they're doing."

Driss looked up with bloodshot eyes. "Treese, is it worth it? Why are we going on?"

Treese gave him an inscrutable look, then turned away. "Get some sleep."

Not till long afterward did Driss ponder the significance of the "shincracker's" touch.

Jonn insisted that Driss ride in the wagon, setting aside protests. Amarl was not above riding Glue and jumped at this chance to get out of the wagon. "Rolind's gettin' creepy!" he muttered to Thilrec as they hitched the team. "Talks about 'the recent campaign' to who knows who. Looks right past you and carries on this long, doodily conversation!"

Driss had trouble sleeping, as had the others. Never again would he hear a youngster cry without shuddering. It didn't help to be shut in with Griselle and Celine's grief, but they had to be somewhere.

No meaning in it, not one damned shred. Not like those kids back in Lorenth trying to save their grandmother. That at least made some sense. But this ... Why ... why? Benzel and Vilda, Nessa and Steph were children he'd loved and played with and corrected when they needed it. He had *known* these kids. He couldn't shrug and walk away from this tragedy, leaving strangers to bear their pain as best they could. This was his pain.

Horrible things happened to children all the time. He knew that. He'd known it when he peered down that dreadful earthcrack, full of bones, human bones, *small* human bones. The amphitheater with its raised platform, a place for hundreds, maybe thousands of people to watch children being thrown into an earthcrack. Was that connected with zill, too? Or was it just another of Sigurth's infinite abominations? If he'd had any sense at all, he'd have turned the group around right then and headed back to Swendia.

What holiday had Sigurth corrupted for his earthcrack celebration? He twisted Middle Night with its beautiful symbol of candles into an obscenity, a horror. *Claeman isn't like Sigurth. An adversary, yes, but not like Sigurth. Celine at the basket shop with the Russetmen and little girl—she saw the difference. And that Russet soldier on the shale slide. He had every right to run me down for suspicious activities. But no—he saluted me. Sigurth's men would've heaved rocks.*

Driss rolled over, trying to block out Griselle's empty wailing and Celine's tuneless dirge at the other end of the wagon.

Even Glinneth rose specter-like to condemn him. What had become of him? Driss closed his eyes. *If he's dead, I'm to blame. I killed him. Death by a jumped conclusion at the grove. Connecting there might've made all the difference. Glinneth, Glinneth . . . I didn't know! I should have, though. Scars. That's the clue. I should've known way back. Sigurth—soldier, commander-in-chief of all T'ribboners—has no scars.*

Vilda knew your scars. You called them "marks of love." "My enemy made them out of hatred," you said, "but I bear them in love. Sometimes even good soldiers can't keep enemies from children, but the marks remind me to do my best."

Oh, Glinneth! You did your best to help us, but what did I do? Threw a spoiled-brat tantrum. Sold you to Sigurth. Jumped at his bait and fell flat on the wrong side.

The wrong side . . . What's the right side? Which side had Glinneth been on? Against Sigurth—that's clear. And he had been with Russetmen heading north. Driss winced as under a sharp lash. *But he wasn't against me, and I'd bet anything he knew I'm in Arlony to rob Claeman. For certain he knew I sold him out. With Glinneth gone, I'm alone, alone against both Sigurth and Claeman. One destroys; the other watches . . . waits . . .*

Well, I'm for Drissan! I'll keep going. Like the general at Harloon Paddock, I'll fight through to the rosillum and laugh at 'em all. I won't give up my dream!

He dropped into an uneasy slumber and endured again the whole hideous nightmare. He was riding through darkness toward a fire-belching earthcrack. Benzel and Vilda were on the point of being thrown in, but Steph and Nessa were trying to hold them, screaming for Driss. His horse that was somehow Glinneth made torturous progress through a thick, viscous substance, and the children's shrieks grew unbearable. When

Driss could take no more, he threw himself off the horse and struggled toward a goblet of rosillum. But as he grasped the delicate stem, zill boiled down its gleaming sides and began to melt his hand. He watched in disbelief as his fingers, then palm and wrist twinkled painlessly into nothingness. Slavering wolfcats snarled at his heels, herding him along an erratic path toward an impenetrable orange net. He could not stop, he could not escape. As he writhed under the inexorable orange, his screams joined those of the children, reverberating . . . beating upon him . . .

"Drissan, Drissan . . . don't! Please don't!" Celine held him in her arms, and the two lay sobbing as the wagon jounced along the desolate road.

27

"The tinker and his woman—both put to bed with a shovel nigh a year or more. Some old mother fried 'em a mess of fancy mushrooms." The red-tongued hag cackled, thin nose hanging like a dried kuhnel pod. "I must git me that recipe. He, he, he!"

Shuddering uncontrollably, Charri turned from the old woman's hovel, her stomach twisting. The tinker's wife—her last solid lead—dead! No family, no relatives, at least none the old crock would tell her about.

She stumbled along a garbage-strewn street in this forsaken corner of Chadwich and slumped behind a tumbledown horse shed, scarcely mindful of the composition of the mound on which she sat. For these many miles, Chadwich had been a lodestone, the magnetic force of hope. Now the stone had crumbled, the fine pieces drifting out of reach in the cyclonic pitch of this fevered city.

Alone. Nowhere to go in a place where hardly anyone stood still. No one to turn to: no one could be trusted. Little food amidst a glittering banquet. Little money in a boomtown made rich on liggeth, where even miners—those lucky enough to survive—lived in luxury. Not even a plan, where schemes simmered over fires of greed.

Her fleeting contact with Glinneth had touched off hope, but unless she could find him again, the remaining embers would turn to ash.

When she started out, her quest for a name had seemed dangerous but reasonable. Here, though, against the starkness of Chadwich, it appeared silly, foolish. Why did she even need a name? She'd answered to Charri for nearly twenty-four years; why put herself through more pain and struggle?

Glinneth told her she had a name. "Go to my home," he said. Go . . . but where, and how? Short of stealing, she could eat for only a few more days. Even if she took to begging, would anyone in this self-absorbed city give her so much as a handful of the rotted manure on which she sat?

She stared unseeing at a half-dozen woe birds pecking the base of the pile. *Just go.* He had not said go back or up or down; should she keep going west? She couldn't go back, not through that dreadful, fire-tormented region.

Driss was heading west, too . . .

She rose from the tangle of weeds that had fed off the ancient heap and walked hurriedly as though to flee the furnace of emotion within her that no amount of self-control seemed able to put out. Driss . . . Driss. In her thoughts, in every pair of guida boots, in passing horsemen. And always in her dreams, leaning toward her but never quite touching her lips. He never would, of course. Even Uncle wouldn't. "That mouth is fit for only one thing," he said. Would Driss think the same? Would she mind it less if it were Driss instead of Uncle? What would she be willing to do for Driss?

Shame rose in her face and commanded her thoughts to stop. Was this corrupt city affecting her, leading her step by step into its own depravity?

Most of the passing faces seemed joyless, despite plush robes, gold chains, and gemstones set in rosillum. Almost everyone's skin carried a yellow cast, the deadly kiss of liggeth.

An ugly city, Chadwich, for all its opulence. Here, ninety-one years ago, on the eastern edge of a vast plain between two ranges of mountains, the Great Earthquake forever altered what had been a quiet, pastoral region and started a new calendar. Throughout the city one could still see rocky extrusions jutting inappropriately—broken bones that would never heal.

Man-made ugliness abounded, as well. Immediately following the quake, a flock of enterprising vultures had converged, wheeling over the lingering diastrophic tremors, impatient to scavenge liggeth from the torn and tortured earth. Entrepreneurs threw up buildings of haphazard design that time and layers of soot had not improved. The leathery, drought-loving trees that grew in this region had quietly succumbed to fumes and the trample of commerce, and now their skeletons dotted the streets, grotesque monuments to the town's mad lust for liggeth, money, and sex. Even the tough, stringy plains grass, once eager to bind up wounded soil, had relinquished the city to slow disintegration.

Against Chadwick's frenetic bustle, Charri had neither destination nor purpose, and a lone woman in such a city needed both. Roanna, silly as she'd been, had at least made her less vulnerable.

Poor Roanna. What had become of her? After hunting as long as she dared through the village to which she'd sent the child, Charri could only hope that nothing worse than a thickheaded farm lad had lured her away. She tried to silence the niggling accusation that she had wanted Roanna out of the way when Glinneth came.

Charri had been warned. How could she have forgotten those frightening words overheard on her way for water in Lorenth? "She'd be a prize, that girl," the Russet soldier had said. "Make sure she don't get outta sight."

She had forgotten that someone was watching the girl and had let her go without thinking. Would she now have two phantoms stalking her? The village lay a scarce mile from the kung grove. Charri had seen it nestled against the hill and had watched nearly the entire way as Roanna appeared and disappeared among winding contours. No one was on the road, no hint of trouble anywhere. The river of destruction that had swept them along the previous day was staying within the banks of distant, more well-traveled roads. There in that peaceful backwater, danger seemed remote.

When Charri herself had reached the hamlet, nothing suggested an alternative to the farm-lad theory. The unthinkable simply hadn't occurred to her. Here in Chadwick, though, the unthinkable screamed from every side. A lineup of sad-eyed girls in front of a gaming house put a new spin on Durk's ominous warnings. Passing men whistled and joked or pretended to check the game schedule. The girls strutted and fanned their goods, saucily drawing their tongues in and out. The bolder ones tackled a potential client with a kiss and a leg wrap, hoping for the magic whisper, "Tonight, love!"

Charri's eyes held pity. *Look at them. Powerless, flat-chested children. What do they have but feather fans and impudence to hide behind? The things they must have to put up with from their men . . .* She thought again of the shredded, strewn roadway she had driven along with Durk. *Yes, there are things worse than anything I've had to . . . than Uncle . . .*

A momentary ebb in traffic sapped the line, and the girls struck tired, mournful postures. Their flesh peddlers, however, were on them in an instant, slapping starch into their thin bodies. Then with eyes still tight on them, the men went back to contending for position, hurling insults across crates of fighting cocks and a string of quarreling pit bulls. Their pecking order seemed proportional to the degree of fear they struck in their girls. Charri closed her eyes against the harrowing images she'd seen along the way. Why—*why* had she given up so quickly on Roanna?

When she opened them again, she saw a rakish, fair-haired man across the street, watching her. A dark robe edged with spun gold fell partway over breeches of the softest fawn. It sat comfortably on broad shoulders accented by wide, intricately plaited ribbons. With casual urbanity he stood, foot crossed, a mocking smile twisting his handsome face.

Charri started and turned away, pulling at her shawl. She hurried in the opposite direction, but with no place to go, she stopped, only to see him even closer, this time leaning against the pocked wall of an abandoned shop.

She whirled in panic. Which way was west, which the quickest route out of Chadwich, no matter what direction? She tried again to escape, but a dozen steps found her way blocked, the stranger's smile still taunting her.

"Where go you, my pretty? Have you lost your way? Perhaps I can help." His voice, facetiously gentle, abraded every nerve. Where had she heard it?

She tried to turn away, but his hand caught her arm, twisting it just enough to still her.

"Ah, my dear, you must be careful in a town such as this. One as comely as you is in jeopardy. You need protection, someone to see you through hard times, hard places." He pulled the shawl from her face, and Charri felt she'd been stripped naked. She returned stare for stare, head held high, trying not to panic.

"Charri."

His slimy familiarity made her skin crawl. Who was he? How did he know her name? Where . . . ?

"Charri. How beautiful . . . such smooth, exquisite skin."

His hand played around the edges of her scar, and she steeled herself against its searing heat.

Leaning close, he whispered conspiratorially, "You have no name," then stood back to survey its effect.

Her eyes widened, her heart pounded, but she remained stiff and silent.

"Come, my dear, not only shall you have a name, you shall wear a queen's garment, eat at my table, be at ease in my mansion. Did Glinneth promise that? He has been—shall we say—incapacitated, you know. He sent me to take care of you. Even your companion, silly child, is no longer with you, her foolishness put to . . . practical use. But we won't go into that now."

Before the words had time to sink in, he continued his thrusts.

"I know something else, too," he murmured. "That small boy with a collar around his neck, a collar of ribbons, beautifully plaited, marking him for . . . shall we say, a special purpose. You remember him, don't you? The poor lad wanted help, but you pushed him away." His voice rose to a mocking falsetto. "'I have nothing to give!' you said."

Charri's face went white and buildings began to spin.

"Charri, my dear, don't take on so. What sort of life do you suppose he had at the tavern, hm? You saw his condition. But the ribbon collar—yes. The mark of emancipation to a higher destiny. From the dust of his wretched bones flows the roseate nectar of *zill.* Surely, you'd agree that the unparalleled pleasures of zill are worth the loss of such a miserable scrap of humanity."

Charri clenched her teeth and eyes against the surge of memory, a tidal-wave recollection long suppressed. She'd been five at the time. In one dreadful hour she observed just what the "unparalleled pleasures" of zill could do. Rozil, her guardian called it, not zill. But it was zill, she was sure. She herself had been overlooked in the general mayhem, tucked as she was in a tiny nook of refuge. For what seemed an eternity of blood and screaming, blended with bellowed ecstasy, she had held her breath and chewed her fist to fight back her own screams. *Unparalleled pleasure...*

"My dear, you look ill. I'm here to help you. I would never turn you away. Besides, what recourse have you?" He toyed with her hair and neck.

Automatically, woodenly, Charri clutched her shawl tighter, if only to forfend nausea.

"Your love has no use for you. Drissan is busy chasing the wind. With the women he's accustomed to, do you suppose he'd have interest in the likes of you?" Again, he fondled her face. This time his fingers froze her skin.

"Come along, my pet. I can claim you, you know; that's what you want, isn't it? I'll more than make up for all you've lost—your baby, your love, your hope, your name . . . your self. You shall have money, fine clothes, power over rich and influential men. Just say the word, and it will happen this very day. Will you come?"

His eyes glittered, but he stood back to allow her room.

Charri remained paralyzed, a block of ice, unable to move, to think, to respond. He had stripped her beyond nakedness. He saw her; he knew her, knew her thoughts, knew about zill. How? *How* did he know? The old crone? Roanna? *Please let me go!* And why such an offer? She was not rich or beautiful or influential. Was she just a challenge, a conquest to laugh over in public latrines? Yes, that's where she'd heard the voice. *Please, please...*

As she tottered there in her shattered state, the man suddenly seemed less offensive, certainly strong, virile, overwhelmingly attractive.

The third man.

One of the three she trusted implicitly, one she could not trust, and one she feared almost to the point of trust. Whatever his motive, this one would do as he said, give what he promised. As false and hideous as he was, she could feel it; she could depend upon it. Glinneth, on the other hand . . . *Glinneth, what happened? Are you even alive?* At best, he was a shimmering mirage, Driss a silk-seed blown before the wind. Desperation demanded dependability, no matter how packaged. Was despair less hungry?

Not daring to raise her eyes higher, she studied the man's feet with their guida boots, so like Driss's, the soft fawn breeches sheathing thigh and leg muscles. A man's legs.

Step by step . . .

She shuddered. What was she *thinking?* Coming from within herself, it frightened her more than anything the man had said, more than her thoughts about Driss. That furnace, at least, had dampened to a controllable flame. But this horror before her . . . That she could be taken in by a fine robe—a robe cloaking, not bulging thigh muscles, but charred bones of dead children. Not just the waif she had turned away, but beyond him, bones and dead children everywhere: innocents stumbling into a violence that consumes them and discards the remains like grape seeds spat to the wind.

She drew a trembling breath. What she had already lost, already done, could never be found or undone. But deep under her hunger and weariness, there was more—however little it might amount to—still more to lose. She looked at him, wanting to shout but only managing a whisper.

"No."

Turning quickly, she hurried away, covering her face as she ran.

Rasping laughter echoed behind her. "I'll see you again, without doubt. Just ask for Sigurth!"

28

"It's as simple as that: with no feed for the animals, we start losing them. Floxie was fat as a wine barrel at the start. Now look at his ribs. His hooves are sore."

"I know, I know, Treese." Driss rubbed his head uncomfortably. "But what do we do? We could get rid of some and have fewer mouths, but we're barely getting by as it is. We need the team and saddle horses, and without the mules, we can't haul rosillum. So what's the answer?"

Treese shrugged glumly. "I dunno. I notice your fleabag isn't suffering any."

"You want him in exchange for Floxie?" Driss snapped. You wouldn't think of swapping a few weeks ago. Maybe you'd like to take over the whole expedition and—"

"Cut it—both of you!" Jonn snapped. "We got problems enough without bitching. We have to go into Chadwich for food; we'll get horse feed, too."

"Go right ahead," Treese retorted, striding off. "I'm taking a nap."

"Oh, great!" Driss exploded. "Take a nap and leave three of us to haul food and horse feed! You know we can't take the team, and the—"

"Stow it, Driss." Jonn pulled him back. "Let him sleep."

Driss turned on Jonn. "Get your hands off me! I'm in charge, and he'll go if I have to kick his shins from here to there!"

Jonn looked at him impassively, then shrugged and turned away. "Keltie and I are riding to Chadwich. If you want to stay and fight it out with Treese, I'll put Amarl on Glue. A knucklehead teenager is better than two adult brats any day."

The argument heated up. Griselle, never quick to read the weather, chose the moment of Treese's passage for a fresh outburst of grief, with unfortunate results. Celine moved in with fire in her eyes, and the conflagration spread. But while tempers blistered, Celine withdrew into her own well-worn lament.

"Oh, children, children . . .
Nessa, my beautiful girl-child,
You dreamed your death; you saw it coming.
Benzel . . . Vilda . . . Steph . . .
You trusted us;
we let you down.
Some parents kick their babies,
let them lie in filth.
We don't do that. We sent you away,
let them steal you.
Oh, children, little ones everywhere,
Why must you suffer so?"

Treese, having transformed Griselle's grief into clawing, spitting anger, now came at Celine, teeth gritted, hand raised. Jonn was there in an instant, eyes blazing. His hot grip on Treese's wrist erased the height difference between the two men, and after a momentary stare-down, Treese broke free and slouched away.

In the end it was Jonn who stayed to oversee the smoldering peace, letting Bren take his mare.

Driss, Bren, and Keltie rode off in stony silence.

While still a good distance from Chadwich, the plain began to mutate into the rounded mounds that marked the hem of major earthquake damage. What little rain fell in this region had worn deep rivulets in these multi-colored heaps, softening sharp edges, melting hills into desert bitterness.

Most of the active liggeth mines lay to the north and west of Chadwich, but on this southeast approach the men found traces of aborted mining ventures. An old road wound past decayed mine shafts, collapsed shacks, and mountains of mining rubble.

A broad, rocky jumble marked a fifty-foot drop where the ground had split off. Suddenly, Bren pulled up and pointed to the right. "Look!" he whispered.

Atop the escarpment, a lone rider sat looking intently at smoke or dust rising from below.

Driss stiffened. "A Russetman! Are there others?"

They could see no one else.

"I don't think he's spotted us," said Keltie. "If we keep goin', quiet like, we can hide in those rocks up ahead."

"But what then?" asked Driss. "Do we wait till he goes away, or do we try to slip by? And how much cover will those rocks give? Looks like the trail barely squeezes through."

"Well, so what?" Keltie returned with a touch of annoyance. "Why would he want us, anyway? Somethin' special about us that every last Russetman in the country has nothin' to do but chase us? Seems to me you're gettin' a bit—"

"Shut up!" returned Driss savagely, making Keltie jump. "We're not taking chances. Just do as I say."

"Okay, okay!" Keltie shrugged.

They moved cautiously toward the towering rocks that guarded a sharp bend in the trail. As Driss had suspected, they found no place to hide. The trail wound along the base of the cliff in full sight of the Russet soldier. They could either turn back and make a wide detour around the rocks or keep going and hope he wasn't interested.

While pondering their situation, they moved to an overlook that opened on the whole Chadwich panorama. The city rose in the distance, the road staggering toward it through a hodgepodge of earthquake and mining debris. Below them, tight to the cliff, lay an old outpost or supply depot with the remains of what might have been a large storehouse. The only remnant was a single wall propped by a sagging timber. A blackened fire pit some yards away had evidently consumed the other walls.

Wind-fanned flames from this pit now pursued smoke this way and that. A metal rod lay propped on a rock, one end in the fire. Several figures moved about—three men and a boy not much smaller than Amarl. The lad was naked, the object of a brutal chase by the men, one of whom wielded a long, cattle-driver's whip.

Their plan was clear. The remaining wall, perpendicular to the cliff and tied to it by impenetrable thornbush, formed enough of a box to guarantee their prey. Therefore, they were in no hurry. Laughing, they feinted, cracked the whip alarmingly, then fell back to enjoy the screams and pleas of their quarry.

Keltie's face became tight and red. "I'll kill 'em!"

He seemed about to attempt a single-handed rescue. Driss put a hand on his arm. "Wait. You're too angry to think straight."

Keltie continued to stare, breathing heavily and jiggling his foot abstractedly in the stirrup.

Driss's shoulders sagged. He knew his own pain and knew Keltie's to be every bit as bad. Keltie had loved the kids. He had played tricks on them and used them to play tricks on everyone else. He had wept unashamedly that terrible night as they mobilized for flight. Maybe the three of them could rescue the boy below, but they'd have to work out a plan. And there was the Russetman to consider.

Every so often, one of the men below went to the fire to inspect the rod that looked like a brand with two outwardly curved prongs.

"You know what that is, don't you?" Bren muttered.

Driss shook his head. "No, what?"

"A V-iron."

"V-iron? What's that?"

"Hah!" Keltie leaned forward, sudden interest breaking up anger. "Hah! So that's what Amarl meant with his 'you-know-whats'! I couldn't figure what he was talkin' about. That's all he'd say—'you know, you know what.' But now—"

"Yes," Driss broke in, drawing a big breath. "I know what, all right! This kid is about to be awarded the permanent badge of a male bitch."

They sat silent, eyes riveted on the scene below. Keltie's foot reverted to jiggling.

A sudden noise brought their heads around. The Russet soldier was bearing down at a fast gallop. The men sat frozen, not knowing whether to flee down the trail or to take him on. But before they could decide, they heard the rider's low, hoarse cry, "Way for Claeman! Way for Claeman!"

The men scrambled clear as best they could. The soldier swept past, eyes glinting fiercely.

"Whoosh!" exclaimed Keltie. "See, I told you—"

"Shut up!" Driss snapped. "Move out of the way. I can't see."

They watched the rider detour from the trail. He moved carefully behind boulders to remain hidden from the men below. At the bottom he stopped to watch the fox-and-rabbit chase once again, stroking his impatient horse. Then, wrapping the reins around his saddle horn, he clapped heels to his mount and disappeared behind a boulder for an instant. When he reappeared, he was low on the horse's neck, heading straight for the whip. This he grabbed, bowling over the wielder. Then he turned his horse back toward the boy. The terrified lad tried to run, but the soldier grabbed him and heaved him over his thigh and the horse's neck. With his whip hand he pulled the horse to an uneasy standstill. The surprised bullies rallied and moved toward him in pursuit. But at the right instant, he swung around and galloped parallel to the long, sagging wall. The whip flashed out and grabbed the lone supporting timber. With a yank that nearly brought horse, rider, and passenger to the ground, the timber gave way, and the wall came down like a giant fly swatter on three angry bees.

The spectators sat stunned. Bren and Driss said nothing, and Keltie could say only, "Man! Man!"

The Russetman continued a few hundred feet before stopping to check for action behind him. Then he slid off his horse and eased the boy to the ground, cradling him in his arms. After a moment he rummaged through his saddlebag, pulling out a water jug and a garment of some sort. As the boy drank long, the soldier continued to kneel, examining him for injuries. With great tenderness, he drew the garment over the lad, then helped him into the saddle and clambered up behind, arms around him in support.

As the two rode off toward Chadwich, Driss headed Glue down the trail. "Let's get out of here before those slime snakes crawl out from under the wall."

Keltie could not stop talking about the astonishing feat of courage and horsemanship. Bren responded in kind, but Driss remained silent and grim.

"What's the matter?" Keltie asked finally. "You sore about somethin'? Did you want the three grawnies to get their boy?"

"Of course not."

"You jealous of the Russetman? You couldn't a done that."

"No, I'm not," Driss snapped. But after a moment, he cleared his throat, his voice rough. "Where was he when our kids needed him?"

Keltie's jaw clamped shut.

29

A sulphurous cloud—the banner of liggeth—hovered over Chadwich. As a fuel, liggeth surpassed coal in efficiency and was scarce enough to justify its price. Those connected with mining in any way had instant wealth. And of course, the miner that hit a pocket of rosillum could live two lifetimes with no financial worries.

With so much money around, food prices were high. Bren shook his head over the cost of flour and fool beans, the staples Thilrec depended on to stretch their shrinking purse. Fruit and vegetables required a king's ransom, and even common foods lay beyond their reach. "Might's well eat our money!" Keltie grumbled.

Chadwich had no marketplace like Lorenth, no mosaic of booths, rugs, and market-drunk children. Instead, gilded shops lined the streets, each with its special odor of shoes, candles, spices, or cloth. Merchants hid deep inside, clinging to the illusion of safety, while thieves prowled the city—cats after grain-fed birds.

As the men moved from store to store, an endless parade of fine horses and carriages helped alleviate cost-of-eating depression. Light runabouts; velvet-cushioned coaches with high-stepping teams; one-man sulkies behind long-legged trotters. Keltie's eyes bugged. "Forget shoppin'! Who needs food when you got this to look at?"

They had to have food, though, and in desperation bought a three-measure sack of flour and a half-kol of beans, rehearsing their defense before Thilrec.

The route back to the horses took them past houses painted in broad, garish stripes. "Stripes and flat roofs," Keltie said. "All they need is bows to make 'em into presents. Not every roof is flat, but I don't remember seein' any in Lorenth or Greentree or other towns."

"Less snow here," said Driss, "so you don't need pitched roofs. In Cassia where it's hotter, they'll probably all be flat."

On passing the courtyard of a high-toned stable, their eyes were drawn to a cream-colored carriage receiving a final polish at the hands of a coachman in matching livery. The men moved in for a closer look and stood in awe. Keltie reached out reverently toward the gleaming surface but jumped back at a crusty bark from the lackey.

Just then, two men brought forth a pair of dancing, straining horses—a heavy carriage breed, deep gold with creamy manes and intricately braided tails. "Cresserlains, maybe?" Bren murmured incredulously. Dark, gold-trimmed harness complemented the horses' color. With difficulty, the three attendants backed the high-strung team into position and fastened the traces.

Bren fairly slavered. "What wouldn't I give to hold those reins!" he moaned. "Just one quick spin around the square."

After horses and attendants had expressed mutual contempt for each other, the carriage passed through the gateway to make entrance on the world, a magnificent spectacle that brought stares from even the jaded inhabitants of Chadwich.

"What tycoon is that rig for, I wonder?" Driss mused. "Let's see where it's headed. We got time."

After a short distance, the team pulled up in front of a small, luxurious house. "No stripes!" Bren exclaimed. "And a proper roof."

"She better be ready!" the coachman growled. "This pair takes to standing like a pig takes to dancing."

The silver-studded door opened almost immediately, and a dark-haired woman swept toward the carriage. Her dress, white with black piping across the bodice, fell in folds under a white velvet cloak. A high collar framed the marble of her skin. She stopped before entering the carriage and turned as though posing on cue for an audience.

Driss and Bren gasped simultaneously. "Rona!"

She spotted them at the same moment and stepped toward them with programmed grace. "Drissan! *Wilcuma!* How nice to see you! And Keltie . . . Bren. Where are the others? Are they with you?"

Driss's heart pounded as he took the heavily ringed hand. "How are you, Rona? You've done well, I see."

"That's sayin' half a word!" Keltie muttered.

"Oh, yes. Very well." Rona laughed. "I made my . . . connections, as I told you—you did get my note?—and here I am."

Her smile was too bright, her laugh too forced. Driss frowned.

By this time, the horses had failed the standing test, and Rona turned in annoyance. "Candor, can't you keep those beasts still, or at least on the ground? They're a disgrace! Bren, dear," she purred, turning to the men, "why don't you show Candor how such horses are to be managed. Get them straightened out while we talk a few moments. Then we'll all go for a ride."

Bren was on the seat and holding the embossed reins before the coachman had time to switch execrations from horses to mistress. With practiced hand he eased the team down the street in a high-stepping trot, chuckling at his dirty clothing and unkempt appearance against such equipage. He exchanged no words with the vinegar coachman and simply gave himself over to the excellence of the animals and his skill in handling them. After as wide a circle as he could justify, he brought them back at a flashy, controlled canter and pulled up with style.

"Ah, Bren, if only I had someone like you! All you lack is the proper attire. I don't suppose you could be lured from this mad junket of Driss's to become my personal horse manager. Ah, well—" She turned deliberately from the covetousness in Bren's eyes. "We'll talk of it later. Take us for a ride now. I don't really know where. This place is so—"

She stopped abruptly and chewed her lip, then turned to Driss for help in entering the carriage, tittering over fancied awkwardness.

Her prattle both annoyed and worried Driss. She had obviously risen in the world, but something was wrong. She would say nothing about how she'd come into such opulence, and she seemed to be trying hard to turn him from his plans. "I know you want rosillum, Driss, but if you stay here, you'll have everything rosillum could give and more, even."

He took her hand mischievously. "Does the 'more' include you?"

With a tight smile she changed the subject by asking after the others.

Driss's face clouded. "They're doing okay. We . . . lost the children on Middle Night, and the women . . . all of us took it hard."

Rona looked straight ahead. "Yes . . . I heard about that, and about Gl—" She broke off abruptly, then murmured mechanically, "I'm sorry."

Driss swung around. "How did you hear about it?"

She looked away, rubbing her fingers nervously. "It's—common knowledge; you know how things get around. Bren, darling—" She leaned forward. "Driss tells me you're low on horse feed. Stop ahead, on the right, at that loading platform. We'll order grain. How many bags can you take?"

Keltie and Driss spoke in unison. "Two apiece?"

"Jangles can manage that," Bren said, "but I doubt Glue could, and Lina bucks under extra weight. Though the difference between my weight and Jonn's would give us another bag." He laughed wryly "We might get away with five, but they'll slow us down. Even four is better than what we have. We have to think of the flour and beans, too."

"Where did you leave your horses? I'll have the bags delivered there. Now." She smiled fetchingly. "Let's go someplace where we can eat and talk—if we can pry Bren away from the carriage!"

Driss nodded vaguely, annoyed by Bren's fawning reverence.

Rona led them up a narrow stone staircase to a room above a wine shop. "Here we are." She beamed, allowing the men to precede her.

The room was tiny and dark, lit only by six wall lamps. It could not have accommodated more than its one camblor table and half-dozen chairs. Near the shuttered window a low stand held a striking arrangement of pink and lavender flowers. Above a sideboard, the only other piece of furniture, a purple and blue tapestry depicted the contorted grace of a dying stag. Overhead, carved camblor beams made a final statement of elegance.

When they stepped into the room, Rona frowned, and a pair of sullen girls jumped apprehensively from their table preparations. "You know I dislike stuffy rooms!" Rona said. She swept to the window and threw open the inlaid panels, almost knocking over the bouquet.

The maids turned away miserably.

"I simply can't believe—" she began, then stopped abruptly and shrugged apologetically. "Well, now we can at least see what we're eating."

The table was laid for intimate dining, and as they drew back their chairs, Driss's eyes lit at sight of his favorite foods, superbly prepared. "Look at this! Even Thilrec would have to hustle to match this meal!"

Despite the excellent food, something bothered Driss, something he couldn't put his finger on. He shook it off, however, and gave himself to repairing an empty stomach.

Between courses, Rona again tried to dissuade him from his journey. "I've always admired your ability, Driss. You'd be at the top in no time. All the money, all the power a man could crave. You'd lack nothing, not even fine horses," she added, tipping her head coyly at Bren.

Bren bent toward her hungrily. Driss kicked him under the table.

"You're crazy!" Driss responded to Rona. "Here I am, within inches of my dream, and you want me to give it up. Sure, there are things here and money to be had in liggeth, but I'd be a fool to quit now for second best."

"But it's not second best, Driss. Like I said in my note, it's the business deal of a lifetime, better than your dream could ever be. You have to admit—your way hasn't gone awfully well."

That much he did have to admit—to himself, but not to Rona.

"Where will you go from here?"

Driss patted her condescendingly. "No good, honey: we don't talk about that—remember?"

"Well, stay away from Cassia. There's a war there. The place is swarming with Claeman's men. It's worth your life to walk through town. So they say. I haven't been there myself. You're better off here where it's safe."

"Safe?" Driss said bitterly. "Is any place safe, for that matter? Don't worry about us, Rona. We'll be all right. Just a short jump to the jackpot!"

After they'd eaten and drunk their fill, the servers cleared the table of all but glasses and a new bottle of wine, then withdrew speedily.

Rona opened the bottle and poured three portions, slopping some on the tablecloth. "Come, Driss, Bren, Keltie. Drink to my health or maybe even to the horses." Again, she smiled winsomely at Bren. "After a such a party, don't I deserve a toast?"

Another warning signal went off in Driss. He eyed her closely, noting her unnatural color and unsteady hand. He began to tease. "Rona, my lovely gazelle, you walked out on us; why should we drink to you? Enough that we didn't turn our backs on your finery."

"You're trying to make me angry." She pouted prettily. "But it won't work. Now drink a toast like good boys."

"I'm not thirsty. We've had too much already."

Keltie nudged him. "Come on, Driss; lead a toast and let's get outta here. It'll be heading into morning before we're back, as it is."

Driss, though, put a hand on Keltie's arm. "Rona, what's this wine? Is it zill?" He studied her closely.

She started at the word, but Driss saw only confusion in her face. She knew of zill, he could tell, but not what it was. "All right, we'll drink to you, Rona—after you drink to us. After all, we hauled you part way—got you started, so to speak." He dumped her remaining wine on the tablecloth and refilled the glass from the new bottle.

Rona, mouth frozen in surprise, watched the stain spread under food scraps and rumpled napkins. Her face turned white, then red and awkward. "Driss, you're so funny!" she gabbled with that uncharacteristic, high-pitched laugh. "What'd you do that for? You're teasing me, aren't you, just like you used to. Don't be such a shilly," she went on, suddenly feigning intoxication. "I've had too . . . too *mush*. You never liked me looped. You were alwaysh afraid I might mark you, like somebody we know marked Treeshe. She was drunk, too, you know."

"Who was drunk?" Driss asked, frowning. "Who marked Treese?"

"Oh, you didn't know?" She tittered. "I shoulda . . . I shoulda— Oh, dear boy, we had sush good times together." She draped herself on his shoulder and pawed at him.

When repeated efforts left Driss unmoved and unsmiling, she rose and rushed to the door. "Excuse me—I'm going to be sick!"

As the door slammed, the three looked at each other, then at the wine. "You think it's been messed with?" asked Keltie.

"I'm sure of it," Driss asserted. "This whole business stinks. Come to think of it," he said, the picture suddenly focusing, "she laid for us at the very start. Lured us with the carriage and team, then hooked us by 'just happening' to walk out her front door. She wasn't going anywhere; she was waiting for us, to bring us to this little dinner party. Why else would they have prepared my favorite foods?"

Keltie pushed back his chair suddenly. "Let's get out of here."

Driss, his flesh crawling, remained seated. "She's locked us in—you can bet on that."

30

"A storm's coming. I feel it in my bones!"

"Oh, Rolind, I don't think so." Celine squinted against the sun without any great enthusiasm. "The sky's as clear as it's ever been. I wish one were coming: we need water bad enough." She rubbed her face wearily, hoping the old soldier had switched his worry from an imaginary attack to the weather.

"This storm won't bring water—only tears. We must ready our defenses, see to fortifications. The enemy knows our position and will soon be upon us." He paced crisply around the coarse vegetation of the campsite, crico ring and doll secured under his left arm.

Celine sighed with dull patience. "I don't know what else we can do, Rolind. You already talked to Jonn and Treese, and they're watching. Maybe when Driss and the others get back, they'll have news. This waterhole—if you can call it that—is in the middle of nothing. We'd notice someone coming. Why don't you help Amarl? He's out looking for fodder. See off to the right?"

Celine shook her head as Rolind marched toward the lethargic form in the distance. "I don't know," she sighed to Griselle, who had an armful of precious sticks for their daily fire. "He seems so sure. Do you suppose there's something in what he says? We've had tears enough . . ." Her voice faltered.

"Don't start bawlin' again!" Griselle snapped. "You think you're the only one has lost anything!"

"I wish we hadn't come." Celine's words mirrored the bleak landscape.

"Huh! You think you're the only one thinkin' that? If you hadn't come, I wouldn't of come, and Vilda'd be alive. It's your fault Vilda's dead."

"My fault! You decided to come before I— Oh, never mind." She returned to her inward staring. "Maybe I am to blame. Why did I come? Jonn wouldn't've come if I'd said no, but he wanted to. We needed what rosillum would bring. A bigger house, a wagon that doesn't fall apart every trip to town, clothes for the kids, clothes for us—" She sighed and picked at her skirt. "A little color, a little elegance—something not brown."

"But you always wear brown. You wouldn't be Jonn and Celine if you didn't wear brown."

Celine glanced up to see if Griselle was joking, then fell back into dreariness. "When you can hardly buy shoes for the children . . ."

She straightened and set her jaw, then looked toward the two scavengers on the plain. "I was talking about Rolind."

"You were not. You were talkin' about—"

"No, when he said a storm is coming."

"Huh! Loony as a piepecker. Do you know what he was doin' early this afternoon? Diggin' breastworks, he said. Pilin' rocks and sand and sticks. Sticks, mind you! Anybody knows there aren't enough sticks to build a bird trap, let alone fortifications. Guess what Thilrec had to say about taking over perfectly good firewood!"

"I can guess, all right!" Celine flared. "Thilrec and Amarl ride him to death, and all you do is gabble. No wonder he's strange. Leave him alone!"

"Oh, you stink!"

Griselle inspected a scab on her right elbow, then said, "I wish I could get those toys away! Gives you the creeps the way he guards 'em. That's what he was doin', y'know, with his breastworks. Puts the toys in the hole, then marches up and down in front." She mimed his stiff gait. "He shouldn't have that gun, neither. Maybe he'll start thinkin' we're the enemy!"

"Well, he won't kill many of us," Celine replied tartly. "Jonn says that after those rabbits the other night, we're down to only three or four bullets."

"Well, if he's gotta kill somebody, who could we do without? Not me or Bren. Not Driss. And Thilrec cooks for us. That leaves you, Jonn, Treese, Keltie, and Amarl to stand up to him."

* * *

Traffic outside the wine shop had dwindled, and now only an occasional passerby broke the midnight silence.

Inside the upper room, Driss began laughing soundlessly, holding his sides until tears ran. Keltie and Bren stared, bewildered, until he pointed to the open window.

"Rona may be well constructed, but there's not a lot upstairs! She locked the door but forgot the escape hatch!"

Bren and Keltie ran to the window and peered cautiously over the deserted street. "You're right!" Keltie exclaimed. "Bit of a drop but basically a piece of pie. Even dirt to land on. And I don't see a soul."

"Another trap, maybe?" Bren suggested.

Driss paused, then shrugged. "Could be. If so, it won't matter how quick we fall into it; if not, speed is our best friend. Rona's bound to come back with her boss, and its not too hard to guess who that might be."

"Who's first?" Keltie looked from one to the other, soft light playing across his cleft chin.

"I'll go," Driss offered, but Bren pulled him back.

"You're the brain. If we hit trouble, maybe you can worm out some other way."

Keltie, the heaviest, backed over the sill holding Driss's arms, with Bren anchoring Driss. He dropped silently and rolled but got up quickly, ready to run. Seeing nothing, he motioned.

"Maybe they're waiting till we all get down," Driss said.

Bren grinned. "One way to find out. Here goes!"

He landed on his feet and had hardly straightened when Driss came down beside him. They listened a moment but heard nothing except a carter's lorry rumbling through town.

"Which way?" whispered Keltie. "Wasn't payin' attention before."

Driss hesitated, then pointed, satisfied with Bren's corroborating nod.

They slid quietly through the streets, but as they neared Rona's house, Driss pulled to a halt. Shrieks and whining sobs issued from open windows. "Whoo!" Keltie exclaimed. "She's in top form!"

"At least the action's here," Driss whispered, "and not the upper room. Let's get closer." He shouldered through the hedge around her house.

"You're crazy!" hissed Keltie. "Just askin' for trouble!"

"Ow! Prickly! Maybe so, but it helps to know what size trouble."

Hunkering against the foundation, they rubbed scratched arms and listened to the storm over their heads.

"Get it yourself! I did what I could. At least I know it's not here in Chadwich. He's stubborn. I told you that. What's rosillum to you, anyway?"

Driss smiled grimly. *I was right! She was off-balance with us. Now she's tight as a harp string. Whatever—or whoever—you're afraid of, old girl, you deserve it and more!*

"You? With your tastes?" a man responded. "Belittling rosillum? Really, my dear, you surprise me!"

A second man near the window spoke up. "I keep telling you, sir, we know just where the others are."

Bren poked Driss. "The coachman!" he whispered. "Couldn't miss that cold-blooded—"

"Yes, Candor, I keep hearing you. But you keep forgetting. As much as I want the rosillum— From what Rona says, it could be one of the richest strikes ever. Pockets are rare at best and always small, yet here's as much as twelve people can carry away. But as much as I want that rosillum, I want Driss even more."

"What will you do with him?" Rona quavered. "You promised to set him up and give him—" She broke off with a scream.

Her inquisitor matched volume. "Don't suppose you can lead me by the nose like you could Drissan! You're mine: don't forget it!"

"You lied to me!" Rona shrieked. "You made promises, and now—"

"Promises! I give you a simple task. You fail, then come looking for favors. You could've gotten me the rosillum, you could've gotten me Driss. You failed both tasks." His voice dropped to disgust. "I should've put you on the street at the start. Candor!"

"Yes, sir."

"Now is the time to speak of where the rest of the group is."

"Yes, sir. I know where they are, sir, and I got thirty men ready to ride at a word. A gambler's chance the map's there, anyhow, not on Rona's rabbits. Even if we don't find the map, won't hurt to have the whole bunch in hand."

"Quite right. At very least, they'd dangle handsomely in front of Glinneth."

Driss's heart leaped to his already-tight throat. *What's he saying? Glinneth is alive?*

"Too bad the kids are gone," Candor continued regretfully. "No end of possibilities with children. I been working on this idea, you know. Turn them into weapons. Cute, innocent children. Can be placed anywhere without rousing suspicion. This group, for instance; right now they'd take in any youngster that came along."

"Oh? How weapons and how manufactured?"

"Well, you beat them, deprive them of food and sleep—toughen them, you see. Then start teaching them how to kill and maim, small jobs at first—a bug or a bird, say. They do okay, they get rewarded; if they balk—"

"Candor, you amaze me. You could disgust a pig out of its slop. How long before your men can muster?"

Sunrise, man, sunrise! prompted Driss silently, his heart pounding.

"An hour at most, on target in two."

Damn! "Let's go!" Driss turned, then stopped as Candor went on.

"Do you want us to kill or capture the three here first?"

"No *killing*, Candor." The voice took on overtones of explaining simple facts to a simple mind. "Drissan is nothing to me dead. I want him alive. I want to claim him. And Candor—"

"Yes, sir?"

"If it's not too much of a comedown for your exotic tastes, you may have the two women to do as you want. Killer moms, perhaps—hm?"

The men crept toward a break in the shrubbery, Driss fighting nausea. They did not see another figure on the far side of the house that wriggled through the hedge and ran doubled-over down the street.

They lost time disagreeing over the most direct route to the horses. Driss prevailed, but they came close to bumping into Candor running toward what looked to be a large stable. As he sounded the call, they froze, then slipped by in the ensuing pandemonium as peevish soldiers tumbled out of a dead sleep and tangled with each other.

"Bunch of snakes!" Driss muttered.

Bren grunted. "Vipers—all knotted together. It'll take two hours for 'em just to untangle and get their clothes on."

"Who we dealing with, anyhow—Sigurth or Claeman?" asked Keltie, his voice taut.

Driss looked at him. "What do you mean? That was Sigurth in the house. Didn't you know that?"

"Yeah, I know. But at least one of 'em inside that stable was a Russetman. I saw him."

"You sure?"

"Positive. Dark face, uniform—I know it was."

"Humph. Maybe they've teamed up against us. When Sigurth tosses Rona on the street, maybe Claeman'll send one of his boys to have a go at her. Spread the benefits around."

"Yeah, Rona" Keltie said eagerly, as though glad for something other than the unspeakable to focus on.

"She set us up," Driss said, "then waved my name in front of Sigurth, pretending she cared. Sigurth's right about where she belongs. I'd like to see her tricked out like those tarts by the gaming house . . ." He trailed off, then shrugged. "Sigurth or Claeman—doesn't matter. We got one hour to get our people moving."

They wondered if the horses might have been stolen and breathed a sigh at Jangles soft nicker. They saddled up and stowed their meager purchases, but as they put foot to stirrup, Bren cried, "Wait! The grain!

Driss shook his head. "We don't have time! We're down to less than an hour."

Bren, though, groped stubbornly around a pile of rocks, then crowed. "Here it is! Six bags, two for each horse!"

"Can't do it; it'll kill 'em!" Driss exclaimed. "Especially Glue. They might make it at a walk, but we have to ride too fast."

"We need the grain, Driss." Urgency tightened Bren's voice. "What good is it to save everyone if the horses starve? Take three sacks, anyway, or two maybe, and leave Glue out altogether."

Driss finally agreed to two, if only to prevent further delay. Cumbered with only the flour and fool beans, he went ahead to warn the others.

Jonn was watching when Driss rode in, Glue lathered and trembling and blowing. "Where are Keltie and Bren?" he asked apprehensively.

"They're coming with grain, but we got to move fast. A raiding party is less than an hour behind. Everyone asleep?"

"Yes, but the team's harnessed and horses saddled. When you didn't come, we thought we might need to leave in a hurry. We can be out in fifteen minutes."

It took less than that, even in the dark. By the time Bren and Keltie arrived, the team was hitched, the mules loaded, the bedding stowed. Amarl transferred the grain to the wagon while Bren and Keltie watered their thirsty mounts and prepared to leave.

"Everyone here? Count off: its too dark to see. Where are the women? I want to know where the women are."

"You havin' a hot flash?" said Griselle. "You been wantin' to know every two minutes."

"Where's Rolind?" Celine cried.

"He's not in the wagon?"

"He jumped out when you came, ordering us to sound the trumpet. But I don't know where he went. All day he's been expecting an attack."

"Rolind!" Keltie shouted. "Rolind! We're ready to leave. Hurry!"

Leathery leaves clattered against the silence.

Griselle grabbed Driss's arm. "I bet he's on the other side, at his breastworks. I don't know if you'll get him, though. He'll probably shoot. He's got four bullets, Celine said."

Driss blew an impatient breath. "Keltie, Treese. Let's go. We can't humor him this time."

"No, Driss!" Griselle cried. "Not you! Send Jonn or Amarl. We can't lose—"

"She's *horrible!*" shrieked Celine. "She has it all planned who Rolind should kill! She and Bren—"

"Stop it, both of you!" Driss exploded. "Get in the wagon, and don't say another word. If anyone gets killed, it won't be by either of your say-so."

Grayness in the east had begun to give definition to the scraggly brush that marked the water hole. The three could just make out the ramrod figure pacing back and forth, gun clamped against his side.

"Rolind," Driss called out, "we're—"

"Who goes there?" Rolind swung around, weapon at the ready.

"It's Driss, Treese, and Keltie. Come along, Rolind. We need to retreat in orderly fashion. We want to avoid a rout. Mount the wagon so we can go."

"I'll not retreat. I'll fight to the last man."

Treese strode forward. "Rolind, let's have the gun. This isn't a game were playing."

"War is no game, son!" the old man roared. "Stand or I'll fire!"

Treese continued on but dropped in consternation when Rolind fired into the air.

"Rolind!" Driss bawled. "You can't shoot us! Were your friends!"

Jonn and Bren ran up, ignoring the outcry from Celine and Griselle. "What's he doing?"

"Where's the other gun?" Driss asked Jonn.

"In the wagon, but it won't do any good. He's got the bullets, what there are of them. One less now."

"Couldn't we fake it?" Bren asked.

Jonn shook his head. "It would only get him thinking we really are the enemy."

Driss sighed, looking anxiously toward Chadwich. "We can't wait. No sign of them yet, but they're supposed to be on their way by now."

Keltie chuckled grimly. "Maybe they did need two hours to get dressed!"

Driss tried once more. "Rolind, if you don't come with us, we'll have to leave you. We have no choice."

"Retreat, lad. I'll hold them off. They'll not touch you. Go quickly!"

Driss detected a softening tone, but when he moved, the gun stiffened.

"All right," he said reluctantly, "let's go."

They moved out and circled in front of Rolind, watching numbly as he paraded up and down, the love-worn doll propped inside the battered crico ring. "Staden—hom—hou—hree, staden—hom—hou—hree . . ."

Celine sobbed disconsolately, her wounded heart again laid open.

Griselle picked the scab off her elbow.

31

All that morning, the group had little heart for talk. Driss and Keltie were particularly quiet, with Candor as well as Rolind on their minds. By unspoken agreement they said nothing to the others of what they had heard.

At first they feared that the cloud of dust, which finally moved out from Chadwich, would turn in their direction. They set a good pace but were forced to slacken for the sake of the three hard-ridden horses.

By noon they felt confident enough to stop at a damp basin where Treese and Amarl dug down to muddy but drinkable water for the animals. Driss and Jonn climbed a rocky prominence and squinted across the plain from where they'd come. "With Rolind's three bullets," said Driss, "the T'ribboners most likely had three bodies to deal with instead of us to chase." He paused, jaw working. "He kept his word, Jonn. 'Retreat, lad,' he said. 'I'll hold them off. They'll not touch you.' "

"Maybe four," said Jonn. "He had a knife. And if he managed to get one of their guns, he—"

"Stop, Jonn. Let's go eat. Enough that they're not following."

Celine was still red-eyed, and all were somber. While they ate, they talked about Rolind, almost as a sacrament of remembering. They skirted the obvious, however—his deep love for the children.

Finally, after a heavy silence, Jonn brought it out.

"Rolind was a strange duck. Like Steph, he . . . saw things the rest of us missed. Maybe we didn't know what we were getting when we took him along. He could make you mad, and probably we made fun of him too much. But I guess . . ." He swallowed hard. "I guess—deep down—we wish we had his courage, or maybe just his chance to do it again, to defend the children . . . to lay down our lives for them."

He paused to gain control. "I'd have saved him if I could, but I . . . I envy his peace of mind. He marched boldly to the end of his road for the sake of the kids."

As they got under way again, their spirits began to lift and rose higher than in many a day. Driss and Keltie joked about Rona—but with no reference to Candor's "idea." "You never know what's in the package when you take on a woman." Driss laughed.

"Yeah." Keltie replied. "Like they say, the skeleton of a beautiful woman's still nuthin' but a skeleton."

"Well, she got what she wanted. Serves her right."

"What d'you suppose Sigurth'll do to her—after she's no good to him, I mean?"

"Who cares?" Driss's mouth tightened. "She chose her bed; so it had a scorpion in it."

Treese grunted. "Are we talking about the woman who had you dancing all over the mountain because she wasn't around for you to ride?"

Keltie hooted. "You think this is sour grapes on lemon! You should of heard him after we jumped out of her little spider trap!"

Driss glared at the road ahead, and Treese smiled to himself before slipping back into melancholy.

Of the three who had gone to Chadwich, Bren seemed quickest to recover, Rona's carriage and team helping to recondition his thoughts. "Man, they were rippers! I've driven some great teams—eight-horse tandems, even—but nothin' like that! That dressed-up dooby, though—he knew horses like this forsaken desert knows water!"

Keltie's foot went to jiggling in his stirrup. "I ever see that 'dressed-up dooby' . . ." he muttered to Driss.

Driss clenched his jaw, angry at his impotence, angry at Bren, angry at Keltie for raking the coals. But he managed a taut laugh. "You'll have your team, Bren. We're not far now. Tomorrow Cassia, another two days to the mine. Then it's ours!"

They found an unexpectedly fine place to camp that night. Good water and adequate forage lay in a small, grass-lined pocket. Their bloodshot eyes found rest in shrubs and flowers, even a scrubby tree or two, after miles of gray, featureless plain. Amarl cut into a bag of the grain thrown hastily on back of the wagon and gave the animals due reward for their day's labor.

At the end of an especially creative supper, Bren rolled back in happy agony. "Thilrec, if all else fails, you and I—we'll go knock on Rona's door. I'll do the horses, you can cook!"

Exhausted from the strain of the two previous days, they bedded early. Bren closed his eyes, his face deep-lined. "If all else fails, nothin'," he growled to Griselle; "if *anything* else fails."

Griselle lay silent for a moment. "Anything else fails," she said, "I'm with you. And I know just how to do it. The perfect plan, even better'n anything Driss could come up with." Bren, already slipping through the door of sleep, only grunted, but when she whispered her scheme in his ear, his eyelids popped open with a loud "Yes!" and then slammed shut for the night.

They slept soundly till first light.

Treese was first to hear the strange noise. He sat up to listen, then punched Thilrec. "What is it? A wild animal?"

By this time Griselle was awake and shaking Bren, rousing him with difficulty. But when the roaring and groaning cut through his sleep-fogged brain, he leaped up. "The horses! They're down!"

He sprinted to the nearest and ran his hand over the distended belly. Jonn's mare Lina lay nearby, writhing and groaning in similar distress. Swearing angrily, he raced to the back of the wagon and snatched the nearly empty grain bag, then strode to where Amarl lay swaddled in sleep, yanking the boy to his feet.

"Look what you done, you cracker-brained dunce! You killed the horses!"

He whirled and shouted to the others, who were staggering in confusion. "Try to get 'em up and walking. Maybe we can save some!"

But it was too late. All but the mules had eaten and drunk their way into severe colic. Jangles and Floxie were already dead, and the other four could not be raised.

Driss sat by Glue, stroking the horse's neck. "You silly, ugly, misbegotten camel, you should've known better. If you were Strada, I could understand. But you were . . . different," he faltered. "Jumped like a deer, got me a cow to milk . . . Why didn't you have sense enough to quit eating?"

The animal shivered and groaned, a wrenching, hollow sound. *What a way to die!* Driss thought. He'd put him out of his misery if Rolind hadn't bagged the bullets.

He did have a knife. Could he do it, though?

Driss drew the blade from his thigh holster and tested its sharpness. After staring at it a long while, he wrapped his arms one last time around the horse's neck . . . and detected just the slightest backward movement of his ears.

"Goodbye, old friend . . . Your Excellency," he whispered and put the blade to the quivering throat.

Sometime the following night—how they did it nobody could quite figure out—Bren, Griselle, and Thilrec disappeared with the mules, the wagon, and most of the food.

32

The Cassia war, an ugly, festering pocket of hostility, had in recent weeks ground to an uneasy stalemate. Claeman's Russetmen wound in and out of Bethzur, the brooding fortress atop the mountain scant miles to the west. If not in full control of Cassia, they were at least a visible presence throughout the city. Sigurth's T'ribboners moved discreetly between Cassia and their headquarters to the north. Numbers alone made them a serious threat. Although little fighting was going on at the moment, Sigurth kept things off balance in this strategic metropolis close to the center of Claeman's power.

In the early hours of morning before the time of color, a horseman rode in from the desert and picked his way along the edge of town. Coming upon a figure huddled against a wall, seemingly asleep, he whistled a distinctive, five-note pattern. The figure answered in kind, with a short embellishment. The rider dismounted and approached cautiously until he could make out the features of the other. The two gripped each other's arms.

"Durk, what news?" the rider asked. "How did it go in Chadwich?"

The "sleeper" grinned. "Dandy. They got off in good time. I wish you could have seen the T'ribboner muster, Vlian. Just as Candor cried the alert, I popped into the barracks."

"You didn't! That's madness! If you'd been captured or recognized . . ."

"They were too sleepy." Durk grinned roguishly. "I was in and out before they quit bumping into each other. It slowed 'em just enough. Actually, the big problem was keeping the horses from getting pinched."

"Glue get stolen? The others, maybe, but not him. But that's neither here nor there, now. Have you heard? The horses got at the grain and died."

"You're joking!"

"No. Day before yesterday. On top of that, the cook and two others headed back to Chadwich with the mules and wagon."

Vlian stroked his mare's nose. "Rose to Sigurth's bait, so it seems."

"Huwee!" said Durk. "That'll hobble the group some! The cook, you say." Sudden interest lit his eyes. "Which two went with him?"

"The teamster and his wife."

"Bren and Griselle. Yes!" Durk punched the air triumphantly. "Didn't I say some were gold and some empty? The last of the empties!"

"So the rest are gold, hm? Think they'll all stick?"

Durk shrugged. "Maybe. Maybe not. No horses, short rations, little water. A test even gold might choke on. How are they managing?"

"They're coming along, carrying what they can," said Vlian. "They travel mostly at night when it's cool. Should get here this morning. Any news on the woman?"

"She's due in, too, but we'll keep her out of the way."

The rider clapped his companion on the shoulder. "You're doing well, Durk. Our charges are headed in. Won't be long now!"

They shook hands in parting, but as Vlian remounted, a small container slipped from his pocket. The horse, swinging around to counter-balance the weight of mounting, stepped on it, denting the lid.

"I still say our best bet is to find Clettie and get help from her."

"Wonderful!" snapped Treese. "Find Clettie—in a city this size!"

"Can't we have another drink?" Amarl whined piteously. "What good is one water jug?"

"Better than none," Keltie growled, slapping a fly.

Upon nearing Cassia, a new concern diverted their attention. Armed Russetmen were stopping in-going traffic on the main thoroughfare. "What're they doin'?" Amarl asked uneasily.

"I dunno," Keltie shrugged. "Askin' questions, searchin' . . . who knows? A foot inspection, maybe?" He lifted an eyebrow in Amarl's direction.

They halted uncertainly.

"We could wait till night and try to sneak in," Celine proposed.

"No good," Driss replied. "The water won't hold. Plus we'd have to dig for shade. It's already hot."

"How about one of us—no, that's no better." Jonn shook his head.

"Let's cut toward those buildings to the right," Driss suggested.

"No getting through there," Treese growled. "The buildings make a solid wall as far as you can see. Even if we did find an alley, they probably got—"

"I know, I know. I just want a place to think. Nobody's around, not even any windows on this side."

The morning sun had not yet swung out of the northeast, and the group dropped wearily in a thin band of shade. They passed the water jug with a wary eye on Amarl.

Celine hunched over her drawn-up legs, rubbing her feet and surveying the expanse they had crossed. "I never walked that far in my whole life!" she groaned. "My skin's peeling off in sheets, even where it's not burned. Are your lips cracked as bad as mine? The children would never—" She broke off, curling inward even further.

"Don't start that!" Jonn snapped.

Suddenly, Celine straightened her legs and leaned forward. "What's that shiny thing over there? No, on the ground, to the right."

"A piece of Cassia junk," Treese grunted sourly.

None of the others showed any curiosity, and even Jonn had withdrawn to his inner stronghold, so Celine crawled over to pick it up. "Huh. A little can. It's been bashed; I don't know if it'll open. The lid wiggles a little. Maybe if I . . . there!"

She peered at the contents curiously. "Huh. Some brownish stuff. Doesn't smell like anything," she said, sniffing experimentally.

Treese leaned over. "Let me see that," he ordered, taking it from her. He studied it carefully, the others looking on with interest. He touched a finger to it and surveyed the color, then rubbed it on the back of his hand.

"Ha!" crowed Driss. "Do you suppose . . . ?"

Treese nodded. "I'm sure of it. Russet grease!"

This opened a brand-new possibility, and with only a few minutes' discussion about possible complications from no uniforms, they began applying this skin-darkening substance to their unshaven faces. Except for Celine. They hadn't seen any dark-faced women and felt it wiser that she be under their "protection."

"Ouch!" yelped Driss. "This stuff packs a wallop!"

"What d'you mean? I don't feel nothin'." Keltie rubbed his dimpled chin briskly.

"Doesn't it sting?"

"No. Feels cool. Great for desert-fried skin!" He wiped the color down his neck and glanced over at Driss, then whipped around for a closer look.

"Whee! I guess it's botherin' you. Your nose and cheeks are bubbly!"

"Let me see." Celine drew his face around. "Oh, Driss! Get it off, quick!"

She pulled a piece of cloth from her basket. Wiping carefully, she removed the grease, but most of the color remained. "They're not blisters—more like warts."

"Oh, great! Perfect disguise. Just the thing to go meet an old lover! At least it doesn't sting now."

But he felt a deeper sting. Driss's face had always been his fortune. In one stroke he had become a different person.

He thought of Charri.

The masquerade worked splendidly, hardly anyone giving a second glance, despite their scruffy appearance. They sauntered along narrow streets lined with ancient, flat-roofed buildings that sagged against each other. "Like walking back in history!" Jonn exclaimed.

Amarl, craning his neck at a pretty girl, fell off the curb.

Driss pulled the boy to his feet and nodded. "Well, Cassia is Arlony's oldest city. Probably an offshoot village from Bethzur."

"What's that statue?" Celine pointed ahead. "Another war memorial? Not as ugly as the one in Lorenth. No, that one wasn't ugly." She thought of the gray-furred soldier-sweeper. "This one's a woman. Let's see what it says. Isn't it strange reading history from the enemy's perspective? Of course, Arlony isn't our enemy now, but back then . . . The inscription must be on the other side."

Keltie looked at the statue thoughtfully. "Maybe she's Triona."

The memorial dated from early in the Green Wars. When the city fell to Swendian forces, a loyal courtesan hid a number of Russet infiltrators, gave them critical information, then helped them escape. At a later time when an army from Bethzur attacked the city, Russet soldiers rescued her and her family, thus rewarding their loyalty to Claeman.

Amarl stared silently. "This? Not ugly?" He rubbed his nose the length of his arm. "What's a courtesan?"

Driss looked at Jonn with raised eyebrows. "Yes. Well. Courtesan. Has a nice sound to it."

Jonn smiled wryly. "I think she's one of your good lusty whores, Driss. A genteel whore, born and bred for the upper crust."

"Really? I guess the economy's been good in this town."

"It's not ugly." Celine slid around their remarks. "It's just been banged on and weathered. And bad air. It stinks around here. No, that makes me sound like Griselle. Celine lifted her head. "I'm proud that a woman—courtesan or whatever—did such a brave— Yikes!" she squealed, scrambling toward Jonn. "That cart hit the monument right where we'd been standing! If we hadn't come around to read the plaque . . ."

"The guy was thieving," said Jonn. "I saw him. Not only are we back in time, we're backing up in other ways. The place is a sewer!"

Keltie brightened. "Maybe he was breakin' the law by just havin' fun, like Garrick said. Each city gets worse, it seems. Nothin' like this in Swendia, and I been around. Lorenth wasn't too bad, but Mifflin, Chadwich, now here. How come? The closer to Bethzur, the worse it gets. Makes you wonder about Claeman."

"Maybe that's why they got a war here," Amarl suggested.

The four men looked at him.

"What do you mean, Amarl?" Driss asked in some amazement.

This unexpected admittance to adult conversation set Amarl to squirming. "Well . . . not much." He paused as though hoping attention would drift away. When they waited, he went on. "Well, I think maybe there's two things it could be . . . maybe. Could be Claeman's real bad, like you say. Or—" He hitched his trousers and scratched his head, uneasy over the consequences of one small observation. "Or it could be it ain't him is bad; it's the guys tryin' to take over the place . . . guys that roast mice." He glanced sideways at Keltie.

Driss frowned. "What?"

"Nuthin. Forget it. I'm just sayin' it could be one, or it could be the other. The closer to the good guys, the hotter the fight . . . maybe."

When even more silence met him, he dropped his head and shuffled along. "Most likely it's what you say."

"No, no," Jonn said quickly, scrambling into his teacher role. "An excellent bit of headwork, Amarl. You laid out the two logical possibilities very adequately."

Amarl shrugged, not sure if he had Jonn's approval or disapproval.

The problem of where to go pressed heavily.

"We can't just stand in the middle of the city and holler for Clettie!" moaned Celine. "We have to ask. Oh, Driss," she said, trying unsuccessfully not to laugh, "your poor nose. It looks like a hairfruit!"

Jonn turned on her. "Shut up!"

Celine jumped at this unaccustomed sharpness from her husband.

"Stick to the problem. If we don't get food or money, we're sunk."

Celine sighed and studied the people around them. After a moment, she pulled Jonn to a stop. "I'm going to that woman over there." She pointed.

"Now, wait a minute," Driss remonstrated. "Why her, and so sudden?"

"She looks like she'd talk to me, that's all. You have a better plan?"

Driss shrugged. "What can we lose?"

Celine drew several nervous breaths and tried to collect loose strands of hair. Only once since the children's death, in the tiny bubble of euphoria that came with talking about Rolind, had she combed and tied her thick, honey coils. The death of the horses had burst the bubble, and again she lost heart for grooming. Now, though, she regretted her slackness.

The woman she was approaching might have been attractive as a child, but she wore the pinched look of one whose survival depended on shrewdness. Yet Celine saw beneath street hardness. She eased toward the woman and began a friendly overture.

"Hweo. I can't seem to find the town well. Could you point me in the right direction?"

The woman nodded and looked two different ways. "That way's quickest," she said, pointing, "but I hear tell there's to be a flogging this morning. Maybe you should steer clear and go down this street here—see? Then when you get to the statue—"

"I know where you mean. We . . . I passed it a few minutes ago. Must've been closer than I thought."

"Well, you turn right and go maybe three, four blocks and turn right again. You'll see it from there."

"Thanks so much. I'm not good at directions, but I should be able to follow that. Appreciate your help."

The woman nodded, but before she could turn away, Celine eased closer. "You know, while you were talking, I couldn't help admiring your hair. The sun hit it just right and turned it into a gold cloud. Mine just doesn't seem to go right anymore." She tucked a strand deprecatingly.

After a moment of calculated study, the woman responded guardedly to Celine, and they began to talk. Her name was

Garryn, and the two chatted about the unrelenting heat, the most recent skirmishes, the difficulty in getting reasonably priced food these days.

Finally, Celine gathered courage to inquire about Clettie.

"Yeah, I know her," Garryn replied carefully. "A friend, you say?" Her eyebrows raised a little.

"Well—a friend of a friend. Actually, I never met her but was told to look her up. Can you tell me where she lives?"

Again Garryn gave her a strange look. "You huntin' for work, honey?"

"Oh, no. We're . . . I'm just passing through."

Garryn studied Celine a moment longer, then shrugged. "If you're sure it's Clettie you want, I can take you part ways on—close enough, anyways, to point out the house. Or do you want to go to the well first?"

"No, the well can wait. At least I know where it is."

The two set off down the street, the men following at a discreet distance. Garryn seemed to know everyone. She nodded to various soldiers—Claeman's and Sigurth's alike—exchanging what seemed to Celine to be veiled or even coded quips.

"I can't get used to seeing T'ribboners and Russetmen side by side like this," Celine remarked. "I'm from Swendia, and I guess I don't understand what's going on. I heard they are fighting each other. What kind of crazy war is this?"

Garryn nodded. "Crazy—you said it! But if you was to look close, they ain't side by side, not at all. After you been here a bit, you get so's you fish up patterns—who goes where—as well as signals that send you divin' for cover. I hear a lot from . . . different ones, so I've learnt what to watch for, and how much Russetmen'll put up with before they smack back. But whatever y'do, honey," she warned, keeping her eyes straight ahead, "stay off the street after dark. That's as plain as I can say it."

At the far end of the city's busiest thoroughfare, Garryn stopped and pointed. "See that roundish hump over there? The only house not flat. That's Clettie's place. I think you'll find her there, but be careful." She grasped Celine's arm as though to divine her motives. "You're sure it's Clettie you want? You don't look . . ." Her voice trailed off, and she shook her head.

Despite Celine's assurances, Garryn remained doubtful, but with a warm squeeze and a vague offer of further help, she was gone.

Celine took a big breath and looked around. Sure enough, the others had kept pace and were coming toward her. She moved toward Clettie's, humming nervously. As Driss drew even, she whispered, "That's it right there, the round place. But there's something funny. Be careful, Driss. Maybe you should tell her Garryn sent you."

Driss nodded and looked anxiously toward the yellow claybrick dome. "Just wish I had a good meal under my belt for this!"

Clettie herself, wrapped shapelessly, her hair in disarray, answered his knock, opening the door first a crack, then wide. In the dim light from an overhead window Driss could see a circular, bench-lined foyer with doors going off. The room was filthy and cluttered with odd bits of rope and chain.

Clettie appeared to have just wakened. "Well! This is a surprise!" she said of the dark face.

"Hello, Clettie."

"Honey, you're a sight!" Her voice, no longer mellow as Driss had known it, rasped harshly. "Not many of your kind come by, but I can see you'd have a time on your own. Costs more in daytime, y'know. The girls are asleep. Come back tonight—unless you don't dare—" She stopped and jerked her head around. "What's that?" She strode toward a bench and kicked at a shapeless mound underneath.

The mound squirmed and cried out.

Clettie ripped away a covering and dragged a girl of about sixteen from under the bench, hauled her partway up and threw her across the floor. "Trying to get away again? Well, *get this through your head.*" She yanked the girl's hair back and shouted into a face that bore multiple bruises. "You stay here till you die—if you live that long. You belong to me!"

She let go of the hair and helped the sobbing girl up almost gently. "Back to bed now. You need all the sleep you can get."

Driss stared in horror, trying to comprehend what was going on. This wasn't Clettie, the alluring woman he had bedded with. Something *was* wrong, and Celine didn't know the half of it.

"Clettie, you don't recognize me, do you? It's Driss."

She started and looked closely, then laughed raucously. "Drissan! I can't believe it!"

"Clettie, I need help. Remember I told you I was going for the big time? Well, I'm almost there, but we've had some bad breaks. We need food and a little money to see us through."

She cocked her head. "And who's providing the big time? Claeman himself? There's nothing after Cassia, honey—nothing but orange!"

Her eyes narrowed suspiciously. "You've got grease on your face. You one of them now?"

"Of course not! We found some outside the city and thought it'd be a good way to sneak in, but it reacted on me, somehow."

"I guess! You're hideous! When did you last shave, even? I wouldn't have you any time of day or night!"

"Clettie, I'm not asking for that. For old times' sake, can you help me? When I get the goods, I'll pay you back, and then some. I don't forget friends."

Her voice turned hard. "Honey, guys who come here have money in their hands. They don't ask me for it. You got jack, I can fix you up; you don't have any—"

"Clettie—"

"Forget it. Don't even ask."

"Clettie, it's rosillum I'm after. It's practically in my hands! I can—"

"I don't care if it's gold lumps on your nose. I run a business that's every bit as good as rosillum. How'd you find me, anyway?"

"A woman named Garryn told us. Said she knew you."

Again she shrieked. "Garryn sent you! Thinks she's funny! I run this end of the city, she does the other—for peanuts! I go for the stuff she's too soft for. If she won't have you, Drissan, it's the end of your line. Now, get out. And don't come back unless you're dripping with rosillum!"

One look at Driss's sagging shoulders told the story.
"It's the end," Jonn said finally. "So close, yet so far."

33

The sun shone russet through the western haze as Charri crept into Cassia, head covered against heat and stares. The city boiled around her: drovers moving animals to safety, street brawlers hurling rocks, an accident tangling horses and drays; animal screams, human curses, and a fetid odor over all. Desperately afraid, she slunk from shadow to shadow in a frantic search for water first, food second. She noted a mound of garbage and willed it to stay there until her greater need had been met.

Finally, she passed a granite-faced woman carrying a brimming pail of water. Not daring to speak, Charri retraced the dribbles, and by the time the trail dried she was within sight of the public well. She held back from the evening draw of water and waited, faint, weary, until most—but not all—had left: it would not do to be conspicuous, even by being last.

Thirst assuaged and small flask filled, she began to search for food. Dusk was turning the city gray and grim, and she became increasingly anxious. She had hoped by this time to have found refuge for the night. Durk's words haunted her: "Whatever you do, don't stay outdoors overnight in any of the towns west of here." Her experience with Sigurth had frightened her badly, but without something to eat, she doubted she could go on.

Go on—but where? To an alternate death, most likely. Driss remained a fragile hope, but her chance of finding him, even if he were in the city, was slim indeed.

She headed back to where she'd seen the fresh garbage, afraid that darkness would rob her of even this.

As she slid along crumbling building fronts, her foot struck something soft. A package lay on the ground, dropped, perhaps, by a shopper. It smelled of food, and her hands trembled. Slipping it under her cloak, she hurried to a dark corner and tore feverishly at the cord. It loosened at last, and with tears of relief she bit into a still-warm, thick-crusted meat pie. New energy poured through her veins as she ate. And just in time: the approach of patrolling soldiers drove her into the night. In her haste she dropped her supper remains but dared not stop.

Thus began her nightmare. Soldiers, flesh-peddlers, prostitutes, gangs, drunks—the city became a howling, shrieking vortex, with Charri, so it seemed, at the epicenter.

She fled down lanes, through broken fences, over low walls. Finally—inexorably—she found herself trapped in an alley next to a house curved high against the still-pale sky. A clay-brick wall blocked her escape from approaching footsteps.

Searching frantically, she discovered a small door beneath the dome's staircase. As two men entered the alley, she pushed at the opening and dove through like a street rat. The door wouldn't shut tight, but she was hidden. Footsteps thundered overhead as she lay trembling in dusty darkness.

But within minutes, the unknown hazards of her hiding place became of little concern. Those two men were only the start of a long parade up the steps. Gradually, reluctantly, incredulously, Charri comprehended the nature of her refuge. Had her little cave been crawling with snakes and spiders, it could not have horrified her more. What started beyond imagining got worse as the night wore on. Charri covered her ears, but sound leaked through. This unwilling participation in pain for pleasure knifed her brain, wrenched her stomach, and bent her body to the ground. Her own screams might have blocked the others, but she could not afford even that small relief. She had to be still—and listen. One cry especially, a tiny, unending wail hidden under the swell of older, more experienced agonies, made her fiercely glad that her own child was forever safe from such a place.

Her only diversion, if it could be called that, came in watching the faces of men who made Uncle seem like a love-struck ground dog. Cruel, brutish expressions: lust made flesh. Charri found a strange fascination in trying to fathom such depravity.

She wondered if prostitutes ever tried to mark their clients as Celine had instructed her. Why not? If it didn't work, they couldn't possibly be worse off. No, she decided, men who came here would have so many marks that nothing could be proved. These women had no recourse—none but death.

Near dawn, a shave-head T'ribboner leaped the steps and shouted through the upper door. "Glinneth's outside the city!" he cried. "Coming here!"

Twin bolts paralyzed Charri. He was alive, despite Sigurth's hints to the contrary! But coming *here?*

The house erupted like mice before a snake. She couldn't tell if the women left, too, or if they had been left prostrate—dead, even—after such a night. Might they be as eager to meet Glinneth as she?

She had to see him. His face would tell. After studying the night's procession, she could never misjudge a man's intentions. She would watch his approach. If he came to destroy the house, she'd gladly run to him. If he came like the rest . . . the hellhole would become her sepulchre.

New voices cut through her plans. Several Russetmen stood talking at the top of the alley.

"Where is she?" one of them asked.

"Under the steps. Been there all night."

"Get her out. Get rid of her. He'll be here shortly."

No! Charri cried silently. *Where can I go? Where can I hide? I must see him!*

There was no place. She fell over crates and sacks but could not make herself vanish before the sun's rays thrust dagger-like through the doorway.

"Come along, lovey," a dark-faced soldier ordered. "No use fussing."

She fought and screamed and bit the hand that held her.

"Ow! She's a wild one! Who'd a thought such a mouse'd scrap so! Won't help you any. Be a good girl, now."

They half carried, half dragged her down the alley toward the west end of town, she fighting the whole way.

At the edge of the city, she only half noticed an assembly of troops. Suddenly, a figure on a heavy-maned gray horse caught her eye. She stopped struggling and stared. Even though a distance away, the horseman size and shape could not be mistaken.

"Oh!" she cried to no one in particular. "Oh! I didn't know! I'm sorry. I didn't know . . ."

She turned a hasty, apologetic smile on her escorts, straining for release from their grasp. He had sent for her. He'd come to rescue her from that terrible place, to take her to his home. A fierce joy welled up in her breast. *Glinneth! Oh, Glinneth!*

The soldiers, however, were not letting go. They didn't understand. They dragged her past the assembled army toward the desolate wasteland that lay between Cassia and Claeman's mountain fortress.

Charri renewed her struggle and began to scream. "No! You must let me go! Glinneth!"

She watched in stunned disbelief as the man on the great horse lifted his arm to signal the start of some dreadful retribution. *Why* didn't he turn? Surely he heard her. Any moment now he'd swing around and at the very least shout where she should go. It would cost him less than a minute.

"Glinneth!"

The enormous gray stallion could scarcely contain himself—nostrils blazing, neck arched thick and muscular, legs tight springs. He reared twice, then settled to the impatient drumbeat of war.

Charri's desperation carried across the dusty theater, cutting through the noise of bit and leather, and Glinneth seemed to falter and look her way. Her heart leaped with hope, then turned to ash as with resolute discipline he laid rein to the dappled neck and roared his command. Arm thrust forward, he thundered past her toward Cassia, his face altered and inscrutable.

Charri sank into the soldiers' impassive grasp, then found herself on the ground, alone and desolate, with nothing but dust and a woe bird's throaty lament drifting across the empty arena. She lay unmoving, eyes staring, willing death to fall on her from the sky.

The dark-clad woe bird on its scraggled perch stopped moaning and hopped to the ground near Charri's head. He scratched about, ticking softly as though counting each seed he turned up.

Glinneth knew about Roanna. He knew about the little boy with the ribbon collar. That was it. Sigurth had found her out; why would it be kept from Glinneth? Her shame, her hardness of heart had become an appalling crime, painted crimson across the sky: I CAN'T HELP YOU . . . I HAVE NOTHING TO GIVE . . . NOTHING . . . NOTHING . . .

Oh, Glinneth, I'm sorry . . .

The sun beat remorselessly on her prostrate form, but it refused the final cup. Though hope was dead, her body lived and demanded attention.

The woe bird scratched the hot soil in seeming random circles, but each round brought him closer to the shadow cast by Charri's body. From his perspective, the chances were about even that this unexpected bit of shade would either provide relief or devour him. He finally took the plunge and plucked courage as well as carbohydrates from the refreshing shadow. His ticking accelerated, perhaps a woe bird's way of whistling in the dark.

Hope was dead in Charri's heart, but something else had died, as well, something deep inside. Another thread tugged darkly. Death itself she might welcome, but that unspeakable fate bound up in Sigurth drove her to the only expedient left: Driss.

She had seen the map that long-ago morning in the kung grove. Jonn had blundered by showing it to her, but having seen it, she would try to intercept Driss at the old liggeth mine. He might help her just out of kindness, but she couldn't count on it.

Those beautiful feelings about sex, salvaged from shame, had deceived her, and somewhere in Chadwich she had buried her Driss fantasies once and for all. Even Glinneth had turned away in revulsion. She knew now. Men—the best and the worst—would either ignore her or use her. But that basic fact of life could be turned to her advantage. Driss might be bought. Driss—not his kindness, not his zest—Driss the man might be bought. Scruple had died deep inside, and she was willing to pay. Driss's price could never be higher than Sigurth's.

The ticking stopped, and the bird lifted his head. Perhaps in response to some distant call or another male in his territory, his dark throat quivered a doleful requiem. Charri raised her head at the sound but caught only a swirl of dust as he flew off.

The morning air soothed her bruised and swollen face. A long climb lay ahead, but she had always found a task to be good medicine for heartache. That, and Durk's words concerning Glinneth ticking beneath every weary step: *Keep in mind that he's a soldier!*

34

Driss looked at the others and shook his head stubbornly. "Sure, Clettie turned us out, but it's not the end. We have only *ten miles to go!*"

"Yeah," Treese shot back, "ten miles—straight up! Without food, the climb alone would kill us, even if we could make it past a solid wall of Russetmen. If we reach the mine, all Claeman has to do is lean out his bedroom window and pick us off one by one."

Celine sighed. "Let's go back and find Garryn. Maybe she'll give us something."

Driss looked at her. "You know what she is? She's a bawd, like Clettie. A madam. Some friend you found!"

Celine's eyes widened in horror. "No! I don't believe it! She was *nice!*"

"Clettie could be lying," Keltie offered.

Driss snorted. "She could at that, but why would she?"

"What choice do we have?" asked Celine. "We don't dare talk to anyone else."

Reluctantly, Driss agreed to give it a try.

Their way was blocked by a restless gathering of people, some shouting angrily, some weeping, all grim. A sudden hush fell, followed by a sharp *whap* and cry of anguish. "Oh, no!" exclaimed Celine at a second whap and scream. "We should've gone the other way. This is a flogging! Garryn told me to keep away."

Treese saw in three seconds all he cared to. As Amarl craned for a look, he grabbed the boy and turned him around, face hard. "Let's get out of here."

"What could anyone do to deserve that?" asked Keltie stiffly.

"I don't know," moaned Celine. "Garryn didn't say. Oh, it's awful!" She put her hands over her ears and started crying. Jonn put his arm around her, his face like granite.

For a moment Driss felt he might pass out. Though not as tall as Treese, he had glimpsed the man, naked except for a thin strip around his loins, hands bound to a pole, feet secured. He saw the rod fall, the twisting, animal agony of the prisoner. He saw the stern, whip-wielding Russetman. He saw other Russetmen ringing the scene, silent, implacable. He saw a crudely printed sign.

"A child molester, it says."

Keltie froze momentarily while his mind rearranged its inventory of anger. "Too good for him, if that's what he done. Too good." He walked in silence for a moment, then added, "Shoulda splatted him with a toppled wall, like the grawnies outside Chadwich."

"It's awful, no matter what he did," said Celine. "They don't whip people in Swendia. Why would they do it here?"

Driss shrugged, his face pale. "I don't know, but I'll tell you one thing: I wouldn't be in a hurry to accuse somebody of a crime here. They make you watch. Right up front. There's a man and woman, and a girl about Nessa's— Anyway, they must be the ones. A soldier is standing behind them, not letting them turn away. Whatever else you think about Russetmen, they serve up justice on a pretty basic platter."

They found Garryn near where they'd seen her before, and her face showed relief when she spotted Celine.

This time, Celine laid everything out. "These are my friends." She waved toward the four men.

Garryn tensed.

"It's all right," Celine assured her. We found some face grease and used it to get into the city. Clettie won't do anything for us, so we came back to see if . . . Did you mean what you said about help? We mostly need food. Ours was stolen two days ago. We expect to have plenty of money in a couple of days, but until then, we have to borrow."

Garryn sized up the furrowed, unshaven faces uncertainly. The silence lengthened.

"Please, Garryn." Celine grasped her arm. "We have nowhere else to turn!"

Driss moved forward and cleared his throat. "I gather from Clettie's . . . remarks," he said, selecting his words carefully, "that you don't have it easy."

Garryn looked up, wary of sympathy.

"I know times are hard, but we ask only a little."

Garryn studied their faces, one by one, searching through her store of street wisdom. "Okay," she agreed finally, "I can give some food, but that's it. Then you leave me alone. Okay?"

They thanked her profusely. "We won't forget you," Driss said. "It will come back to you."

She shook her head. "No. I don't want nothin' back. I ask only one thing. You guys wear russet, just as a cover. But it's the right color. Believe me—I know. Everything in me says, someday, somehow, Claeman's gonna win this damn crazy war. If ever you get the chance, put in a word for me, will you?" Her eyes, suddenly plaintive and vulnerable, searched their faces, then dropped. "I ain't . . . proud of what I do, but there's things I won't have no part in—if I starve!" she added fiercely.

Driss caught his breath as he weighed the significance of her words against Clettie's "big stuff" and the girl she had caught trying to escape. He looked at Garryn with new respect. "Claeman's the last person we want to see," he said, "but I'll remember. I will not forget your kindness."

"Come now." She led them to an ancient villa and pushed open a rusted gate that led onto what seemed at first a wide, dark passageway. A path, however, threaded through a number of decaying statues and benches—a garden of sorts tucked between the high walls of adjacent buildings.

Amarl, immediately behind Garryn, eyed the hemming walls apprehensively, thereby missing a twist in the path. He walked straight into the outstretched arms of a wooden lady with real clothing draped provocatively over her weathered body.

He bounced back in confusion. "Oops! Sorry. You okay? I wasn't— Oh." He brushed his nose, hitched his pants, and shuffled a dance step. "Doo-de-doo-de-doo-de-doo . . ." He bowed gallantly and was hauled away by Treese.

The entrance to the establishment was another challenge. Traces of gilt on the ornate surround spoke of former glory, but now large cracks made the building appear off-balance. The doorway itself was low with a thick lintel. Amarl bent properly to clear it but straightened three inches too soon. Clutching his head, he pitched forward across the tiny room, fetching up against a soft pile on the far wall. He lay there groaning, two sides of his damaged body finding comfort from the cool stone floor and the cushioning mound.

Until the mound moved. A languid arm reached across his chest. "Mm—honey. Come . . . come!" The hand traveled southward.

Amarl went rigid. His eyes swelled to melon size. With scarcely a bend of any joint, he popped to his feet and made for the doorway. Only Driss's intervention saved his head from another bashing.

"Ho, the woman killer!" Keltie crowed.

Even Treese smiled as he intoned, " 'He knows every move, he rides like a deer, he speaks a secret language!' Great work, Amarl!"

Garryn took Amarl's head between her hands and kissed him playfully. Then she knelt beside the blanketed form, already back in sleep.

"Dargi . . . Dargi." She shook the woman gently. "Wake up. These people are going to eat; we need your pad to sit on."

The woman moaned and turned over. Garryn stroked her hair regretfully but continued shaking. "Up, Dargi. Move to the next room. You can come back later. Come on. I'll help you."

Celine touched Garryn's shoulder. "We don't mind if she stays. We can sit on the floor. We're hot; it'll feel good."

But Garryn shook her head. "No, she can move. "Dargi," she said more firmly. "Now."

Slowly, eyes curtained, the woman rose in her blanket and moved to a door once heavily ornamented but now only old and scarred.

"Thank you, Dargi. Now for some bread." She followed the sleepy woman and returned in a few minutes with two loaves, a pitcher, and an apology. "Food's scarce these days, and I got . . . other hungry mouths."

Driss sat on the still-warm pad and leaned his head against the splintery wall. Like Celine, he would have preferred the cooler floor, but he could hardly refuse such costly honor. Garryn moved among them, filling and holding out a single cup. Driss nibbled his portion of bread, deliberately resisting the urge to wolf it down. Wolfing would not do. This meal—cheap, dry bread and warmish water—had more integrity than any banquet he could remember. He thought of Rona's contrivance, and his mouth twisted. Here in the dingy anteroom of a run-down brothel, served by a marginal madam, he felt peace for the first time since the mountain refuge. There was dignity here, respect—love, even. *There's things I won't have no part in—if I starve!* Garryn did what she had to to make a living—a nasty business at best—but she had drawn a line, taken a stand, fiercely protective of the girls in her care. Would she know about zill, at least enough to keep her girls safe? Would she watch a flogging for something done to her girls? If so, she had a stronger stomach than he had.

As Garryn held out yet another cupful, Driss scrutinized her. Despite her glorious hair, she had none of Clettie's soft sensuousness. Her eyes burned almost as intensely as Jonn's; her thin, hard face was made up to disguise wrinkles. *She's older than she looks. And tired. If she's been up all night, what's she doing out during the day? She's got scars, too. Bet she can give as well as get. She's kind—never mentioned my warty face—but I'd hate to step over her line. What a life! Is she that much different from Clettie? They both feed on men, build their empires on women's bodies. Could they both kill, if it came to that? Clettie without doubt. But Garryn? Yes. She'd do what she had to. Like Glinneth, she's got scars.*

Scars . . . lines. Glinneth had scars, but he didn't draw lines. Not at dying, anyway. Maybe some lines he'd draw, but there were none on that hellish hill . . .

"Finish up, Driss." Jonn's voice cut through his reverie. "We need to push on and take advantage of this food."

Driss sighed and picked up his remaining bread.

"Where you headed?" Garryn inquired.

Driss chewed rapidly to get an answer out, but Jonn spoke for him. "West," he said.

"West?" Garryn raised her eyebrows, then looked at Celine as much as to say, "Honey, what are you doin', messin' with these crazies?" She held her peace, though, and went on to instruct them on the best way to get out of town. "There's some Russetmen you got to watch out for, and some as won't bother." She hesitated. "I know 'em, but it's hard to give it to somebody else. I best go with you—a ways, anyhow."

Driss shook his head. "No. Please. You're tired. You've already done all we could ask. We'll get through somehow."

Garryn sagged wearily but then straightened. "I'll go with you. Come." She began pulling them to their feet.

As the others gathered their things, Driss took Garryn's wrists and looked at her in silence. Finally he spoke. "Garryn, you've given us . . . me . . . a great gift. This has been a tough day—we even happened on that flogging." He smiled wanly. "But you took us in and treated us . . . differently." He drew a big breath and bit his lip. *"Thank you* is all I can say." He looked at her another moment, watching her eyes fill up, then took her in his arms and hugged her a long time.

They passed again through the "garden," Amarl bowing to each buxom statue. When the gate clunked behind them, Garryn became alert and watchful. *The cost of kindness,* thought Driss. *No lines drawn here.*

She threaded the streets with the languid grace of a dancer, a hand here, winking there. Near the edge of town, her body tensed, she halted the group. "Wait here," she whispered, then moved toward two men.

The others watched as she spoke to them. She showed none of the familiarity that had marked other encounters, but these men were obviously not strangers. After pointing down the thoroughfare and seeing them off in that direction, she hurried back.

"Quick, now. The way is clear."

"Who were they?" Jonn asked. "They didn't have dark faces; not Russetmen, at least."

"Russet officers," Garryn replied. "Officers don't—"

Keltie turned on Jonn. "How can you be so dumb!" he scolded. "Don't you *remember?* Ol' Garrick'd turn in his grave."

"Go, while there's time." Garryn swung them in the right direction. "They'll be watchin' close at the stone pillars, but if you mix in the crowd, you'll be okay. Now, Celine—" She addressed the men. "She bein' a woman won't have no trouble goin', or if you want her to stay . . ." She paused significantly, then pushed them on their way, giving Amarl an extra pat.

Arms out, Amarl leaped and whirled into the flow of traffic, with Driss, Treese, and Keltie scrambling after him in alarm. "Just what we need—a red flag bobbing up and down," Treese muttered.

"Damn!" said Driss. "I forgot to ask her about zill."

Jonn and Celine followed behind, engaged in conversation. Keltie walked backwards, watching them, and began to sing softly:

Two brown birds, comin' through the green.
Two brown birds couldn't be seen.
Two brown birds tied in brown together.
Two brown birds all of a feather.

Driss looked up quizzically, but Keltie grinned and danced a quickstep.

The group passed unchallenged through the monolithic stone gate and paused minutes later to regroup.

Jonn caught up with them. He was alone.

35

Treese left the following night, taking the round container with him. Amarl saw him go but didn't wake the others. "Said he didn't feel like takin' orders from a toad. Said he'd rather chance it in Cassia and maybe make it to Chadwich later on."

This rankled and absorbed more energy than Driss had to spare. The three that remained—Jonn, Keltie, and Amarl—knew better than to try to talk around it, and the decimated band crept up the mountain in silence.

They counted distance in reverse—nine more miles, eight more miles, then seven. Their way wound through barren canyons, across windswept shelves, over great mounds of whirling sand. Bethzur, Claeman's fortress, could not yet be seen, but the mountain, ears laid back, reared above them, breathing coppery clouds.

Though it meant tougher going, they avoided the road. Not only would the actual distance shrink by eliminating switchbacks, they would be less vulnerable to stop-and-search maneuvers. They might have blended easily among the flow of service personnel and soldiers, especially with their skin still dark. But it seemed logical that only familiar faces could approach the fortress unchallenged. Even off the road, they occasionally had to duck behind rocks to avoid ranging soldiers.

Claeman's men had an unusual way of communicating. From time to time a whistle bounced eerily against the hills. The band came to recognize three or four basic patterns, but the echo, depending on the particular arrangement of the landscape, made each message unique. Driss considered trying to decode the system, just to help pass time and reduce the agony, but his tired mind sent its regrets.

Thirst dogged them, and more than once they were reduced to digging and straining mud. Slowly, slowly, over two long, hungry days, they crept closer to their goal—the abandoned liggeth shaft that lay a scarce half mile from the thick wall of Bethzur.

Driss continued to chafe over Treese. Without pack animals, they needed every able body to carry rosillum. Though Treese normally bled vinegar, Driss never once doubted his loyalty. Discounting Treese's usual crustiness, Driss couldn't think of a single signal that might have tipped him off if he'd paid closer attention. Nor did he believe the line Treese had given Amarl. He wasn't that shallow. In fact, when he thought about it, Treese had twice been downright demonstrative. Driss's return from the plank detour marked the first instance; the second came last night. Both times Treese had laid his hand on Driss's shoulder. Given his devotion to distance between men, the gesture held great import. Had it been his way of saying goodbye?

Actually, Amarl was the big surprise. They all had expected "the featherheader," as Treese called him, to be the first to fall away, even before Garrick. Yet here he was, sticking through to this final, bitter ascent. The lad had suffered more than any of them over the horses' colic, but he came through his disgrace intact, thanks to timely intervention.

Driss had watched him closely that first day. Amarl survived the initial fury through his usual ploy of a silly grin and vacant stare. But when the tempest let up, the boy quietly began to destroy himself. Without emotion, without words, he took to hazardous acts, first banging his head on the tailgate of the wagon, then teasing the mules until he got kicked (and batted by Keltie for being so stupid). After he half-heartedly tried to jump a steep cut and rolled himself bloody to the bottom, Driss took the matter in hand.

He hauled Amarl up the slope with little help, if not actual resistance, from the boy. After cleaning and repairing multiple cuts, Driss grabbed the lad's shirt and stood him up.

"Amarl, look at me."

The boy stared at two sets of feet.

"Look at me, I said!" Driss's tone sharpened.

Amarl's head lifted almost imperceptibly.

"At me, not my knees!" He forced Amarl's chin up.

Amarl looked everywhere except into Driss's eyes until Driss squeezed his jaw just enough to make him wince.

"That's better. Now, listen. The horses are dead. There's nothing any of us can do about it. Do you understand that?"

Amarl eyes quickly dropped and were as quickly brought back by another squeeze.

"I want you to say it: 'The horses are dead, and there's nothing we can do about it.' Say it!"

Again the rebellious drop, again the tightened hand.

"Lemme go," Amarl mumbled through Driss's hand.

"No. You're going to say these words: 'The horses are dead; there's nothing we can do about it.' The sooner you say it, the sooner I'll let go."

Driss relaxed his hand just a bit and allowed Amarl to shift and fidget. But his eyes would brook no escape.

Finally, Amarl opened his mouth to speak, but no sound would come. He tried again, breathing heavily. Then, after clearing his throat, he began.

"'The . . . horses are . . . are . . .' I can't, Driss; I can't say it!" His eyes pleaded. Perspiration dripped off his face.

Driss remained adamant. "You can say it. You will."

Amarl cleared his throat again. " 'The horses are . . . hum . . . the horses are dead, and . . . there's nuthin' . . .' " His mouth began to screw out of shape. " '. . . nuthin' . . . nuthin' we can do . . .' "

The dam broke, and Driss held the boy's head tight to his own chest. "Nothing we can do, Amarl; nothing. It's over; it's behind us. From here on—behind us. Rosillum in front, dead horses behind."

That night when Bren and Thilrec spirited away wagon and mules, the death of the horses had suddenly become of both greater and lesser import.

As they neared the top, the air became a luminous fog, almost apricot in color, making breathing difficult and forcing frequent rests. Hope, however, fed their strength as they passed key landmarks noted on the map.

"There's twin needles!" exclaimed Jonn. "Can't be more than a half mile now!"

"Don't forget the road," Keltie reminded him. "We have to cross to get to the mine. Be our luck to meet a whole battalion right there."

"You standing in for Treese?" asked Driss caustically. "We'll get over. What's a road, after all we've been through?"

After another hour's climb, Driss called a halt. "Let's rest. The fortress should be in sight over that next rise."

They dropped in varying postures and lay as dead for a full ten minutes. Amarl was the first to move. He ground his hands into his eyes, scratched his head thoroughly, then took off his boots to rub his feet. "I stink," he muttered. He sat cross-legged, examining the Arlony birthmark on the bottom of his foot. "Y'know, I seen him before," he remarked irrelevantly.

"Who?" Keltie grunted.

"Glinneth."

"Yeah, me too. At the crico game. Big deal."

"But I didn't go to the crico game. Remember?"

"Yeah, so?"

"Well, I seen him. I'm sure it was the same guy."

Keltie, tiring of a conversation that seemed to be going nowhere, began whistling experimentally. He tried to copy the patterns echoing around them, then began improvising embellishments that wove in and out in musical counterpoint. Driss lay absorbed in this tiny moment of peace.

Suddenly Jonn scrambled to a crouch. "Stop!" he commanded softly. "Soldiers!"

"Uh-oh!" whispered Keltie. "Now I've done it!"

They saw a number of Russetmen drop from the roadway to their left and fan out as though searching for something.

"Was it the whistlin'?" Keltie asked anxiously. "I didn't think anyone'd notice with all the rest of it."

Driss shrugged. "Who knows? I don't think they've seen us. Back up slowly. We just passed a tipped rock I think we can get under. Head down, Amarl."

They wriggled into a dusty tunnel and lay silent as two of the soldiers worked down the rocky incline to where the group had just rested.

". . . came from this area. They're here somewhere."

"Maybe. But it'd take a battalion to ferret them out. A chicken hunt, you ask me."

The four held their breath and watched in taut fascination as dusty guida boots crunched less than two feet from their faces, kicking up little salvos of dust.

Driss closed his eyes, suddenly drained of everything. He was tired . . . hungry. His trusted comrade had abandoned him for no reason at all. He had once asked Treese if the quest was worth the terrible price. Treese had shrugged ambiguously. Maybe it had taken all this time to find an answer.

Maybe . . . maybe he left because Griselle left. Had Griselle really marked Treese, as Rona hinted? She was capable. Treese had little use for her; that was clear. He'd been more cross-grained than ever since the three renegades took off with the mules. Treese was a proud man. Being marked as a rapist by a weak-faced nit like Griselle would be hard to bear. Such an insult from Rona would have angered him, but from Griselle . . . What man could tolerate that? There was no telling what she might do. Bren would side with her, of course. A master teamster, yes, but loyalty to the team didn't necessarily factor in. Perhaps for Treese, rosillum would only set him up for endless blackmail.

Driss closed his eyes against the complications that had risen out of the group's tangled love affairs. *Love*—bah! Who of them knew the first thing about love? He had joked about Uncle's twisted sex life, but was his own version better? Rona the magnificent, the jewel on his right arm. How far had they gotten before the glitter began flaking off? Hardly past the border. There he was, dangling in an earthcrack, and she wouldn't endanger her precious robe to help him out. Good in bed, but many days he'd have been glad to fold her up with the blankets till the next night.

Before Rona, Clettie. Less beautiful but more capable and astute. Too astute, actually. Her gift, even then, was managing men, and now he realized that she'd turned it into a vocation. He'd gotten a belly full of her "managing." Always trying to bind him, body and soul, with wine and caresses and special favors. Even this slab of rock he was under felt no less constricting than her arms had felt. A prison's a prison, no matter the shape of its bars. That night in Lorenth, pleasant enough at the time, had been one long silent struggle to keep her hand out of the rosillum pot. Damn Garrick for his big mouth!

The crunch of boots faded, and as Driss stared at the rock, his ears began to hum, a buzz that swallowed all other sound. A sense of detachment raised him out of his stone crypt, higher and higher until only cool rays on the fringe of the sun bathed him in light. He could have stopped floating. Enough of his mind was still on the ground to realize he had only to close his eyes or turn his head to break the spell. But this seemed important, a "pay-attention" sort of feeling. Whatever was coming over him held some terrible import that could either kill him or change him beyond recognition.

A face took shape before him, a woman's face. No one he knew. The line of her cheek and chin, the teasing set of her mouth—she surpassed both Clettie and Rona and certainly Charri. Lovely, alluring, she came tantalizingly close, lips opening to his.

But as he watched, fascinated, her skin began to age, then to decay, and finally, she lost flesh altogether. "The skeleton of a beautiful woman is still nuthin' but a skeleton," Keltie had remarked. Was this hideous ghoul looming over him in fact the only face of love any of them had known? The cicada-like buzz intensified; the face floated toward him and came upon him in deadly embrace. It sucked tight to his mouth, leaching air from his lungs until everything grew dark. The only face of love . . . the only face of love . . . His head threatened to split from the insect noise.

Keltie cut the sound. "I think they've gone," he whispered. "The whistles seem near the road now. Probably callin' it off . . . Driss? You okay?"

Driss finally got enough breath to mumble affirmatively, but he closed his eyes and was afraid to open them. After testing his breathing apparatus, he crept out and looked around. "I think it's all right, if we keep to the rocks."

They continued cautiously, expecting a heavy guard near the citadel itself. But as they neared the road the actual number of soldiers seemed fewer than below. Even the whistling had ceased.

They could see the wall clearly now, even through the fog. Was the fortress an extension of the mountain, or the mountain an extension of the fortress? Could there be one without the other?

The crossing proved uneventful, and without trouble they located the mine road, now sliced by a rockslide. Their hearts beat faster as they scrambled across. When they got within a hundred yards of a great heap of mine tailings, they listened warily but could hear nothing but horses neighing, the clatter of vehicles on the road, and the cheerful song of some far-off troubadour.

The entrance to the mine had been carefully hidden, and they were grateful for Uncle's detailed instructions. After anxious moments of poking among scattered stones, Keltie finally whooped, "Here it is! Feel the cold air!"

Again they stopped to look and listen but heard nothing.

"It'll be a job moving these rocks," Jonn observed ruefully.

"Mm," Driss grunted, studying the jumble. "A stout stick would help right now, but we don't have one. I guess we just start heaving. Keep your ears open, though," he warned. "This is no time to be careless!"

They struggled and panted for an hour, resting and watching by turn. Finally, they had made a hole large and stable enough to squeeze into the dark passageway.

"We never thought about light!" exclaimed Keltie.

"*You* never thought about light," Driss returned with a chuckle. "Uncle said there'd be plenty from a cave-in too high and soft to use as an entrance. In fact," he said as he felt his way along the dank, sloping corridor, "I see light ahead! We made it, guys, *we made it!*"

A hundred feet further brought them into a large chamber, partly collapsed, partly supported by pillars of undisturbed, liggeth-streaked rock. A broad streamer of sunlight filtered across tapestried bats, past pillared sentinels, to a great heap, glowing and shimmering, seemingly alive.

Amarl's eyes bugged. Keltie and Jonn knelt outside the pillared cage in awed silence, while Driss murmured ecstatically, "Look at it, guys. Look at it! *Rosegold!*"

"Ours! All ours!" squeaked Amarl unbelievingly.

"Yes, ours," returned Driss. He looked at them with love and pride. "Words can't say how much I appreciate you guys—each one." His voice thickened. "We've struggled a long way and lost just about everything, but you stuck with me. This is our reward!" He studied the rosillum with emotion. "We're rich beyond belief, even if we carry away only part."

Amarl rolled over and groaned. "I can't think about carryin'. I can hardly carry myself!"

Driss laughed. "One taste of rosillum, Amarl, and you'll fly down the mountain with a hundred pounds on your back! What's a little messed-up rosillum for the sake of strength when we have so much?"

"Let's have it, then. I'm starving!" Keltie whooped. "How do we get at it, with these columns in the way?"

They fell silent, surveying the setup. The rosillum lay in a corner behind two large liggeth pillars. The spaces between had been cordoned off with additional stone columns, leaving a series of slots too narrow for even Amarl to squeeze through.

"We could dismantle one of the columns, maybe." Worry began to settle familiarly in the angles of Jonn's face.

Driss examined them carefully. "They're too solid. I doubt even a sledgehammer would budge them, much less bare hands."

He suddenly found it hard to breathe, this time under a band tight across his chest. Uncle's maniacal laughter echoed through the dusty chamber, his last fiendish joke—not on his cronies, but on Driss, who had caught him at his secret "sport." *I guarantee you'll find it, son, and it's all yours—as much as you can carry away!*

36

Fog shrouded the hot sun. As Charri toiled upwards, soft, lambent air sought to cool the furnace of despair that fired her reckless assault on the mountain. Blood oozed from the latest cut. She had fallen countless times, but physical pain could not override the utter desolation driving her up the hill. Derelict, set adrift by events she had no control over, she cast all before the winds of anguish. If her thundering heart gave out before she reached the mine, so much the better: she would gain release from her fruitless quest.

She kept to the road except where footpaths cut across hairpins. Traffic flowed invisibly around her. The angry red of her scar signaled distress, and an occasional tradesman stopped as though to help. Charri, however, pushed on, not seeing, not caring what anyone saw. Hope was gone. Yet this very futility drove her relentlessly until it seemed that nothing would be left of her but charred remains.

"Face it, Driss. We're licked." Keltie kicked at the rocks they had thrown ineffectively against the columns, his face damp from exertion.

Driss turned on him. "We're not licked. There's got to be a way! I'm not getting within ten feet of the prize, only to walk away!"

The sun had moved from the rosillum, leaving a drab, shapeless lump in the shadow. They stared at it morosely.

"What's the use?" Amarl sighed. "By the time we figure it out, we'll be too pooped to do anything."

"Look," Driss snarled, "nothing's stopping you from leaving right now." His angry glance took them all in. "Go ahead. Go back to Cassia. Go find Sigurth. Maybe he's handing out free food today—just for quitters!" He turned away angrily, his eyes stabbing the ceiling with its arabesque of restless bats.

Careful, Driss; what are your chances if they do leave?

He swung back, hands open and pleading. "Use your heads, men! Think what it means to give up now!"

He walked a tight circle, crumpling his hair. "Maybe we could pare one of the liggeth columns," he suggested more calmly, "this smallest one. It's hard, but not like rock, and if we all worked at it . . . At the very least we could look for a stick long enough to poke the rosillum and hope it picks up something to lick. Even a little energy—"

Keltie snorted. "How many sticks did you see on the way up here? No tree within twenty miles. Brambles, but no sticks."

Driss sighed and went back to rubbing his head. After a moment he pulled out his knife and began scraping the pillar he had singled out. The blade snapped.

"Blast!" He threw down the handle and paced tensely.

Jonn stiffened. "Stop! I hear something!"

They crouched defensively as footsteps, accompanied by muffled cries, echoed in the passageway.

"Driss, Driss, Driss . . . oh, please be here!"

The men looked at each other. "A woman!" Amarl whispered wonderingly.

They watched in fascination as the figure stumbled into view, face blood-streaked and grimy, eyes burned hollows, clothing shredded. She halted at the entrance, wildly searching the dim cavern. Her eye fell on the four huddled near the corner.

"Driss!" She moved toward them and sank to her knees in wretched relief. "I found you! Oh, Driss, I need . . . help . . ." Her voice trailed into anguished sobs.

Driss rose, his face drained of color. "Charri!" he gasped.

As she lay weeping before him, the cumulation of his own adversity crested in a noxious, bituminous tide. A bitter smile twisted his lips.

"You came to the wrong man, Charri. I'm a dry well, an empty pitcher. I'm as ugly as you are, now. Look at me!"

She raised from the floor and peered at his face, but without comprehension. She shook her head. "You don't understand. I have nowhere, no one to go to!"

Driss's voice rose. "It's you that doesn't understand. I'm hanging by the end of my tail!"

Charri's eyes shone unnaturally bright; her words tumbled over each other. "Driss, you wanted a woman. You once wanted me, but I didn't—"

His harsh laugh cut her off. "I—wanted—a woman! What a joke! Now that I'm repulsive like you, you think that's what I want? You think that'll take the place of rosillum, that a little sex will get us back down the mountain? Honey, if you want sex, go back to Cassia. There's plenty there. Look up Clettie—dome-shaped house at the north edge of town. She'll give you all you ever wanted and more besides!"

Charri's eyes glassed over.

Driss saw but pressed on venomously. "And if that's not enough, go to Sigurth. He's the big man in sex. You might even get your own house and a cream carriage with matching team! And zill. He'll have zill for you, too."

He pulled her up roughly and spun her toward the entrance. "I can't help you, Charri. I got troubles of my own. Get somebody else to bail you out. *I have nothing to give you!*"

Charri fell back as though he had lashed her with a whip. Then with a wild, shrieking wail, she stumbled blindly up the dark corridor. A lone bat saw her to the door.

Driss sat alone in the crypt, staring vacantly at the mocking, impregnable treasure. A few minutes earlier, Jonn had placed a parting hand on his shoulder, after trying to persuade him to leave with them.

His hopes, his plans, his grand scheme for Great Zelland. "There's a fortune to be made in mining and trading," he had told Jonn. "And Wooten. I know Wooten would take off. The harsher the climate, the finer the wool. With rosillum to fund ships and supplies, our investment would double—maybe triple—in no time."

That's what he'd said to Jonn.

And his other plans. Two or three fine houses. Fine clothes. Fine horses. Fine carriages. Fine women.

Fine women. There was a laugh, as clever a bit of illusion as one could imagine. Was the rest of the list illusory, too?

Was rosillum a delusion? It was here; it was his. He'd spent everything he had for that ugly, shapeless pile of mineral. He had scaled his alp and stood victorious at the top, but the top could not be carried off.

Everything gone . . . money, equipment, horses, manpower; worst of all, the children. Even his looks. *I'm as ugly as you are. Look at me—look at me—look at me . . .*

You wanted a woman. That's what Charri said. I needed women back then, a necessity right up with food and drink. How long ago . . . ?

There'd been plenty of women to start with—before Rona, before Clettie, long before. . . .

You once wanted me . . .

Yes, I wanted you, but you didn't want me. The first woman who ever refused me on principle. But . . . you did want me. Every fiber of your body reached out. You wanted me then, you needed me now. And today, in this bat hole, I refused . . .

Driss closed his eyes, trying to shut out a horror that gnawed like a starving rat at the thread of his composure. She didn't understand. She didn't see what I'm up against. *I'm hanging by the end of my tail over an earthcrack. Nowhere to go, no one to help me . . .*

His breath caught in a sob, and he writhed against the implacable gnawing.

I can't help you. I have nothing to give! I said that to her. I said those words—a whip that drove her away!

The thread broke. He crashed into the depths. *She wanted ME—not what I could give! She wanted me to hold her, to comfort her. I could have been the Middle Night pitcher of water. I could've poured myself over her . . . sealed her love. No, I threw ashes in her face. "Go to Clettie, go to Sigurth. Be one of his 'good, lusty whores' . . . " Oh, Charri, my darling, what have I done? The real treasure . . . right here, and I threw it away! What is rosillum next to the love of a worthy woman? If nothing else, we could've held each other . . . died together. Charri, oh, Charri . . .*

The light faded, the bats departed from the little hole above as Driss stared into the blackness of his soul. Slowly—as slowly as the return of day—resolve brought life to his body. His options were few, but he still had choices. He could, of course, stay where he was till he withered away to bat guano, or he could crawl outside and wait for deathbirds to pick his bones. Once outdoors, though, he'd be game for other predators. Who would get him first—Sigurth or Claeman? Did he care? Like the skeleton of a beautiful woman, dead bones are still dead, no matter who makes them that way.

He could beat them both to the punch, walk up to whoever came first and say, "Go ahead. Kill me." No pleading, no groveling—just a good, quick death.

It wouldn't work, though. Well . . . it might with Claeman—he was still an unknown—but never with Sigurth. For whatever reason, Sigurth wanted to claim him alive, and he'd get his kicks if it meant wringing blood, ounce by ounce, from Driss's body.

Maybe . . . maybe Driss could milk some good out of the situation. He could go to Sigurth and, if nothing else, simply die with Charri. He'd seen enough to know that neither of their lives was worth a nod from Sigurth; a quick death was probably the best they could hope for. But if that didn't work and Sigurth insisted on claiming Driss, he might use that as leverage to buy Charri's life as Glinneth had bought his. As insignificant as Charri was in the broad scheme of things, Driss was in fact far less. He'd allow Sigurth to claim him in exchange for Charri—and try not to think about what Sigurth's claim might actually mean. Yes, Charri was the one to save, no matter what.

Yes, the thing to do. He rose and without a backward glance crept from the mine, leaning like an old man on walls and rocks.

Wind roared in his ears and swept orange dust against his face. The fortress loomed on his left. This Bethzur, this brooding house on a rock, was anchored to the weathered core of an ancient volcano, the arteries and organs of which had hardened eons ago into liggeth and rosillum.

The road ran parallel to the high, patterned stone wall. Driss kept to the thoroughfare, heedless of traffic, mindless of danger. Weak, light-headed, heavy-hearted, he staggered drunkenly.

Death was setting in. He felt cold, paralyzed. Not physical death; he was hungry but not starving, tired but not exhausted. No, this was a deeper death, the death of his life.

But this wasn't his first encounter; he saw that now. All his life he'd been chasing death, blinded by the illusion of a strong body and good looks. He had begun to catch up with death on his way up this mountain. There under the rock where they had hidden from Russetmen, the loathsome woman came upon him, imprinting the true nature of beauty on his mouth. Disillusionment—the first layer of death that demolished the trappings of power and influence.

Inside the mine his dream had died—the second layer. Now, was this third layer, this staggering toward destruction, the death of hope? If so, he was making the best of it, perhaps in saving Charri through his own destruction.

Where the road made its first hairpin turn to the right, he stopped to rest. Maybe the men had stopped there on their way down. What would happen to them? Jonn . . . Keltie . . . Amarl . . . They were weak, too, their only hope, to stumble down the mountain without interference. Garryn—yes, she'd give them food.

As he sat, Driss noticed a well-traveled path not far from the road, leading from what appeared to be a service tunnel at the corner of the fortress to a cliff nearby. He watched dully as several men with buckets and packs emptied the contents of their burdens over the edge. The fortress dump? A faint glimmer rose to his eyes as he viewed this refuse disposal. The men looked mostly simple but happy enough. And well fed.

Hunger spawned an idea.

Clambering over the boulders separating path from roadway, he waited for the next carrier, a gangling, slack-jawed youth with a pail of "night slops." Driss would rather have intercepted table scraps for some immediate nourishment, but at this point he couldn't afford to be choosy.

"Good morning, friend! Looks like you didn't get much sleep last night. Too much noise in the quarters, eh?" He laughed and chucked the bewildered lad's arm. "Why don't you let me carry this the rest of the way, and you go back for another load? We'll help each other today."

The boy's jaw dropped even lower as Driss relieved him of his burden and aimed him toward the tunnel. The lad trotted off, mystified but obedient.

Driss sighed with grim satisfaction. *Now—we'll see what comes of this. I'm dirty enough to blend in; whether I can hold up till lunchtime is another matter. Right now even pig slop sounds good. Work till they dole out food, then go face Sigurth.* He took a deep breath and turned to the stinking bucket.

Two russet-clad figures stood before him on the path. "Drissan, you don't belong here. You will come with us, please."

37

Driss closed his eyes upon this final collapse of his grand dream. The ground of his personal landscape lay crumbled beneath his feet, leveled by a cataclysm of higher magnitude than the Great Earthquake at Chadwich. What in terms of goods and ambitions had he brought into Arlony? In the end, not a fool bean was left; not even his freedom remained.

Why, then, did he feel relieved? The war was over; he'd lost. The last thread had broken. Could anything be worse? The war was *over*. Yes, that was it. He could breathe again. No more choices to make, nothing to do but face whatever punishment. No matter how severe the sentence, he deserved it.

Such irony: seven hundred miles of scheming and evasion, maneuvering right to Claeman's doorstep—only to get arrested for trespassing on the dump path!

He shuddered. Trespass might be the immediate charge, but Russetmen had been watching. They knew his scheme. He would most certainly be taken before Claeman, the person he feared above all others. Sigurth had been seen, his evil named. But Claeman remained the implacable unknown. How would he look upon Driss's bold act? It was, in reality, hardly more than a misdemeanor. Though he'd entered the mine without authorization, he had not actually stolen the rosillum. But would Claeman interpret it that way? He'd see things differently. He would know.

What would come of it? A simple flogging, perhaps. Driss's dying flesh became even colder. His legs turned to jelly, and he almost lost the little water he had between his legs. He would turn utterly craven; he knew he would, more terrified than at the plank. They'd drag him to the post, screaming, empty of courage.

What would Claeman do with him? Driss knew Sigurth's specialties: torture, brutalizing children, and of course, earthcrack and High Summer orgies. Could Claeman—the antithesis of such evil—be less extreme? A good, quick end:

that, on the whole, was the thing to wish for. Better, certainly, than a flogging.

He tried to get his numb brain to function—*a gift, maybe. Would that help? Some zill*—then almost laughed. All this time, all this distance, and he still didn't know what the stuff was. He was sure, though, in his circumstance it would make a grand joke if he had some to offer. But lacking zill, he scanned the area for something that might serve as tribute—a flower, an interesting stone. Nothing. Nothing but rock, brambles, and the slop bucket.

The two soldiers, misinterpreting his search, moved to either side.

"Come along. You've nowhere to go but with us."

Strange that the color of their uniforms should strike him at such a moment. He'd seen soldiers many times, of course, but the uniforms had seemed brown or red or even orange as on the rim of the mountain valley. But these were more the color of earth, earth that was alive, the embodiment of red and orange and brown. *Yes, a gift . . . something . . . anything.*

"Wait! I need to take—" But as he moved to pick up the pail, his foot caught on a bramble and put him off balance. Before the men could steady him, he fell sideways, the pail spilling filth over his leg.

The soldiers shook their heads but allowed him to keep the pail.

Again, Driss felt light and free as they wound up the steep road toward the massive gate. Everything and everyone was gone, his sole possession an empty, stinking bucket.

The apricot mist thickened as they neared the great wall. Before, different ones of the group had felt uncomfortable under this colored fog. Treese in particular had growled incessantly. But now it pressed on him and pulled him toward the lowering citadel. He felt his inner resistance crumbling, even as his money and group of followers had eroded. Heart pounding, gasping for breath, Driss writhed against the scourging haze.

"Poison!" he managed to croak. But as he said it, he knew it wasn't so. His captors paid no heed. Oh, that it were true! If only he could escape so easily, even by dying at the hand of Sigurth! *Known!* His soul—normally a close, private thing—flapped like an old, thin cape over his skeleton, for all to see. All that was essentially Driss—zest, capability, daring—was being ground to a fine powder. The final death. He had not reckoned on this dimension of Claeman's power. What once had been a nameless, shapeless fear was now fleshing out. Rocks that moved—suddenly that seemed quite reasonable.

Partway up the hill, a disturbance behind them drew his captors' attention. They stood listening, tense, alert. Sure enough, a complex whistle sent them bounding through the fog, leaving their prisoner standing alone.

Driss stared after them, dumbfounded. Finally he waved weakly, facetiously. "It's okay, fellas. I'll just wait here till you get back!"

He was free—free to run from the searing vapor. *I could get away. I know I could! Claeman bagged his game, then let it go. The tiger in the bush seems to have trumped the squirrel in hand.*

He looked around, indecisive. Was it a trick? He saw no one—no one anywhere.

No one anywhere. No one to stop him, no one to run to. Where could he go? Where in the world could a dead man go? Cassia was a sewer, like Jonn said. He couldn't just pop down, get a little bread from Garryn, then somehow sneak back to Swendia. It wouldn't work. He wouldn't even get off the mountain, let alone recross the entire country unobserved by either Sigurth or Claeman. Besides, after what he'd done to Charri, running away wasn't an option. He had to at least try to find her, even though it meant certain doom—or worse—for them both. If he lived, it could only be on Sigurth's terms. How could he abide becoming a vassal to Sigurth?

Driss closed his eyes with a shudder and in that instant saw it all: *the alternative to Claeman was Sigurth,* a towering good versus a monstrous evil. All along—yes, he saw it clearly now—Claeman was good, for Russetmen were good. He'd seen it. Celine's basket story. The daring rescue outside of Chadwich. The way they laughed. Even the booby-trapped cobbler shop. A Russetman with a sense of humor. Driss had been too nervous to appreciate the comedy, but the little fellow obviously got a kick out of his elaborate scheme to help a crippled cobbler catch a thief. *Well done, little guy!* Driss wished he could shake his hand again, this time with firmer grip.

Yes, Claeman was good, for Russetmen were good. Though the group had joked about Claeman, they all—except for Garrick—intuitively understood his grand design of bringing the country to peace and security. The entire history of Arlony, from the Arls of Keltie's "juice" beginnings, through the Green Wars that secured national interests, to the long Civil War and its present stalemate. The stories he'd heard, of Triona, of the great victory at Harloon Paddock. The courtesan—and Garryn, too, for that matter. These two whores understood that only the Cletties of their profession were beneath them. Yet from the bottom of their social well where one can look up in broad daylight and see stars, they caught—more clearly, perhaps, than respectable people—a glimpse of that far-off, unfathomable good that was worth risking their daily bread and even their lives for.

Yes, the alternative to Claeman's good was unmitigated evil. Driss abhorred the ritual horror that was Sigurth, but was he himself any better? He saw that all along, little choices—of each person in the group, for that matter—had marked them for one camp or the other. His whole scheme—not just in Arlony, but the totality of his life—had been built on deceit and lust. In the end, the great dream turned as black as licked rosillum.

Yes, at last he knew good and evil. But what could he do about it? Admitting mistakes was foreign to him. Like the time the food box ripped his arm. Driss had tried to turn Jonn's apology, "I'm sorry, Driss; I thought you had it," into an admission of guilt. "Saying you're sorry means you did something wrong. You should've looked before letting go." To him, *sorry* meant *shame,* an ever-tightening vise of guilt. And pointing the finger elsewhere wasn't his only ploy: as children on First Night, he and Jonn had staged coughing fits when the group discussed the year's "fame or sorry shame."

Today, though, he had come of age. No longer was First Night a ritualistic mumbling of words to humor the old ones. Comprehending those simple songs put him on the knife-edge of good and evil, and Claeman was allowing him a final, ultimate decision. Yes, he could escape, he could run away from Claeman; that was the hell of it.

He looked again at the swirling tunnel directly ahead. Not a living soul was in sight. Only the croak of a deathbird wheeling overhead broke the windblown silence. Doom lay in either direction, but he could still make a last free act of will in determining his fate. All it required was one step . . . then another . . . and another.

Inside the gateway the fog became a filmy curtain of flame that whipped around him remorselessly. The sum of his life's choices seemed to rise in leaping conflagration: the scramble for money and women, cheap sex, the loss of lives entrusted to him. Most terrible of all, because most inexcusable, was the obscenity he'd hurled upon Charri. Her principles had been right all along. Principle held genuine love steady and true. A woman who loved according to principle would never do as Rona had done. Charri had offered him a precious, fragile gift, and he'd hurled it at the bats.

Even this could have been borne had it stopped there. Deeper still, to the core of his heart, the indictment burned. *Is Sigurth so terrible? You, Drissan—Driss the callous, Driss the cruel.* He heard again the terrible fate he'd wished on Rona. He saw again the distressed ground dog whose life he could have saved with little effort. Instead, he'd abandoned the animal to a slow, ghastly death. *Choices. One camp or another.* And Charri, always Charri . . . Where once he'd looked at his twisted, shrunken image reflected in water, he now stared into a cesspool. *You, Driss—you are Sigurth.* In desperation he clung to the night-slops bucket.

An anomaly rose with the stench. *Why am I holding this thing? I need a gift, not an insult.*

Then the solution came clear.

"Please . . . take it!" he shouted hoarsely and held the pail high under the incandescence. "Take it! I'm here in this pail. The pail is me, my 'sorry shame!' It's all I . . ."

He could go no further. He hunched to the ground, sobs wrenching his body, aware only that the dirt in his mouth tasted sweet.

38

How long he lay he could not say. Only gradually did he become aware of being held—tightly, soothingly—while a broken voice murmured over and over, "Drissan, Drissan . . . you've come at last. Why did you wait so long? Hush, now. You're safe. Hush, Drissan."

Driss was five years old again. During a day at the fair he had gotten separated from his parents, and for what seemed like hours he endured the terror of lostness. When strangers finally placed him in his father's arms, he felt then as he felt now. In the arms of this "father" he could not open his eyes, nor could he move from the broad, comforting chest. He who had once possessed "sovereign command" now wept as that child of years ago.

Spent at last, he lay back, gathering courage to look up.

He saw little except a blurred image, but something was terribly wrong.

In terms of physical strength, one hand of this person could crush the life from Driss's body. His presence spoke power. But out of strength came gentleness, tenderness, and—most unsettling of all—knowledge, like the hidden conversation at the crico match, like Steph knowing horses' minds.

This man knows me! Panic stabbed his gut.

"Drissan," the rumbling voice declared, "your name means 'known,' " though Driss had said nothing aloud. "I know your pain, your longings, your sorrow, your shame. I know, lad—and I love you."

Something in the unsteady voice stung Driss to his feet, ready to flee, if necessary. The man stood, too, and a face, badly burned, came into focus.

Driss's knees almost gave way. "Glinneth!" he cried, turning white.

"Ay, lad." Glinneth stood back, strangely vulnerable. "Ay. Have I become repulsive to you?"

Driss grabbed his head to hold together a disintegrating brain. He winced at the angry scars on his friend's face and arms and what he could see of his chest. He reached out gingerly, as though to experience the pain, to retrieve it, undo it somehow. The cost, the dreadful, *needless* price Glinneth paid so Driss and the others could escape that night. Willingly, for love alone, he had climbed that hill, placed himself in Sigurth's hands, stood before that terrible fire, endured—

Driss twisted away, chest heaving, then as suddenly turned back. "I . . . did this to you," he whispered. "Because of me, you had to . . ." Like Amarl, he had trouble speaking the words. His fingers trembled across a slash of magenta that should have been beard. "I did it by not waiting at the top of the rise . . . If I'd accepted your money and help . . ." He stopped to clear his throat. "And that awful night, so we could get away . . ." His voice would not stay steady.

What if Glinneth hadn't come? Driss would have charged in blind fury up the hill. T'ribboners would have dragged him toward the searing flames. What then of his noble intentions? He, who couldn't even cross a wide plank without help, who couldn't bear to think about a flogging, could he have stood under Sigurth's molten wax, even for the children? "Sorry shame," indeed!

Sorry shame . . . sorry shame. Outside the fortress he thought that seeing himself as he actually was had reduced him to dust. Now he was between the stones of yet a finer mill. He had to face this incomprehensible love that had freely covered his shame, had to look it in the eye. Groveling or flogging himself or getting mules to kick him would be easier to endure. Amarl knew how it was. He had tried everything when the horses died. Driss had done right by him to force him past guilt, but now he himself was under the same stone, and he couldn't believe how much it hurt. He couldn't do it . . . but he had to. One more sentence: he had to say it. "Glinneth, those burns . . . should've been . . . mine." He tried to lift his eyes. "My life . . . Please . . . can you forgive . . . ?" He'd said it. He'd said the words, and now his eyes and every straining muscle pleaded.

"It's done, lad," the soft voice said. "And there's the end of it."

Tentatively, almost timidly, Glinneth held out his arms, and with a strangled cry Driss fell into the bear-like embrace. He buried his head on the enormous shoulder, his body shaking. They rocked back and forth, tears streaming down both faces.

"It's all right, laddie, it's all right. You're home, now," Glinneth murmured over and over.

Finally, he stepped back and drew a tremulous breath, cupping great hands around Driss's head and surveying his face. "Ah, lad, you've suffered much—and not just hunger and exhaustion."

Driss dropped his eyes, suddenly conscious of his lumpy skin.

Glinneth, however, uncomfortable with gloom, tousled Driss's dusty curls. "Come. We'll get you cleaned and decked more suitably."

Glinneth supported Driss through a maze of stone corridors to a small room, surprisingly homely and stark in a place such as Bethzur. Yet the rough floor and paneling, the simple table positioned close to a small fireplace seemed made for absorbing stress. Glinneth eased Driss into the only chair and swathed his shivering body in a soft blanket that most likely was Wooten. Though not thick and plush like Driss's cloak, the warmth and fine texture could come from nothing else.

"Can you remain awake, lad, until—"

But Driss felt a dim unease. "Glinneth, I . . ." He looked at the luxury in his lap, trying to force his brain to articulate its objection.

"What is it, lad? Food will be here shortly. Is that it?"

"No, not food. The blanket . . ." The connection came through, and he unwrapped his legs. "It's too nice. My clothes. They're filthy. It'll be ruined. I'll just sit on the hearth and—"

"No, lad. I'll not hear of it." Glinneth pushed him back in the chair and tucked him closely. "You're cold, weak. What's a blanket, fine or plain, against need? Ah, here comes food. Not a feast, mind you. Your stomach would not thank me for such fare.

A little broth, a few bites of hard bread, taken slowly— Soon enough you'll be ready for feasting!

An old soldier shuffled into the room, his crushed-paper skin permanently darkened by years of grease. He nodded cheerfully to Driss and turned a leathery smile on Glinneth, then set a fragrant, steaming tureen on the table. With a hand that shook alarmingly, he ladled a small amount into a mug and carried it to Driss.

Driss closed his eyes and sipped gratefully. When had he last eaten all he wanted? Was it the meal with Rona? He thought about that strange evening, the food selected for his benefit. He took another sip from the mug. Nothing, *nothing* on Rona's gourmet table could come close to the pleasure of this clear gold liquid. Not even zill, whatever it was. It warmed his stomach, it warmed his heart. Strength flowed to his limbs.

"Glinneth," he asked. "Please—what is zill? I've heard about it but never could find out . . ."

Glinneth's eyes dropped a moment, then met Driss's with infinite sadness. "Zill. What can be said of it? Little, perhaps, is best." He sighed. "First you need ask what rosillum is. No rosillum, no zill. Incomparable beauty and power in rosillum— yes. Yet an embezzler, a waster of lives. Beauty distorted to horror. This you know, lad; you know well."

Driss closed his eyes against a twisting within.

"A wine of unsurpassed beauty and taste—that's zill. But it's also the blood of death, a drink that begets unquenchable thirst, that brews the blackest midnight out of high noon. That too is zill. Enough that you know only rosillum. You've been spared zill, a poisonous swamp of misery and depravity. Few know of zill. Not much flows in the land, but what does becomes a fire storm." He paused. "Sigurth would have you believe it a new pleasure, but it's old, as old as murder, and every bit as deadly."

Driss stared into the fire. When he did speak his voice picked through words as though putting together a puzzle. "I was spared zill. I was spared Sigurth. I was spared Clae— No, I can't say that yet. But you—you who have every reason to hate me, to kill me, even, knowing what you do— Why all this for me? Why so . . . kind? Do you want something . . . a task, perhaps?"

Glinneth smiled and rocked on his heels. "Someone else asked the very question when first you came into Arlony. No, lad, you've completed your 'task.' You made your choice, and now wholeness will work its health, not just in you, but in everything around you, despite the great conflict. The war goes on, but it cannot destroy those who choose to be whole."

Glinneth ran a hand across Driss's back. "I'll see to your bath. Set zill and tasks aside for now and eat, but slowly, no more than your stomach will receive. Ferrel here will take you when you're ready."

As the eating room was plain, the bathing room was elegant. A high, vaulted ceiling hung with tropical vines curved over a steaming cistern. "Hot spring," Ferrel told Driss in his old-leather voice. "From deep in the earth. Same temperature summer and winter." The cistern overflowed into a rich-hued, polished stone tub. A pad, a shade lighter than the tub itself, softened the bottom and slanting backrest. Cold water from a brass pipe tempered the cistern's heat, but only to a degree to leave skin intact. The swirling water exited through a slot on the lower end.

Driss groaned in ecstasy as he lowered himself into the kneading waters. He closed his eyes under Ferrel's ministering hands, partly to avoid looking at his own protruding bones. It would take more than broth and bread to pad them out.

After a good soak while being shaved, followed by a thorough scrubbing, Driss emerged into an enfolding wrap to have what skin remained to him scoured dry. Ferrel then treated his desert-parched skin with warm oil, applying salve to his cracked lips.

Then after inspecting his handiwork, he led Driss through a stone archway to an adjoining dressing room. A single camblor beam supported the ceiling, and rich draperies stood aside to allow the sun full run of the room. A thick rug, as light as the ceiling, warmed henna-colored flagstones.

Glinneth was waiting, and he himself trimmed Driss's hair and dressed him in a gold robe of incredible softness. On his head went a matching band centered with a rich brown gemstone. Three gold circlets gathered the cloth of his right sleeve.

"Ahh. Look at you!" With pride, Glinneth led Driss to a carved mirror and watched, amused, as Driss struggled with this first look at his warty face, especially against the sumptuous clothing.

Finally, Driss laughed. "It's me—a fancied-up toad!"

But Glinneth shook his head. "No, lad, it's not you, but the picture speaks some truth. Even for someone known, wholeness can't come unless the person is first emptied of hindrances." His mouth bent upwards.

Solemnly, Driss studied the face in the mirror. "Yes, this is better. With my normal face I'd be right back to . . . to its demands. I wouldn't be free. The *burden* of good looks."

Glinneth nodded approvingly. "Ay, lad, you've learned about the burden. Wholeness lies beyond the burden, though. Here, I'll fix it." He twisted open a small, round box, familiar in its deformity.

Driss drew back. "No! What are you doing?" He stopped abruptly, a stricken look frozen in place.

Glinneth raised scorched eyebrows and waited.

Driss closed his eyes and ran a hand across his face.

The older man chuckled and began applying the grease. "The burden and its pain flow from the likes of Sigurth. We must go through it to get beyond it."

Driss winced under the familiar sting but gritted his teeth. "*We*, you say. Your face is burned but not marred like mine. There's a diff—"

"Hah! Marred, my breastplate! You bear a different mark, the image of Claeman, the mark of freedom! Here. See for yourself." Again he positioned Driss in front of the mirror.

After a glance, Driss stepped back and turned away, unable to speak. Was this the image of Claeman? Not only was his skin not dark as he expected, not only were the unsightly lumps gone, his face had taken on a glow that outshone even his clothing.

"So much for the 'marred' look," said Glinneth. "You're well rid of Sigurth's reflection. But, come. Enough of faces.

We're known by far more than that! One last garment before you rest."

Smiling broadly, Glinneth stepped to a closet. Like a child revealing a long-kept secret, he drew out a midnight-blue cloak with silver plaiting across one shoulder. "Too warm for summer wear, perhaps, but—"

Driss drew a sharp, unbelieving breath. "My Wooten! That's my Wooten! Where'd you get it?"

Then he knew. "This is Glue, isn't it?" he whispered, receiving the garment and stroking its softness. "Glue come back.... 'Your Excellency.' The name—Steph had it right. Excellent horse, noble animal." He held the cloak to his face, closing his eyes under its silky feel. He straightened after a moment, then, almost as a sacrament, laid it gently in Glinneth's arms. "Thank you." His eyes filled. "Thank you."

Glinneth put an arm around him. "You're weary," he said. "Come now. Come to a place of rest."

Glinneth drew Driss along fortress passageways. As their footsteps echoed off stone, Driss reflected on this interior perspective of Claeman's fortress. Outside had been fear and despair, the ruinous, scourging fog; inside were safety and warmth—stately beauty, even—and security in his status as friend of Glinneth. True, he hadn't yet stood before Claeman, and he was under no illusion that he would be spared that confrontation. At least, though, he'd have the benefit of sleep. And if he were granted only one word to say, it must be on behalf of Garryn. He had promised. Despite her profession in that terrible city, she was a good woman; even Claeman must see that. Maybe a monument would be raised to her someday.

He noted the friendly banter as they squeezed by a small band of Russetmen. Obvious esteem, clothed in a joke, passed between these men and their leader. *I was right,* Driss observed silently; *the way people laugh shows the kind of persons they are.*

Once outside, they headed toward a green place in the distance. A series of broad stone steps brought them to a sunken garden deep within a cool, shrubby surround. Water from a quiet spring eased across a narrow ledge, lowering itself carefully down tiny tree roots that hung bare and dripping. A low, pillowed couch nestled in a carpet of moss banking the tiny stream. Flowers in every shade of yellow, from pale cream to the tawny rust of soldiers' tunics, scattered a fragrance that dug at Driss's deepest longings.

He halted on the steps, overwhelmed, then reached out as though to grasp the memories and phantom images that rode the perfume. When his hands returned empty, he looked anxiously at Glinneth.

"This . . . place!" he whispered hoarsely.

"Ay, lad." Glinneth smiled. "It's for you. You know it well. Stay now, and rest. Durk will play a tune to start your sleep, and a drink of the water should sustain you through troubling dreams." He pointed to a rosillum goblet near the couch. "Rest well. I'll send someone after a bit."

He hesitated. "First, though—" His eyes were solemn in love. "Drissan," he asked, "what is my name?"

Driss, strangely unnerved, smiled foolishly as Amarl might have done. "Your name is Glinneth."

"No, lad, no longer Glinneth to you. I am Claeman—he who claims. I claimed you once through fire; now I claim you through pouring."

As Driss reeled under this revelation, Claeman bent to scoop water with a hand the size of a pitcher.

Seal my heart in love,
Seal my love in flame,
Mark my love,
Set my love,
Nor death can mar its claim.

The water trickling over Driss's head touched the melted wax of his heart. He drew deep breaths against a lifetime of Middle Night emotion.

"Claeman!" he whispered hoarsely. The man folded him again in his great arms, then was gone.

Driss fell on the couch, his closed eyes wet. The music of the shepherd's pipe once again spun its illusion, his inner vision wheeling dizzily. He was bone-weary, too tired to drink even from a rosillum goblet. Rest . . .

The hypnotic effect of haunting music, trickling water, and maddening perfume carried him from this place of tranquility, back along the orange road, past those haulers of waste, beyond the entrance to the liggeth mine, back . . . back . . . past three dusty men and a broken, weeping woman trudging eastward toward Swendia. Keltie, Amarl, Jonn, Celine . . . *Gold—pure gold; not empty. Faithful to the end. They just didn't know. They didn't know about the fiery tunnel. They went on by.* His heart yearned after them, to bring them back. "Through the tunnel! Through the tunnel! That's where wholeness dwells!" But the music drove him on.

He returned to the old spring with its floating blossoms, so like this one, but found it empty of peace. No rest here. (Why hadn't he drunk of that goblet?) Fair May clawed at his heart, his loins twisting with an ache no woman's body could satisfy. No, he needed to join, not body to body, but mind to mind, heart to heart.

The need became desperate. He was alone. Even if he waited for them, the others would not stop on their way home, not even Jonn, homely, faithful Jonn. A man could die from aloneness, as well as from lust.

His heart pounded under this attack of May, a steel band around his chest. With a desolate cry, he sat up, eyes wide and wild.

A woman knelt beside him, compassionate but apprehensive. She wore a pale green, diaphanous robe tied with a rope of fine-woven gold. From her neck hung a jewel of unusual color and shape. In its depth, delicate veins drew the eye inward.

With a mother's practice, the woman hushed and soothed as Driss fought for control. She held the cup to his lips.

Strength surged through him from the vibrant water.

He lay back, his eyes searching her face. Yes, the scar was there, but it had mellowed, her beauty transcending it.

She was here! She, too, had been rescued. How had it happened with her? Glinneth wouldn't have drawn her through the tunnel, that dreadful furnace that immolated such as Driss.

Not Charri. No, he'd have gone looking for her, perhaps finding her desolate, half-dead on the road. He'd have taken her in his arms, covering her shame, healing her brokenness, consoling her torment. *Oh, Charri!* Driss writhed inwardly, not daring to speak. *I could have . . . I should have . . . Please forgive me!*

Her face was not vindictive, yet something was bothering her. Like him, she had been restored and mended; he had received his Wooten, she the green dress she so desired. What did she still lack?

He looked again at her jewel and fingered it, examining intently.

There, at its center, he found her name.

Sad, yearning eyes locked into his, and he drew a sharp breath, his heart thudding. Of the two of them, he alone knew.

Driss reached out and drew trembling fingers down her cheek, across her mouth. "A second chance!" he whispered in awe. "I *can* help you, I *can* give. You are 'Cari' . . . my heart, my love!"

About the Author

ELEANOR K. GUSTAFSON
An author of both fiction and nonfiction since 1978, MIDDLE NIGHT is her third novel. The first two, APPALACHIAN SPRING and WILD HARVEST, were published by Zondervan Books.

A GRADUATE OF WHEATON COLLEGE IN ILLINOIS
In many of her stories, the author explores the overarching cosmic struggle between good and evil and its effect on ordinary people. She has enjoyed a variety of experiences—horses, tree farming, music, hands-on house building, travel—all of which have helped bring color and humor to her fiction.

A TREE FARMER
Mrs. Gustafson and her husband divide their time between Haverhill, Massachusetts where he teaches philosophy, and the family forest in Chester, Vermont. She is at work in both locations on her next novel.